C0-AXD-636

THE WORKS OF
HERMAN MELVILLE

STANDARD EDITION
VOLUME
IV

MARDI

AND A VOYAGE THITHER

BY

HERMAN MELVILLE

IN TWO VOLUMES

VOL. II

NEW YORK

RUSSELL & RUSSELL · INC

1963

#5341574

PS
2384
.M37
1963
v.2

THE STANDARD EDITION OF
THE WORKS OF HERMAN MELVILLE
IN SIXTEEN VOLUMES
REISSUED, 1963, BY RUSSELL & RUSSELL, INC.
L. C. CATALOG CARD NO: 63–18862

PRINTED IN THE UNITED STATES OF AMERICA

CONTENTS

v

Cabrini College Library
21617
Radnor, Pa.

CONTENTS

MARDI

CHAPTER I

MARAMMA

WE were now voyaging straight for Maramma; where
lived and reigned, in mystery, the high pontiff of the
adjoining isles : prince, priest, and god, in his own proper
person : great lord paramount over many kings in Mardi ;
his hands full of sceptres and crosiers.

Soon, rounding a lofty and insulated shore, the great
central peak of the island came in sight ; domineering
over the neighbouring hills ; the same aspiring pinnacle
descried in drawing near the Archipelago in the *Chamois*.

' Tall Peak of Ofo ! ' cried Babbalanja, ' how comes it
that thy shadow so broods over Mardi ; flinging new
shades upon spots already shaded by the hillsides ; shade
upon shade ! '

' Yet so it is,' said Yoomy, sadly, ' that where that
shadow falls, gay flowers refuse to spring ; and men long
dwelling therein become shady of face and of soul. "Hast
thou come from out the shadows of Ofo ? " inquires the
stranger, of one with a clouded brow.'

' It was by this same peak,' said Mohi, ' that the nimble
god Roo, a great sinner above, came down from the skies,
a very long time ago. Three skips and a jump, and he
landed on the plain. But alas, poor Roo ! though easy
the descent, there was no climbing back.'

' No wonder, then,' said Babbalanja, ' that the peak is

inaccessible to man. Though, with a strange infatuation, many still make pilgrimages thereto ; and wearily climb and climb, till slipping from the rocks, they fall headlong backward, and oftentimes perish at its base.'

' Ay,' said Mohi, ' in vain, on all sides of the peak, various paths are tried ; in vain new ones are cut through the cliffs and the brambles :—Ofo yet remains inaccessible.'

' Nevertheless,' said Babbalanja, ' by some it is believed, that those who by dint of hard struggling climb so high as to become invisible from the plain ; that these have attained the summit ; though others much doubt whether their becoming invisible is not because of their having fallen, and perished by the way.'

' And wherefore,' said Media, ' do you mortals undertake the ascent at all ? why not be content on the plain ? and even if attainable, what would you do upon that lofty, clouded summit ? Or how can you hope to breathe that rarefied air, unfitted for your human lungs ? '

' True, my lord,' said Babbalanja ; ' and Bardianna asserts that the plain alone was intended for man ; who should be content to dwell under the shade of its groves, though the roots thereof descend into the darkness of the earth. But, my lord, you well know, that there are those in Mardi who secretly regard all stories connected with this peak as inventions of the people of Maramma. They deny that anything is to be gained by making a pilgrimage thereto. And for warranty, they appeal to the sayings of the great prophet Alma.'

Cried Mohi, ' But Alma is also quoted by others, in vindication of the pilgrimages to Ofo. They declare that the prophet himself was the first pilgrim that thitherward journeyed : that from thence he departed to the skies.'

Now, excepting this same peak, Maramma is all rolling hill and dale, like the sea after a storm ; which then

seems not to roll, but to stand still, poising its mountains.
Yet the landscape of Maramma has not the merriness of
meadows ; partly because of the shadow of Ofo, and
partly because of the solemn groves in which the Morais
and temples are buried.

According to Mohi, not one solitary tree bearing fruit,
not one esculent root, grows in all the isle ; the population
wholly depending upon the large tribute remitted from
the neighbouring shores.

' It is not that the soil is unproductive,' said Mohi, ' that
these things are so. It is extremely fertile ; but the
inhabitants say that it would be wrong to make a bread-
fruit orchard of the holy island.'

' And hence, my lord,' said Babbalanja, ' while others
are charged with the business of their temporal welfare,
these Islanders take no thought of the morrow ; and
broad Maramma lies one fertile waste in the lagoon.'

CHAPTER II

COMING close to the island, the pennons and trappings of
our canoes were removed; and Vee-Vee was commanded
to descend from the shark's-mouth; and for a time to
lay aside his conch. In token of reverence, our paddlers
also stripped to the waist; an example which even Media
followed; though, as a king, the same homage he rendered
was at times rendered himself.

At every place hitherto visited joyous crowds stood
ready to hail our arrival; but the shores of Maramma
were silent, and forlorn.

Said Babbalanja, ' It looks not as if the lost one were
here.'

At length we landed in a little cove nigh a valley, which
Mohi called Uma; and here in silence we beached our
canoes.

But presently there came to us an old man, with a
beard white as the mane of the pale horse. He was clad
in a midnight robe. He fanned himself with a fan of
faded leaves. A child led him by the hand, for he was
blind, wearing a green plantain leaf over his plaited
brow.

Him, Media accosted, making mention who we were,
and on what errand we came: to seek out Yillah, and
behold the isle.

Whereupon Pani, for such was his name, gave us a
courteous reception; and lavishly promised to discover
sweet Yillah; declaring that in Maramma, if anywhere,

4

the long-lost maiden must be found. He assured us, that throughout the whole land he would lead us ; leaving no place, desirable to be searched, unexplored.

And so saying, he conducted us to his dwelling, for refreshment and repose.

It was large and lofty. Near by, however, were many miserable hovels, with squalid inmates. But the old man's retreat was exceedingly comfortable ; especially abounding in mats for lounging ; his rafters were bowed down by calabashes of good cheer.

During the repast which ensued, blind Pani, freely partaking, enlarged upon the merit of abstinence ; declaring that a thatch overhead, and a cocoa-nut tree, comprised all that was necessary for the temporal welfare of a Mardian. More than this, he assured us was sinful.

He now made known that he officiated as guide in this quarter of the country ; and that as he had renounced all other pursuits to devote himself to showing strangers the island, and more particularly the best way to ascend lofty Ofo, he was necessitated to seek remuneration for his toil.

'My lord,' then whispered Mohi to Media, 'the great prophet Alma always declared, that, without charge, this island was free to all.'

'What recompense do you desire, old man ? ' said Media to Pani.

'What I seek is but little :—twenty rolls of fine tappa ; two score mats of best upland grass ; one canoe-load of bread-fruit and yams ; ten gourds of wine ; and forty strings of teeth ;—you are a large company, but my requisitions are small.'

'Very small,' said Mohi.

'You are extortionate, good Pani,' said Media. 'And what wants an aged mortal like you with all these things ? '

'I thought superfluities were worthless; nay, sinful,' said Babbalanja.

'Is not this your habitation already more than abundantly supplied with all desirable furnishings?' asked Yoomy.

'I am but a lowly labourer,' said the old man, meekly crossing his arms, 'but does not the lowliest labourer ask and receive his reward? and shall I miss mine?—But I beg charity of none. What I ask, I demand; and in the dread name of great Alma, who appointed me a guide.' And to and fro he strode, groping as he went.

Marking his blindness, whispered Babbalanja to Media, 'My lord, methinks this Pani must be a poor guide. In his journeys inland his little child leads him; why not, then, take the guide's guide?'

But Pani would not part with the child.

Then said Mohi in a low voice, 'My lord Media, though I am no appointed guide; yet will I undertake to lead you aright over all this island; for I am an old man, and have been here oft by myself; though I cannot undertake to conduct you up the Peak of Ofo, and to the more secret temples.'

Then Pani said, 'And what mortal may this be, who pretends to thread the labyrinthine wilds of Maramma? Beware!'

'He is one with eyes that see,' made answer Babbalanja.

'Follow him not,' said Pani, 'for he will lead thee astray; no Yillah will he find; and having no warrant as a guide, the curses of Alma will accompany him.'

Now, this was not altogether without effect; for Pani and his fathers before him had always filled the office of guide.

Nevertheless, Media at last decided, that, this time, Mohi should conduct us; which being communicated to Pani, he desired us to remove from his roof. So withdrawing to the skirt of a neighbouring grove, we lingered awhile, to refresh ourselves for the journey in prospect.

As we here reclined, there came up from the seaside a party of pilgrims, but newly arrived.

Apprised of their coming, Pani and his child went out to meet them ; and standing in the path he cried, ' I am the appointed guide ; in the name of Alma I conduct all pilgrims to the temples.'

' This must be the worthy Pani,' said one of the strangers, turning upon the rest.

' Let us take him, then, for our guide,' cried they ; and all drew near.

But upon accosting him, they were told that he guided none without recompense.

And now, being informed that the foremost of the pilgrims was one Divino, a wealthy chief of a distant island, Pani demanded of him his requital.

But the other demurred ; and by many soft speeches at length abated the recompense to three promissory cocoa-nuts, which he covenanted to send Pani at some future day.

The next pilgrim accosted was a sad-eyed maiden, in decent but scanty raiment ; who without seeking to diminish Pani's demands promptly placed in his hands a small hoard of the money of Mardi.

' Take it, holy guide,' she said, ' it is all I have.'

But the third pilgrim, one Fanna, a hale matron, in handsome apparel, needed no asking to bestow her goods. Calling upon her attendants to advance with their burdens, she quickly unrolled them ; and wound round and round Pani, fold after fold of the costliest tappas ; and filled both his hands with teeth ; and his mouth with some savoury marmalade ; and poured oil upon his head ; and knelt and besought of him a blessing.

' From the bottom of my heart I bless thee,' said Pani ;

and still holding her hands exclaimed, ' Take example from this woman, oh Divino ; and do ye likewise, ye pilgrims all ! '

' Not to-day,' said Divino.

' We are not rich, like unto Fanna,' said the rest.

Now, the next pilgrim was a very old and miserable man ; stone blind, covered with rags ; and supporting his steps with a staff.

' My recompense,' said Pani.

' Alas ! I have naught to give. Behold my poverty.'

' I cannot see,' replied Pani ; but feeling of his garments, he said, ' Thou wouldst deceive me ; hast thou not this robe and this staff ? '

' Oh ! merciful Pani, take not my all ! ' wailed the pilgrim. But his worthless gaberdine was thrust into the dwelling of the guide.

Meanwhile, the matron was still enveloping Pani in her interminable tappas.

But the sad-eyed maiden, removing her upper mantle, threw it over the naked form of the beggar.

The fifth pilgrim was a youth of an open, ingenuous aspect ; and with an eye, full of eyes ; his step was light.

' Who art thou ? ' cried Pani, as the stripling touched him in passing.

' I go to ascend the peak,' said the boy.

' Then take me for guide.'

' No, I am strong and lithesome. Alone must I go.'

' But how knowest thou the way ? '

' There are many ways : the right one I must seek for myself.'

' Ah, poor deluded one,' sighed Pani ; ' but thus is it ever with youth ; and rejecting the monitions of wisdom, suffer they must. Go on, and perish ! '

Turning, the boy exclaimed—' Though I act counter to

thy counsels, oh Pani, I but follow the divine instinct in me.'

'Poor youth!' murmured Babbalanja. 'How earnestly he struggles in his bonds. But though rejecting a guide, still he clings to that legend of the peak.'

The rest of the pilgrims now tarried with the guide, preparing for their journey inland.

CHAPTER III

THEY PASS THROUGH THE WOODS

REFRESHED by our stay in the grove, we rose, and placed ourselves under the guidance of Mohi ; who went on in advance.

Winding our way among jungles, we came to a deep hollow, planted with one gigantic palm shaft, belted round by saplings springing from its roots. But, Laocoon-like, sire and sons stood locked in the serpent folds of gnarled, distorted banians ; and the banian-bark, eating into their vital wood, corrupted their veins of sap, till all those palm nuts were poisoned chalices.

Near by stood clean-limbed, comely manchineels, with lustrous leaves and golden fruit. You would have deemed them Trees of Life ; but underneath their branches grew no blade of grass, no herb, nor moss ; the bare earth was scorched by heaven's own dews, filtrated through that fatal foliage.

Farther on, there frowned a grove of blended banian boughs, thick-ranked manchineels, and many a upas ; their summits gilded by the sun ; but below, deep shadows, darkening night-shade ferns, and mandrakes. Buried in their midst, and dimly seen among large leaves, all halberd-shaped, were piles of stone, supporting falling temples of bamboo. Thereon frogs leaped in dampness, trailing round their slime. Thick hung the rafters with lines of pendent sloths ; the upas-trees dropped darkness round ; so dense the shade, nocturnal birds found there perpetual night, and throve on poisoned air. Owls

10

hooted from dead boughs ; or, one by one, sailed by on
silent pinions ; cranes stalked abroad, or brooded in the
marshes ; adders hissed ; bats smote the darkness ;
ravens croaked ; and vampires, fixed on slumbering
lizards, fanned the sultry air.

CHAPTER IV

Now, those doleful woodlands passed, straightway converse was renewed, and much discourse took place concerning Hivohitee, pontiff of the isle.

For, during our first friendly conversation with Pani, Media had inquired for Hivohitee, and sought to know in what part of the island he abode.

Whereto Pani had replied, that the pontiff would be invisible for several days to come ; being engaged with particular company.

And upon further inquiry, as to who were the personages monopolising his hospitalities, Media was dumb when informed, that they were no other than certain incorporeal deities from above, passing the Capricorn Solstice at Maramma.

As on we journeyed, much curiosity being expressed to know more of the pontiff and his guests, old Mohi, familiar with these things, was commanded to enlighten the company. He complied ; and his recital was not a little significant of the occasional credulity of chroniclers.

According to his statement, the deities entertained by Hivohitee belonged to the third class of immortals. These, however, were far elevated above the corporeal demi-gods of Mardi. Indeed, in Hivohitee's eyes, the greatest demi-gods were as gourds. Little wonder, then, that their superiors were accounted the most genteel characters on his visiting list.

These immortals were wonderfully fastidious and dainty

12

as to the atmosphere they breathed ; inhaling no sublunary air, but that of the elevated interior ; where the
pontiff had a rural lodge for the special accommodation of impalpable guests ; who were entertained at very
small cost ; dinners being unnecessary, and dormitories
superfluous.

But Hivohitee permitted not the presence of these
celestial grandees to interfere with his own solid comfort.
Passing his mornings in highly intensified chat, he thrice
reclined at his ease ; partaking of a fine plantain pudding,
and pouring out from a calabash of celestial old wine ;
meanwhile, carrying on the flow of soul with his guests.
And truly, the sight of their entertainer thus enjoying
himself in the flesh, while they themselves starved on the
ether, must have been exceedingly provoking to these
aristocratic and aerial strangers.

It was reported, furthermore, that Hivohitee, one of
the haughtiest of pontiffs, purposely treated his angelical
guests thus cavalierly ; in order to convince them that,
though a denizen of earth, a sublunarian ; and in respect
of heaven, a mere provincial, he (Hivohitee) accounted
himself full as good as seraphim from the capital ; and
that too at the Capricorn Solstice, or any other time of
the year. Strongly bent was Hivohitee upon humbling
their supercilious pretensions.

Besides, was he not accounted a great god in the land ?
supreme ? having power of life and death ? essaying the
deposition of kings ? and dwelling in moody state, all by
himself, in the goodliest island of Mardi ? Though here,
be it said, that his assumptions of temporal supremacy
were but seldom made good by express interference with
the secular concerns of the neighbouring monarchs ; who,
by force of arms, were too apt to argue against his claims
to authority ; however, in theory, they bowed to it. And
now, for the genealogy of Hivohitee ; for eighteen hundred

and forty-seven Hivohitees were alleged to have gone
before him. He came in a right line from the divine
Hivohitee I. : the original grantee of the empire of men's
souls and the first swayer of a crosier. The present
pontiff's descent was unquestionable ; his dignity having
been transmitted through none but heirs-male ; the whole
procession of high priests being the fruit of successive
marriages between uterine brother and sister. A conjunction deemed incestuous in some lands, but, here,
held the only fit channel for the pure transmission of
elevated rank.

Added to the hereditary appellation, Hivohitee, which
simply denoted the sacerdotal station of the pontiffs, and
was but seldom employed in current discourse, they were
individualised by a distinctive name, bestowed upon them
at birth. And the degree of consideration in which they
were held may be inferred from the fact, that during the
lifetime of a pontiff, the leading sound in his name was
banned to ordinary uses. Whence, at every new accession
to the archiepiscopal throne, it came to pass that multitudes of words and phrases were either essentially modi-
fied, or wholly dropped. Wherefore, the language of
Maramma was incessantly fluctuating ; and had become
so full of jargonings, that the birds in the groves were
greatly puzzled ; not knowing where lay the virtue of
sounds so incoherent.

And, in a good measure, this held true of all tongues
spoken throughout the Archipelago ; the birds marvelling
at mankind, and mankind at the birds ; wondering how
they could continually sing ; when, for all man knew to
the contrary, it was impossible they could be holding
intelligent discourse. And thus, though for thousands
of years, men and birds had been dwelling together in
Mardi, they remained wholly ignorant of each other's
secrets ; the Islander regarding the fowl as a senseless

songster, forever in the clouds ; and the fowl him, as a screeching crane, destitute of pinions and lofty aspirations.

Over and above numerous other miraculous powers imputed to the pontiffs as spiritual potentates, there was ascribed to them one special privilege of a secular nature : that of healing with a touch the bites of the ravenous sharks swarming throughout the lagoon. With these they were supposed to be upon the most friendly terms ; according to popular accounts, sociably bathing with them in the sea ; permitting them to rub their noses against their priestly thighs ; playfully mouthing their hands, with all their tiers of teeth.

At the ordination of a pontiff, the ceremony was not deemed complete until, embarking in his barge, he was saluted high priest by three sharks drawing near ; with teeth turned up, swimming beside his canoe.

These monsters were deified in Maramma ; had altars there ; it was deemed worse than homicide to kill one. ' And what if they destroy human life ? ' say the Islanders, ' are they not sacred ? '

Now many more wonderful things were related touching Hivohitee ; and though one could not but doubt the validity of many prerogatives ascribed to him, it was nevertheless hard to do otherwise, than entertain for the pontiff that sort of profound consideration which all render to those who indisputably possess the power of quenching human life with a wish.

CHAPTER V

THEY VISIT THE GREAT MORAI

As garrulous guide to the party, Braid-Beard soon brought us nigh the great Morai of Maramma, the burial-place of the pontiffs, and a rural promenade, for certain idols there inhabiting.

Our way now led through the bed of a shallow water-course ; Mohi observing, as we went, that our feet were being washed at every step ; whereas, to tread the dusty earth would be to desecrate the holy Morai, by trans-ferring thereto the base soil of less sacred ground.

Here and there, thatched arbours were thrown over the stream, for the accommodation of devotees ; who, in these consecrated waters, issuing from a spring in the Morai, bathed their garments, that long life might ensue. Yet, as Braid-Beard assured us, sometimes it happened that divers feeble old men, zealously donning their raiment immediately after immersion, became afflicted with rheumatics ; and instances were related of their falling down dead in this their pursuit of longevity.

Coming to the Morai, we found it enclosed by a wall ; and while the rest were surmounting it, Mohi was busily engaged in the apparently childish occupation of collecting pebbles. Of these, however, to our no small surprise, he presently made use, by irreverently throwing them at all objects to which he was desirous of directing attention. In this manner was pointed out a black boar's head, suspended from a bough. Full twenty of these sentries were on post in the neighbouring trees.

Proceeding, we came to a hillock of bone-dry sand, resting upon the otherwise loamy soil. Possessing a secret, preservative virtue, this sand had, ages ago, been brought from a distant land, to furnish a sepulchre for the pontiffs ; who here, side by side, and sire by son, slumbered all peacefully in the fellowship of the grave. Mohi declared, that were the sepulchre to be opened, it would be the resurrection of the whole line of high priests. 'But a resurrection of bones, after all,' said Babbalanja, ever osseous in his allusions to the departed.

Passing on, we came to a number of runic-looking stones, all over hieroglyphical inscriptions, and placed round an elliptical aperture ; where welled up the sacred spring of the Morai, clear as crystal, and showing through its waters, two tiers of sharp, tusk-like stones ; the mouth of Oro, so called ; and it was held, that if any secular hand should be immersed in the spring, straight upon it those stony jaws would close.

We next came to a large image of a dark-hued stone, representing a burly man, with an overgrown head, and abdomen hollowed out, and open for inspection ; therein, were relics of bones. Before this image we paused. And whether or no it was Mohi's purpose to make us tourists quake with his recitals, his revelations were far from agreeable. At certain seasons, human beings were offered to the idol, which being an epicure in the matter of sacrifices, would accept of no ordinary fare. To ensure his digestion, all indirect routes to the interior were avoided : the sacrifices being packed in the ventricle itself.

Near to this image of Doleema, so called, a solitary forest tree was pointed out ; leafless and dead to the core. But from its boughs hung numerous baskets, brimming over with melons, grapes, and guavas. And daily these baskets were replenished.

As we here stood, there passed a hungry figure, in

ragged raiment : hollow cheeks, and hollow eyes. Wistfully he eyed the offerings ; but retreated ; knowing it was sacrilege to touch them. There, they must decay, in honour of the god Ananna ; for so this dead tree was denominated by Mohi.

Now, as we were thus strolling about the Morai, the old chronicler elucidating its mysteries, we suddenly spied Pani and the pilgrims approaching the image of Doleema ; his child leading the guide.

'This,' began Pani, pointing to the idol of stone, 'is the holy god Ananna who lives in the sap of this green and flourishing tree.'

'Thou meanest not, surely, this stone image we behold ? ' said Divino.

'I mean the tree,' said the guide. 'It is no stone image.'

'Strange,' muttered the chief ; ' were it not a guide that spoke, I would deny it. As it is, I hold my peace.'

'Mystery of mysteries ! ' cried the blind old pilgrim ; ' is it, then, a stone image that Pani calls a tree ? Oh, Oro, that I had eyes to see, that I might verily behold it, and then believe it to be what it is not ; that so I might prove the largeness of my faith ; and so merit the blessing of Alma.'

'Thrice sacred Ananna,' murmured the sad-eyed maiden, falling upon her knees before Doleema, 'receive my adoration. Of thee, I know nothing, but what the guide has spoken. I am but a poor, weak-minded maiden, judging not for myself, but leaning upon others that are wiser. These things are above me. I am afraid to think. In Alma's name, receive my homage.'

And she flung flowers before the god.

But Fanna, the hale matron, turning upon Pani, exclaimed, 'Receive more gifts, oh guide.' And again she showered them upon him.

Upon this, the wilful boy who would not have Pani for his guide, entered the Morai; and perceiving the group before the image, walked rapidly to where they were. And beholding the idol, he regarded it attentively, and said, 'This must be the image of Doleema; but I am not sure.'

'Nay,' cried the blind pilgrim, 'it is the holy tree Ananna, thou wayward boy.'

'A tree? whatever it may be, it is not that; thou art blind, old man.'

'But though blind, I have that which thou lackest.'

Then said Pani, turning upon the boy, 'Depart from the holy Morai, and corrupt not the hearts of these pilgrims. Depart, I say; and, in the sacred name of Alma, perish in thy endeavours to climb the peak.'

'I may perish there in truth,' said the boy, with sadness; 'but it shall be in the path revealed to me in my dream. And think not, oh guide, that I perfectly rely upon gaining that lofty summit. I will climb high Ofo with hope, not faith; oh, mighty Oro, help me!'

'Be not impious,' said Pani; 'pronounce not Oro's sacred name too lightly.'

'Oro is but a sound,' said the boy. 'They call the supreme god, Ati, in my native isle; it is the soundless thought of him, oh guide, that is in me.'

'Hark to his rhapsodies! Hark, how he prates of mysteries, that not even Hivohitee can fathom.'

'Nor he, nor thou, nor I, nor any; Oro, to all, is Oro the unknown.'

'Why claim to know Oro, then, better than others?'

'I am not so vain; and I have little to substitute for what I cannot receive. I but feel Oro in me, yet cannot declare the thought.'

'Proud boy! thy humility is a pretence; at heart, thou deemest thyself wiser than Mardi.'

'Not near so wise. To believe is a haughty thing ; my very doubts humiliate me. I weep and doubt ; all Mardi may be right ; and I too simple to discern.'

'He is mad,' said the chief Divino ; 'never before heard I such words.'

'They are thoughts,' muttered the guide.

'Poor fool ! ' cried Fanna.

'Lost youth ! ' sighed the maiden.

'He is but a child,' said the beggar. 'These whims will soon depart ; once I was like him ; but, praise be to Alma, in the hour of sickness I repented, feeble old man that I am ! '

'It is because I am young and in health,' said the boy, 'that I more nourish the thoughts, that are born of my youth and my health. I am fresh from my Maker, soul and body unwrinkled. On thy sick couch, old man, they took thee at advantage.'

'Turn from the blasphemer,' cried Pani. 'Hence ! thou evil one, to the perdition in store.'

'I will go my ways,' said the boy, ' but Oro will shape the end.'

And he quitted the Morai.

After conducting the party round the sacred enclosure, assisting his way with his staff, for his child had left him, Pani seated himself on a low, mossy stone, grimly surrounded by idols ; and directed the pilgrims to return to his habitation ; where ere long he would rejoin them.

The pilgrims departed, he remained in profound meditation ; while, backward and forward, an invisible ploughshare turned up the long furrows on his brow.

Long he was silent ; then muttered to himself, 'That boy, that wild, wise boy, has stabbed me to the heart. His thoughts are my suspicions. But he is honest. Yet I harm none. Multitudes must have unspoken meditations as well as I. Do we then mutually deceive ? Off masks, mankind, that I may know what warranty of fellowship with others my own thoughts possess. Why, upon this one theme, oh Oro! must all dissemble? Our thoughts are not our own. Whate'er it be, an honest thought must have some germ of truth. But we must set, as flows the general stream; I blindly follow, where I seem to lead; the crowd of pilgrims is so great, they see not there is none to guide.—It hinges upon this: Have we angelic spirits? But in vain, in vain, oh Oro! I essay to live out of this poor, blind body, fit dwelling for my sightless soul. Death, death:—blind, am I dead? for blindness seems a consciousness of death. Will my grave be more dark than all is now?—From dark to dark!—What is this subtle something that is in me, and eludes me? Will it have no end? When, then, did it begin? All, all is chaos! What is this shining light in heaven, this sun they tell me of? Or, do they lie? Methinks, it might blaze convictions; but I brood and grope in blackness; I am dumb with doubt; yet, 'tis not doubt, but worse: I doubt my doubt. Oh, ye all-wise spirits in the air, how can ye witness all this woe, and give no sign? Would, would that mine were a settled doubt, like that wild boy's, who without faith, seems full of it. The undoubting doubter believes the most. Oh! that I were he. Methinks that daring boy hath Alma in him, struggling to be free. But those pilgrims: that trusting girl.—What, if they saw me as I am? Peace, peace, my soul; on, mask, again.'

And he staggered from the Morai.

Cabrini College Library
21617
Radnor, Pa.

CHAPTER VI

THEY DISCOURSE OF THE GODS OF MARDI, AND BRAID-BEARD TELLS OF ONE FONI

WALKING from the sacred enclosure, Mohi discoursed of the plurality of gods in the land, a subject suggested by the multitudinous idols we had just been beholding.

Said Mohi, ' These gods of wood and of stone are nothing in number to the gods in the air. You breathe not a breath without inhaling, you touch not a leaf without ruffling a spirit. There are gods of heaven, and gods of earth ; gods of sea and of land ; gods of peace and of war ; gods of rock and of fell ; gods of ghosts and of thieves ; of singers and dancers ; of lean men and of house-thatchers. Gods glance in the eyes of birds, and sparkle in the crests of the waves ; gods merrily swing in the boughs of the trees, and merrily sing in the brook. Gods are here, and there, and everywhere ; you are never alone for them.'

' If this be so, Braid-Beard,' said Babbalanja, ' our inmost thoughts are overheard ; but not by eavesdroppers. However, my lord, these gods to whom he alludes, merely belong to the semi-intelligibles, the divided unities in unity, this side of the First Adyta.'

' Indeed ? ' said Media.

' Semi-intelligible, say you, philosopher ? ' cried Mohi. ' Then, prithee, make it appear so ; for what you say seems gibberish to me.'

' Babbalanja,' said Media, ' no more of your abstrusities ; what know you mortals of us gods and demi-gods ?

22

But tell me, Mohi, how many of your deities of rock and fell think you there are ? Have you no statistical table ? '

'My lord, at the lowest computation, there must be at least three billion trillion of quintillions.'

'A mere unit !' said Babbalanja. 'Old man, would you express an infinite number ? Then take the sum of the follies of Mardi for your multiplicand ; and for your multiplier the totality of sublunarians that never have been heard of since they became no more ; and the product shall exceed your quintillions, even though all their units were nonillions.'

'Have done, Babbalanja !' cried Media ; 'you are showing the sinister vein in your marble. Have done. Take a warm bath, and make tepid your cold blood. But come, Mohi, tell us of the ways of this Maramma ; something of the Morai and its idols, if you please.'

And straightway Braid-Beard proceeded with a narration, in substance as follows :—

It seems, there was a particular family upon the island, whose members, for many generations, had been set apart as sacrifices for the deity called Doleema. They were marked by a sad and melancholy aspect, and a certain involuntary shrinking, when passing the Morai. And though, when it came to the last, some of these unfortunates went joyfully to their doom, declaring that they gloried to die in the service of holy Doleema ; still, were there others, who audaciously endeavoured to shun their fate ; upon the approach of a festival, fleeing to the innermost wilderness of the island. But little availed their flight. For swift on their track sped the hereditary butler of the insulted god, one Xiki, whose duty it was to provide the sacrifices. And when crouching in some covert, the fugitive spied Xiki's approach, so fearful did he become of the vengeance of the deity he sought to evade, that renouncing all hope of escape, he would burst from his lair, exclaiming, ' Come on, and kill ! ' baring his breast for the javelin that slew him.

The chronicles of Maramma were full of horrors.

In the wild heart of the island, was said still to lurk the remnant of a band of warriors, who, in the days of the sire of the present pontiff, had risen in arms to dethrone him, headed by Foni, an upstart prophet, a personage distinguished for the uncommon beauty of his person. With terrible carnage, these warriors had been defeated ; and the survivors, fleeing into the interior, for thirty days were pursued by the victors. But though many were overtaken and speared, a number survived ; who, at last, wandering forlorn and in despair, like demoniacs, ran wild in the woods. And the Islanders, who at times penetrated into the wilderness, for the purpose of procuring rare herbs, often scared from their path some spectre, glaring through the foliage. Thrice had these demoniacs been discovered prowling about the inhabited portions of the isle ; and at daybreak, an attendant of the holy Morai once came upon a frightful figure, doubled with age, helping itself to the offerings in the image of Doleema. The demoniac was slain ; and from his ineffaceable tattooing it was proved that this was no other than Foni, the false prophet ; the splendid form he had carried into the rebel fight, now squalid with age and misery.

CHAPTER VII

THEY VISIT THE LAKE OF YAMMO

FROM the Morai, we bent our steps toward an unoccupied
arbour; and here, refreshing ourselves with the viands
presented by Borabolla, we passed the night. And next
morning proceeded to voyage round to the opposite
quarter of the island; where, in the sacred lake of Yammo,
stood the famous temple of Oro, also the great gallery of
the inferior deities.

The lake was but a portion of the smooth lagoon, made
separate by an arm of wooded reef, extending from the
high western shore of the island, and curving round
toward a promontory, leaving a narrow channel to the
sea, almost invisible, however, from the land-locked
interior.

In this lake were many islets, all green with groves. Its
main shore was a steep acclivity, with jutting points, each
crowned with mossy old altars of stone, or ruinous
temples, darkly reflected in the green, glassy water;
while, from its long line of stately trees, the low reef-side
of the lake looked one verdant bluff.

Gliding in upon Yammo, its many islets greeted us like
a little Mardi; but ever and anon we started at long lines
of phantoms in the water, reflections of the long line of
images on the shore.

Toward the islet of Dolzono we first directed our way;
and there we beheld the great gallery of the gods; a
mighty temple, resting on one hundred tall pillars of palm,
each based, below the surface, on the buried body of a

25

man ; its nave one vista of idols ; names carved on their
foreheads : Ogro, Tripoo, Indrimarvoki, Parzillo, Vivivi,
Jojijojorora, Jorkraki, and innumerable others.

Crowds of attendants were new-grouping the images.

' My lord, you behold one of their principal occupations,'
said Mohi.

Said Media : ' I have heard much of the famed image of
Mujo, the Nursing Mother ;—can you point it out, Braid-
Beard ? '

' My lord, when last here, I saw Mujo at the head of
this file ; but they must have removed it ; I see it not
now.'

' Do these attendants, then,' said Babbalanja, ' so
continually new-marshal the idols, that visiting the gallery
to-day, you are at a loss to-morrow ? '

' Even so,' said Braid-Beard. ' But behold, my lord,
this image is Mujo.'

We stood before an obelisk-idol, so towering, that
gazing at it, we were fain to throw back our heads.
According to Mohi, winding stairs led up through its legs ;
its abdomen a cellar, thick-stored with gourds of old wine ;
its head a hollow dome ; in rude alto-relievo, its scores of
hillock-breasts were carved over with legions of baby
deities, frog-like sprawling ; while, within, were secreted
whole litters of infant idols, there placed to imbibe
divinity from the knots of the wood.

As we stood, a strange subterranean sound was heard,
mingled with a gurgling as of wine being poured. Looking
up, we beheld, through arrow-slits and port-holes, three
masks cross-legged seated in the abdomen, and holding
stout wassail. But instantly upon descrying us, they
vanished deeper into the interior ; and presently was
heard a sepulchral chant, and many groans and grievous
tribulations.

Passing on, we came to an image, with a long anaconda-like posterior development, wound round and round its own neck.

'This must be Oloo, the god of Suicides,' said Babbalanja.

'Yes,' said Mohi, 'you perceive, my lord, how he lays violent tail upon himself.'

At length, the attendants having, in due order, new-disposed the long lines of sphinxes and griffins, and many-limbed images, a band of them, in long flowing robes, began their morning chant :—

> Awake, Rarni ! awake, Foloona !
> Awake, unnumbered deities !

with many similar invocations, to which the images made not the slightest rejoinder. Not discouraged, however, the attendants now separately proceeded to offer up petitions on behalf of various tribes, retaining them for that purpose.

One prayed for abundance of rain, that the yams of Valapee might not wilt in the ground ; another for dry sunshine, as most favourable for the present state of the bread-fruit crop in Mondoldo.

Hearing all this, Babbalanja thus spoke : ' Doubtless, my lord Media, besides these petitions we hear, there are ten thousand contradictory prayers ascending to these idols. But methinks the gods will not jar the eternal progression of things by any hints from below ; even were it possible to satisfy conflicting desires.'

Said Yoomy : ' But I would pray, nevertheless, Babbalanja ; for prayer draws us near to our own souls, and purifies our thoughts.   Nor will I grant that our supplications are altogether in vain.'

Still wandering among the images, Mohi had much to say, concerning their respective claims to the reverence of the devout.

For though, in one way or other, all Mardians bowed to the supremacy of Oro, they were not so unanimous concerning the inferior deities; those supposed to be intermediately concerned in sublunary things. Some nations sacrificed to one god; some to another; each maintaining that their own god was the most potential.

Observing that all the images were more or less defaced, Babbalanja sought the reason.

To which, Braid-Beard made answer, that they had been thus defaced by hostile devotees; who quarrelling in the great gallery of the gods, and getting beside themselves with rage, often sought to pull down, and demolish each other's favourite idols.

' But behold,' cried Babbalanja, ' there seems not a single image unmutilated. How is this, old man ? '

' It is thus. While one faction defaces the images of its adversaries, its own images are in like manner assailed ; whence it comes that no idol escapes.'

' No more, no more, Braid-Beard,' said Media. ' Let us depart, and visit the islet, where the god of all these gods is enshrined.'

CHAPTER VIII

DEEP, deep, in deep groves, we found the great temple of
Oro, Spreader-of-the-Sky, and deity supreme.

While here we silently stood eyeing this Mardi-renowned
image, there entered the fane a great multitude of its
attendants, holding pearl shells on their heads, filled with
a burning incense. And ranging themselves in a crowd
round Oro, they began a long-rolling chant, a sea of
sounds ; and the thick smoke of their incense went up to
the roof.

And now approached Pani and the pilgrims ; followed,
at a distance, by the wilful boy.

' Behold great Oro,' said the guide.

' We see naught but a cloud,' said the chief Divino.

' My ears are stunned by the chanting,' said the blind
pilgrim.

' Receive more gifts, oh guide ! ' cried Fanna the
matron.

' Oh Oro ! invisible Oro ! I kneel,' slow murmured the
sad-eyed maid.

But now, a current of air swept aside the eddying
incense ; and the wilful boy, all eagerness to behold the
image, went hither and thither ; but the gathering of
attendants was great, and at last he exclaimed, ' Oh
Oro ! I cannot see thee, for the crowd that stands between
thee and me.'

' Who is this babbler ? ' cried they with the censers,
one and all turning upon the pilgrims ; ' let him speak no

29

more ; but bow down, and grind the dust where he stands ; and declare himself the vilest creature that crawls. So Oro and Alma command.'

'I feel nothing in me so utterly vile,' said the boy, 'and I cringe to none. But I would as lief *adore* your image, as that in my heart, for both mean the same ; but more, how can I ? I love great Oro, though I comprehend him not. I marvel at his works, and feel as nothing in his sight ; but because he is thus omnipotent, and I a mortal, it follows not that I am vile. Nor so doth he regard me. We do ourselves degrade ourselves, not Oro us. Hath not Oro made me ? And therefore am I not worthy to stand erect before him ? Oro is almighty, but no despot. I wonder ; I hope ; I love ; I weep ; I have in me a feeling nigh to fear, that is not fear ; but wholly vile I am not ; nor can we love and cringe. But Oro knows my heart, which I cannot speak.'

'Impious boy,' cried they with the censers, 'we will offer thee up before the very image thou contemnest. In the name of Alma, seize him.'

And they bore him away unresisting.

'Thus perish the ungodly,' said Pani to the shuddering pilgrims.

And they quitted the temple, to journey toward the Peak of Ofo.

'My soul bursts !' cried Yoomy. 'My lord, my lord, let us save the boy.'

'Speak not,' said Media. 'His fate is fixed. Let Mardi stand.'

'Then let us away from hence, my lord ; and join the pilgrims ; for, in these inland vales, the lost one may be found, perhaps at the very base of Ofo.'

'Not there ; not there,' cried Babbalanja. 'Yillah may have touched these shores ; but long since she must have fled.'

CHAPTER IX

THEY DISCOURSE OF ALMA

SAILING to and fro in the lake, to view its scenery, much discourse took place concerning the things we had seen ; and far removed from the censer-bearers, the sad fate that awaited the boy was now the theme of all.

A good deal was then said of Alma, to whom the guide, the pilgrims, and the censer - bearers had frequently alluded, as to some paramount authority.

Called upon to reveal what his chronicles said on this theme, Braid-Beard complied ; at great length narrating, what now follows condensed.

Alma, it seems, was an illustrious prophet, and teacher divine ; who, ages ago, at long intervals, and in various islands, had appeared to the Mardians under the different titles of Brami, Manko, and Alma. Many thousands of moons had elapsed since his last and most memorable avatar, as Alma on the Isle of Maramma. Each of his advents had taken place in a comparatively dark and benighted age. Hence, it was devoutly believed, that he came to redeem the Mardians from their heathenish thrall ; to instruct them in the ways of truth, virtue, and happiness ; to allure them to good by promises of beatitude hereafter ; and to restrain them from evil by denunciations of woe. Separated from the impurities and corruptions, which in a long series of centuries had become attached to everything originally uttered by the prophet, the maxims, which as Brami he had taught, seemed similar to those inculcated by Manko. But as Alma, adapting his lessons to the improved condition of humanity, the divine prophet had more completely unfolded his scheme ; as Alma, he had made his last revelation.

This narration concluded, Babbalanja mildly observed, ' Mohi : without seeking to accuse you of uttering false-hoods ; since what you relate rests not upon testimony of your own ; permit me, to question the fidelity of your account of Alma. The prophet came to dissipate errors, you say ; but superadded to many that have survived the past, ten thousand others have originated in various constructions of the principles of Alma himself. The prophet came to do away all gods but one ; but since the days of Alma, the idols of Maramma have more than quadrupled. The prophet came to make us Mardians more virtuous and happy ; but along with all previous good, the same wars, crimes, and miseries, which existed in Alma's day, under various modifications are yet extant. Nay : take from your chronicles, Mohi, the history of those horrors, one way or other, resulting from the doings of Alma's nominal followers, and your chronicles would not so frequently make mention of blood. The prophet came to guarantee our eternal felicity ; but according to what is held in Maramma, that felicity rests on so hard a proviso, that to a thinking mind, but very few of our sinful race may secure it. For one, then, I wholly reject your Alma ; not so much because of all that is hard to be understood in his histories ; as because of obvious and undeniable things all round us ; which, to me, seem at war with an unreserved faith in his doctrines as pro-mulgated here in Maramma. Besides, everything in this isle strengthens my incredulity ; I never was so thorough a disbeliever as now.'

' Let the winds be laid,' cried Mohi, ' while your rash confession is being made in this sacred lake.'

Said Media : ' Philosopher ; remember the boy, and they that seized him.'

' Ah ! I do indeed remember him. Poor youth ! in his agony, how my heart yearned toward his. But that very prudence which you deny me, my lord, prevented me from saying aught in his behalf. Have you not observed, that until now, when we are completely by ourselves, I have refrained from freely discoursing of what we have seen in this island ? Trust me, my lord, there is no man, that bears more in mind the necessity of being either a believer or a hypocrite in Maramma, and the imminent peril of being honest here, than I, Babbalanja. And have I not reason to be wary, when in my boyhood, my own sire was burnt for his temerity ; and in this very isle ? Just Oro ! it was done in the name of Alma,—what wonder then, that, at times, I almost hate that sound. And from those flames, they devoutly swore he went to others,—horrible fable ! '

Said Mohi : ' Do you deny, then, the everlasting torments ? '

' 'Tis not worth a denial. Nor by formally denying it, will I run the risk of shaking the faith of thousands, who in that pious belief find infinite consolation for all they suffer in Mardi.'

' How ? ' said Media ; ' are there those who soothe themselves with the thought of everlasting flames ? '

' One would think so, my lord, since they defend that dogma more resolutely than any other. Sooner will they yield you the isles of Paradise, than it. And in truth, as liege followers of Alma, they would seem but right in clinging to it as they do ; for, according to all one hears in Maramma, the great end of the prophet's mission seems to have been the revealing to us Mardians the existence of horrors, most hard to escape. But better we were all annihilated, than that one man should be damned.'

Rejoined Media : ' But think you not, that possibly, Alma may have been misconceived ? Are you certain that doctrine is his ? '

' I know nothing more than that such is the belief in this land. And in these matters I know not where else to go for information. But, my lord, had I been living in those days when certain men are said to have been actually possessed by spirits from hell, I had not let slip the opportunity—as our forefathers did—to cross-question them concerning the place they came from.'

' Well, well,' said Media, ' your Alma's faith concerns not me : I am a king, and a demi-god ; and leave vulgar torments to the commonalty.'

' But it concerns me,' muttered Mohi ; ' yet I know not what to think.'

' For me,' said Yoomy, ' I reject it. Could I, I would not believe it. It is at variance with the dictates of my heart ; instinctively my heart turns from it, as a thirsty man from gall.'

' Hush ; say no more,' said Mohi ; ' again we approach the shore.'

CHAPTER X

MOHI TELLS OF ONE RAVOO, AND THEY LAND TO VISIT
HEVANEVA, A FLOURISHING ARTISAN

HAVING seen all worth viewing in Yammo, we departed,
to complete the circumnavigation of the island by
returning to Uma without reversing our prows. As we
glided along, we passed many objects of interest, concerning which Mohi, as usual, was very diffuse.

Among other things pointed out, were certain little
altars, like milestones, planted here and there upon bright
bluffs, running out into the lagoon. Dedicated respectively to the guardian spirits of Maramma, these altars
formed a chain of spiritual defences ; and here were
presumed to stand post the most vigilant of warders ;
dread Hivohitee, all by himself, garrisoning the impregnable interior.

But these sentries were only subalterns, subject to the
beck of the pontiff ; who frequently sent word to them
concerning the duties of their watch. His mandates
were entrusted to one Ravoo, the hereditary pontifical
messenger, a long-limbed varlet, so swift of foot that
he was said to travel like a javelin. ' Art thou Ravoo,
that thou so pliest thy legs ? ' say these Islanders, to one
encountered in a hurry.

Hivohitee's postman held no oral communication with
the sentries. Dispatched round the island with divers
bits of tappa, hieroglyphically stamped, he merely deposited one upon each altar ; superadding a stone, to
keep the missive in its place ; and so went his rounds.

35

Now, his route lay over hill and over dale, and over many a coral rock ; and to preserve his feet from bruises, he was fain to wear a sort of buskin, or boot, fabricated of a durable tappa, made from the thickest and toughest of fibres. As he never wore his buskins except when he carried the mail, Ravoo sorely fretted with his Hessians ; though it would have been highly imprudent to travel without them. To make the thing more endurable, therefore, and, at intervals, to cool his heated pedals, he established a series of stopping-places, or stages ; at each of which a fresh pair of buskins, hanging from a tree, were taken down and vaulted into by the ingenious traveller. Those relays of boots were exceedingly convenient ; next, indeed, to being lifted upon a fresh pair of legs.

'Now, to what purpose that anecdote ? ' demanded Babbalanja of Mohi, who in substance related it.

'Marry ! 'tis but the simple recital of a fact ; and I tell it to entertain the company.'

'But has it any meaning you know of ? '

'Thou art wise ; find out,' retorted Braid-Beard.

'But what comes of it ? ' persisted Babbalanja.

'Beshrew me, this senseless catechising of thine,' replied Mohi ; 'naught else, it seems, save a grin or two.'

'And pray, what may you be driving at, philosopher ? ' interrupted Media.

'I am intent upon the essence of things ; the mystery that lieth beyond ; the elements of the tear which much laughter provoketh ; that which is beneath the seeming ; the precious pearl within the shaggy oyster. I probe the circle's centre ; I seek to evolve the inscrutable.'

'Seek on ; and when aught is found, cry out, that we may run to see.'

'My lord the king is merry upon me. To him my more subtle cogitations seem foolishness. But believe me, my lord, there is more to be thought of than to be seen.

There is a world of wonders insphered within the spontaneous consciousness ; or, as old Bardianna hath it, a
mystery within the obvious, yet an obviousness within
the mystery.'

' And did I ever deny that ? ' said Media.'

' As plain as my hand in the dark,' said Mohi.

' I dreamed a dream,' said Yoomy.

' They banter me ; but enough ; I am to blame for
discoursing upon the deep world wherein I live. I am
wrong in seeking to invest sublunary sounds with celestial
sense. Much that is in me is incommunicable by this
ether we breathe. But I blame ye not.' And wrapping
round him his mantle, Babbalanja retired into its most
private folds.

Ere coming in sight of Uma, we put into a little bay, to
pay our respects to Hevaneva, a famous character there
dwelling, who, assisted by many journeymen, carried on
the lucrative business of making idols for the surrounding
isles.

Know ye, that all idols not made in Maramma, and
consecrated by Hivohitee ; and, what is more, in strings
of teeth paid down for to Hevaneva ; are of no more
account than logs, stocks, or stones. Yet does not the
cunning artificer monopolise the profits of his vocation ;
for Hevaneva being but the vassal of the pontiff, the
latter lays claim to King Leo's share of the spoils, and
secures it.

The place was very prettily lapped in a pleasant dell,
nigh to the margin of the water ; and here were several
spacious arbours ; wherein, prostrate upon their sacred
faces, were all manner of idols, in every imaginable stage
of statuary development.

With wonderful industry the journeymen were plying
their tools :—some chiselling noses ; some trenching for
mouths ; and others, with heated flints, boring for ears :

a hole drilled straight through the occiput, representing the auricular organs.

'How easily they are seen through,' said Babbalanja, taking a sight through one of the heads.

The last finish is given to their godships, by rubbing them all over with dried slips of consecrated shark skin, rough as sand-paper, tacked over bits of wood.

In one of the farther arbours, Hevaneva pointed out a goodly array of idols, all complete and ready for the market. They were of every variety of pattern ; and of every size ; from that of a giant, to the little images worn in the ears of the ultra devout.

'Of late,' said the artist, 'there has been a lively demand for the image of Arbino, the god of fishing ; the present being the principal season for that business. For Nadams (Nadam presides over love and wine), there has also been urgent call ; it being the time of the grape ; and the maidens growing frolicsome withal, and devotional.'

Seeing that Hevaneva handled his wares with much familiarity, not to say irreverence, Babbalanja was minded to learn from him what he thought of his trade ; whether the images he made were genuine or spurious ; in a word, whether he believed in his gods.

His reply was curious. But still more so, the marginal gestures wherewith he helped out the text.

'When I cut down the trees for my idols,' said he, ' they are nothing but logs ; when upon those logs, I chalk out the figures of my images, they yet remain logs ; when the chisel is applied, logs they are still ; and when all complete, I at last stand them up in my studio, even then they are logs. Nevertheless, when I handle the pay, they are as prime gods as ever were turned out in Maramma.'

'You must make a very great variety,' said Babbalanja.

'All sorts, all sorts.'

' And from the same material, I presume.'

' Ay, ay, one grove supplies them all. And, on an average, each tree stands us in full fifty idols. Then, we often take second-hand images in part pay for new ones. These we work over again into new patterns ; touching up their eyes and ears ; resetting their noses ; and more especially new-footing their legs, where they always decay first.'

Under sanction of the pontiff, Hevaneva, in addition to his large commerce in idols, also carried on the highly lucrative business of canoe-building ; the profits whereof, undivided, he dropped into his private exchequer. But Mohi averred, that the pontiff often charged him with neglecting his images for his canoes. Be that as it may, Hevaneva drove a thriving trade at both avocations. And in demonstration of the fact, he directed our attention to three long rows of canoes, upheld by wooden supports. They were in perfect order ; at a moment's notice, ready for launching ; being furnished with paddles, out-riggers, masts, sails, and a human skull, with a short handle thrust through one of its eyes, the ordinary bailer of Maramma ; besides other appurtenances, including on the prow a duodecimo idol to match.

Owing to a superstitious preference bestowed upon the wood and work of the sacred island, Hevaneva's canoes were in as high repute as his idols ; and sold equally well.

In truth, in several ways one trade helped the other. The larger images being dug out of the hollow part of the canoes ; and all knotty odds and ends reserved for the idol earrings.

' But after all,' said the artificer, ' I find a readier sale for my images than for my canoes.'

' And so it will ever be,' said Babbalanja.—' Stick to thy idols, man ! a trade more reliable than the baker's.'

CHAPTER XI

A NURSERY TALE OF BABBALANJA'S

HAVING taken to our canoes once again, we were silently sailing along, when Media observed, 'Babbalanja; though I seldom trouble myself with such thoughts, I have just been thinking, how difficult it must be, for the more ignorant sort of people, to decide upon what particular image to worship as a guardian deity, when in Maramma, it seems, there exists such a multitude of idols, and a thousand more are to be heard of.'

'Not at all, your highness. The more ignorant the better. The multitude of images distracts them not. But I am in no mood for serious discourse; let me tell you a story.'

'A story! hear him: the solemn philosopher is desirous of regaling us with a tale! But pray, begin.'

'Once upon a time, then,' said Babbalanja, indifferently adjusting his girdle, 'nine blind men, with uncommonly long noses, set out on their travels to see the great island on which they were born.'

'A precious beginning,' muttered Mohi. 'Nine blind men setting out to see sights.'

Continued Babbalanja: 'Staff in hand, they travelled; one in advance of the other; each man with his palm upon the shoulder next him; and he with the longest nose took the lead of the file. Journeying on in this manner, they came to a valley, in which reigned a king called Tammaro. Now, in a certain enclosure toward the head of the valley, there stood an immense wild banian-tree; all over moss,

and many centuries old, and forming quite a wood in
itself ; its thousand boughs striking into the earth, and
fixing there as many gigantic trunks.   With Tammaro,
it had long been a question which of those many trunks
was the original and true one ; a matter that had puzzled
the wisest heads among his subjects ; and in vain had
a reward been offered for the solution of the perplexity.
But the tree was so vast, and its fabric so complex ; and
its rooted branches so similar in appearance ; and so
numerous, from the circumstance that every year added
to them, that it was quite impossible to determine the
point.   Nevertheless, no sooner did the nine blind men
hear that there was a reward offered for discovering the
trunk of a tree, standing all by itself, than, one and all,
they assured Tammaro that they would quickly settle
that little difficulty of his ; and loudly inveighed against
the stupidity of his sages, who had been so easily posed.
So, being conducted into the enclosure, and assured that
the tree was somewhere within, they separated their
forces, so as at wide intervals to surround it at a distance ;
when feeling their way, with their staves and their noses,
they advanced to the search, crying out—" Pshaw ! make
room there ; let us wise men feel of the mystery."   Presently, striking with his nose one of the rooted branches,
the foremost blind man quickly knelt down ; and feeling
that it struck into the earth, gleefully shouted : " Here
it is ! here it is ! "   But almost in the same breath, his
companions, also, each striking a branch with his staff or
his nose, cried out in like manner, " Here it is ! here it is ! "
Whereupon they were all confounded : but directly, the
man who first cried out thus addressed the rest : " Good
friends, surely you 're mistaken.   There is but one tree in
the place, and here it is."   " Very true," said the others,
all together ; " there is only *one* tree ; but *here* it is."
" Nay," said the others, " it is *here*! " and so saying, each

blind man triumphantly felt of the branch, where it
penetrated into the earth. Then again said the first
speaker : " Good friends, if you will not believe what I
say, come hither, and feel for yourselves." " Nay, nay,"
replied they, " why seek further ? *here* it is ; and nowhere
else can it be." " You blind fools, you, you contradict
yourselves," continued the first speaker, waxing wroth ;
" how can you each have hold of a separate trunk, when
there is but one in the place ? " Whereupon, they re-
doubled their cries, calling each other all manner of oppro-
brious names, and presently they fell to beating each
other with their staves, and charging upon each other
with their noses. But soon after, being loudly called
upon by Tammaro and his people ; who all this while had
been looking on ; being loudly called upon, I say, to clap
their hands on the trunk, they again rushed for their
respective branches ; and it so happened, that, one and
all, they changed places ; but still cried out, " *Here* it is ;
here it is ! " " Peace ! peace ! ye silly blind men," said
Tammaro. " Will ye without eyes presume to see more
sharply than those who have them ? The tree is too much
for us all. Hence ! depart from the valley." '

' An admirable story,' cried Media. ' I had no idea
that a mere mortal, least of all a philosopher, could acquit
himself so well. By my sceptre, but it is well done !
Ha, ha ! blind men round a banian ! Why, Babbalanja,
no demi-god could surpass it. Taji, could you ? '

' But, Babbalanja, what under the sun mean you by
your blind story ! ' cried Mohi. ' Obverse, or reverse, I
can make nothing out of it.'

' Others may,' said Babbalanja. ' It is a polysensuum,
old man.'

' A pollywog ! ' said Mohi.

CHAPTER XII

LANDING TO VISIT HIVOHITEE THE PONTIFF, THEY EN-
COUNTER AN EXTRAORDINARY OLD HERMIT; WITH
WHOM YOOMY HAS A CONFIDENTIAL INTERVIEW, BUT
LEARNS LITTLE

GLIDING on, suddenly we spied a solitary Islander putting out in his canoe from a neighbouring cove.

Drawing near, the stranger informed us that he was just from the face of the great pontiff, Hivohitee, who, having dismissed his celestial guests, had retired to his private sanctuary. Upon this, Media resolved to land forthwith, and under the guidance of Mohi, proceed inland, and pay a visit to his Holiness.

Quitting the beach, our path penetrated into the solitudes of the groves. Skirting the way were tall casaurinas, a species of cypress, standing motionless in the shadows, as files of mutes at a funeral. But here and there they were overrun with the adventurous vines of the convolvulus, the Morning Glory of the Tropics, whose tendrils, bruised by the twigs, dropped milk upon the dragon-like scales of the trees.

This vine is of many varieties. Lying perdu, and shunning the garish sun through the day, one species rises at night with the stars; bursting forth in dazzling constellations of blossoms, which close at dawn. Others, slumbering through the darkness, are up and abroad with their petals, by peep of morn; and after inhaling its breath, again drop their lids in repose. While a third species, more capricious, refuse to expand at all, unless

43

in the most brilliant sunshine, and upon the very tops of
the loftiest trees. Ambitious flowers ! that will not blow,
unless in high places, with the bright day looking on and
admiring.

Here and there we passed open glades in the woods,
delicious with the incense of violets. Balsamic ferns,
stirred by the breeze, fanned all the air with aromas.
These glades were delightful.

Journeying on, we at length came to a dark glen so
deftly hidden by the surrounding copses, that were it not
for the miasma thence wafted, an ignorant wayfarer
might pass and repass it, time and again, never dreaming
of its vicinity.

Down into the gloom of this glen we descended. Its
sides were mantled with noxious shrubs, whose exhalations,
half-way down, unpleasantly blended with the piny breeze
from the uplands. Through its bed ran a brook, whose
encrusted margin had a strange metallic lustre, from the
polluted waters here flowing ; their source a sulphur
spring, of vile flavour and odour, where many invalid
pilgrims resorted.

The woods all round were haunted by the dismal
cawings of crows ; tap, tap, the black hawk whetted his
bill on the boughs ; each trunk stalked a ghost ; and from
those trunks Hevaneva procured the wood for his idols.

Rapidly crossing this place, Yoomy's hands to his ears,
old Mohi's to his nostrils, and Babbalanja vainly trying to
walk with closed eyes, we toiled among steep, flinty rocks,
along a wild, zigzag pathway ; like a mule-track in the
Andes, not so much onward as upward ; Yoomy above
Babbalanja, my lord Media above him, and Braid-Beard,
our guide, in the air, above all.

Strewn over with cinders, the vitreous marl seemed
tumbled together, as if belched from a volcano's throat.

Presently, we came to a tall, slender structure, hidden

among the scenic projections of the cliffs, like a monument in the dark, vaulted ways of an abbey. Surrounding it, were five extinct craters. The air was sultry and still, as if full of spent thunderbolts.

Like a Hindoo pagoda, this bamboo edifice rose story above story ; its many angles and points decorated with pearl shells suspended by cords. But the uppermost story, some ten toises in the air, was closely thatched from apex to floor ; which summit was gained by a series of ascents.

What eremite dwelleth here, like St. Stylites at the top of his column ?—a question which Mohi seemed all eagerness to have answered.

Dropping upon his knees, he gave a peculiar low call : no response. Another : all was silent. Marching up to the pagoda, and again dropping upon his knees, he shook the bamboos till the edifice rocked, and its pearl shells jingled, as if a troop of Andalusian mules, with bells round their necks, were galloping along the defile.

At length the thatch aloft was thrown open, and a head was thrust forth. It was that of an old, old man ; with steel-gray eyes, hair and beard, and a horrible necklace of jawbones.

Now, issuing from the pagoda, Mohi turned about to gain a view of the ghost he had raised ; and no sooner did he behold it than, with King Media and the rest, he made a marked salutation.

Presently, the eremite pointed to where Yoomy was standing ; and waved his hand upward ; when Mohi informed the minstrel, that it was St. Stylites' pleasure that he should pay him a visit.

Wondering what was to come, Yoomy proceeded to mount ; and at last arriving toward the top of the pagoda, was met by an opening, from which an encouraging arm assisted him to gain the ultimate landing.

Here, all was murky enough ; for the aperture from which the head of the apparition had been thrust was now closed ; and what little twilight there was came up through the opening in the floor.

In this dismal seclusion, silently the hermit confronted the minstrel ; his gray hair, eyes, and beard all gleaming, as if streaked with phosphorus ; while his ghastly gorget grinned hideously, with all its jaws.

Mutely Yoomy waited to be addressed ; but hearing no sound, and becoming alive to the strangeness of his situation, he meditated whether it would not be well to subside out of sight, even as he had come—through the floor. An intention which the eremite must have anticipated ; for of a sudden, something was slid over the opening ; and the apparition seating itself thereupon, the twain were in darkness complete.

Shut up thus, with an inscrutable stranger posted at the only aperture of escape, poor Yoomy fell into something like a panic ; hardly knowing what step to take next. As for endeavouring to force his way out, it was alarming to think of ; for aught he knew, the eremite, availing himself of the gloom, might be bristling all over with javelin points.

At last, the silence was broken.

' What see you, mortal ? '

' Chiefly darkness,' said Yoomy, wondering at the audacity of the question.

' I dwell in it. But what else see you, mortal ? '

' The dim gleaming of thy gorget.'

' But that is not me. What else dost thou see ? '

' Nothing.'

' Then thou hast found me out, and seen all ! Descend.'

And with that, the passage-way opened, and groping through the twilight, Yoomy obeyed the mandate, and retreated ; full of vexation at his enigmatical reception.

On his alighting, Mohi inquired whether the hermit was not a wonderful personage.

But thinking some sage waggery lurked in the question ; and at present too indignant to enter into details, the minstrel made some impatient reply ; and winding through a defile, the party resumed its journey.

Straggling behind, to survey the strange plants and flowers in his path, Yoomy became so absorbed, as almost to forget the scene in the pagoda ; yet every moment expected to be nearing the stately abode of the pontiff.

But suddenly, the scene around grew familiar ; the path seemed that which had been followed just after leaving the canoes ; and at length the place of debarkation was in sight.

Surprised that the object of our visit should have been thus abandoned, the minstrel ran forward, and sought an explanation.

Whereupon, Mohi lifted his hands in amazement ; exclaiming at the blindness of the eyes, which had beheld the supreme pontiff of Maramma, without knowing it.

The old hermit was no other than the dread Hivohitee ; the pagoda, the inmost oracle of the isle.

CHAPTER XIII

BABBALANJA ENDEAVOURS TO EXPLAIN THE MYSTERY

THIS Great Mogul of a personage, then ; this woundy Ahasuerus ; this man of men ; this same Hivohitee, whose name rumbled among the mountains like a peal of thunder, had been seen face to face, and taken for naught but a bearded old hermit, or, at best, some equivocal conjurer.

So great was his wonderment at the time, that Yoomy could not avoid expressing it in words.

Whereupon thus discoursed Babbalanja :

' Gentle Yoomy, be not astounded that Hivohitee is so far behind your previous conceptions. The shadows of things are greater than themselves ; and the more exaggerated the shadow, the more unlike to the substance.'

' But knowing now, what manner of person Hivohitee is,' said Yoomy, ' much do I long to behold him again.'

But Mohi assured him it was out of the question ; that the pontiff always acted toward strangers as toward him (Yoomy) ; and that but one dim blink at the eremite was all that mortal could obtain.

Debarred thus from a second and more satisfactory interview with one, concerning whom his curiosity had been violently aroused, the minstrel again turned to Mohi for enlightenment ; especially touching that magnate's Egyptian reception of him in his aerial den.

Whereto, the chronicler made answer, that the pontiff affected darkness because he liked it : that he was a ruler of few words, but many deeds ; and that, had Yoomy

48

been permitted to tarry longer with him in the pagoda, he would have been privy to many strange attestations of the divinity imputed to him. Voices would have been heard in the air, gossiping with Hivohitee ; noises inexplicable proceeding from him ; in brief, light would have flashed out of his darkness.

' But who has seen these things, Mohi ? ' said Babbalanja ; ' have you ? '

' Nay.'

' Who then ?—Media ?—Anyone you know ? '

' Nay : but the whole Archipelago has.'

' Thus,' exclaimed Babbalanja, ' does Mardi, blind though it be in many things, collectively behold the marvels, which one pair of eyes sees not.'

CHAPTER XIV

TAJI RECEIVES TIDINGS AND OMENS

SLOWLY sailing on, we were overtaken by a shallop ; whose inmates grappling to the side of Media's, said they came from Borabolla.

Dismal tidings !—My faithful follower's death.

Absent overnight, that morning early, he had been discovered lifeless in the woods, three arrows in his heart. And the three pale strangers were nowhere to be found. But a fleet canoe was missing from the beach.

Slain for me ! my soul sobbed out. Nor yet appeased Aleema's manes ; nor yet seemed sated the avengers' malice ; who, doubtless, were on my track.

But I turned ; and instantly the three canoes had been reversed ; and full soon, Jarl's dead hand in mine, had not Media interposed.

' To death, your presence will not bring life back.'

' And we must on,' said Babbalanja. ' We seek the living, not the dead.'

Thus they overruled me ; and Borabolla's messengers departed.

Soon evening came, and in its shades, three shadows,— Hautia's heralds.

Their shallop glided near.

A leaf tri-foiled was first presented ; then another, arrow-shaped.

Said Yoomy, ' Still I swiftly follow, behind revenge.'

Then were showered faded, pallid daffodils.

Said Yoomy, ' Thy hopes are blighted all.'

' Not dead, but living with the life of life. Syrens ! I heed ye not.'

They would have showered more flowers ; but crowding sail we left them.

Much converse followed. Then, beneath the canopy all sought repose. And ere long slouched sleep drew nigh, tending dreams innumerable; silent dotting all the downs; a shepherd with his flock.

CHAPTER XV

DREAMS

DREAMS! dreams! golden dreams: endless, and golden, as the flowery prairies that stretch away from the Rio Sacramento, in whose waters Danae's shower was woven; —prairies like rounded eternities: jonquil leaves beaten out; and my dreams herd like buffaloes, browsing on to the horizon, and browsing on round the world; and among them, I dash with my lance, to spear one, ere they all flee.

Dreams! dreams! passing and repassing, like Oriental empires in history; and sceptres wave thick, as Bruce's pikes at Bannockburn; and crowns are plenty as marigolds in June. And far in the background, hazy and blue, their steeps let down from the sky, loom Andes on Andes, rooted on Alps; and all round me, long rushing oceans, roll Amazons and Oronocos; waves, mounted Parthians; and, to and fro, toss the wide woodlands: all the world an elk, and the forests its antlers.

But far to the south, past my Sicily suns and my vineyards, stretches the Antarctic barrier of ice: a China wall, built up from the sea, and nodding its frosted towers in the dun, clouded sky. Do Tartary and Siberia lie beyond? Deathful, desolate dominions those; bleak and wild the ocean, beating at that barrier's base, hovering 'twixt freezing and foaming; and freighted with navies of icebergs,— warring worlds crossing orbits; their long icicles projecting like spears to the charge. Wide away stream the floes of drift ice, frozen cemeteries of skeletons and bones.

52

White bears howl as they drift from their cubs ; and the grinding islands crush the skulls of the peering seals.

But beneath me, at the Equator, the earth pulses and beats like a warrior's heart ; till I know not, whether it be not myself. And my soul sinks down to the depths, and soars to the skies ; and comet-like reels on through such boundless expanses, that methinks all the worlds are my kin, and I invoke them to stay in their course. Yet, like a mighty three-decker, towing argosies by scores, I tremble, gasp, and strain in my flight, and fain would cast off the cables that hamper.

And like a frigate, I am full with a thousand souls ; and as on, on, on, I scud before the wind, many mariners rush up from the orlop below, like miners from caves ; running shouting across my decks ; opposite braces are pulled ; and this way and that, the great yards swing round on their axes ; and boisterous speaking trumpets are heard ; and contending orders, to save the good ship from the shoals. Shoals, like nebulous vapours, shoring the white reef of the Milky Way, against which the wrecked worlds are dashed ; strewing all the strand with their Himmaleh keels and ribs.

Ay : many, many souls are in me. In my tropical calms, when my ship lies tranced on Eternity's main, speaking one at a time, then all with one voice : an orchestra of many French bugles and horns, rising and falling and swaying, in golden calls and responses.

Sometimes, when these Atlantics and Pacifics thus undulate round me, I lie stretched out in their midst : a landlocked Mediterranean, knowing no ebb, nor flow. Then again, I am dashed in the spray of these sounds ; an eagle at the world's end, tossed skyward, on the horns of the tempest.

Yet, again, I descend, and list to the concert.

Like a grand, ground swell, Homer's old organ rolls its

vast volumes under the light frothy wave-crests of Anac-
reon and Hafiz; and high over my ocean, sweet Shake-
speare soars, like all the larks of the spring. Throned on
my seaside, like Canute, bearded Ossian smites his hoar
harp, wreathed with wildflowers, in which warble my
Wallers; blind Milton sings bass to my Petrarchs and
Priors, and laureates crown me with bays.

In me, many worthies recline, and converse. I list to
St. Paul who argues the doubts of Montaigne; Julian the
Apostate cross-questions Augustine; and Thomas à
Kempis unrolls his old black letters for all to decipher.
Zeno murmurs maxims beneath the hoarse shout of
Democritus; and though Democritus laugh loud and
long, and the sneer of Pyrrho be seen; yet, divine Plato,
and Proclus, and Verulam are of my counsel; and
Zoroaster whispered me before I was born. I walk a
world that is mine; and enter many nations, as Mungo
Park rested in African cots; I am served like Bajazet:
Bacchus my butler, Virgil my minstrel, Philip Sidney my
page. My memory is a life beyond birth; my memory,
my library of the Vatican, its alcoves all endless perspec-
tives, eve-tinted by cross-lights from Middle Age oriels.

And as the great Mississippi musters his watery nations:
Ohio, with all his leagued streams; Missouri, bringing
down in torrents the clans from the highlands; Arkansas,
his Tartar rivers from the plain;—so, with all the past
and present pouring in me, I roll down my billow from afar.

Yet not I, but another: God is my Lord; and though
many satellites revolve around me, I and all mine revolve
round the great central Truth, sun-like, fixed and lumin-
ous forever in the foundationless firmament.

Fire flames on my tongue; and though of old the
Bactrian prophets were stoned, yet the stoners in oblivion
sleep. But whoso stones me, shall be as Erostratus, who
put torch to the temple; though Genghis Khan with

Cambyses combine to obliterate him, his name shall be extant in the mouth of the last man that lives. And if so be, down unto death, whence I came, will I go, like Xenophon retreating on Greece, all Persia brandishing her spears in his rear.

My cheek blanches white while I write ; I start at the scratch of my pen ; my own mad brood of eagles devours me ; fain would I unsay this audacity ; but an iron-mailed hand clenches mine in a vice, and prints down every letter in my spite. Fain would I hurl off this Dionysius that rides me ; my thoughts crush me down till I groan ; in far fields I hear the song of the reaper, while I slave and faint in this cell. The fever runs through me like lava ; my hot brain burns like a coal ; and like many a monarch, I am less to be envied than the veriest hind in the land.

CHAPTER XVI

MEDIA AND BABBALANJA DISCOURSE

OUR visiting the pontiff at a time previously unforeseen somewhat altered our plans. All search in Maramma for the lost one proving fruitless, and nothing of note remaining to be seen, we returned not to Uma ; but proceeded with the tour of the lagoon.

When day came, reclining beneath the canopy, Babbalanja would fain have seriously discussed those things we had lately been seeing, which, for all the occasional levity he had recently evinced, seemed very near his heart.

But my lord Media forbade ; saying that they necessarily included a topic which all gay, sensible Mardians, who desired to live and be merry, invariably banished from social discourse.

' Meditate as much as you will, Babbalanja, but say little aloud, unless in a merry and mythical way. Lay down the great maxims of things, but let inferences take care of themselves. Never be special ; never, a partisan. In safety, afar off, you may batter down a fortress ; but at your peril you essay to carry a single turret by escalade. And if doubts distract you, in vain will you seek sympathy from your fellow-men. For upon this one theme, not a few of you free-minded mortals, even the otherwise honest and intelligent, are the least frank and friendly. Discourse with them, and it is mostly formulas, or prevarications, or hollow assumption of philosophical indifference, or urbane hypocrisies, or a cool, civil deference to the dominant belief ; or still worse, but less common,

a brutality of indiscriminate scepticism.   Furthermore,
Babbalanja, on this head, final, last thoughts you mortals
have none ; nor can have ; and, at bottom, your own
fleeting fancies are too often secrets to yourselves ; and
sooner may you get another's secret, than your own.
Thus with the wisest of you all ; you are ever unfixed.
Do you show a tropical calm without ? then, be sure a
thousand contrary currents whirl and eddy within.   The
free, airy robe of your philosophy is but a dream, which
seems true while it lasts ; but waking again into the
orthodox world, straightway you resume the old habit.
And though in your dreams you may hie to the uttermost
Orient, yet all the while you abide where you are.   Babbalanja, you mortals dwell in Mardi, and it is impossible
to get elsewhere.'

Said Babbalanja : 'My lord, you school me. But though
I dissent from some of your positions, I am willing to
confess that this is not the first time a philosopher has
been instructed by a man.'

' A demi-god, sir ; and therefore I the more readily
discharge my mind of all seriousness, touching the subject
with which you mortals so vex and torment yourselves.'

Silence ensued.   And seated apart, on both sides of the
barge, solemnly swaying, in fixed meditation, to the roll
of the waves, Babbalanja, Mohi, and Yoomy drooped
lower and lower, like funeral plumes ; and our gloomy
canoe seemed a hearse.

CHAPTER XVII

THEY REGALE THEMSELVES WITH THEIR PIPES

'Ho! mortals! mortals!' cried Media. 'Go we to bury our dead? Awake, sons of men! Cheer up, heirs of immortality! Ho, Vee-Vee! bring forth our pipes: we 'll smoke off this cloud.'

Nothing so beguiling as the fumes of tobacco, whether inhaled through hookah, narghil, chibouque, Dutch porcelain, pure Principe, or Regalia. And a great oversight had it been in King Media, to have omitted pipes among the appliances of this voyage that we went. Tobacco in rouleaus we had none; cigar nor cigarette; which little the company esteemed. Pipes were preferred; and pipes we often smoked; testify, oh Vee-Vee, to that! But not of the vile clay of which mankind and Etruscan vases were made, were these jolly fine pipes of ours. But all in good time.

Now, the leaf called tobacco is of divers species and sorts. Not to dwell upon vile Shag, Pigtail, Plug, Nail-rod, Negrohead, Cavendish, and misnamed Lady's-twist, there are the following varieties: Gold-leaf, Oronoco, Cimaroza, Smyrna, Bird's-eye, James-river, Sweet-scented, Honey-dew, Kentucky, Cnaster, Scarfalati, and famed Shiraz, or Persian. Of all of which, perhaps the last is the best.

But smoked by itself, to a fastidious wight, even Shiraz is not gentle enough. It needs mitigation. And the cunning craft of so mitigating even the mildest tobacco was well understood in the dominions of Media. There,

in plantations ever covered with a brooding, blue haze,
they raised its fine leaf in the utmost luxuriance ; almost
as broad as the broad fans of the broad-bladed banana.
The stalks of the leaf withdrawn, the remainder they cut
up, and mixed with soft willow-bark, and the aromatic
leaves of the betel.

' Ho, Vee-Vee ! bring forth the pipes,' cried Media.
And forth they came, followed by a quaint, carved cocoa-
nut, agate-lidded, containing ammunition sufficient for
many stout charges and primings.

Soon we were all smoking so hard that the canopied
howdah, under which we reclined, sent up purple wreaths
like a Michigan wigwam. There we sat in a ring, all
smoking in council—every pipe a halcyon pipe of peace.

And among those calumets, my lord Media's showed
like the turbaned Grand Turk among his Bashaws. It
was an extraordinary pipe, be sure ; of right royal
dimensions. Its mouthpiece an eagle's beak ; its long
stem a bright, red-barked cherry-tree branch, partly
covered with a close network of purple-dyed porcupine
quills ; and toward the upper end, streaming with
pennons, like a Versailles flagstaff of a coronation day.
These pennons were managed by halyards ; and after
lighting his prince's pipe, it was little Vee-Vee's part to
run them up toward the mast-head, or mouthpiece, in
token that his lord was fairly under weigh.

But Babbalanja's was of a different sort ; an immense,
black, serpentine stem of ebony, coiling this way and that,
in endless convolutions, like an anaconda round a traveller
in Brazil. Smoking this hydra, Babbalanja looked as if
playing upon the trombone.

Next, gentle Yoomy's. Its stem, a slender, golden
reed, like musical Pan's ; its bowl very merry with tassels.

Lastly, old Mohi the chronicler's. Its Death's-head
bowl forming its latter end, continually reminding him of

his own. Its shank was an ostrich's leg, some feathers
still waving nigh the mouthpiece.

'Here, Vee-Vee! fill me up again,' cried Media, through
the blue vapours sweeping round his great gonfalon, like
plumed Marshal Ney, waving his baton in the smoke of
Waterloo ; or thrice gallant Anglesea, crossing his wooden
leg mid the reek and rack of the Apsley House banquet.

Vee-Vee obeyed ; and quickly, like a howitzer, the
pipe-bowl was reloaded to the muzzle, and King Media
smoked on.

'Ah! this is pleasant indeed,' he cried. 'Look, it's a
calm on the waters, and a calm in our hearts, as we inhale
these sedative odours.'

'So calm,' said Babbalanja ; 'the very gods must be
smoking now.'

'And thus,' said Media, 'we demi-gods hereafter shall
cross-legged sit, and smoke out our eternities. Ah, what
a glorious puff! Mortals, methinks these pipe-bowls of
ours must be petrifactions of roses, so scented they seem.
But, old Mohi, you have smoked this many a long year ;
doubtless, you know something about their material—the
Froth-of-the-Sea they call it, I think—ere my handicraft
subjects obtain it, to work into bowls. Tell us the tale.'

'Delighted to do so, my lord,' replied Mohi, slowly
disentangling his mouthpiece from the braids of his
beard. 'I have devoted much time and attention to the
study of pipe-bowls, and groped among many learned
authorities, to reconcile the clashing opinions concerning
the origin of the so-called Farnoo, or Froth-of-the-Sea.'

'Well, then, my old centenarian, give us the result of
your investigations. But smoke away : a word and a
puff : go on.'

'May it please you, then, my right worshipful lord, this
farnoo is an unctuous, argillaceous substance ; in its
natural state, soft, malleable, and easily worked as the

cornelian-red clay from the famous pipe quarries of the
wild tribes to the north.   But though mostly found
buried in terra-firma, especially in the isles toward the
east, this farnoo, my lord, is sometimes thrown up by
the ocean ; in seasons of high sea, being plentifully found
on the reefs.   But, my lord, like amber, the precise nature
and origin of this farnoo are points widely mooted.'

' Stop there ! ' cried Media ; ' our mouthpieces are of
amber ; so, not a word more of the Froth-of-the-Sea, until
something be said to clear up the mystery of amber.
What is amber, old man ? '

' A still more obscure thing to trace than the other, my
worshipful lord.   Ancient Plinnee maintained that originally it must be a juice, exuding from balsam firs and pines ;
Borhavo that, like camphor, it is the crystallised oil of
aromatic ferns ; Berzilli, that it is the concreted scum of
the lake Cephioris ; and Vondendo, against scores of
antagonists, stoutly held it a sort of bituminous gold,
trickling from antediluvian smugglers' caves, nigh the sea.'

' Why, old Braid-Beard,' cried Media, placing his pipe
in rest, ' you are almost as erudite as our philosopher here.'

' Much more so, my lord,' said Babbalanja ; ' for Mohi
has somehow picked up all my worthless forgettings,
which are more than my valuable rememberings.'

' What say you, wise one ? ' cried Mohi, shaking his
braids, like an enraged elephant with many trunks.

Said Yoomy : ' My lord, I have heard that amber is
nothing less than the congealed tears of broken-hearted
mermaids.'

' Absurd, minstrel,' cried Mohi.   ' Hark ye ; I know
what it is.   All other authorities to the contrary, amber is
nothing more than gold-fishes' brains, made waxy, then
firm, by the action of the sea.'

' Nonsense ! ' cried Yoomy.

' My lord,' said Braid-Beard, waving his pipe, ' this

thing is just as I say. Imbedded in amber, do we not find
little fishes' fins, porpoise teeth, seagulls' beaks and
claws ; nay, butterflies' wings, and sometimes a topaz ?
And how could that be, unless the substance was first
soft ? Amber is gold-fishes' brains, I say.'

'For one,' said Babbalanja, ' I 'll not believe that, till
you prove to me, Braid-Beard, that ideas themselves are
found imbedded therein.'

'Another of your crazy conceits, philosopher,' replied
Mohi, disdainfully ; ' yet, sometimes plenty of strange
black-letter characters have been discovered in amber.'
And throwing back his hoary old head, he jetted forth his
vapours like a whale.

'Indeed ? ' cried Babbalanja. ' Then, my lord Media, it
may be earnestly inquired, whether the gentle laws of the
tribes before the Flood, were not sought to be embalmed
and perpetuated between transparent and sweet-scented
tablets of amber.'

'That, now, is not so unlikely,' said Mohi ; ' for old
King Rondo the Round once set about getting him a
coffin-lid of amber ; much desiring a famous mass of it
owned by the ancestors of Donjalolo of Juam. But no
navies could buy it. So Rondo had himself urned in a
crystal.'

'And that immortalised Rondo, no doubt,' said Babbalanja.   ' Ha ! ha ! pity he fared not like the fat porpoise
frozen and tombed in an iceberg ; its icy shroud drifting
south, soon melted away, and down, out of sight, sunk the
dead.'

'Well, so much for amber,' cried Media.   ' Now, Mohi,
go on about farnoo.'

'Know, then, my lord, that farnoo is more like ambergris than amber.'

'Is it ? then, pray, tell us something on that head.
You know all about ambergris, too, I suppose.'

'Everything about all things, my lord. Ambergris is found both on land and at sea. But especially, are lumps of it picked up on the spicy coasts of Jovanna ; indeed, all over the atolls and reefs in the eastern quarter of Mardi.'

'But *what* is this ambergris, Braid-Beard ? ' said Babbalanja.

'Aquovi, the chemist, pronounced it the fragments of mushrooms growing at the bottom of the sea ; Voluto held that, like naphtha, it springs from fountains down there. But it is neither.'

'I have heard,' said Yoomy, ' that it is the honeycomb of bees, fallen from flowery cliffs into the brine.'

'Nothing of the kind,' said Mohi. ' Do I not know all about it, minstrel ? Ambergris is the petrified gallstones of crocodiles.'

'What ! ' cried Babbalanja, ' comes sweet - scented ambergris from those musky and chain-plated river cavalry ? No wonder, then, their flesh is so fragrant ; their upper jaws as the visors of vinaigrettes.'

'Nay, you are all wrong,' cried King Media.

Then, laughing to himself : ' It 's pleasant to sit by, a demi-god, and hear the surmisings of mortals, upon things they know nothing about ; theology, or amber, or ambergris, it 's all the same. But then, did I always out with everything I know, there would be no conversing with these comical creatures.

'Listen, old Mohi ; ambergris is a morbid secretion of the spermaceti whale ; for like you mortals, the whale is at times a sort of hypochondriac and dyspeptic. You must know, subjects, that in antediluvian times, the spermaceti whale was much hunted by sportsmen, that being accounted better pastime than pursuing the behemoths on shore. Besides, it was a lucrative diversion. Now, sometimes, upon striking the monster, it would start off in a dastardly fright, leaving certain fragments in its wake. These fragments the hunters picked up, giving over the chase for a while. For in those days, as now, a quarter-quintal of ambergris was more valuable than a whole ton of spermaceti.'

' Nor, my lord,' said Babbalanja, ' would it have been wise to kill the fish that dropped such treasures : no more than to murder the noddy that laid the golden eggs.'

' Beshrew me ! a noddy it must have been,' gurgled Mohi through his pipe-stem, ' to lay golden eggs for others to hatch.'

' Come, no more of that now,' cried Media. ' Mohi, how long think you may one of these pipe-bowls last ? '

' My lord, like one's cranium, it will endure till broken. I have smoked this one of mine more than half a century.'

' But unlike our craniums, stocked full of concretions,' said Babbalanja, ' our pipe-bowls never need clearing out.'

' True,' said Mohi, ' they absorb the oil of the smoke, instead of allowing it offensively to encrust.'

' Ay, the older the better,' said Media, ' and the more delicious the flavour imparted to the fumes inhaled.'

' Farnoos forever ! my lord,' cried Yoomy. ' By much smoking, the bowl waxes russet and mellow, like the berry-brown cheek of a sunburnt brunette.'

' And as like smoked hams,' cried Braid-Beard, ' we veteran old smokers grow browner and browner ; hugely do we admire to see our jolly noses and pipe-bowls mellowing together.'

' Well said, old man,' cried Babbalanja ; ' for, like a good wife, a pipe is a friend and companion for life. And whoso weds with a pipe is no longer a bachelor. After many vexations, he may go home to that faithful counsellor, and ever find it full of kind consolations and suggestions. But not thus with cigars or cigarettes : the acquaintances of a moment, chatted with in by-places, whenever they come handy ; their existence so fugitive, uncertain, unsatisfactory. Once ignited, nothing like longevity pertains to them. They never grow old. Why, my lord, the stump of a cigarette is an abomination ; and two of them crossed are more of a *memento mori* than a brace of thigh-bones at right angles.'

' So they are, so they are,' cried King Media. ' Then, mortals, puff we away at our pipes. Puff, puff, I say. Ah ! how we puff ! But thus we demi-gods ever puff at our ease.'

' Puff, puff, how we puff,' cried Babbalanja. ' But life itself is a puff and a wheeze. Our lungs are two pipes which we constantly smoke.'

' Puff, puff ! how we puff,' cried old Mohi. ' All thought is a puff.'

' Ay,' said Babbalanja, ' not more smoke in that skull-bowl of yours than in the skull on your shoulders : both ends alike.'

' Puff ! puff ! how we puff,' cried Yoomy. ' But in every puff there hangs a wreath. In every puff off flies a care.'

' Ay, there they go,' cried Mohi, ' there goes another— and there, and there ;—this is the way to get rid of them, my worshipful lord ; puff them aside.'

' Yoomy,' said Media, ' give us that pipe song of thine. Sing it, my sweet and pleasant poet. We 'll keep time with the flageolets of ours.'

So with pipes and puffs for a chorus, thus Yoomy sang :—

> Care is all stuff :—
>   Puff ! Puff !
> To puff is enough :—
>   Puff ! Puff !
> More musky than snuff,
> And warm is a puff :—
>   Puff ! Puff !

Here we sit mid our puffs,
Like old lords in their ruffs,
Snug as bears in their muffs :—
    Puff ! Puff !
Then puff, puff, puff,
For care is all stuff,
Puffed off in a puff.—
    Puff ! Puff !

' Ay, puff away,' cried Babbalanja, ' puff, puff, so we
are born, and so die.   Puff, puff, my volcanoes : the great
sun itself will yet go out in a snuff, and all Mardi smoke
out its last wick.'

' Puffs enough,' said King Media.   ' Vee-Vee ! haul
down my flag.   There, lie down before me, oh Gonfalon !
and, subjects, hear,—when I die, lay this spear on my
right, and this pipe on my left, its colours at half-mast ;
so shall I be ambidexter, and sleep between eloquent
symbols.'

CHAPTER XVIII

'ABOUT prows there, ye paddlers,' cried Media. 'In this fog we 've been raising, we have sailed by Padulla, our destination.'

Now, Padulla was but a little island, tributary to a neighbouring king; its population embracing some hundreds of thousands of leaves, and flowers, and butterflies, yet only two solitary mortals; one, famous as a venerable antiquarian : a collector of objects of Mardian vertu ; a cognoscenti, and dilettante in things old and marvellous ; and for that reason, very choice of himself.

He went by the exclamatory cognomen of 'Oh-Oh'; a name bestowed upon him by reason of. the delighted interjections with which he welcomed all accessions to his museum.

Now, it was to obtain a glimpse of this very museum that Media was anxious to touch at Padulla.

Landing, and passing through a grove, we were accosted by Oh-Oh himself ; who, having heard the shouts of our paddlers, had sallied forth, staff in hand.

The old man was a sight to see ; especially his nose ; a remarkable one. And all Mardi over, a remarkable nose is a prominent feature : an ever obvious passport to distinction. For, after all, this gaining a name is but the individualising of a man ; as well achieved by an extraordinary nose as by an extraordinary epic. Far better, indeed ; for you may pass poets without knowing them. Even a hero, is no hero without his sword ; nor Beelzebub

himself a lion, minus that lasso-tail of his, wherewith he
catches his prey. Whereas, he who is famous through
his nose, it is impossible to overlook. He is a celebrity
without toiling for a name. Snugly ensconced behind
his proboscis, he revels in its shadow, receiving tributes
of attention wherever he goes.

Not to enter at large upon the topography of Oh-Oh's
nasal organ, all must be content with this ; that it was
of a singular magnitude, and boldly aspiring at the end ;
an exclamation point in the face of the wearer, forever
wondering at the visible universe. The eyes of Oh-Oh
were like the creature's that the Jew abhors : placed
slanting in his head, and converging their rays toward
the mouth ; which was no mouth, but a gash.

I mean not to be harsh, or unpleasant upon thee,
Oh-Oh ; but I must paint thee as thou wert.

The rest of his person was crooked, and dwarfed, and
surmounted by a hump that sat on his back like a burden.
And a weary load is a hump, Heaven knows, only to be
cast off in the grave.

Thus old, and antiquated, and gable-ended, was the
tabernacle of Oh-Oh's soul. But his person was housed
in as curious a structure. Built of old boughs of trees
blown down in the groves, and covered over with unruly
thatching, it seemed, without, some ostrich nest. But
within, so intricate, and grotesque, its brown alleys and
cells, that the interior of no walnut was more labyrinthine.

And here, strewn about, all dusty and disordered, were
the precious antiques, and *curios*, and obsoletes, which
to Oh-Oh were dear as the apple of his eye, or the memory
of departed days.

The old man was exceedingly importunate in directing
attention to his relics ; concerning each of which he had
an endless story to tell. Time would fail ; nay, patience,
to repeat his legends. So, in order, here follow the most
prominent of his rarities :—

The identical Canoe, in which, ages back, the god Unja came
from the bottom of the sea.

(Very ponderous ; of lignum-vitæ wood.)

A stone Flower Pot, containing in the original soil Unja's
last footprints, when he embarked from Mardi for parts
unknown.

(One footprint unaccountably reversed.)

The Jawbones of Tooroorooloo, a great orator in the days
of Unja.

(Somewhat twisted.)

A quaint little Fish Hook.

(Made from the finger-bones of Kravi the Cunning.)

The mystic Gourd ; carved all over with cabalistic triangles,
and hypogriffs ; by study of which a reputed prophet
was said to have obtained his inspiration.

(Slightly redolent of vineyards.)

The complete Skeleton of an immense Tiger Shark ; the
bones of a pearl-shell diver's leg inside.

(Picked off the reef at low tide.)

An inscrutable, shapeless block of a mottled-hued, smoke-
dried wood.

(Three unaccountable holes drilled through the
middle.)

A sort of ecclesiastical Fasces, being the bony blades of nine
sword-fish, basket-hilted with shark's jaws, braided round
and tasselled with cords of human hair.

(Now obsolete.)

The mystic Fan with which Unja fanned himself when in
trouble.

(Woven from the leaves of the Water Lily.)

A Tripod of a Stork's Leg, supporting a nautilus shell,
containing the fragments of a bird's egg ; into which
was said to have been magically decanted the soul of a
deceased chief.

(Unfortunately crushed in by atmospheric pressure.)

Two clasped Right Hands, embalmed ; being those of twin
warriors, who thus died on a battlefield.
(Impossible to sunder.)

A curious Pouch, or Purse, formed from the skin of an
albatross' foot, and decorated with three sharp claws,
naturally pertaining to it.
(Originally the property of a notorious old Tooth-per-
Tooth.)

A long tangled lock of Mermaid's Hair, much resembling the
curling silky fibres of the finer seaweed.
(Preserved between fins of the dolphin.)

A Mermaid's Comb for the toilet. The stiff serrated crest
of a cock storm-petrel.
(Oh-Oh was particularly curious concerning mermaids.)

Files, Rasps, and Pincers, all bone, the implements of an
eminent Chiropodist, who flourished his tools before the
flood.
(Owing to the excessive unevenness of the surface in
those times, the diluvians were peculiarly liable to
pedal afflictions.)

The back Tooth that Zoro the Enthusiast, in token of grief,
recklessly knocked out at the decease of a friend.
(Worn to a stump and quite useless.)

These wonders inspected, Oh-Oh conducted us to an
arbour to show us the famous telescope, by help of which
he said he had discovered an ant-hill in the moon. It
rested in the crotch of a bread-fruit tree ; and was a
prodigiously long and hollow trunk of a palm ; a scale
from a sea-kraken its lens.

Then returning to his cabinet, he pointed to a bamboo
microscope, which had wonderfully assisted him in his
entomological pursuits.

' By this instrument, my masters,' said he, ' I have satisfied myself that in the eye of a dragon-fly there are precisely twelve thousand five hundred and forty-one triangular lenses ; and in the leg of a flea scores on scores of distinct muscles. Now, my masters, how far think you a flea may leap at one spring ? Why, two hundred times its own length ; I have often measured their leaps, with a small measure I use for scientific purposes.'

' Truly, Oh-Oh,' said Babbalanja, ' your discoveries must ere long result in something grand ; since you furnish such invaluable data for theorists. Pray, attend, my lord Media. If, at one spring, a flea leaps two hundred times its own length, then, with the like proportion of muscles in his calves, a bandit might pounce upon the unwary traveller from a quarter of a mile off. Is it not so, Oh-Oh ? '

' Indeed, but it is, my masters. And one of the greatest consolations I draw from these studies is the ever-strengthening conviction of the beneficent wisdom that framed our Mardi. For did men possess thighs in pro-portion to fleas, verily, the wicked would grievously leap about, and curvet in the isles.'

' But Oh-Oh,' said Babbalanja, ' what other discoveries have you made ? Hast yet put a usurer under your lens, to find his conscience ? or a libertine, to find his heart ? Hast yet brought your microscope to bear upon a downy peach, or a rosy cheek ? '

' I have,' said Oh-Oh, mournfully ; ' and from the moment I so did, I have had no heart to eat a peach, or salute a cheek.'

' Then dash your lens ! ' cried Media.

' Well said, my lord. For all the eyes we get beyond our own but minister to infelicity. The microscope disgusts us with our Mardi ; and the telescope sets us longing for some other world.'

CHAPTER XIX

THEY GO DOWN INTO THE CATACOMBS

WITH a dull flambeau, we now descended some narrow stone steps to view Oh-Oh's collection of ancient and curious manuscripts, preserved in a vault.

'This way, this way, my masters,' cried Oh-Oh, aloft, swinging his dim torch. 'Keep your hands before you ; it 's a dark road to travel.'

'So it seems,' said Babbalanja, wide-groping, as he descended lower and lower. 'My lord, this is like going down to posterity.'

Upon gaining the vault, forth flew a score or two of bats, extinguishing the flambeau, and leaving us in darkness, like Belzoni deserted by his Arabs in the heart of a pyramid. The torch at last relumed, we entered a tomb-like excavation, at every step raising clouds of dust ; and at last stood before long rows of musty, mummyish parcels, so dingy-red, and so rolled upon sticks, that they looked like stiff sausages of Bologna ; but smelt like some fine old Stilton or Cheshire.

Most ancient of all was a hieroglyphical 'Elegy on the Dumps,' consisting of one thousand and one lines ; the characters,—herons, weeping willows, and ravens, supposed to have been traced by a quill from the sea-noddy.

Then there were plenty of rare old ballads :—

'King Kroko, and the Fisher Girl.'
'The Fight at the Ford of Spears.'
'The Song of the Skulls.'

72

And brave old chronicles that made Mohi's mouth water :—

'The Rise and Setting of the Dynasty of Foofoo.'
'The Heroic History of the Noble Prince Dragoni ; show-
    ing how he killed ten Pinioned Prisoners with his
    Own Hand.'
'The whole Pedigree of the King of Kandidee, with that
    of his famous horse, Znorto.'

And Tarantula books :—

'Sour Milk for the Young, by a Dairyman.'
'The Devil adrift, by a Corsair.'
'Grunts and Groans, by a Mad Boar.'
'Stings, by a Scorpion.'

And poetical productions :—

'Suffusions of a Lily in a Shower.'
'Sonnet on the last Breath of an Ephemera.'
'The Gad-fly, and Other Poems.'

And metaphysical treatises :—

'Necessitarians not Predestinarians.'
'Philosophical Necessity and Predestination One Thing
    and The Same.'
'Whatever is not, is.'
'Whatever is, is not.'

And scarce old memoirs :—

'The One Hundred Books of the Biography of the Great
    and Good King Grandissimo.'
'The Life of old Philo, the Philanthropist, in one Chapter.'

And popular literature :—

'A most Sweet, Pleasant, and Unctuous Account of the
    Manner in which Five-and-Forty Robbers were torn
    asunder by Swiftly-Going Canoes.'

And books by chiefs and nobles :—

'The Art of Making a Noise in Mardi.'

'On the Proper Manner of Saluting a Bosom Friend.'
'Letters from a Father to a Son, inculcating the Virtue of Vice.'
'Pastorals by a Younger Son.'
'A Catalogue of Chieftains who have been Authors, by a Chieftain who disdains to be deemed an Author.'
'A Canto on a Cough caught by my Consort.'
'The Philosophy of Honesty, by a late Lord, who died in disgrace.'

And theological works :—

'Pepper for the Perverse.'
'Pudding for the Pious.'
'Pleas for Pardon.'
'Pickles for the Persecuted.'

And long and tedious romances with short and easy titles :—

'The Buck.'
'The Belle.'
'The King and the Cook, or the Cook and the King.'

And books of voyages :—

'A Sojourn among the Anthropophagi, by One whose Hand was eaten off at Tiffin among the Savages.'
'Franko : its King, Court, and Tadpoles.'
'Three Hours in Vivenza, containing a Full and Impartial Account of that Whole Country : by a Subject of King Bello.'

And works of nautical poets :—

'Sky-Sail-Pole Lyrics.'

And divers brief books, with panic-striking titles :—

'Are you safe ? '
'A Voice from Below.'
'Hope for none.'
'Fire for all.'

And pamphlets by retired warriors :—

'On the Best Gravy for Wild Boar's Meat.'
'Three Receipts for Bottling New Arrack.'
'To Brown Bread-Fruit without Burning.'
'Advice to the Dyspeptic.'
'On Starch for Tappa.'

All these manuscripts were highly prized by Oh-Oh. He averred that they spoke of the mighty past, which he reverenced more than the paltry present, the dross and sediment of what had been.

Peering into a dark crypt, Babbalanja drew forth a few crumbling, illegible, black-letter sheets of his favourite old essayist, brave Bardianna. They seemed to have formed parts of a work, whose title only remained— 'Thoughts, by a Thinker.'

Silently Babbalanja pressed them to his heart. Then at arm's length held them, and said, ' And is all this wisdom lost ? Cannot the divine cunning in thee, Bardianna, transmute to brightness these sullied pages ? Here, perhaps, thou didst dive into the deeps of things, treating of the normal forms of matter and of mind ; how the particles of solids were first moulded in the interstices of fluids ; how the thoughts of men are each a soul, as the lung-cells are each a lung ; how that death is but a mode of life ; while midmost is the Pharzi.—But all is faded. Yea, here the Thinker's thoughts lie cheek by jowl with phrasemen's words. Oh Bardianna ! these pages were offspring of thee, thought of thy thought, soul of thy soul. Instinct with mind, they once spoke out like living voices ; now, they're dust ; and would not prick a fool to action. Whence then is this ? If the fogs of some few years can make soul linked to matter naught ; how can the unhoused spirit hope to live when mildewed with the damps of death.'

Piously he folded the shreds of manuscript together kissed them, and laid them down.

Then approaching Oh-Oh, he besought him for one leaf, one shred of those most precious pages, in memory of Bardianna, and for the love of him.

But learning who he was, one of that old Ponderer's commentators, Oh-Oh tottered toward the manuscripts ; with trembling fingers told them over, one by one, and said—' Thank Oro ! all are here.—Philosopher, ask me for my limbs, my life, my heart, but ask me not for these. Steeped in wax, these shall be my cerements.'

All in vain ; Oh-Oh was an antiquary.

Turning in despair, Babbalanja spied a heap of worm-eaten parchment covers, and many clippings and parings. And whereas the rolls of manuscripts did smell like unto old cheese ; so these relics did marvellously resemble the rinds of the same.

Turning over this pile, Babbalanja lighted upon something that restored his good-humour. Long he looked it over delighted ; but bethinking him that he must have dragged to day some lost work of the collection, and much desirous of possessing it, he made bold again to ply Oh-Oh ; offering a tempting price for his discovery.

Glancing at the title—' A Happy Life '—the old man cried—' Oh, rubbish ! rubbish ! take it for nothing.'

And Babbalanja placed it in his vestment.

The catacombs surveyed, and daylight gained, we inquired the way to Ji-Ji's, also a collector, but of another sort ; one miserly in the matter of teeth, the money of Mardi.

At the mention of his name, Oh-Oh flew out into scornful philippics upon the insanity of that old dotard, who hoarded up teeth, as if teeth were of any use, but to purchase rarities. Nevertheless, he pointed out our path ; following which, we crossed a meadow.

CHAPTER XX

BABBALANJA QUOTES FROM AN ANTIQUE PAGAN; AND
EARNESTLY PRESSES IT UPON THE COMPANY THAT
WHAT HE RECITES IS NOT HIS, BUT ANOTHER'S

JOURNEYING on, we stopped by a gurgling spring, in a
beautiful grove; and here we stretched out on the grass,
and our attendants unpacked their hampers to provide
us a lunch.

But as for that Babbalanja of ours, he must needs go
and lunch by himself, and, like a cannibal, feed upon an
author; though in other respects he was not so partial
to bones.

Bringing forth the treasure he had buried in his bosom,
he was soon buried in it; and motionless on his back,
looked as if laid out, to keep an appointment with his
undertaker.

'What, ho! Babbalanja!' cried Media from under a
tree, 'don't be a duck, there, with your bill in the air;
drop your metaphysics, man, and fall to on the solids.
Do you hear?'

'Come, philosopher,' said Mohi, handling a banana,
'you will weigh more after you have eaten.'

'Come, list, Babbalanja,' cried Yoomy, 'I am going to
sing.'

'Up! up! I say,' shouted Media again. 'But go, old
man, and wake him: rap on his head, and see whether
he be in.'

Mohi, obeying, found him at home; and Babbalanja
started up.

'In Oro's name, what ails you, philosopher ? See you
Paradise, that you look so wildly ? '

'A Happy Life ! a Happy Life ! ' cried Babbalanja, in
an ecstasy. 'My lord, I am lost in the dream of it, as
here recorded. Marvellous book ! its goodness transports
me. Let me read :—" I would bear the same mind,
whether I be rich or poor, whether I get or lose in the
world. I will reckon benefits well placed as the fairest
part of my possession, not valuing them by number or
weight, but by the profit and esteem of the receiver ;
accounting myself never the poorer for anything I give.
What I do shall be done for conscience, not ostentation.
I will eat and drink, not to gratify my palate, but to
satisfy nature. I will be cheerful to my friends, mild and
placable to my enemies. I will prevent an honest request,
if I can foresee it ; and I will grant it, without asking. I
will look upon the whole world as my country ; and upon
Oro, both as the witness and the judge of my words and
my deeds. I will live and die with this testimony : that
I loved a good conscience ; that I never invaded another
man's liberty ; and that I preserved my own. I will
govern my life and my thoughts, as if the whole world
were to see the one, and to read the other ; for what does
it signify, to make anything a secret to my neighbour,
when to Oro all our privacies are open." '

'Very fine,' said Media.

'The very spirit of the first followers of Alma, as recorded in the legends,' said Mohi.

'Inimitable,' said Yoomy.

Said Babbalanja : 'Listen again :—" Righteousness is
sociable and gentle ; free, steady, and fearless ; full of
inexhaustible delights." And here again, and here, and
here :—" The true felicity of life is to understand our duty
to Oro."—" True joy is a serene and sober motion."
And here, and here,—my lord, 'tis hard quoting from this

book ;—but listen—" A peaceful conscience, honest
thoughts, and righteous actions are blessings without
end, satiety, or measure. The poor man wants many
things ; the covetous man, all. It is not enough to know
Oro, unless we obey him." '

' Alma all over,' cried Mohi ; ' sure, you read from his
sayings ? '

' I read but odd sentences from one, who though he lived
ages ago, never saw, scarcely heard of Alma. And mark
me, my lord, this time I improvise nothing. What I have
recited, is here. Mohi, this book is more marvellous than
the prophecies. My lord, that a mere man, and a heathen,
in that most heathenish time, should give utterance to such
heavenly wisdom, seems more wonderful than that an
inspired prophet should reveal it. And is it not more
divine in this philosopher, to love righteousness for its
own sake, and in view of annihilation, than for pious sages
to extol it as the means of everlasting felicity ? '

' Alas,' sighed Yoomy, ' and does he not promise us any
good thing when we are dead ? '

' He speaks not by authority. He but woos us to
goodness and happiness here.'

' Then, Babbalanja,' said Media, ' keep your treasure
to yourself. Without authority, and a full right hand,
Righteousness better be silent. Mardi's religion must
seem to come direct from Oro, and the mass of you mortals
endeavour it not, except for a consideration, present or to
come.'

' And call you that righteousness, my lord, which is but
the price paid down for something else ? '

' I called it not righteousness ; it is religion so called.
But let us prate no more of these things ; with which I, a
demi-god, have but little in common. It ever impairs
my digestion. No more, Babbalanja.'

' My lord ! my lord ! out of itself, Religion has nothing

to bestow.   Nor will she save us from aught, but from the
evil in ourselves.   Her one grand end is to make us wise ;
her only manifestations are reverence to Oro and love to
man ;   her only, but ample reward, herself.   He who has
this, has all.   He who has this, whether he kneel to an
image of wood, calling it Oro ;   or to an image of air,
calling it the same ;   whether he fasts or feasts ;   laughs
or weeps ;—that man can be no richer.   And this religion,
faith, virtue, righteousness, good, whate'er you will, I
find in this book I hold.   No written page can teach me
more.'

' Have you that, then, of which you speak, Babbalanja ?
Are you content, there where you stand ? '

' My lord, you drive me home.   I am not content.   The
mystery of mysteries is still a mystery.   How this author
came to be so wise, perplexes me.   How he led the life he
did, confounds me.   Oh, my lord, I am in darkness, and
no broad blaze comes down to flood me.   The rays that
come to me are but faint cross lights, mazing the obscurity
wherein I live.   And after all, excellent as it is, I can be no
gainer by this book.   For the more we learn, the more we
unlearn ;   we accumulate not, but substitute ;   and take
away more than we add.   We dwindle while we grow ;
we sally out for wisdom, and retreat beyond the point
whence we started ;   we essay the Fondiza, and get but
the Phe.   Of all simpletons, the simplest !   Oh ! that I
were another sort of fool than I am, that I might restore
my good opinion of myself.   Continually I stand in the
pillory, am broken on the wheel, and dragged asunder by
wild horses.   Yes, yes, Bardianna, all is in a nut, as thou
sayest ;   but all my back teeth cannot crack it ;   I but crack
my own jaws.   All round me, my fellow-men are new-
grafting their vines, and dwelling in flourishing arbours ;
while I am forever pruning mine, till it is become but a
stump.   Yet in this pruning will I persist ;   I will not add,

I will diminish ; I will train myself down to the standard of what is unchangeably true. Day by day I drop off my redundancies ; ere long I shall have stripped my ribs ; when I die, they will but bury my spine. Ah ! where, where, where, my lord, is the everlasting Tekana ? Tell me, Mohi, where the Ephina ? I may have come to the Penultimate, but where, sweet Yoomy, is the Ultimate ? Ah, companions ! I faint, I am wordless :—something,— nothing,—riddles,—does Mardi hold her ? '

' He swoons ! ' cried Yoomy.

' Water ! water ! ' cried Media.

' Away ! ' said Babbalanja serenely, ' I revive.'

CHAPTER XXI

THEY VISIT A WEALTHY OLD PAUPER

CONTINUING our route to Ji-Ji's, we presently came to a miserable hovel. Half projecting from the low, open entrance, was a bald overgrown head, intent upon an upright row of dark-coloured bags :—pelican pouches—prepared by dropping a stone within, and suspending them, when moist.

Ever and anon, the great head shook with a tremulous motion, as one by one, to a clicking sound from the old man's mouth, the strings of teeth were slowly drawn forth, and let fall, again and again, with a rattle.

But perceiving our approach, the old miser suddenly swooped his pouches out of sight ; and, like a turtle into its shell, retreated into his den. But soon he decrepitly emerged upon his knees, asking what brought us thither ? —to steal the teeth, which lying rumour averred he possessed in abundance ? And opening his mouth, he averred he had none ; not even a sentry in his head.

But Babbalanja declared, that long since he must have drawn his own dentals, and bagged them with the rest.

Now this miserable old miser must have been idiotic ; for soon forgetting what he had but just told us of his utter toothlessness, he was so smitten with the pearly mouth of Hohora, one of our attendants (the same for whose pearls, little King Peepi had taken such a fancy), that he made the following overture to purchase its contents : namely : one tooth of the buyer's, for every three

82

of the seller's. A proposition promptly rejected, as involving a mercantile absurdity.

'Why?' said Babbalanja. 'Doubtless, because that proposed to be given is less than that proposed to be received. Yet, says a philosopher, this is the very principle which regulates all barterings. For where the sense of a simple exchange of quantities, alike in value?'

'Where, indeed?' said Hohora with open eyes; 'though I never heard it before, that's a staggering question. I beseech you, who was the sage that asked it?'

'Vivo, the Sophist,' said Babbalanja, turning aside.

In the hearing of Ji-Ji, allusion was made to Oh-Oh, as a neighbour of his. Whereupon he vented much slavering opprobrium upon that miserable old hump-back; who accumulated useless monstrosities; throwing away the precious teeth, which otherwise might have sensibly rattled in his own pelican pouches.

When we quitted the hovel, Ji-Ji, marking little Vee-Vee, from whose shoulder hung a calabash of edibles, seized the hem of his garment and besought him for one mouthful of food; for nothing had he tasted that day.

The boy tossed him a yam.

CHAPTER XXII

YOOMY SINGS SOME ODD VERSES, AND BABBALANJA QUOTES
FROM THE OLD AUTHORS RIGHT AND LEFT

SAILING from Padulla, after many pleasant things had been said concerning the sights there beheld, Babbalanja thus addressed Yoomy—' Warbler, the last song you sung was about moonlight, and paradise, and fabulous pleasures evermore : now, have you any hymns about earthly felicity ? '

' If so, minstrel,' said Media, ' jet it forth, my fountain, forthwith.'

' Just now, my lord,' replied Yoomy, ' I was singing to myself, as I often do, and by your leave, I will continue aloud.'

' Better begin at the beginning, I should think,' said the chronicler, both hands to his chin, beginning at the top to new-braid his beard.

' No : like the roots of your beard, old Mohi, all beginnings are stiff,' cried Babbalanja. ' We are lucky in living midway in eternity. So sing away, Yoomy, where you left off,' and thus saying he unloosed his girdle for the song, as Apicius would for a banquet.

' Shall I continue aloud, then, my lord ? '

My lord nodded, and Yoomy sang :—

> Full round, full soft, her dewy arms,—
> Sweet shelter from all Mardi's harms !

' Whose arms ? ' cried Mohi.

Sang Yoomy :—

> Diving deep in the sea,
>   She takes sunshine along :
> Down flames in the sea,
>   As of dolphins a throng.

' What mermaid is this ? ' cried Mohi.
Sang Yoomy :—

> Her foot, a falling sound,
> That all day long might bound.
>   Over the beach,
>   The soft sand beach,
>   And none would find
>   A trace behind.

' And why not ? ' demanded Media, ' why could no trace be found ? '

Said Braid-Beard, ' Perhaps owing, my lord, to the flatness of the mermaid's foot. But no ; that cannot be ; for mermaids are all vertebræ below the waist.'

' Your fragment is pretty good, I dare say, Yoomy,' observed Media, ' but as Braid-Beard hints, rather flat.'

' Flat as the foot of a man with his mind made up,' cried Braid-Beard. ' Yoomy, did you sup on flounders last night ? '

But Yoomy vouchsafed no reply, he was ten thousand leagues off in a revery : somewhere in the Hyades perhaps.

Conversation proceeding, Braid-Beard happened to make allusion to one Rotato, a portly personage, who, though a sagacious philosopher, and very ambitious to be celebrated as such, was only famous in Mardi as the fattest man of his tribe.

Said Media, ' Then, Mohi, Rotato could not pick a quarrel with Fame, since she did not belie him. Fat he was, and fat she published him.'

'Right, my lord,' said Babbalanja, 'for Fame is not always so honest. Not seldom to be famous, is to be widely known for what you are not, says Alla-Malolla. Whence it comes, as old Bardianna has it, that for years a man may move unnoticed among his fellows; but all at once, by some chance attitude, foreign to his habit, become a trumpetful for fools; though, in himself, the same as ever. Nor has he shown himself yet; for the entire merit of a man can never be made known; nor the sum of his demerits, if he have them. We are only known by our names; as letters sealed up, we but read each other's superscriptions.

'So with the commonalty of us Mardians. How then with those beings who every way are but too apt to be riddles. In many points the works of our great poet Vavona, now dead a thousand moons, still remain a mystery. Some call him a mystic; but wherein he seems obscure, it is, perhaps, we that are in fault; not by pre-meditation spoke he those archangel thoughts, which made many declare, that Vavona, after all, was but a crack-pated god, not a mortal of sound mind. But had he been less, my lord, he had seemed more. Saith Fulvi, " Of the highest order of genius, it may be truly asserted, that to gain the reputation of superior power, it must partially disguise itself; it must come down, and then it will be applauded for soaring." And furthermore, " that there are those who falter in the common tongue, because they think in another; and these are accounted stutterers and stammerers." '

'Ah! how true!' cried the Warbler.

'And what says the archangel Vavona, Yoomy, in that wonderful drama of his, " The Souls of the Sages? "— " Beyond most barren hills, there are landscapes ravishing; with but one eye to behold; which no pencil can portray." What wonder then, my lord, that Mardi itself is so blind. "Mardi is a monster," says old Bardianna, "whose eyes are fixed in its head, like a whale's; it can see but two ways, and those comprising but a small arc of a perfect vision. Poets, heroes, and men of might are all around this monster Mardi. But stand before me on stilts, or I will behold you not, says the monster; brush back your hair; inhale the wind largely; lucky are all men with dome-like foreheads; luckless those with pippin-heads; loud lungs are a blessing; a lion is no lion that cannot roar." Says Aldina, "There are those looking on, who know themselves to be swifter of foot than the racers, but are confounded with the simpletons that stare."'

'The mere carping of a disappointed cripple,' cried Mohi. 'His biographer states that Aldina had only one leg.'

'Braid-Beard, you are witty,' said Babbalanja, adjusting his robe. 'My lord, there are heroes without armies, who hear martial music in their souls.'

'Why not blow their trumpets louder, then,' cried Media, 'that all Mardi may hear?'

'My lord Media, too, is witty, Babbalanja,' said Mohi.

Breathed Yoomy, 'There are birds of divinest plumage, and most glorious song, yet singing their lyrics to themselves.'

Said Media, 'The lark soars high, cares for no auditor, yet its sweet notes are heard here below. It sings, too, in company with myriads of mates. Your soliloquists, Yoomy, are mostly herons and owls.'

Said Babbalanja, 'Very clever, my lord; but think you not there are men eloquent, who never babble in the market-place?'

'Ay, and arrant babblers at home. In few words, Babbalanja, you espouse a bad cause. Most of you mortals are peacocks; some having tails, and some not;

those who have them will be sure to thrust their plumes in your face ; for the rest, they will display their bald cruppers, and still screech for admiration. But when a great genius is born into Mardi, he nods, and is known.'

' More wit, but, with deference, perhaps less truth, my lord. Say what you will, fame is an accident; merit a thing absolute. But what matter ? Of what available value reputation, unless wedded to power, dentals, or place ? To those who render him applause, a poet's may seem a thing tangible ; but to the recipient, 'tis a fantasy ; the poet never so stretches his imagination, as when striving to comprehend what it is ; often, he is famous without knowing it.'

' At the sacred games of Lazella,' said Yoomy, ' slyly crowned from behind with a laurel fillet, for many hours, the minstrel Jarmi wandered about ignorant of the honours he bore. But enlightened at last, he doffed the wreath ; then, holding it at arm's length, sighed forth— " Oh, ye laurels ! to be visible to me, ye must be removed from my brow ! " '

' And what said Botargo,' cried Babbalanja, ' hearing that his poems had been translated into the language of the remote island of Bertranda ?—" It stirs me little ; already, in merry fancies, have I dreamed of their being trilled by the blessed houris in paradise ; I can only imagine the same of the damsels of Bertranda." Says Boldo, the Materialist—" Substances alone are satisfactory." '

' And so thought the mercenary poet, Zenzi,' said Yoomy. ' Upon receiving fourteen ripe yams for a sonnet, one for every line, he said to me—" Yoomy, I shall make a better meal upon these than upon so many compliments." '

' Ay,' cried Babbalanja, ' " Bravos," saith old Bardianna, " but induce flatulency." '

Said Media, ' And do you famous mortals, then, take no pleasure in hearing your bravos ? '

' Much, my good lord ; at least such famous mortals, so enamoured of a clamorous notoriety, as to bravo for themselves, when none else will huzza ; whose whole existence is an unintermitting consciousness of self ; whose very persons stand erect and self-sufficient as their infallible index, the capital letter I ; who relish and comprehend no reputation but what attaches to the carcass ; who would as lief be renowned for a splendid moustache as for a splendid drama : who know not how it was that a personage, to posterity so universally celebrated as the poet Vavona, ever passed through the crowd unobserved ; who deride the very thunder for making such a noise in Mardi, and yet disdain to manifest itself to the eye.'

' Wax not so warm, Babbalanja ; but tell us, if to his contemporaries Vavona's person was almost unknown, what satisfaction did he derive from his genius ? '

' Had he not its consciousness ?—an empire boundless as the West. What to him were huzzas ? Why, my lord, from his privacy, the great and good Logodora sent liniment to the hoarse throats without. But what said Bardianna, when they dunned him for autographs ?— " Who keeps the register of great men ? who decides upon noble actions ? and how long may ink last ? Alas ! Fame has dropped more rolls than she displays ; and there are more lost chronicles than the perished books of the historian Livella." But what is lost forever, my lord, is nothing to what is now unseen. There are more treasures in the bowels of the earth than on its surface.'

' Ah ! no gold,' cried Yoomy, ' but that comes from dark mines.'

Said Babbalanja, ' " Bear witness, ye gods ! " cries fervent old Bardianna, " that besides disclosures of good and evil undreamed of now, there will be other and more astounding revelations hereafter, of what has passed in Mardi unbeheld." '

' A truce to your everlasting pratings of old Bardianna,' said King Media ; ' why not speak your own thoughts, Babbalanja ? then would your discourse possess more completeness ; whereas, its warp and woof are of all sorts, —Bardianna, Alla-Malolla, Vavona, and all the writers that ever have written. Speak for yourself, mortal ! '

' May you not possibly mistake, my lord ? for I do not so much quote Bardianna, as Bardianna quoted me, though he flourished before me ; and no vanity, but honesty to say so. The catalogue of true thoughts is but small ; they are ubiquitous ; no man's property ; and unspoken, or bruited, are the same. When we hear them, why seem they so natural, receiving our spontaneous approval ? why do we think we have heard them before ? Because they but reiterate ourselves ; they were in us before we were born. The truest poets are but mouth-pieces ; and some men are duplicates of each other ; I see myself in Bardianna.'

' And there, for Oro's sake, let it rest, Babbalanja ; Bardianna in you, and you in Bardianna forever ! '

CHAPTER XXIII

WHAT MANNER OF MEN THE TAPPARIANS WERE

THE canoes sailed on. But we leave them awhile. For our visit to Ji-Ji, the last visit we made, suggests some further revelations concerning the dental money of Mardi.

Ere this, it should have been mentioned, that throughout the Archipelago there was a restriction concerning incisors and molars as ornaments for the person ; none but great chiefs, brave warriors, and men distinguished by rare intellectual endowments, orators, romancers, philosophers, and poets, being permitted to sport them as jewels. Though, as it happened, among the poets there were many who had never a tooth, save those employed at their repasts ; which, coming but seldom, their teeth almost corroded in their mouths. Hence, in commerce, poets' teeth were at a discount.

For these reasons, then, many mortals blent with the promiscuous mob of Mardians, who, by any means, accumulated teeth, were fain to assert their dental claims to distinction, by clumsily carrying their treasures in pelican pouches slung over their shoulders ; which pouches were a huge burden to carry about, and defend. Though, in good truth, from any of these porters, it was harder to wrench his pouches, than his limbs. It was also a curious circumstance that at the slightest casual touch, these bags seemed to convey a simultaneous thrill to the owners.

Besides these porters, there were others, who exchanged their teeth for richly stained calabashes, elaborately carved canoes, and, more especially, for costly robes and

turbans ; in which last, many outshone the noblest-born
nobles. Nevertheless, this answered not the end they
had in view ; some of the crowd only admiring what they
wore, and not them ; breaking out into laudation of the
inimitable handiwork of the artisans of Mardi.

And strange to relate, these artisans themselves often
came to be men of teeth and turbans, sporting their
bravery with the best. A circumstance which accounted
for the fact, that many of the class above alluded to were
considered capital judges of tappa and tailoring.

Hence, as a general designation, the whole tribe went by
the name of Tapparians ; otherwise, Men of Tappa.

Now, many moons ago, according to Braid-Beard, the
Tapparians of a certain cluster of islands, seeing themselves hopelessly confounded with the plebeian race of
mortals; such as artificers, honest men, bread-fruit bakers,
and the like ; seeing, in short, that nature had denied
them every inborn mark of distinction ; and furthermore,
that their external assumptions were derided by so many
in Mardi, these self-same Tapparians, poor devils, resolved
to secede from the rabble ; form themselves into a community of their own ; and conventionally pay that
homage to each other which universal Mardi could not be
prevailed upon to render to them.

Jointly, they purchased an island, called Pimminee, toward the extreme west of the lagoon ; and thither they
went ; and framing a code of laws—amazingly arbitrary,
considering they themselves were the framers—solemnly
took the oath of allegiance to the commonwealth thus
established. Regarded section by section, this code of
laws seemed exceedingly trivial ; but taken together,
made a somewhat imposing aggregation of particles.

By this code, the minutest things in life were all ordered
after a specific fashion. More especially one's dress was
legislated upon, to the last warp and woof. All girdles

must be so many inches in length, and with such a number of tassels in front. For a violation of this ordinance, before the face of all Mardi, the most dutiful of sons would cut the most affectionate of fathers.

Now, though like all Mardi, kings and slaves included, the people of Pimminee had dead dust for grandsires, they seldom reverted to that fact; for, like all founders of families, they had no family vaults. Nor were they much encumbered by living connections; connections, some of them appeared to have none. Like poor Logan the last of his tribe, they seemed to have monopolised the blood of their race, having never a cousin to own.

Wherefore it was, that many ignorant Mardians, who had not pushed their investigations into the science of physiology, sagely divined, that the Tapparians must have podded into life like peas, instead of being otherwise indebted for their existence. Certain it is, they had a comical way of backing up their social pretensions. When the respectability of his clan was mooted, Paivai, one of their bucks, disdained all reference to the Domesday Book, and the ancients. More reliable evidence was had. He referred the anxious world to a witness, still alive and hearty,—his contemporary tailor; the varlet who cut out his tappa doublets, and rejoiced his soul with good fits.

' Ah ! ' sighed Babbalanja, ' how it quenches in one the thought of immortality, to think that these Tapparians, too, will hereafter claim each a niche ! '

But we rove. Our visit to Pimminee itself will best make known the ways of its denizens.

CHAPTER XXIV

THEIR ADVENTURES UPON LANDING AT PIMMINEE

A LONG sail over, the island of Pimminee came in sight;
one dead flat, wreathed in a thin, insipid vapour.

' My lord, why land ? ' said Babbalanja ; ' no Yillah
is here.'

' 'Tis my humour, Babbalanja.'

Said Yoomy, ' Taji would leave no isle unexplored.

As we neared the beach, the atmosphere became still
closer and more languid. Much did we miss the refreshing
balm which breathed in the fine breezy air of the open
lagoon. Of a slender and sickly growth seemed the trees ;
in the meadows, the grass grew small and mincing.

Said Media, ' Taji, from the accounts which Braid-
Beard gives, there must be much to amuse in the ways
of these Tapparians.'

' Yes,' said Babbalanja, ' their lives are a continual
farce, gratuitously performed for the diversion of Mardi.
My lord, perhaps we had best doff our dignity, and land
among them as persons of lowly condition ; for then, we
shall receive more diversion, though less hospitality.'

' A good proposition,' said Media.

And so saying, he put off his robe for one less pre-
tentious.

All followed suit ; Yoomy doffing turban and sash ; and
at last, completely metamorphosed, we looked like
Hungarian gypsies.

Voyaging on, we entered a bay, where numbers of
menials were standing in the water, engaged in washing

94

the carved work of certain fantastic canoes, belonging to the Tapparians, their masters.

Landing at some distance, we followed a path that soon conducted us to a betwisted dwelling of bamboos, where, gently, we knocked for admittance. So doing, we were accosted by a servitor, his portliness all in his calves. Marking our appearance, he monopolised the threshold, and gruffly demanded what was wanted.

'Strangers, kind sir, fatigued with travel, and in need of refreshment and repose.'

'Then hence with ye, vagabonds!' and with an emphasis he closed the portal in our face.

Said Babbalanja, turning, 'You perceive, my lord Media, that these varlets take after their masters; who feed none but the well-fed, and house none but the well-housed.'

'Faith! but they furnish most rare entertainment, nevertheless,' cried Media. 'Ha! ha! Taji, we had missed much had we missed Pimminee.'

As this was said, we observed, at a distance, three menials running from seaward, as if conveying important intelligence.

Halting here and there, vainly seeking admittance at other habitations, and receiving nothing but taunts for our pains, we still wandered on; and at last came upon a village, toward which those from the seaside had been running.

And now, to our surprise, we were accosted by an eager and servile throng.

'Obsequious varlets,' said Media, 'where tarry your masters?'

'Right royal, and thrice worshipful Lord of Odo, do you take us for our domestics? We are Tapparians, may it please your illustrious highness; your most humble and obedient servants. We beseech you, supereminent sir, condescend to visit our habitations, and partake of our cheer.'

Then turning upon their attendants, ' Away with ye, hounds ! and set our dwellings in order.'

' How know ye me to be king ? ' asked Media.

' Is it not in your serene highness's regal port, and eye ? '

' 'Twas their menials,' muttered Mohi, ' who from the paddlers in charge of our canoes must have learned who my lord was, and published the tidings.'

After some further speech, Media made a social surrender of himself to the foremost of the Tapparians, one Nimni ; who, conducting us to his abode, with much deference introduced us to a portly old Begum, and three slender damsels ; his wife and daughters.

Soon, refreshments appeared :—green and yellow compounds, and divers enigmatical dainties ; besides vegetable liqueurs of a strange and alarming flavour served in fragile little leaves, folded into cups, and very troublesome to handle.

Excessively thirsty, Babbalanja made bold to inquire for water ; which called forth a burst of horror from the old Begum, and minor shrieks from her daughters ; who declared, that the beverage to which remote reference had been made was far too widely diffused in Mardi to be at all esteemed in Pimminee.

' But though we seldom imbibe it,' said the old Begum, ceremoniously adjusting her necklace of cowrie-shells, ' we occasionally employ it for medicinal purposes.'

' Ah, indeed ? ' said Babbalanja.

' But oh ! believe me ; even then, we imbibe not the ordinary fluid of the springs and streams ; but that which in afternoon showers softly drains from our palm-trees into the little hollow or miniature reservoir beneath its compacted roots.'

A goblet of this beverage was now handed Babbalanja ;

but having a curious, gummy flavour, it proved anything but palatable.

Presently, in came a company of young men, relatives of Nimni. They were slender as skysail-poles ; standing in a row, resembled a picket-fence ; and were surmounted by enormous heads of hair, combed out all round, variously dyed, and evened by being singed with a lighted wisp of straw. Like milliners' parcels, they were very neatly done up ; wearing redolent robes.

'How like the woodlands they smell,' whispered Yoomy.

'Ay, marvellously like sap,' said Mohi.

One part of their garniture consisted of numerous tasselled cords, like those of an aiguillette, depending from the neck, and attached here and there about the person. A separate one, at a distance, united their ankles. These served to measure and graduate their movements ; keeping their gestures, paces, and attitudes within the pre-scribed standard of Tapparian gentility. When they went abroad they were preceded by certain footmen, who placed before them small, carved boards, whereon their masters stepped ; thus avoiding contact with the earth. The simple device of a shoe, as a fixture for the foot, was unknown in Pimminee.

Being told, that Taji was lately from the sun, they mani-fested not the slightest surprise ; one of them incidentally observing, however, that the eclipses there must be a sad bore to endure.

CHAPTER XXV

A, I, AND O

THE old Begum went by the euphonious appellation of Ohiro-Moldona-Fivona ; a name, from its length, deemed highly genteel ; though scandal averred that it was nothing more than her real name transposed ; the appellation by which she had been formerly known, signifying a ' Getter-up-of-Fine-Tappa.' But as this would have let out an ancient secret, it was thought wise to disguise it.

Her daughters respectively revelled in the pretty diminutives of A, I, and O ; which, from their brevity, comical to tell, were considered equally genteel with the dame's.

The habiliments of the three Vowels must not be omitted. Each damsel garrisoned an ample, circular farthingale of canes, serving as the framework whereon to display a gaily-dyed robe. Perhaps their charms entrenched themselves in these impregnable petticoats, as feeble armies fly to fortresses, to hide their weakness, and better resist an onset.

But polite and politic it is to propitiate your hostess. So seating himself by the Begum, Taji led off with earnest inquiries after her welfare. But the Begum was one of those who relieve the diffident from the embarrassment of talking ; all by themselves carrying on conversation for two. Hence, no wonder that my lady was esteemed invaluable at all assemblies in the groves of Pimminee ; contributing so largely to that incessant din, which is held the best test of the enjoyment of the company, as making them deaf to the general nonsense, otherwise audible.

Learning that Taji had been making the tour of certain islands in Mardi, the Begum was surprised that he could have thus hazarded his life among the barbarians of the East. She desired to know whether his constitution was not impaired by inhaling the unrefined atmosphere of those remote and barbarous regions. For her part, the mere thought of it made her faint in her innermost citadel ; nor went she ever abroad with the wind at east, dreading the contagion which might lurk in the air.

Upon accosting the three damsels, Taji very soon discovered that the tongue which had languished in the presence of the Begum was now called into active requisition to entertain the Polysyllables, her daughters. So assiduously were they occupied in silent endeavours to look sentimental and pretty, that it proved no easy task to sustain with them an ordinary chat. In this dilemma, Taji diffused not his remarks among all three ; but discreetly centred them upon O. Thinking she might be curious concerning the sun, he made some remote allusion to that luminary as the place of his nativity. Upon which, O inquired where that country was of which mention was made.

'Some distance from here ; in the air above ; the sun that gives light to Pimminee, and Mardi at large.'

She replied, that if that were the case she had never beheld it ; for such was the construction of her farthingale that her head could not be thrown back, without impairing its set. Wherefore, she had always abstained from astronomical investigations.

Hereupon, rude Mohi laughed out. And that lucky laugh happily relieved Taji from all further necessity of entertaining the Vowels. For at so vulgar and, in Pimminee, so unwonted a sound as a genuine laugh, the three startled nymphs fainted away in a row, their

round farthingales falling over upon each other, like a file
of empty tierces.   But they presently revived.

Meanwhile, without stirring from their mats, the polite
young bucks in the aiguillettes did nothing but hold semi-
transparent leaves to their eyes, by the stems ; which
leaves they directed downward, toward the disordered
hems of the farthingales ; in wait, perhaps, for the revelation of an ankle, and its accompaniments. What the
precise use of these leaves could have been, it would be
hard to say, especially as the observers invariably peeped
over and under them.

The calamity of the Vowels was soon followed by the
breaking up of the party ; when, evening coming on, and
feeling much wearied with the labour of seeing company
in Pimminee, we retired to our mats ; there finding that
repose which ever awaits the fatigued.

CHAPTER XXVI

A RECEPTION DAY AT PIMMINEE

NEXT morning, Nimni apprised us that throughout the day he proposed keeping open house, for the purpose of enabling us to behold whatever of beauty, rank, and fashion, Pimminee could boast; including certain strangers of note from various quarters of the lagoon, who doubtless would honour themselves with a call.

As inmates of the mansion, we unexpectedly had a rare opportunity of witnessing the final toilets of the Begum and her daughters, preparatory to receiving their guests.

Their four farthingales were placed standing in the middle of the dwelling; when their future inmates, arrayed in rudimental vestments, went round and round them, attaching various articles of finery, dyed scarfs, ivory trinkets, and other decorations. Upon the propriety of this or that adornment, the three Vowels now and then pondered apart, or together consulted. They talked and they laughed; they were silent and sad; now merry at their bravery; now pensive at the thought of the charms to be hidden.

It was O who presently suggested the expediency of an artful fold in their draperies, by the merest accident in Mardi, to reveal a tantalising glimpse of their ankles, which were thought to be pretty.

But the old Begum was more active than any; by far the most disinterested in the matter of advice. Her great object seemed to be to pile on the finery at all hazards;

and she pointed out many as yet vacant and unappropriated spaces, highly susceptible of adornment.

At last, all was in readiness ; when, taking a valedictory glance at their entrenchments, the Begum and damsels simultaneously dipped their heads, directly after emerging from the summit, all ready for execution.

And now to describe the general reception that followed. In came the Roes, the Fees, the Lol-Lols, the Hummee-Hums, the Bidi-Bidies, and the Dedidums ; the Peenees, the Yamoyamees, the Karkies, the Fanfums, the Diddle-dees, and the Fiddlefies ; in a word, all the aristocracy of Pimminee ; people with exceedingly short names ; and some all name, and nothing else. It was an imposing array of sounds ; a circulation of ciphers ; a marshalling of tappas ; a getting together of grimaces and furbelows ; a masquerade of vapidities.

Among the crowd was a bustling somebody, one Gaddi, arrayed in much apparel to little purpose ; who, singling out Babbalanja, for some time adhered to his side, and with excessive complaisance, enlightened him as to the people assembled.

'*That* is rich Marmonora, accounted a mighty man in Pimminee ; his bags of teeth included, he is said to weigh upwards of fourteen stone ; and is much sought after by tailors for his measure, being but slender in the region of the heart. His riches are great. And that old vrow is the widow Roo ; very rich ; plenty of teeth ; but has none in her head. And *this* is Finfi ; said to be not very rich, and a maid. Who would suppose she had ever beat tappa for a living ? '

And so saying, Gaddi sauntered off ; his place by Babbalanja's side being immediately supplied by the damsel Finfi. That vivacious and amiable nymph at once proceeded to point out the company, where Gaddi had left off ; beginning with Gaddi himself, who, she insinuated, was a mere parvenu, a terrible infliction upon society, and not near so rich as he was imagined to be.

Soon we were accosted by one Nonno, a sour, saturnine personage. ' I know nobody here ; not a soul have I seen before ; I wonder who they all are.' And just then he was familiarly nodded to by nine worthies abreast. Whereupon Nonno vanished. But after going the rounds of the company, and paying court to many, he again sauntered by Babbalanja, saying, ' Nobody, nobody ; nobody but nobodies ; I see nobody I know.'

Advancing, Nimni now introduced many strangers of distinction, parading their titles after a fashion, plainly signifying that he was bent upon convincing us that there were people present at this little affair of his who were men of vast reputation ; and that we erred if we deemed him unaccustomed to the society of the illustrious.

But not a few of his magnates seemed shy of Media and their laurels. Especially a tall robustuous fellow, with a terrible javelin in his hand, much notched and splintered, as if it had dealt many a thrust. His left arm was gallanted in a sling, and there was a patch upon his sinister eye. Him Nimni made known as a famous captain, from King Piko's island (of which anon), who had been all but mortally wounded somewhere, in a late desperate though nameless encounter.

' Ah,' said Media as this redoubtable withdrew, ' Fofi is a cunning knave ; a braggart, driven forth by King Piko for his cowardice. He has blent his tattooing into one mass of blue, and thus disguised must have palmed himself off here in Pimminee for the man he is not. But I see many more like him.'

' Oh ye Tapparians,' said Babbalanja, ' none so easily humbugged as humbugs. Taji : to behold this folly makes one wise. Look, look ; it is all round us. Oh Pimminee, Pimminee ! '

CHAPTER XXVII

BABBALANJA FALLETH UPON PIMMINEE TOOTH AND NAIL

THE levee over, waiving further civilities, we took
courteous leave of the Begum and Nimni, and, proceeding to the beach, very soon were embarked.

When all were pleasantly seated beneath the canopy,
pipes in full blast, calabashes revolving, and the paddlers
quietly urging us along, Media proposed that, for the
benefit of the company, someone present, in a pithy, whiffy
sentence or two, should sum up the character of the
Tapparians ; and ended by nominating Babbalanja to
that office.

' Come, philosopher : let us see in how few syllables you
can put the brand on those Tapparians.'

' Pardon me, my lord, but you must permit me to
ponder awhile ; nothing requires more time, than to be
brief. An example : they say that in conversation old
Bardianna dealt in nothing but trisyllabic sentences. His
talk was thunder peals : sounding reports, but long
intervals.'

' The devil take old Bardianna. And would that the
gravedigger had buried his Ponderings along with his
other remains. Can none be in your company, Babbalanja, but you must perforce make them hob-a-nob with
that old prater ? A brand for the Tapparians ! that is
what we seek.'

' You shall have it, my lord. Full to the brim of themselves, for that reason, the Tapparians are the emptiest of
mortals.'

104

' A good blow and well planted, Babbalanja.'

' In sooth, a most excellent saying ; it should be carved upon his tombstone,' said Mohi, slowly withdrawing his pipe.

' What ! would you have my epitaph read thus :— " Here lies the emptiest of mortals, who was full of himself ? " At best, your words are exceedingly ambiguous, Mohi.'

' Now have I the philosopher,' cried Yoomy, with glee. ' What did someone say to me, not long since, Babbalanja, when in the matter of that sleepy song of mine, Braid-Beard bestowed upon me an equivocal compliment ? Was I not told to wrest commendation from it, though I tortured it to the quick ? '

' Take thy own pills, philosopher,' said Mohi.

' Then would he be a great original,' said Media.

' Tell me, Yoomy,' said Babbalanja, ' are you not in fault ? Because I sometimes speak wisely, you must not imagine that I should always act so.'

' I never imagined that,' said Yoomy, ' and, if I did, the truth would belie me. It is you who are in fault, Babbalanja ; not I, craving your pardon.'

' The minstrel's sides are all edges to-day,' said Media.

' This, then, thrice gentle Yoomy, is what I would say,' resumed Babbalanja ; ' that since we philosophers bestow so much wisdom upon others, it is not to be wondered at, if now and then we find what is left in us too small for our necessities. It is from our very abundance that we want.'

' And from the fool's poverty,' said Media, ' that he is opulent ; for his very simplicity is sometimes of more account than the wisdom of the sage. But we were discoursing of the Tapparians. Babbalanja : sententiously you have acquitted yourself to admiration ; now amplify, and tell us more of the people of Pimminee.'

' My lord, I might amplify forever.'

'Then, my worshipful lord, let him not begin,' interposed Braid-Beard.

'I mean,' said Babbalanja, 'that all subjects are inexhaustible, however trivial ; as the mathematical point, put in motion, is capable of being produced into an infinite line.'

'But forever extending into nothing,' said Media. 'A very bad example to follow. Do you, Babbalanja, come to the point, and not travel off with it, which is too much your wont.'

'Since my lord insists upon it then, thus much for the Tapparians, though but a thought or two of many in reserve. They ignore the rest of Mardi, while they themselves are but a rumour in the isles of the East ; where the business of living and dying goes on with the same uniformity, as if there were no Tapparians in existence. They think themselves Mardi in full ; whereas, by the mass, they are stared at as prodigies ; exceptions to the law, ordaining that no Mardian shall undertake to live, unless he set out with at least the average quantity of brains. For these Tapparians have no brains. In lieu, they carry in one corner of their craniums a drop or two of attar of roses ; charily used, the supply being small. They are the victims of two incurable maladies : stone in the heart, and ossification of the head. They are full of fripperies, fopperies, and finesses ; knowing not, that nature should be the model of art. Yet, they might appear less silly than they do, were they content to be the plain idiots which at bottom they are. For there be grains of sense in a simpleton, so long as he be natural. But what can be expected from them ? They are irreclaimable Tapparians ; not so much fools by contrivance of their own, as by an express, though inscrutable decree of Oro's. For one, my lord, I cannot abide them.'

Nor could Taji.

In Pimminee were no hilarious running and shouting :
none of the royal good cheer of old Borabolla ; none of the
mysteries of Maramma ;   none of the sentiment and
romance of Donjalolo ; no rehearsing of old legends : no
singing of old songs ; no life ; no jolly commotion : in
short, no men and women; nothing but their integuments ;
stiff trains and farthingales.

CHAPTER XXVIII

BABBALANJA REGALES THE COMPANY WITH SOME SANDWICHES

IT was night. But the moon was brilliant, far and near illuminating the lagoon.

Over silvery billows we glided.

'Come, Yoomy,' said Media, 'moonlight and music for aye—a song! a song! my bird of paradise.'

And folding his arms, and watching the sparkling waters, thus Yoomy sang :—

> A ray of the moon on the dancing waves
> Is the step, light step, of that beautiful maid :
> Mardi, with music, her footfall paves,
> And her voice, no voice, but a song in the glade.

'Hold!' cried Media, 'yonder is a curious rock. It looks black as a whale's hump in blue water, when the sun shines.'

'That must be the Isle of Fossils,' said Mohi. 'Ay, my lord, it is.'

'Let us land, then,' said Babbalanja.

And none dissenting, the canoes were put about, and presently we debarked.

It was a dome-like surface, here and there fringed with ferns, sprouting from clefts. But at every tide the thin soil seemed gradually washing into the lagoon.

Like antique tablets, the smoother parts were moulded in strange devices :—Luxor marks, Tadmor ciphers, Palenque inscriptions. In long lines, as on Denderah's

108

architraves, were bas-reliefs of beetles, turtles, ant-eaters, armadilloes, guanos, serpents, tongueless crocodiles :—a long procession, frosted and crystallised in stone, and silvered by the moon.

'Strange sight !' cried Media. 'Speak, antiquarian Mohi.'

But the chronicler was twitching his antiquarian beard, nonplussed by these wondrous records. The cowled old father, Piaggi, bending over his calcined Herculanean manuscripts, looked not more at fault than he.

Said Media, ' Expound *you*, then, sage Babbalanja.'

Muffling his face in his mantle, and his voice in sepulchral tones, Babbalanja thus :—

' These are the leaves of the book of Oro. Here we read how worlds are made ; here read the rise and fall of Nature's kingdoms. From where this old man's farthest histories start, these unbeginning records end. These are the secret memoirs of times past ; whose evidence, at last divulged, gives the grim lie to Mohi's gossipings, and makes a rattling among the dry-bone relics of old Maramma.'

Braid-Beard's old eyes flashed fire. With bristling beard, he cried, ' Take back the lie you send ! '

' Peace ! everlasting foes,' cried Media, interposing, with both arms outstretched. ' Philosopher, probe not too deep. All you say is very fine, but very dark. I would know something more precise. But, prithee, ghost, unmuffle ! chatter no more ! wait till you 're buried for that.'

' Ay, death's cold ague will set us all shivering, my lord. We 'll swear our teeth are icicles.'

' Will you quit driving your sleet upon us ? have done : expound these rocks.'

' My lord, if you desire, I 'll turn over these stone tablets till they 're dog-eared.'

' Heaven and Mardi !—Go on, Babbalanja.'

' 'Twas thus. These were tombs burst open by volcanic throes ; and hither hurled from the lowermost vaults of the lagoon. All Mardi's rocks are one wide resurrection. But look. Here, now, a pretty story 's told. Ah, little thought these grand old lords that lived and roared before the Flood that they would come to this. Here, King Media, look and learn.'

He looked ; and saw a picture petrified, and plain as any on the pediments of Petra.

It seemed a stately banquet of the dead, where lords in skeletons were ranged around a board heaped up with fossil fruits, and flanked with vitreous vases, grinning like empty skulls. There they sat, exchanging rigid courtesies. One's hand was on his stony heart ; his other pledged a lord who held a hollow beaker. Another sat, with earnest face beneath a mitred brow. He seemed to whisper in the ear of one who listened trustingly. But on the chest of him who wore the mitre, an adder lay, close-coiled in flint.

At the farther end was raised a throne, its canopy surmounted by a crown, in which now rested the likeness of a raven on an egg.

The throne was void. But half-concealed by drapery, behind the goodliest lord, sideway leaned a figure diademed, a lifted poniard in its hand :—a monarch fossilised in very act of murdering his guest.

' Most high and sacred majesty ! ' cried Babbalanja, bowing to his feet.

While all stood gazing on this sight, there came two servitors of Media's, who besought of Babbalanja to settle a dispute concerning certain tracings upon the islet's other side.

Thither we followed them.

Upon a long layer of the slaty stone were marks of ripplings of some now waveless sea ; mid which were tri-toed footprints of some huge heron, or wading fowl.

Pointing to one of which, the foremost disputant thus spoke : ' I maintain that these are three toes.'

' And I, that it is one foot,' said the other.

' And now decide between us,' joined the twain.

Said Babbalanja, starting, ' Is not this the very question concerning which they made such dire contention in Maramma, whose tertiary rocks are chiselled all over with these marks ?   Yes ; this it is, concerning which they once shed blood.   This it is, concerning which they still divide.'

' Which of us is right ? ' again demanded the impatient twain.

' Unite, and both are right ; divide, and both are wrong. Every unit is made up of parts, as well as every plurality. Nine is three threes ; a unit is as many thirds ; or, if you please, a thousand thousandths ; no special need to stop at thirds.'

' Away, ye foolish disputants ! ' cried Media.   ' Full before you is the thing disputed.'

Strolling on, many marvels did we mark ; and Media said : ' Babbalanja, you love all mysteries ; here's a fitting theme.   You have given us the history of the rock ; can your sapience tell the origin of all the isles ? how Mardi came to be ? '

' Ah, that once mooted point is settled.   Though hard at first, it proved a bagatelle.   Start not, my lord ; there are those who have measured Mardi by perch and pole, and with their wonted lead sounded its utmost depths. Listen : it is a pleasant story.   The coral wall which circumscribes the isles but continues upward the deep buried crater of the primal chaos.   In the first times this crucible was charged with vapours nebulous, boiling over fires volcanic.   Age by age, the fluid thickened ; dropping, at long intervals, heavy sediment to the bottom ; which layer on layer concreted, and at length, in crusts, rose toward the surface.   Then, the vast volcano burst ; rent

the whole mass ; upthrew the ancient rocks ; which now
in divers mountain tops tell tales of what existed ere
Mardi was completely fashioned. Hence many fossils
on the hills, whose kith and kin still lurk beneath the vales.
Thus Nature works, at random warring, chaos a crater,
and this world a shell.'

Mohi stroked his beard.

Yoomy yawned.

Media cried, ' Preposterous ! '

' My lord, then take another theory—which you will—
the celebrated sandwich system. Nature's first condition
was a soup, wherein the agglomerating solids formed
granitic dumplings, which, wearing down, deposited the
primal stratum made up of series, sandwiching strange
shapes of molluscs, and zoophytes ; then snails, and
periwinkles :—marmalade to sip, and nuts to crack, ere
the substantials came.

' And next, my lord, we have the fine old time of the
Old Red Sandstone sandwich, clapped on the underlying
layer, and among other dainties, imbedding the first course
of fish,—all quite in rule,—sturgeon-forms, cephalaspis,
glyptolepis, pterichthys; and other finny things, of flavour
rare, but hard to mouth for bones. Served up with these
were sundry greens,—lichens, mosses, ferns, and fungi.

' Now comes the New Red Sandstone sandwich : marly
and magnesious, spread over with old patriarchs of
crocodiles and alligators,—hard carving these,—and
prodigious lizards, spine-skewered, tails tied in bows, and
swimming in saffron saucers.'

' What next ? ' cried Media.

' The Ool, or Oily sandwich :—rare gormandising then ;
for oily it was called, because of fat old joints, and hams,
and rounds, and barons of sea-beeves and walruses, which
then crowned the stratum-board. All piled together,
glorious profusion !—fillets and briskets, rumps, and

saddles, and haunches ; shoulder to shoulder, loin 'gainst sirloin, ribs rapping knuckles, and quarter to none. And all these sandwiched right over all that went before. Course after course, and course on course, my lord ; no time to clear the wreck ; no stop nor let ; lay on and slash ; cut, thrust, and come.

' Next the Chalk or Coral sandwich ; but 'no dry fare for that ; made up of rich side-courses,—eocene, miocene, and pliocene. The first was wild game for the delicate,— bantam larks, curlews, quails, and flying weasels ; with a slight sprinkling of pilaus,—capons, pullets, plovers, and garnished with petrels' eggs. Very savoury, that, my lord. The second side-course—miocene—was out of course, flesh after fowl :—marine mammalia,—seals, grampuses, and whales, served up with seaweed on their flanks, hearts and kidneys devilled, and fins and flippers fricasseed. All very nice, my lord. The third side-course, the pliocene, was goodliest of all :—whole-roasted ele-phants, rhinoceroses, and hippopotamuses, stuffed with boiled ostriches, condors, cassowaries, turkeys. Also barbecued mastodons and megatheriums, gallantly served up with fir-trees in their mouths, and tails cock-billed.

' Thus fared the old diluvians : arrant gormandisers and beef-bolters. We Mardians famish on the superficial strata of deposits ; cracking our jaws on walnuts, filberts, cocoa-nuts, and clams. My lord, I 've done.'

' And bravely done it is. Mohi tells us that Mardi was made in six days ; but you, Babbalanja, have built it up from the bottom in less than six minutes.'

' Nothing for us geologists, my lord. At a word we turn you out whole systems, suns, satellites, and asteroids included. Why, my good lord, my friend Annonimo is laying out a new Milky Way, to intersect with the old one, and facilitate cross-cuts among the comets.'

And so saying, Babbalanja turned aside.

CHAPTER XXIX

THEY STILL REMAIN UPON THE ROCK

'Gogle-goggle, fugle-fi, fugle-fogle-orum,' so hummed to himself Babbalanja, slowly pacing over the fossils.

'Is he crazy again ? ' whispered Yoomy.

'Are you crazy, Babbalanja ? ' asked Media.

'From my very birth have I been so, my lord ; am I not possessed by a devil ? '

'Then I 'll e'en interrogate him,' cried Media.—'Hark ye, sirrah ;—why rave you thus in this poor mortal ? '

' 'Tis he, not I. I am the mildest devil that ever entered man ; *in propria persona*, no antlers do I wear ; my tail has lost its barb, as at last your Mardian lions lose their caudal horns.'

'A very sing-song devil, this. But, prithee, who are you, sirrah ? '

'The mildest devil that ever entered man ; *in propria persona*, no antlers do I wear ; my tail has lost its barb, as at last your Mardian lions lose their caudal horns.'

'A very iterating devil, this. Sirrah ! mock me not. Know ye aught yet unrevealed by Babbalanja ? '

'Many things I know, not good to tell ; whence they call me Azzageddi.'

'A very confidential devil, this ; that tells no secrets. Azzageddi, can I drive thee out ? '

'Only with this mortal's ghost :—together we came in, together we depart.'

'A very terse and ready devil, this. Whence come you, Azzageddi ? '

114

' Whither my catechist must go—a torrid clime, cut by a hot equator.'

' A very keen and witty devil, this. Azzageddi, whom have you there ? '

' A right down merry, jolly set, that at a roaring furnace sit and toast their hoofs for aye ; so used to flames, they poke the fire with their horns, and light their tails for torches.'

' A very funny devil, this. Azzageddi, is not Mardi a place far pleasanter than that from whence you came ? '

' Ah, home ! sweet, sweet home ! would, would that I were home again ! '

' A very sentimental devil, this. Azzageddi, would you had a hand,—I 'd shake it.'

' Not so with us ; who, rear to rear, shake each other's tails, and courteously inquire, " Pray, worthy sir, how now stands the great thermometer ? " '

' The very prince of devils, this.'

' How mad our Babbalanja is,' cried Mohi. ' My lord, take heed ; he 'll bite.'

' Alas ! alas ! ' sighed Yoomy.

' Hark ye, Babbalanja,' cried Media, ' enough of this : doff your devil, and be a man.'

' My lord, I cannot doff him ; but I 'll down him for a time : Azzageddi ! down, imp ; down, down, down ! so : now, my lord, I 'm only Babbalanja.'

' Shall I test his sanity, my lord ! ' cried Mohi.

' Do, old man.'

' Philosopher, our great reef is surrounded by an ocean ; what think you lies beyond ? '

' Alas ! ' sighed Yoomy, ' the very subject to renew his madness.'

' Peace, minstrel ! ' said Media. ' Answer, Babbalanja.'

' I will, my lord. Fear not, sweet Yoomy ; you see how calm I am. Braid-Beard, those strangers that came

to Mondoldo prove isles afar, as a philosopher of old sur-
mised, but was hooted at for his surmisings. Nor is it
at all impossible, Braid-Beard, that beyond their land may
exist other regions, of which those strangers know not ;
peopled with races something like us Mardians ; but perhaps with more exalted faculties, and organs that we lack.
They may have some better seeing sense than ours ;
perhaps, have fins or wings for arms.'

'This seems not like sanity,' muttered Mohi.

'A most crazy hypothesis, truly,' said Media.

'And are all inductions vain ? ' cried Babbalanja.
'Have we mortals naught to rest on, but what we see with
eyes ? Is no faith to be reposed in that inner microcosm,
wherein we see the charted universe in little, as the whole
horizon is mirrored in the iris of a gnat ? Alas ! alas !
my lord, is there no blest Odonphi ? no Astrazzi ? '

'His devil's uppermost again, my lord,' cried Braid-
Beard.

'He's stark, stark mad ! ' sighed Yoomy.

'Ay, the moon's at full,' said Media. 'Ho, paddlers !
we depart.'

CHAPTER XXX

BEHIND AND BEFORE

IT was yet moonlight when we pushed from the islet. But soon, the sky grew dun ; the moon went into a cavern among the clouds ; and by that secret sympathy between our hearts and the elements, the thoughts of all but Media became overcast.

Again discourse was had of that dark intelligence from Mondoldo,—the fell murder of Taji's follower.

Said Mohi, ' Those spectre sons of Aleema must have been the assassins.'

' They harboured deadly malice,' said Babbalanja.

' Which poor Jarl's death must now have sated,' sighed Yoomy.

' Then all the happier for Taji,' said Media. ' But away with gloom ! because the sky is clouded, why cloud your brows ? Babbalanja, I grieve the moon is gone. Yet start some paradox, that we may laugh. Say a woman is a man, or you yourself a stork.'

At this they smiled. When hurtling came an arrow, which struck our stern, and quivered. Another ! and another ! Grazing the canopy, they darted by, and hissing, dived like red-hot bars beneath the waves.

Starting, we beheld a corruscating wake, tracking the course of a low canoe, far flying for a neighbouring mountain. The next moment it was lost within the mountain's shadow and pursuit was useless.

' Let us fly ! ' cried Yoomy.

117

'Peace ! What murderers these ? ' said Media, calmly; ' whom can they seek ?—you, Taji ? '

' The three avengers fly three bolts,' said Babbalanja.

' See if the arrow yet remain astern,' cried Media.

They brought it to him.

' By Oro ! Taji on the barb ! '

' Then it missed its aim. But I will not mine. And whatever arrows follow, still will I hunt on. Nor does the ghost, that these pale spectres would avenge, at all disquiet me. The priest I slew, but to gain her, now lost ; and I would slay again to bring her back. Ah, Yillah ! Yillah.'

All started.

Then said Babbalanja, ' Aleema's sons raved not ; 'tis true, then, Taji, that an evil deed gained you your Yillah : no wonder she is lost.'

Said Media, unconcernedly, ' Perhaps better, Taji, to have kept your secret ; but tell no more ; I care not to be your foe.'

' Ah, Taji ! I had shrank from you,' cried Yoomy, ' but for the mark upon your brow. That undoes the tenor of your words. But look, the stars come forth, and who are these ? A waving iris ! ay, again they come :—Hautia's heralds ! '

They brought a black thorn, buried in withered rosebalm blossoms, red and blue.

Said Yoomy, ' For that which stings, there is no cure.'

' Who, who is Hautia, that she stabs me thus ? '

' And this wild sardony mocks your misery.'

' Away ! ye fiends.'

' Again a Venus-car ; and lo ! a wreath of strawberries ! —Yet fly to me, and be garlanded with joys.'

' Let the wild witch laugh. She moves me not. Neither hurtling arrows nor Circæa flowers appal.'

Said Yoomy, ' They wait reply.'

' Tell your Hautia, that I know her not ; nor care to know.   I defy her incantations ; she lures in vain.   Yillah! Yillah ! still I hope ! '

Slowly they departed ; heeding not my cries no more to follow.

Silence, and darkness fell.

CHAPTER XXXI

BABBALANJA DISCOURSES IN THE DARK

NEXT day came and went; and still we onward sailed. At last, by night, there fell a calm, becalming the water of the wide lagoon, and becalming all the clouds in heaven, veiling the constellations. But though our sails were useless, our paddlers plied their broad stout blades. Thus sweeping by a rent and hoar old rock, Vee-Vee, impatient of the calm, sprang to his crow's nest in the shark's-mouth, and seizing his conch, sounded a blast which ran in and out among the hollows, reverberating with the echoes.

Be sure, it was startling. But more so with respect to one of our paddlers, upon whose shoulders, elevated Vee-Vee, his balance lost, all at once came down by the run. But the heedless little bugler himself was most injured by the fall; his arm nearly being broken.

Some remedies applied, and the company grown composed, Babbalanja thus : ' My lord Media, was there any human necessity for that accident ? '

' None that I know, or care to tell, Babbalanja.'

' Vee-Vee,' said Babbalanja, ' did you fall on purpose ? '

' Not I,' sobbed little Vee-Vee, slinging his ailing arm in its mate.

' Woe ! woe to us all, then,' cried Babbalanja ; ' for what direful events may be in store for us which we cannot avoid.'

' How now, mortal ? ' cried Media ; ' what now ? '

' My lord, think of it. Minus human inducement from without, and minus volition from within, Vee-Vee has met

120

with an accident which has almost maimed him for life.
Is it not terrifying to think of ?   Are not all mortals exposed to similar, nay, worse calamities, ineffably unavoid-
able ?   Woe, woe, I say, to us Mardians !   Here, take my
last breath ; let me give up this beggarly ghost ! '

' Nay,' said Media ; ' pause, Babbalanja.   Turn it not
adrift prematurely.   Let it house till midnight ;   the
proper time for you mortals to dissolve.   But, philosopher,
if you harp upon Vee-Vee's mishap, know that it was
owing to nothing but his carelessness.'

' And what was that owing to, my lord ? '

' To Vee-Vee himself.'

' Then, my lord, what brought such a careless being into
Mardi ? '

' A long course of generations.   He's someone's great-
great-grandson, doubtless ; who was great-great-grandson
to someone else ; who also had grandsires.'

' Many thanks then to your highness ; for you establish
the doctrine of Philosophical Necessity.'

' No.   I establish nothing ; I but answer your questions.'

' All one, my lord : you are a Necessitarian ; in other
words, you hold that everything takes place through
absolute necessity.'

' Do you take me, then, for a fool, and a Fatalist ?
Pardie ! a bad creed for a monarch, the distributor of
rewards and punishments.'

' Right there, my lord.   But, for all that, your highness
is a Necessitarian, yet no Fatalist.   Confound not the
distinct.   Fatalism presumes express and irrevocable
edicts of heaven concerning particular events.   Whereas,
Necessity holds that all events are naturally linked, and
inevitably follow each other, without providential inter-
position, though by the eternal letting of Providence.'

' Well, well, Babbalanja, I grant it all.   Go on.'

' On high authority, we are told that in times past the fall of certain nations in Mardi was prophesied of seers.'

' Most true, my lord,' said Mohi ; ' it is all down in the chronicles.'

' Ha ! ha ! ' cried Media. ' Go on, philosopher.'

Continued Babbalanja, ' Previous to the time assigned to their fulfilment, these prophecies were bruited through Mardi ; hence, previous to the time assigned to their fulfilment, full knowledge of them may have come to the nations concerned. Now, my lord, was it possible for these nations, thus forewarned, so to conduct their affairs, as at the prophesied time, to prove false the events revealed to be in store for them ? '

' However that may be,' said Mohi, ' certain it is, those events did assuredly come to pass :—Compare the ruins of Babbelona with book ninth, chapter tenth, of the Chronicles. Yea, yea, the owl inhabits where the seers predicted ; the jackals yell in the tombs of the kings.'

' Go on, Babbalanja,' said Media. ' Of course those nations could not have resisted their doom. Go on, then : vault over your premises.'

' If it be, then, my lord, that——'

' My very worshipful lord,' interposed Mohi, ' is not our philosopher getting off soundings ; and may it not be impious to meddle with these things ? '

' Were it so, old man, he should have known it. The king of Odo is something more than you mortals.'

' But are we the great gods themselves,' cried Yoomy, ' that we discourse of these things ? '

' No, minstrel,' said Babbalanja ; ' and no need have the great gods to discourse of things perfectly comprehended by them, and by themselves ordained. But you and I, Yoomy, are men, and not gods ; hence is it for us, and not for them, to take these things for our themes. Nor is there any impiety in the right use of our reason,

whatever the issue. Smote with superstition, shall we let
it wither and die out, a dead limb to a live trunk, as the
mad devotee's arm held up motionless for years ? Or
shall we employ it but for a paw, to help us to our bodily
needs, as the brutes use their instinct ? Is not reason
subtile as quicksilver—live as lightning—a neighing
charger to advance, but a snail to recede ? Can we starve
that noble instinct in us, and hope that it will survive ?
Better slay the body than the soul ; and if it be the direst
of sins to be the murderers of our own bodies, how much
more to be a soul-suicide. Yoomy, we are men, we are
angels. And in his faculties, high Oro is but what a man
would be, infinitely magnified. Let us aspire to all things.
Are we babes in the woods, to be scared by the shadows of
the trees ? What shall appal us ? If eagles gaze at the
sun, may not men at the gods ? '

'For one,' said Media, 'you may gaze at me freely.
Gaze on. But talk not of my kinsmen so fluently,
Babbalanja. Return to your argument.'

'I go back then, my lord. By implication, you have
granted, that in times past the future was foreknown of
Oro ; hence, in times past, the future must have been
foreordained. But in all things Oro is immutable.
Wherefore our own future is foreknown and foreordained.
Now, if things foreordained concerning nations have in
times past been revealed to them previous to their taking
place, then something similar may be presumable concerning individual men now living. That is to say, out of
all the events destined to befall any one man, it is not impossible that previous knowledge of some one of these
events might supernaturally come to him. Say, then, it
is revealed to me, that ten days hence I shall, of my own
choice, fall upon my javelin ; when the time comes round
could I refrain from suicide ? Grant the strongest presumable motives to the act ; grant that, unforewarned, I

would slay myself outright at the time appointed : yet, foretold of it, and resolved to test the decree to the uttermost, under such circumstances, I say, would it be possible for me not to kill myself ?   If possible, then predestination is not a thing absolute ; and Heaven is wise to keep secret from us those decrees, whose virtue consists in secrecy.   But if not possible, then that suicide would not be mine, but Oro's.   And, by consequence, not only that act, but all my acts, are Oro's.   In sum, my lord, he who believes that in times past, prophets have prophesied, and their prophecies have been fulfilled ; when put to it, inevitably must allow that every man now living is an irresponsible being.'

' In sooth, a very fine argument very finely argued,' said Media.   ' You have done marvels, Babbalanja.   But hark ye, were I so disposed, I could deny you all over, premises and conclusions alike.   And furthermore, my cogent philosopher, had you published that anarchical dogma among my subjects in Oro, I had silenced you by my spear-headed sceptre instead of my uplifted finger.'

' Then, all thanks and all honour to your generosity, my lord, in granting us the immunities you did at the outset of this voyage.   But, my lord, permit me one word more.   Is not Oro omnipresent—absolutely everywhere ? '

' So you mortals teach, Babbalanja.'

' But so do they *mean*, my lord.   Often do we Mardians stick to terms for ages, yet truly apply not their meanings.'

' Well, Oro is everywhere.   What now ? '

' Then, if that be absolutely so, Oro is not merely a universal onlooker, but occupies and fills all space ; and no vacancy is left for any being, or anything but Oro. Hence, Oro is *in* all things, and himself *is* all things—the time-old creed.   But since evil abounds, and Oro is all things, then he cannot be perfectly good ; wherefore,

Oro's omnipresence and moral perfection seem incompatible.   Furthermore, my lord, those orthodox systems which ascribe to Oro almighty and universal attributes every way, those systems, I say, destroy all intellectual individualities but Oro, and resolve the universe into him. But this is a heresy ; wherefore, orthodoxy and heresy are one.   And thus is it, my lord, that upon these matters we Mardians all agree and disagree together, and kill each other with weapons that burst in our hands.   Ah, my lord, with what mind must blessed Oro look down upon this scene !   Think you he discriminates between the deist and atheist ?   Nay ; for the Searcher of the cores of all hearts well knoweth that atheists there are none.   For in things abstract, men but differ in the sounds that come from their mouths, and not in the wordless thoughts lying at the bottom of their beings.   The universe is all of one mind.   Though my twin-brother sware to me, by the blazing sun in heaven at noonday, that Oro is not ; yet would he belie the thing he intended to express.   And who lives that blasphemes ?   What jargon of human sounds so puissant as to insult the unutterable majesty divine ?   Is Oro's honour in the keeping of Mardi ?— Oro's conscience in man's hands ?   Where our warrant, with Oro's sign-manual, to justify the killing, burning, and destroying, or far worse, the social persecutions we institute in his behalf ?   Ah, how shall these self-assumed attorneys and vicegerents be astounded, when they shall see all heaven peopled with heretics and heathens, and all hell nodding over with mitres !   Ah ! let us Mardians quit this insanity.   Let us be content with the theology in the grass and the flower, in seed-time and harvest.   Be it enough for us to know that Oro indubitably is.   My lord ! my lord ! sick with the spectacle of the madness of men, and broken with spontaneous doubts, I sometimes see but two things in all Mardi to believe :—that I myself exist, and that I can most happily, or least miserably exist, by the practice of righteousness. All else is in the clouds ; and naught else may I learn, till the firmament be split from horizon to horizon. Yet, alas ! too often do I swing from these moorings.'

'Alas ! his fit is coming upon him again,' whispered Yoomy.

'Why, Babbalanja,' said Media, 'I almost pity you. You are too warm, too warm. Why fever your soul with these things ? To no use you mortals wax earnest. No thanks, but curses, will you get for your earnestness. You yourself you harm most. Why not take creeds as they come ? It is not so hard to be persuaded ; never mind about believing.'

'True, my lord ; not very hard ; no act is required ; only passiveness. Stand still and receive. Faith is to the thoughtless, doubts to the thinker.'

'Then, why think at all ? Is it not better for you mortals to clutch error as in a vice, than have your fingers meet in your hand ? And to what end your eternal inquisitions ? You have nothing to substitute. You say all is a lie ; then out with the truth. Philosopher, your devil is but a foolish one, after all. I, a demi-god, never say nay to these things.'

'Yea, my lord, it would hardly answer for Oro himself, were he to come down to Mardi, to deny men's theories concerning him. Did they not strike at the rash deity in Alma ? '

'Then, why deny those theories yourself ? Babbalanja, you almost affect my immortal serenity. Must you for-ever be a sieve for good grain to run through, while you retain but the chaff ? Your tongue is forked. You speak two languages : flat folly for yourself, and wisdom for others. Babbalanja, if you have any belief of your own, keep it ; but, in Oro's name, keep it secret.'

' Ay, my lord, in these things wise men are spectators, not actors ; wise men look on, and say " ay." '

' Why not say so yourself, then ? '

' My lord, because I have often told you, that I am a fool, and not wise.'

' Your highness,' said Mohi, ' this whole discourse seems to have grown out of the subject of Necessity and Free Will. Now, when a boy, I recollect hearing a sage say that these things were reconcilable.'

' Ay ? ' said Media, ' what say you to that, now, Babbalanja ? '

' It may be even so, my lord. Shall I tell you a story ? '

' Azzageddi 's stirring now,' muttered Mohi.

' Proceed,' said Media.

' King Normo had a fool, called Willi, whom he loved to humour. Now, though Willi ever obeyed his lord, by the very instinct of his servitude, he flattered himself that he was free ; and this conceit it was that made the fool so entertaining to the king. One day, said Normo to his fool,—" Go, Willi, to yonder tree, and wait there till I come." " Your majesty, I will," said Willi, bowing beneath his jingling bells ; " but I presume your majesty has no objections to my walking on my hands :—I am free, I hope." " Perfectly," said Normo, " hands or feet, it 's all the same to me ; only do my bidding." " I thought as much," said Willi ; so, swinging his limber legs into the air, Willi, thumb after thumb, essayed progression. But soon, his bottled blood so rushed downward through his neck, that he was fain to turn a somerset and regain his feet. Said he, " Though I am free to do it, it 's not so easy turning digits into toes ; I 'll walk, by gad ! which is my other option." So he went straight forward, and did King Normo's bidding in the natural way.'

' A curious story that,' said Media ; ' whence came it ? '

' My lord, where everything, but one, is to be had :—within.'

' You are charged to the muzzle, then,' said Braid-Beard.

' Yes, Mohi ; and my talk is my overflowing, not my fulness.'

' And what may you be so full of ? '

' Of myself.'

' So it seems,' said Mohi, whisking away a fly with his beard.

' Babbalanja,' said Media, ' you did right in selecting this ebon night for discussing the theme you did ; and truly, you mortals are but too apt to talk in the dark.'

' Ay, my lord, and we mortals may prate still more in the dark when we are dead ; for methinks, that if we then prate at all, 'twill be in our sleep. Ah ! my lord, think not that in aught I 've said this night I would assert any wisdom of my own. I but fight against the armed and crested Lies of Mardi, that like a host assail me. I am stuck full of darts ; but, tearing them from out me, gasping, I discharge them whence they come.'

So saying, Babbalanja slowly drooped, and fell reclining ; then lay motionless as the marble Gladiator, that for centuries has been dying.

CHAPTER XXXII

MY LORD MEDIA SUMMONS MOHI TO THE STAND

WHILE slowly the night wore on, and the now scudding clouds flown past, revealed again the hosts in heaven, few words were uttered save by Media ; who, when all others were most sad and silent, seemed but little moved, or not stirred a jot.

But that night, he filled his flagon fuller than his wont, and drank, and drank, and pledged the stars.

'Here's to thee, old Arcturus ! To thee, old Aldebaran ! who ever poise your wine-red, fiery spheres on high. A health to *thee*, my regal friend, Alphacca, in the constellation of the Crown : lo ! crown to crown, I pledge thee ! I drink to *ye*, too, Alphard ! Markab ! Denebola ! Capella ! —to *ye*, too, sailing Cygnus ! Aquila soaring !—All round, a health to all your diadems ! May they never fade ! nor mine ! '

At last, in the shadowy east, the dawn, like a gray, distant sail before the wind, was descried ; drawing nearer and nearer, till her gilded prow was perceived.

And as in tropic gales, the winds blow fierce, and more fierce, with the advent of the sun ; so with King Media ; whose mirth now breezed up afresh. But, as at sunrise, the sea-storm only blows harder, to settle down at last into a steady wind ; even so, in good time, my lord Media came to be more decorous of mood. And Babbalanja abated his reveries.

For who might withstand such a morn !

As on the night-banks of the far-rolling Ganges, the

royal bridegroom sets forth for his bride, preceded by nymphs, now this side, now that, lighting up all the flowery flambeaux held on high as they pass ; so came the sun, to his nuptials with Mardi :—the hours going on before, touching all the peaks, till they glowed rosy-red.

By reflex, the lagoon, here and there, seemed on fire ; each curling wave-crest a flame.

Noon came as we sailed.

And now, citrons and bananas, cups and calabashes, calumets and tobacco, were passed round ; and we were all very merry and mellow indeed. Smacking our lips, chatting, smoking, and sipping. Now a mouthful of citron to season a repartee ; now a swallow of wine to wash down a precept ; now a fragrant whiff to puff away care. Many things did beguile. From side to side, we turned and grazed, like Juno's white oxen in clover meads.

Soon, we drew nigh to a charming cliff, overrun with woodbines, on high suspended from flowering tamarisk and tamarind trees. The blossoms of the tamarisks, in spikes of small, red bells ; the tamarinds, wide-spreading their golden petals, red-streaked as with streaks of the dawn. Down sweeping to the water, the vines trailed over to the crisp, curling waves,—little pages, all eager to hold up their trains.

Within, was a bower ; going behind it, like standing inside the sheet of the falls of the Genesee.

In this arbour we anchored. And with their shaded prows thrust in among the flowers, our three canoes seemed baiting by the way, like wearied steeds in a hawthorn lane.

High midsummer noon is more silent than night. Most sweet a siesta then. And noon-dreams are day-dreams indeed ; born under the meridian sun. Pale Cynthia begets pale spectre shapes ; and her frigid rays best illuminate white nuns, marble monuments, icy glaciers, and cold tombs.

The sun rolled on. And starting to his feet, arms clasped, and wildly staring, Yoomy exclaimed—' Nay, nay, thou shalt not depart, thou maid !—here, here I fold thee for aye !—Flown ?—A dream ! Then siestas henceforth while I live. And at noon, every day will I meet thee, sweet maid ! And, oh Sun ! set not ; and poppies bend over us, when next we embrace ! '

' What ails that somnambulist ? ' cried Media, rising. ' Yoomy, I say ! what ails thee ? '

' He must have indulged over freely in those citrons,' said Mohi sympathetically, rubbing his fruitery. ' Ho, Yoomy ! a swallow of brine will help thee.'

' Alas,' cried Babbalanja, ' do the fairies then wait on repletion ? Do our dreams come from below, and not from the skies ? Are we angels, or dogs ? Oh, man, man, man ! thou art harder to solve than the Integral Calculus—yet plain as a primer ; harder to find than the philosopher's stone—yet ever at hand ; a more cunning compound than an alchemist's—yet a hundredweight of flesh to a pennyweight of spirit ; soul and body glued together, firm as atom to atom, seamless as the vestment without joint, warp or woof—yet divided as by a river, spirit from flesh ; growing both ways, like a tree, and dropping thy topmost branches to earth, like thy beard or a banian !—I give thee up, oh man ! thou art twain—yet indivisible ; all things—yet a poor unit at best.'

' Philosopher, you seem puzzled to account for the riddles of your race,' cried Media, sideways reclining at his ease. ' Now, do thou, old Mohi, stand up before a demi-god, and answer for all.—Draw nigh, so I can eye thee. What art thou, mortal ? '

' My worshipful lord, a man.'

' And what are men ? '

' My lord, before thee is a specimen.'

' I fear me, my lord will get nothing out of that witness,'
said Babbalanja. ' Pray you, King Media, let another
inquisitor cross-question.'

' Proceed ; take the divan.'

' A pace or two farther off, there, Mohi ; so I can garner
thee all in at a glance.—Attention ! Rememberest thou,
fellow-being, when thou wast born ? '

' Not I. Old Braid-Beard had no memory then.'

' When, then, wast thou first conscious of being ? '

' What time I was teething : my first sensation was an
ache.'

' What dost thou, fellow-being, here in Mardi ? '

' What doth Mardi here, fellow-being, under me ? '

' Philosopher, thou gainest but little by thy questions,'
cried Yoomy, advancing. ' Let a poet endeavour.'

' I abdicate in your favour, then, gentle Yoomy ; let me
smooth the divan for you ;—there : be seated.'

' Now, Mohi, who art thou ? ' said Yoomy, nodding his
bird-of-paradise plume.

' The sole witness, it seems, in this case.'

' Try again, minstrel,' cried Babbalanja.

' Then, what art thou, Mohi ? '

' Even what thou art, Yoomy.'

' He is too sharp or too blunt for us all,' cried King
Media. ' His devil is even more subtle than yours,
Babbalanja. Let him go.'

' Shall I adjourn the court, then, my lord ? ' said
Babbalanja.

' Ay.'

' Oyez ! Oyez ! Oyez ! All mortals having business at
this court, know ye, that it is adjourned till sundown of the
day which hath no to-morrow.'

CHAPTER XXXIII

WHEREIN BABBALANJA AND YOOMY EMBRACE

'How the isles grow and multiply around us!' cried Babbalanja, as turning the bold promontory of an uninhabited shore, many distant lands bluely loomed into view. 'Surely, our brief voyage, may not embrace all Mardi like its reef?'

'No,' said Media, 'much must be left unseen. Nor everywhere can Yillah be sought, noble Taji.'

Said Yoomy, 'We are as birds, with pinions clipped, that in unfathomable and endless woods but flit from twig to twig of one poor tree.'

'More isles! more isles!' cried Babbalanja, erect, and gazing abroad. 'And lo! round all is heaving that infinite ocean. Ah! gods! what regions lie beyond?'

'But whither now?' he cried, as in obedience to Media, the paddlers suddenly altered our course.

'To the bold shores of Diranda,' said Media.

'Ay; the land of clubs and javelins, where the lord seigniors Hello and Piko celebrate their famous games,' cried Mohi.

'Your clubs and javelins,' said Media, 'remind me of the great battle-chant of Narvi—Yoomy!'—turning to the minstrel, gazing abstractedly into the water;— 'awake, Yoomy, and give us the lines.'

'My lord Media, 'tis but a rude, clanging thing; dissonant as if the north wind blew through it. Methinks the company will not fancy lines so inharmonious. Better sing you, perhaps, one of my sonnets.'

' Better sit and sob in our ears, silly Yoomy that thou
art !—no ! no ! none of your sentiment now ; my soul is
martially inclined ; I want clarion peals, not lute war-
blings. So throw out your chest, Yoomy : lift high your
voice ; and blow me the old battle-blast.—Begin, sir
minstrel.'

And warning all that he himself had not composed the
odious chant, Yoomy thus :—

Our clubs ! our clubs !
The thousand clubs of Narvi !
Of the living trunk of the palm-tree made ;
Skull breakers !   Brain spatterers !
Wielded right, and wielded left ;
Life quenchers !   Death dealers !
Causing live bodies to run headless !

Our bows ! our bows !
The thousand bows of Narvi !
Ribs of Tara, god of War !
Fashioned from the light Tola their arrows ;
Swift messengers !   Heart piercers !
Barbed with sharp pearl shells ;
Winged with white tail-plumes ;
To wild death-chants, strung with the hair of wild
maidens !

Our spears ! our spears !
The thousand spears of Narvi !
Of the thunder-riven Moo-tree made :
Tall tree, couched on the long mountain Lana !
No staves for gray-beards ! no rods for fishermen !
Tempered by fierce sea-winds,
Splintered into lances by lightnings,
Long arrows !   Heart seekers !
Toughened by fire their sharp black points !

Our slings ! our slings !
The thousand slings of Narvi !
All tasselled, and braided, and gaily bedecked.
In peace, our girdles ; in war, our war-nets ;
Wherewith catch we heads as fish from the deep !
The pebbles they hurl, have been hurled before,—
Hurled up on the beach by the stormy sea !
Pebbles, buried erewhile in the head of the shark :
To be buried erelong in the heads of our foes !
Home of hard blows, our pouches !
Nest of death-eggs !   How quickly they hatch !

Uplift, and couch we our spears, men !
Ring hollow on the rocks our war clubs !
Bend we our bows, feel the points of our arrows :
Aloft, whirl in eddies our sling-nets ;
To the fight, men of Narvi !
Sons of battle !   Hunters of men !
Raise high your war-wood !
Shout, Narvi ! her groves in the storm !

'By Oro !' cried Media, 'but Yoomy has well-nigh
stirred up all Babbalanja's devils in me.   Were I a mortal,
I could fight now on a pretence.   And did any man say me
nay, I would charge upon him like a spear-point.   Ah,
Yoomy, thou and thy tribe have much to answer for ; ye
stir up all Mardi with your lays.   Your war chants make
men fight ; your drinking songs, drunkards ; your love
ditties, fools.   Yet there thou sittest, Yoomy, gentle as a
dove.—What art thou, minstrel, that thy soft, singing soul
should so master all mortals ?   Yoomy, like me, you
sway a sceptre.'

'Thou honourest my calling overmuch,' said Yoomy ;
'we minstrels but sing our lays carelessly, my lord
Media.'

'Ay : and the more mischief they make.'

'But sometimes we poets are didactic.'

'Didactic and dull; many of ye are but too apt to be prosy unless mischievous.'

'Yet in our verses, my lord Media, but few of us purpose harm.'

'But when all harmless to yourselves, ye may be otherwise to Mardi.'

'And are not foul streams often traced to pure fountains, my lord?' said Babbalanja. 'The essence of all good and all evil is in us, not out of us. Neither poison nor honey lodgeth in the flowers on which, side by side, bees and wasps oft alight. My lord, nature is an immaculate virgin, forever standing unrobed before us. True poets but paint the charms which all eyes behold. The vicious would be vicious without them.'

'My lord Media,' impetuously resumed Yoomy, 'I am sensible of a thousand sweet, merry fancies, limpid with innocence; yet my enemies account them all lewd conceits.'

'There be those in Mardi,' said Babbalanja, 'who would never ascribe evil to others, did they not find it in their own hearts; believing none can be different from themselves.'

'My lord, my lord!' cried Yoomy. 'The air that breathes my music from me is a mountain air! Purer than others am I; for though not a woman, I feel in me a woman's soul.'

'Ah, have done, silly Yoomy,' said Media. 'Thou art becoming flighty, even as Babbalanja, when Azzageddi is uppermost.'

'Thus ever: ever thus!' sighed Yoomy. 'They comprehend us not.'

'Nor me,' said Babbalanja. 'Yoomy: poets both, we differ but in seeming; thy airiest conceits are as the shadows of my deepest ponderings; though Yoomy soars, and Babbalanja dives, both meet at last.   Not a song you sing, but I have thought its thought ; and where dull Mardi sees but your rose, I unfold its petals, and disclose a pearl.   Poets are we, Yoomy, in that we dwell without us ; we live in grottoes, palms, and brooks ; we ride the sea, we ride the sky ; poets are omnipresent.'

CHAPTER XXXIV

OF THE ISLE OF DIRANDA

IN good time the shores of Diranda were in sight. And, introductory to landing, Braid-Beard proceeded to give us some little account of the island, and its rulers.

As previously hinted, those very magnificent and illustrious lord seigniors, the lord seigniors Hello and Piko, who between them divided Diranda, delighted in all manner of public games, especially warlike ones ; which last were celebrated so frequently, and were so fatal in their results, that, notwithstanding the multiplicity of nuptials taking place in the isle, its population remained in equilibrio. But, strange to relate, this was the very object which the lord seigniors had in view ; the very object they sought to compass, by instituting their games. Though, for the most part, they wisely kept the secret locked up.

But to tell how the lord seigniors Hello and Piko came to join hands in this matter.

Diranda had been amicably divided between them ever since the day they were crowned ; one reigning king in the east, the other in the west. But King Piko had been long harassed with the thought, that the unobstructed and indefinite increase of his browsing subjects might eventually denude of herbage his portion of the island. Posterity, thought he, is marshalling her generations in squadrons, brigades, and battalions, and ere long will be down upon my devoted empire. Lo ! her locust cavalry darken the skies ; her light-troop pismires cover the earth. Alas !

my son and successor, thou wilt inhale choke-damp for air, and have not a private corner to say thy prayers.

By a sort of arithmetical progression, the probability, nay, the certainty of these results, if not in some way averted, was proved to King Piko ; and he was furthermore admonished, that war—war to the haft with King Hello—was the only cure for so menacing an evil.

But so it was, that King Piko, at peace with King Hello, and well content with the tranquillity of the times, little relished the idea of picking a quarrel with his neighbour, and running its risks, in order to phlebotomise his redundant population.

' Patience, most illustrious seignior,' said another of his sagacious Ahithophels, 'and haply a pestilence may decimate the people.'

But no pestilence came.   And in every direction the young men and maidens were recklessly rushing into wedlock ; and so salubrious the climate, that the old men stuck to the outside of the turf, and refused to go under.

At last some Machiavel of a philosopher suggested, that peradventure the object of war might be answered without going to war ; that peradventure King Hello might be brought to acquiesce in an arrangement whereby the men of Diranda might be induced to kill off one another voluntarily, in a peaceable manner, without troubling their rulers.   And to this end, the games before mentioned were proposed.

' Egad ! my wise ones, you have hit it,' cried Piko ; ' but will Hello say ay ? '

' Try him, most illustrious seignior,' said Machiavel.

So to Hello went ambassadors ordinary and extra-ordinary, and ministers plenipotentiary and peculiar ; and anxiously King Piko awaited their return.

The mission was crowned with success.

Said King Hello to the ministers, in confidence :—' The very thing, Dons, the very thing I have wanted. My people are increasing too fast. They keep up the succession too well. Tell your illustrious master it 's a bargain. The games ! the games ! by all means.'

So, throughout the island, by proclamation, they were forthwith established ; succeeding to a charm.

And the lord seigniors, Hello and Piko, finding their interests the same, came together like bride and bridegroom ; lived in the same palace ; dined off the same cloth ; cut from the same bread-fruit ; drank from the same calabash ; wore each other's crowns ; and often locking arms with a charming frankness, paced up and down in their dominions, discussing the prospect of the next harvest of heads.

In his old-fashioned way, having related all this, with many other particulars, Mohi was interrupted by Babbalanja, who inquired how the people of Diranda relished the games, and how they fancied being coolly thinned out in that manner.

To which in substance the chronicler replied, that of the true object of the games they had not the faintest conception ; but hammered away at each other, and fought and died together, like jolly good fellows.

' Right again, immortal old Bardianna ! ' cried Babbalanja.

' And what has the sage to the point this time ? ' asked Media.

' Why, my lord, in his chapter on " Cracked Crowns," Bardianna, after many profound ponderings, thus concludes : " In this cracked sphere we live in, then, cracked skulls would seem the inevitable allotments of many. Nor will the splintering thereof cease, till this pugnacious animal we treat of be deprived of his natural maces :

videlicet, his arms. And right well doth man love to bruise and batter all occiputs in his vicinity." '

' Seems to me, our old friend must have been on his stilts that time,' interrupted Mohi.

' No, Braid-Beard. But by way of apologising for the unusual rigidity of his style in that chapter, he says in a note, that it was written upon a straight-backed settle, when he was ill of a lumbago, and a crick in the neck.'

' That incorrigible Azzageddi again,' said Media. ' Proceed with your quotation, Babbalanja.'

' Where was I, Braid-Beard ? '

' Battering occiputs at the last accounts,' said Mohi.

' Ah, yes.—" And right well doth man love to bruise and batter all occiputs in his vicinity ; he but follows his instincts ; he is but one member of a fighting world. Spiders, vixens, and tigers all war with a relish ; and on every side is heard the howls of hyenas, the throttlings of mastiffs, the din of belligerent beetles, the buzzing warfare of the insect battalions : and the shrill cries of lady Tartars rending their lords. And all this existeth of necessity. To war it is, and other depopulators, that we are beholden for elbow-room in Mardi, and for all our parks and gardens, wherein we are wont to expatiate. Come on, then, plague, war, famine and viragos ! Come on, I say, for who shall stay ye ? Come on, and healthfulise the census ! And more especially, oh War ! do thou march forth with thy bludgeon ! Cracked are our crowns by nature, and henceforth forever cracked shall they be by hard raps." '

' And hopelessly cracked the skull that hatched such a tirade of nonsense,' said Mohi.

' And think you not, old Bardianna knew that ? ' asked Babbalanja. ' He wrote an excellent chapter on that very subject.'

'What, on the cracks in his own pate?'

'Precisely. And expressly asserts, that to those identical cracks was he indebted for what little light he had in his brain.'

'I yield, Babbalanja; your old ponderer is older than I.'

'Ay, ay, Braid-Beard; his crest was a tortoise; and this was the motto :—" I bite, but am not to be bitten." '

CHAPTER XXXV

IN good time, we landed at Diranda. And that landing was like landing at Greenwich among the Waterloo pensioners. The people were docked right and left; some without arms; some without legs; not one with a tail; but to a man, all had heads, though rather the worse for wear; covered with lumps and contusions.

Now, those very magnificent and illustrious lord seigniors, the lord seigniors Hello and Piko, lived in a palace, round which was a fence of the cane called Malacca, each picket helmed with a skull, of which there were fifty, one to each cane. Over the door was the blended arms of the high and mighty houses of Hello and Piko: a Clavicle crossed over an Ulna.

Escorted to the sign of the Skull and Cross Bones, we received the very best entertainment which that royal inn could afford. We found our hosts Hello and Piko seated together on a dais or throne, and now and then drinking some claret-red wine from an ivory bowl, too large to have been wrought from an elephant's tusk. They were in glorious good spirits, shaking ivory coins in a skull.

'What says your majesty?' said Piko. 'Heads or tails?'

' Oh, heads, your majesty,' said Hello.

' And heads say I,' said Piko.

And heads it was. But it was heads on both sides, so both were sure to win.

And thus they were used to play merrily all day long; beheading the gourds of claret by one slicing blow with

143

their sickle-shaped sceptres. Wide round them lay empty calabashes, all feathered, red dyed, and betasselled, trickling red wine from their necks, like the decapitated pullets in the old baronial barn-yard at Kenilworth, the night before Queen Bess dined with my lord Leicester.

The first compliments over ; and Media and Taji having met with a reception suitable to their rank, the kings inquired whether there were any good javelin flingers among us : for if that were the case, they could furnish them plenty of sport. Informed, however, that none of the party were professional warriors, their majesties looked rather glum, and by way of chasing away the blues, called for some good old stuff that was red.

It seems, this soliciting guests, to keep their spears from decaying, by cut and thrust play with their subjects, was a very common thing with their illustrious majesties.

But if their visitors could not be prevailed upon to spear a subject or so, our hospitable hosts resolved to have a few speared, and otherwise served up for our special entertainment. In a word, our arrival furnished a fine pretext for renewing their games ; though, we learned, that only ten days previous, upward of fifty combatants had been slain at one of these festivals.

Be that as it might, their joint majesties determined upon another one ; and also upon our tarrying to behold it.

We objected, saying we must depart.

But we were kindly assured that our canoes had been dragged out of the water, and buried in a wood ; there to remain till the games were over.

The day fixed upon was the third subsequent to our arrival ; the interval being devoted to preparations ; summoning from their villages and valleys the warriors of the land ; and publishing the royal proclamations, whereby the unbounded hospitality of the kings' household was freely offered to all heroes whatsoever, who for

the love of arms, and the honour of broken heads, desired
to cross battle clubs, hurl spears, or die game in the royal
valley of Deddo.

Meantime, the whole island was in a state of uproarious
commotion, and strangers were daily arriving.

The spot set apart for the festival was a spacious down,
mantled with white asters ; which, waving in winrows,
lay upon the land, like the cream-surf surging the milk of
young heifers. But that whiteness, here and there, was
spotted with strawberries ; tracking the plain, as if
wounded creatures had been dragging themselves bleeding
from some deadly encounter. All round the down waved
scarlet thickets of sumach, moaning in the wind, like the
gory ghosts environing Pharsalia the night after the battle ;
scaring away the peasants, who with bushel-baskets came
to the jewel-harvest of the rings of Pompey's knights.

Beneath the heaped turf of this down lay thousands of
glorious corpses of anonymous heroes, who here had died
glorious deaths.

Whence, in the florid language of Diranda, they called
this field ' The Field of Glory.'

CHAPTER XXXVI

THEY ATTEND THE GAMES

At last the third day dawned ; and facing us upon entering the plain was a throne of red log-wood, canopied by the foliage of a red-dyed pandanus. Upon this throne, purple-robed, reclined those very magnificent and illustrious lord seigniors, the lord seigniors Hello and Piko. Before them were many gourds of wine ; and crosswise, staked in the sod, their own royal spears.

In the middle of the down, as if by a furrow, a long, oval space was margined off, about which a crowd of spectators were seated. Opposite the throne was reserved a clear passage to the arena, defined by air-lines, indefinitely produced from the levelled points of two spears, so poised by a brace of warriors.

Drawing near, our party was courteously received, and assigned a commodious lounge.

The first encounter was a club-fight between two warriors. Nor casque of steel nor skull of Congo could have resisted their blows, had they fallen upon the mark ; for they seemed bent upon driving each other, as stakes, into the earth. Presently, one of them faltered ; but his adversary rushing in to cleave him down, slipped against a guava-rind ; when the falterer, with one lucky blow, high into the air sent the stumbler's club, which descended upon the crown of a spectator, who was borne from the plain.

' All one,' muttered Piko.

'As good dead as another,' muttered Hello.

146

The second encounter was a hugging match ; wherein two warriors, masked in grizzly-bear skins, hugged each other to death.

The third encounter was a bumping match between a fat warrior and a dwarf. Standing erect, his paunch like a bass-drum before a drummer, the fat man was run at, head-a-tilt, by the dwarf, and sent spinning round on his axis.

The fourth encounter was a tussle between two-score warriors, who, all in a mass, writhed like the limbs in Sebastioni's painting of Hades. After obscuring them-selves in a cloud of dust these combatants, uninjured, but hugely blowing, drew off ; and separately going among the spectators, rehearsed their experience of the fray.

'Braggarts ! ' mumbled Piko.

'Poltroons ! ' growled Hello.

While the crowd were applauding, a sober-sided observer, trying to rub the dust out of his eyes, inquired of an enthusiastic neighbour, 'Pray what was all that about ? '

'Fool ! saw you not the dust ? '

'That I did,' said Sober-Sides, again rubbing his eyes ; 'but I can raise a dust myself.'

The fifth encounter was a fight of single-sticks between one hundred warriors, fifty on a side.

In a line, the first fifty emerged from the sumachs, their weapons interlocked in a sort of wicker-work.   In advance marched a priest, bearing an idol with a cracked cocoa-nut for a head,—Krako, the god of Trepans. Preceded by damsels flinging flowers, now came on the second fifty, gaily apparelled, weapons poised, and their feet nimbly moving in a martial measure.

Midway meeting, both parties touched poles, then re-treated. Very courteous, this ; but tantamount to

bowing each other out of Mardi ; for upon Piko's tossing
a javelin, they rushed in, and each striking his man, all
fell to the ground.

' Well done ! ' cried Piko.

' Brave fellows ! ' cried Hello.

' But up and at it again, my heroes ! ' joined both.
' Lo ! we kings look on, and there stand the bards ! '

These bards were a row of lean, sallow, old men, in
threadbare robes, and chaplets of dead leaves.

' Strike up ! ' cried Piko.

' A stave ! ' cried Hello.

Whereupon, the old croakers, each with a quinsy, sang
thus in cracked strains :—

> Quack !   Quack !   Quack !
> With a toorooloo whack ;
> Hack away, merry men, hack away.
> Who would not die brave,
> His ear smote by a stave ?
> Thwack away, merry men, thwack away !
> 'Tis glory that calls,
> To each hero that falls,
> Hack away, merry men, hack away !
> Quack !   Quack !   Quack !
> Quack !   Quack !
> Quack !

Thus it tapered away.

' Ha, ha ! ' cried Piko, ' how they prick their ears at
that ! '

' Hark ye, my invincibles ! ' cried Hello.   ' That pæan
is for the slain.   So all ye who have lives left, spring to it !
Die and be glorified !   Now 's the time !—Strike up again,
my ducklings ! '

Thus incited, the survivors staggered to their feet ; and
hammering away at each other's sconces, till they rung like
a chime of bells going off with a triple-bob-major, they

finally succeeded in immortalising themselves by quenching their mortalities all round ; the bards still singing.

' Never mind your music now,' cried Piko.

' It 's all over,' said Hello.

' What valiant fellows we have for subjects,' cried Piko.

' Ho ! gravediggers, clear the field,' cried Hello.

' Who else is for glory ? ' cried Piko.

' There stand the bards ! ' cried Hello.

But now there rushed among the crowd a haggard figure,
trickling with blood, and wearing a robe, whose edges
were burned and blacked by fire. Wielding a club, it ran
to and fro, with loud yells menacing all.

A noted warrior this ; who, distracted at the death of
five sons slain in recent games, wandered from valley to
valley, wrestling and fighting.

With wild cries of ' The Despairer ! The Despairer ! '
the appalled multitude fled ; leaving the two kings frozen
on their throne, quaking and quailing, their teeth rattling
like dice.

The Despairer strode toward them ; when, recovering
their senses, they ran ; for a time pursued through the
woods by the phantom.

CHAPTER XXXVII

TAJI STILL HUNTED, AND BECKONED

PREVIOUS to the kings' flight, we had plunged into the
neighbouring woods ; and from thence emerging, entered
brakes of cane, sprouting from morasses. Soon we heard
a whirring, as if three startled partridges had taken wing ;
it proved three feathered arrows, from three unseen hands.

Grazing us, two buried in the ground, but from Taji's
arm the third drew blood.

On all sides round we turned ; but none were seen.

' Still the avengers follow,' said Babbalanja.

' Lo ! the damsels three ! ' cried Yoomy. ' Look
where they come ! '

We joined them by the sumach-wood's red skirts ; and
there, they waved their cherry stalks and heavy bloated
cactus leaves, their crimson blossoms armed with nettles ;
and before us flung shining, yellow tiger-flowers spotted red.

' Blood ! ' cried Yoomy, starting, ' and leopards on
your track ! '

And now the syrens blew through long reeds, tasselled
with their panicles, and waving verdant scarfs of vines,
came dancing toward us, proffering clustering grapes.

' For all now yours, Taji ; and all that yet may come,'
cried Yoomy, ' fly to me ! I will dance away your gloom,
and drown it in inebriation.'

' Away ! woe is its own wine. What may be mine,
that will I endure, in its own essence to the quick. Let
me feel the poniard if it stabs.'

They vanished in the wood ; and hurrying on, we soon
gained sunlight, and the open glade.

CHAPTER XXXVIII

THEY EMBARK FROM DIRANDA

ARRIVED at the Sign of the Skulls, we found the illustrious lord seigniors at rest from their flight, and once more quaffing their claret, all thoughts of the spectre departed. Instead of rattling their own ivory in the heads on their shoulders, they were rattling their dice in the skulls in their hands. And still ' Heads ' was the cry, and ' Heads ' was the throw.

That evening they made known to my lord Media that an interval of two days must elapse ere the games were renewed, in order to reward the victors, bury their dead, and provide for the execution of an Islander, who under the provocation of a blow, had killed a stranger.

As this suspension of the festivities had been wholly unforeseen, our hosts were induced to withdraw the embargo laid upon our canoes. Nevertheless, they pressed us to remain ; saying, that what was to come would far exceed in interest what had already taken place. The games in prospect being of a naval description, embracing certain hand-to-hand contests in the water between shoals of web-footed warriors.

However, we decided to embark on the morrow.

It was in the cool of the early morning, at that hour when a man's face can be known, that we set sail from Diranda ; and in the ghostly twilight our thoughts reverted to the phantom that so suddenly had cleared the plain. With interest we hearkened to the recitals of Mohi ; who, discoursing of the sad end of many brave

151

chieftains in Mardi, made allusion to the youthful Adondo, one of the most famous of the chiefs of the chronicles. In a canoe fight, after performing prodigies of valour, he was wounded in the head, and sunk to the bottom of the lagoon.

'There is a noble monody upon the death of Adondo,' said Yoomy. 'Shall I sing it, my lord ? It is very beautiful ; nor could I ever repeat it without a tear.'

'We will dispense with your tears, minstrel,' said Media, ' but sing it, if you will.'

And Yoomy sang :—

> Departed the pride, and the glory of Mardi :
> The vaunt of her isles sleeps deep in the sea,
> That rolls o'er his corse with a hush.
> His warriors bend over their spears,
> His sisters gaze upward and mourn.
> Weep, weep, for Adondo is dead !
> The sun has gone down in a shower ;
> Buried in clouds the face of the moon ;
> Tears stand in the eyes of the starry skies,
> And stand in the eyes of the flowers ;
> And streams of tears are the trickling brooks,
> Coursing adown the mountains.—
> Departed the pride, and the glory of Mardi :
> The vaunt of her isles sleeps deep in the sea.
> Fast falls the small rain on its bosom that sobs,—
> Not showers of rain, but the tears of Oro.

' A dismal time it must have been,' yawned Media, ' not a dry brook then in Mardi, not a lake that was not moist. Lachrymose rivulets, and inconsolable lagoons ! Call you this poetry, minstrel ? '

' Mohi has something like a tear in his eye,' said Yoomy.

' False ! ' cried Mohi, brushing it aside.

' Who composed that monody ? ' said Babbalanja. ' I have often heard it before.'

'None know, Babbalanja; but the poet must be still singing to himself; his songs bursting through the turf, in the flowers over his grave.'

'But gentle Yoomy, Adondo is a legendary hero, indefinitely dating back. May not his monody, then, be a spontaneous melody, that has been with us since Mardi began? What bard composed the soft verses that our palm boughs sing at even? Nay, Yoomy, that monody was not written by man.'

'Ah! Would that I had been the poet, Babbalanja; for then had I been famous indeed; those lines are chanted through all the isles, by prince and peasant. Yes, Adondo's monody will pervade the ages, like the low undertone you hear, when many singers do sing.'

'My lord, my lord,' cried Babbalanja, 'but this were to be truly immortal;—to be perpetuated in our works, and not in our names. Let me, oh Oro! be anonymously known!'

CHAPTER XXXIX

AN interval of silence was at last broken by Babbalanja.

Pointing to the sun, just gaining the horizon, he exclaimed, ' As old Bardianna says—shut your eyes, and believe.'

' And what may Bardianna have to do with yonder orb ? ' said Media.

' This much, my lord, the astronomers maintain that Mardi moves round the sun ; which I, who never formally investigated the matter for myself, can by no means credit ; unless, plainly seeing one thing, I blindly believe another. Yet even thus blindly does all Mardi subscribe to an astronomical system, which not one in fifty thousand can astronomically prove. And not many centuries back, my lord, all Mardi did equally subscribe to an astronomical system, precisely the reverse of that which they now believe. But the mass of Mardians have not as much reason to believe the first system, as the exploded one ; for all who have eyes must assuredly see, that the sun seems to move, and that Mardi seems a fixture, eternally *here*. But doubtless there are theories which may be true, though the face of things belie them. Hence, in such cases, to the ignorant, disbelief would seem more natural than faith ; though they too often reject the testimony of their own senses for what to them is a mere hypothesis. And thus, my lord, is it, that the mass of Mardians do not believe because they know, but because they know *not*. And they are as ready to receive one thing as another, if it

comes from a canonical source. My lord, Mardi is as an
ostrich, which will swallow aught you offer, even a bar of
iron, if placed endwise. And though the iron be indigestible, yet it serves to fill : in feeding, the end proposed.
For Mardi must have something to exercise its digestion,
though that something be forever indigestible. And as
fishermen for sport, throw two lumps of bait, united by a
cord, to albatrosses floating on the sea ; which are greedily
attempted to be swallowed, one lump by this fowl, the
other by that ; but forever are kept reciprocally going
up and down in them, by means of the cord ; even
so, my lord, do I sometimes fancy, that our theorists
divert themselves with the greediness of Mardians to
believe.'

' Ha, ha,' cried Media, ' methinks this must be Azzageddi who speaks.'

' No, my lord ; not long since, Azzageddi received a
furlough to go home and warm himself for a while. But
this leaves me not alone.'

' How ? '

' My lord,—for the present putting Azzageddi entirely
aside,—though I have now been upon terms of close companionship with myself for nigh five hundred moons, I
have not yet been able to decide who or what I am. To
you, perhaps, I seem Babbalanja ; but to myself, I seem
not myself. All I am sure of is a sort of prickly sensation
all over me, which they call life ; and, occasionally, a
headache or a queer conceit admonishes me, that there is
something astir in my attic. But how know I that these
sensations are identical with myself ? For aught I know,
I may be somebody else. At any rate, I keep an eye on
myself, as I would on a stranger. There is something
going on in me that is independent of me. Many a time
have I willed to do one thing, and another has been done.
I will not say by myself, for I was not consulted about it ;

it was done instinctively. My most virtuous thoughts
are not born of my musings, but spring up in me, like
bright fancies to the poet; unsought, spontaneous.
Whence they come I know not. I am a blind man pushed
from behind; in vain, I turn about to see what propels
me. As vanity, I regard the praises of my friends; for
what they commend pertains not to me, Babbalanja; but
to this unknown something that forces me to it. But why
am I, a middle-aged Mardian, less prone to excesses than
when a youth? The same inducements and allurements
are around me. But no; my more ardent passions are
burned out; those which are strongest when we are least
able to resist them. Thus, then, my lord, it is not so
much outer temptations that prevail over us mortals;
but inward instincts.'

'A very curious speculation,' said Media.—'But,
Babbalanja, have you mortals no moral sense, as they
call it?'

'We have. But the thing you speak of is but an after-
birth; we eat and drink many months before we are
conscious of thoughts. And though some adults would
seem to refer all their actions to this moral sense, yet, in
reality, it is not so; for, dominant in them, their moral
sense bridles their instinctive passions; wherefore, they
do not govern themselves, but are governed by their very
natures. Thus, some men in youth are constitutionally
as staid as I am now. But shall we pronounce them pious
and worthy youths for this? Does he abstain, who is not
incited? And on the other hand, if the instinctive
passions through life naturally have the supremacy over
the moral sense, as in extreme cases we see it developed
in irreclaimable malefactors,—shall we pronounce such,
criminal and detestable wretches? My lord, it is easier
for some men to be saints, than for others not to be
sinners.'

' That will do, Babbalanja ; you are on the verge, take
not the leap !   Go back whence you set out, and tell us of
that other, and still more mysterious Azzageddi ; him
whom you hinted to have palmed himself off on you for
you yourself.'

' Well, then, my lord,—Azzageddi still set aside,—upon
that self-same inscrutable stranger, I charge all those past
actions of mine, which in the retrospect appear to me such
eminent folly, that I am confident it was not I, Babbalanja, now speaking, that committed them.   Nevertheless,
my lord, this very day I may do some act, which at a
future period may seem equally senseless ; for in one lifetime we live a hundred lives.   By the incomprehensible
stranger in me, I say, this body of mine has been rented
out scores of times, though always one dark chamber in
me is retained by the old mystery.'

' Will you never come to the mark, Babbalanja ?   Tell
me something direct of the stranger.   Who, what is he ?
Introduce him.'

' My lord, I cannot.   He is locked up in me.   In a
mask, he dodges me.   He prowls about in me, hither and
thither ; he peers, and I stare.   This is he who talks in my
sleep, revealing my secrets ; and takes me to unheard of
realms, beyond the skies of Mardi.   So present is he
always, that I seem not so much to live of myself, as to be
a mere apprehension of the unaccountable being that is in
me.   Yet all the time this being is I, myself.'

' Babbalanja,' said Media, ' you have fairly turned
yourself inside out.'

' Yes, my lord,' said Mohi, ' and he has so unsettled me,
that I begin to think all Mardi a square circle.'

' How is that, Babbalanja,' said Media, ' is a circle
square ? '

' No, my lord, but ever since Mardi began, we Mardians
have been essaying our best to square it.'

'Cleverly retorted. Now, Babbalanja, do you not imagine that you may do harm by disseminating these sophisms of yours; which like your devil theory, would seem to relieve all Mardi from moral accountability?'

'My lord, at bottom, men wear no bonds that other men can strike off; and have no immunities of which other men can deprive them. Tell a good man that he is free to commit murder,—will he murder? Tell a murderer that at the peril of his soul he indulges in murderous thoughts,—will that make him a saint?'

'Again on the verge, Babbalanja! Take not the leap, I say.'

'I can leap no more, my lord. Already I am down, down, down.'

'Philosopher,' said Media, 'what with Azzageddi, and the mysterious indweller you darkly hint of, I marvel not that you are puzzled to decide upon your identity. But when do you seem most yourself?'

'When I sleep, and dream not, my lord.'

'Indeed?'

'Why then, a fool's cap might be put on you, and you would not know it.'

'The very turban he ought to wear,' muttered Mohi.

'Yet, my lord, I live while consciousness is not mine, while to all appearances I am a clod. And may not this same state of being, though but alternate with me, be continually that of many dumb, passive objects we so carelessly regard? Trust me, there are more things alive than those that crawl, or fly, or swim. Think you, my lord, there is no sensation in being a tree? feeling the sap in one's boughs, the breeze in one's foliage? think you it is nothing to be a world? one of a herd, bison-like, wending its way across boundless meadows of ether? In the sight of a fowl, that sees not our souls, what are our own tokens of animation? That we move, make a noise, have

organs, pulses, and are compounded of fluids and solids.
And all these are in this Mardi as a unit.   Daily the slow,
majestic throbbings of its heart are perceptible on the
surface in the tides of the lagoon.   Its rivers are its veins ;
when agonised, earthquakes are its throes ; it shouts in
the thunder, and weeps in the shower ; and as the body of
a bison is covered with hair, so Mardi is covered with
grasses and vegetation, among which we parasitical things
do but crawl, vexing and tormenting the patient creature
to which we cling.   Nor yet, hath it recovered from the
pain of the first foundation that was laid.   Mardi is alive
to its axis.   When you pour water, does it not gurgle ?
When you strike a pearl shell, does it not ring ?   Think
you there is no sensation in being a rock ?—To exist, is to
be ; to be, is to be something : to be something, is——'
' Go on,' said Media.
' And what is it, to be something ? ' said Yoomy art-
lessly.
' Bethink yourself of what went before,' said Media.
' Lose not the thread,' said Mohi.
' It has snapped,' said Babbalanja.
' I breathe again,' said Mohi.
' But what a stepping-off place you came to then,
philosopher,' said Media.   ' By the way, is it not old
Bardianna who says, that no Mardian should undertake
to walk without keeping one foot foremost ? '
' To return to the vagueness of the notion I have of
myself,' said Babbalanja.
' An appropriate theme,' said Media, ' proceed.'
' My lord,' murmured Mohi, ' is not this philosopher
like a centipede ?   Cut off his head, and still he crawls.'
' There are times when I fancy myself a lunatic,' re-
sumed Babbalanja.
' Ah, now he 's beginning to talk sense,' whispered Mohi.
' Surely you forget, Babbalanja,' said Media.   ' How

many more theories have you ?   First, you are possessed
by a devil ; then rent yourself out to the indweller ; and
now turn yourself into a mad-house.   You are inconsistent.'

' And for that very reason, my lord, *not* inconsistent ;
for the sum of my inconsistencies makes up my consistency.
And to be consistent to one's self is often to be inconsistent to Mardi.   Common consistency implies unchange-
ableness ; but much of the wisdom here below lives in a
state of transition.'

' Ah ! ' murmured Mohi, ' my head goes round again.'

' Azzageddi aside, then, my lord, and also, for the nonce,
the mysterious indweller, I come now to treat of myself as
a lunatic.   But this last conceit is not so much based
upon the madness of particular actions, as upon the whole
drift of my ordinary and hourly ones ; those, in which I
most resemble all other Mardians.   It seems like going
through with some nonsensical whim-whams, destitute of
fixed purpose.   For though many of my actions seem to
have objects, and all of them somehow run into each other ;
yet, where is the grand result ?   To what final purpose do
I walk about, eat, think, dream ?   To what great end,
does Mohi there, now stroke his beard ? '

' But I was doing it unconsciously,' said Mohi, dropping
his hand, and lifting his head.

' Just what I would be at, old man.   " What we do,
we do blindly," says old Bardianna.   Many things we do,
we do without knowing,—as with you and your beard,
Mohi.   And many others we know not, in their true
bearing at least, till they are past.   Are not half our lives
spent in reproaches for foregone actions, of the true nature
and consequences of which, we were wholly ignorant at
the time ?   Says old Bardianna, " Did I not so often feel
an appetite for my yams, I should think everything a
dream " ;—so puzzling to him seemed the things of this

Mardi. But Alla-Malolla goes further. Says he, " Let us club together, fellow-riddles :—Kings, clowns, and intermediates. We are bundles of comical sensations ; we bejuggle ourselves into strange phantasies : we are air, wind, breath, bubbles ; our being is told in a tick." '

' Now, then, Babbalanja,' said Media, ' what have you come to in all this rhapsody ? You everlastingly travel in a circle.'

' And so does the sun in heaven, my lord ; like me, it goes round, and gives light as it goes. Old Bardianna, too, revolved. He says so himself. In his roundabout chapter on " Cycles and Epicycles, with Notes on the Ecliptic," he thus discourseth :—" All things revolve upon some centre, to them, fixed ; for the centripetal is ever too much for the centrifugal. Wherefore, it is a perpetual cycling with us, without progression ; and we fly round, whether we will or no. To stop, were to sink into space. So, over and over we go, and round and round ; double-shuffle, on our axis, and round the sun." In another place, he says :—" There is neither apogee nor perigee, north nor south, right nor left ; what to-night is our zenith, to-morrow is our nadir ; stand as we will, we stand on our heads ; essay to spring into the air, and down we come ; here we stick ; our very bones make glue." '

' Enough, enough, Babbalanja,' cried Media. ' You are a very wise Mardian ; but the wisest Mardians make the most consummate fools.'

' So they do, my lord ; but I was interrupted. I was about to say that there is no place but the universe ; no limit but the limitless ; no bottom but the bottomless.'

CHAPTER XL

OF THE SORCERERS IN THE ISLE OF MINDA

'TIFFIN! tiffin!' cried Media; 'time for tiffin! Up, comrades! and while the mat is being spread, walk we to the bow, and inhale the breeze for an appetite. Hark ye, Vee-Vee! forget not that calabash with the sea-blue seal, and a round ring for a brand. Rare old stuff, that, Mohi; older than you: the circumnavigator, I call it. My sire had a canoe launched for the express purpose of carrying it thrice round Mardi for a flavour. It was many moons on the voyage; the mariners never sailed faster than three knots. Ten would spoil the best wine ever floated.'

Tiffin over, and the blue-sealed calabash all but hid in the great cloud raised by our pipes, Media proposed to board it in the smoke. So, goblet in hand, we all gallantly charged, and came off victorious from the fray.

Then seated again, and serenely puffing in a circle, the circumnavigator meanwhile pleasantly going the rounds, Media called upon Mohi for something entertaining.

Now, of all the old gossips in Mardi, surely our delightful old Diodorus was furnished with the greatest possible variety of histories, chronicles, anecdotes, memoirs, legends, traditions, and biographies. There was no end to the library he carried. In himself, he was the whole history of Mardi, amplified, not abridged, in one volume.

In obedience, then, to King Media's command, Mohi regaled the company with a narrative, in substance as follows :—

In a certain quarter of the Archipelago was an island

called Minda ; and in Minda were many sorcerers, employed in the social differences and animosities of the
people of that unfortunate land.   If a Mindarian deemed
himself aggrieved or insulted by a countryman, he forthwith repaired to one of these sorcerers ; who, for an
adequate consideration, set to work with his spells, keeping
himself in the dark, and directing them against the
obnoxious individual.   And full soon, by certain peculiar
sensations, this individual, discovering what was going on,
would straightway hie to his own professor of the sable art,
who, being well fee'd, in due time brought about certain
counter-charms, so that in the end it sometimes fell out
that neither party was gainer or loser, save by the sum
of his fees.

But the worst of it was, that in some cases all knowledge
of these spells was at the outset hidden from the victim ;
who, hearing too late of the mischief brewing, almost
always fell a prey to his foe ; which calamity was held the
height of the art.   But as the great body of sorcerers were
about matched in point of skill, it followed that the
parties employing them were so likewise.   Hence arose
those interminable contests, in which many moons were
spent, both parties toiling after their common destruction.

Indeed, to say nothing of the obstinacy evinced by their
employers, it was marvellous, the pertinacity of the
sorcerers themselves.   To the very last tooth in their
employer's pouches, they would stick to their spells ; never
giving over till he was financially or physically defunct.

But much as they were vilified, no people in Minda were
half so disinterested as they.   Certain indispensable con-
ditions secured, some of them were as ready to undertake
the perdition of one man as another ; good, bad, or
indifferent, it made little matter.

What wonder, then, that such abominable mercenaries
should cause a mighty deal of mischief in Minda ; privately

going about, inciting peaceable folks to enmities with their neighbours ; and, with marvellous alacrity, proposing themselves as the very sorcerers to rid them of the annoyances suggested as existing.

Indeed, it even happened that a sorcerer would be secretly retained to work spells upon a victim who, from his bodily sensations, suspecting something wrong, but knowing not what, would repair to that self-same sorcerer, engaging him to counteract any mischief that might be brewing. And this worthy would at once undertake the business ; when, having both parties in his hands, he kept them forever in suspense ; meanwhile seeing to it well that they failed not in handsomely remunerating him for his pains.

At one time, there was a prodigious excitement about these sorcerers, growing out of some alarming revelations concerning their practices. In several villages of Minda they were sought to be put down. But fruitless the attempt ; it was soon discovered that already their spells were so spread abroad, and they themselves so mixed up with the everyday affairs of the isle, that it was better to let their vocation alone, than, by endeavouring to suppress it, breed additional troubles. Ah ! they were a knowing and a cunning set, those sorcerers ; very hard to overcome, cajole, or circumvent.

But in the name of the Magi, what were these spells of theirs, so potent and occult ? On all hands it was agreed, that they derived their greatest virtue from the fumes of certain compounds, whose ingredients—horrible to tell— were mostly obtained from the human heart ; and that by variously mixing these ingredients, they adapted their multifarious enchantments.

They were a vain and arrogant race. Upon the strength of their dealing in the dark, they affected even more mystery than belonged to them ; when interrogated con-

cerning their science, would confound the inquirer by
answers couched in an extraordinary jargon, employing
words almost as long as anacondas. But all this greatly
prevailed with the common people.

Nor was it one of the least remarkable things, that oftentimes two sorcerers, contrarily employed upon a Mindarian,
—one to attack, the other to defend,—would nevertheless
be upon the most friendly terms with each other ; which
curious circumstance never begat the slightest suspicions
in the mind of the victim.

Another phenomenon : If from any cause, two sorcerers
fell out, they seldom exercised their spells upon each other ;
ascribable to this, perhaps,—that both being versed in the
art, neither could hope to get the advantage.

But for all the opprobrium cast upon these sorcerers,
part of which they deserved, the evils imputed to them
were mainly, though indirectly, ascribable to the very
persons who abused them ; nay, to the very persons who
employed them ; the latter being by far the loudest in their
vilifyings ; for which, indeed, they had excellent reason.

Nor was it to be denied, that in certain respects the
sorcerers were productive of considerable good. The
nature of their pursuits leading them deep into the arcana
of mind, they often lighted upon important discoveries ;
along with much that was cumbersome, accumulated
valuable examples concerning the inner working of the
hearts of the Mindarians ; and often waxed eloquent in
elucidating the mysteries of iniquity.

Yet was all this their lore graven upon so uncouth,
outlandish, and antiquated tablets, that it was all but
lost to the mass of their countrymen ; and some old
sachem of a wise man is quoted as having said, that their
treasures were locked up after such a fashion, that for
old iron, the key was worth more than the chest and its
contents.

CHAPTER XLI

CHIEFLY OF KING BELLO

'Now Taji,' said Media, 'with old Bello of the Hump, whose island of Dominora is before us, I am at variance.'

'Ah! How so?'

'A dull recital, but you shall have it.'

And forthwith his highness began.

This princely quarrel originated, it seems, in a slight jostling concerning the proprietorship of a barren islet in a very remote quarter of the lagoon. At the outset the matter might have been easily adjusted, had the parties but exchanged a few amicable words. But each disdaining to visit the other, to discuss so trivial an affair, the business of negotiating an understanding was committed to certain plenipos, men with lengthy tongues, who scorned to utter a word short of a polysyllable.

Now, the more these worthies penetrated into the difficulty, the wider became the breach; till what was at first a mere gap, became a yawning gulf.

But that which had perhaps tended more than anything else to deepen the variance of the kings, was hump-backed Bello's dispatching to Odo, as his thirtieth plenipo, a diminutive little negotiator, who all by himself, in a solitary canoe, sailed over to have audience of Media; into whose presence he was immediately ushered.

Darting one glance at him, the king turned to his chieftains, and said: 'By much straining of your eyes, my lords, can you perceive this insignificant manikin? What! are there no tall men in Dominora, that King Bello must needs send this dwarf hither?'

166

And charging his attendants to feed the ambassador extraordinary with the soft pap of the cocoa-nut, and provide nurses during his stay, the monarch retired from the arbour of audience.

' As I am a man,' shouted the despised plenipo, raising himself on his toes, ' my royal master will resent this affront !—A dwarf, forsooth !—Thank Oro, I am no long-drawn giant ! There is as much stuff in me, as in others ; what is spread out in their clumsy carcasses, in me is condensed. I am much in little ! And that much, thou shalt know full soon, disdainful King of Odo ! '

' Speak not against our lord the king,' cried the attendants.

' And speak not ye to me, ye headless spear-poles ! '

And so saying, under sufferance of being small, the plenipo was permitted to depart unmolested ; for all his bravadoes, fobbing his credentials and affronts.

Apprised of his servant's ignoble reception, the choleric Bello burst forth in a storm of passion ; issuing orders for one thousand conch-shells to be blown, and his warriors to assemble by land and by sea.

But bethinking him of the hostilities that might ensue, the sagacious Media hit upon an honourable expedient to ward off an event for which he was then unprepared. With all haste he dispatched to the hump-backed king a little dwarf of his own ; who voyaging over to Dominora in a canoe, sorry and solitary as that of Bello's plenipo, in like manner received the same insults. The effect whereof was to strike a balance of affronts ; upon the principle, that a blow given heals one received.

Nevertheless, these proceedings but amounted to a post-ponement of hostilities ; for soon after, nothing prevented the two kings from plunging into war, but the following judicious considerations. First : Media was almost afraid of being beaten. Second : Bello was almost afraid to

conquer. Media, because he was inferior in men and arms;
Bello, because his aggrandisement was already a subject
of warlike comment among the neighbouring kings.

Indeed, did the old chronicler Braid-Beard speak truth,
there were some tribes in Mardi that accounted this king
of Dominora a testy, quarrelsome, rapacious old monarch;
the indefatigable breeder of contentions and wars; the
elder brother of this household of nations, perpetually
essaying to lord it over the juveniles; and though his
patrimonial dominions were situated to the north of the
lagoon, not the slightest misunderstanding took place
between the rulers of the most distant islands, than this
doughty old cavalier on a throne forthwith thrust his
insolent spear into the matter, though it in no wise
concerned him, and fell to irritating all parties by his
gratuitous interference.

Especially was he officious in the concerns of Porpheero,
a neighbouring island, very large and famous, whose
numerous broad valleys were divided among many rival
kings:—the king of Franko, a small-framed, poodle-haired,
fine, fiery gallant; finical in his tattooing; much given to
the dance and glory;—the king of Ibeereea, a tall and
stately cavalier, proud, generous, punctilious, temperate
in wine; one hand forever on his javelin, the other, in
superstitious homage, lifted to his gods; his limbs all over
marks of stakes and crosses;—the king of Luzianna, a
slender, dark-browed chief; at times wrapped in a moody
robe, beneath which he fumbled something, as if it were a
dagger, but otherwise a sprightly troubadour, given to
serenades and moonlight;—the many chiefs of sunny
Latianna, minstrel monarchs, full of song and sentiment;
fiercer in love than war; glorious bards of freedom; but
rendering tribute while they sang;—the priest-king of
Vatikanna, his chest marked over with antique tattooings;
his crown, a cowl; his rusted sceptre swaying over falling

towers, and crumbling mounds ; full of the superstitious past ; askance, eyeing the suspicious time to come ;—the king of Hapzaboro, portly, pleasant ; a lover of wild boar's meat ; a frequent quaffer from the can ; in his better moods much fancying solid comfort ;—the eight-and-thirty banded kings, chieftains, seigniors, and oligarchies of the broad hill and dale of Tutoni ; clubbing together their domains, that none might wrest his neighbour's ; an earnest race ; deep thinkers, deeper drinkers ; long pipes, long heads ; their wise ones given to mystic cogitations, and consultations with the devil ;—the twin kings of Zandinavia, hardy, frugal mountaineers ; upright of spine and heart ; clad in skins of bears ;—the king of Jutlanda, much like their highnesses of Zandinavia ; a sealskin cap his crown ; a fearless sailor of his frigid seas ;—the king of Muzkovi, a shaggy, icicled white-bear of a despot in the North ; said to reign over millions of acres of glaciers ; had vast provinces of snow-drifts, and many flourishing colonies among the floating icebergs. Absolute in his rule as Predestination in metaphysics, did he command all his people to give up the ghost, it would be held treason to die last. Very precise and foppish in his imperial tastes was this monarch. Disgusted with the want of uniformity in the stature of his subjects, he was said to nourish thoughts of killing off all those below his prescribed standard—six feet, long measure. Immortal souls were of no account in his fatal wars ; since, in some of his serf-breeding estates, they were daily manufactured to order.

Now, to all the above-mentioned monarchs, old Bello would frequently dispatch heralds ; announcing, for example, his unalterable resolution, to espouse the cause of this king against that ; at the very time, perhaps, that their Serene Superfluities, instead of crossing spears, were touching flagons. And upon these occasions, the kings would often send back word to old Bello, that instead of troubling himself with their concerns he might far better attend to his own ; which, they hinted, were in a sad way, and much needed reform.

The royal old warrior's pretext for these and all similar proceedings was the proper adjustment in Porpheero, of what he facetiously styled the ' Equipoise of Calabashes ' ; which he stoutly swore was essential to the security of the various tribes in that country.

' But who put the balance into thy hands, King Bello ? ' cried the indignant nations.

' Oro ! ' shouted the hump-backed king, shaking his javelin.

Superadded to the paternal interest which Bello betrayed in the concerns of the kings of Porpheero, according to our chronicler, he also manifested no less interest in those of the remotest islands.   Indeed, where he found a rich country, inhabited by a people deemed by him barbarous and incapable of wise legislation, he sometimes relieved them from their political anxieties, by assuming the dictatorship over them.   And if incensed at his conduct, they flew to their spears, they were accounted rebels, and treated accordingly.   But as old Mohi very truly observed,—herein, Bello was not alone ; for throughout Mardi, all strong nations, as well as all strong men, loved to govern the weak.   And those who most taunted King Bello for his political rapacity, were open to the very same charge.   So with Vivenza, a distant island, at times very loud in denunciations of Bello, as a great national brigand. Not yet wholly extinct in Vivenza were its aboriginal people, a race of wild Nimrods and hunters, who year by year were driven farther and farther into remoteness, till, as one of their sad warriors said, after continual removes along the log, his race was on the point of being remorselessly pushed off the end.

Now, Bello was a great geographer, and land surveyor, and gauger of the seas. Terraqueous Mardi, he was continually exploring in quest of strange empires. Much he loved to take the altitude of lofty mountains, the depth of deep rivers, the breadth of broad isles. Upon the highest pinnacles of commanding capes and promontories, he loved to hoist his flag. He circled Mardi with his watch-towers : and the distant voyager passing wild rocks in the remotest waters, was startled by hearing the tattoo, or the réveillé, beating from hump-backed Bello's omnipresent drum. Among Antarctic glaciers, his shrill bugle-calls mingled with the scream of the gulls ; and so impressed seemed universal nature with the sense of his dominion, that the very clouds in heaven never sailed over Dominora without rendering the tribute of a shower ; whence the air of Dominora was more moist than that of any other clime.

In all his grand undertakings, King Bello was marvellously assisted by his numerous fleets of war canoes ; his navy being the largest in Mardi. Hence his logicians swore that the entire lagoon was his ; and that all prowling whales, prowling keels, and prowlings sharks were invaders. And with this fine conceit to inspire them, his poets-laureate composed some glorious old salt-water odes, enough to make your very soul sing to hear them.

But though the rest of Mardi much delighted to list to such noble minstrelsy, they agreed not with Bello's poets in deeming the lagoon their old monarch's hereditary domain.

Once upon a time, the paddlers of the hump-backed king meeting upon the broad lagoon certain canoes belonging to the before-mentioned island of Vivenza ; these paddlers seized upon several of their occupants ; and feeling their pulses, declared them born men of Dominora ; and therefore, not free to go whithersoever they would ; for, unless they could somehow get themselves born over again, they

must forever remain subject to Bello. Shed your hair ;
nay, your skin, if you will, but shed your allegiance you
cannot ; while you have bones, they are Bello's. So,
spite of all expostulations and attempts to prove alibis,
these luckless paddlers were dragged into the canoes of
Dominora, and commanded to paddle home their captors.

Whereof hearing, the men of Vivenza were thrown into
a great ferment ; and after a mighty pow-wow over their
council fire, fitting out several double-keeled canoes, they
sallied out to sea, in quest of those, whom they styled the
wholesale corsairs of Dominora.

But lucky perhaps it was, that at this juncture, in all
parts of Mardi, the fleets of the hump-backed king were
fighting, gunwale and gunwale, alongside of numerous
foes ; else there had borne down upon the canoes of the
men of Vivenza so tremendous an armada, that the very
swell under its thousand prows might have flooded their
scattered proas forever out of sight.

As it was, Bello dispatched a few of his smaller craft to
seek out, and incidentally run down the enemy ; and
without returning home, straightway proceed upon more
important enterprises.

But it so chanced that Bello's crafts, one by one meeting the foe, in most cases found the canoes of Vivenza
much larger than their own ; and manned by more men,
with hearts bold as theirs ; whence, in the ship-duels that
ensued, they were worsted ; and the canoes of Vivenza,
locking their yard-arms into those of the vanquished,
very courteously gallanted them into their coral harbours.

Solely imputing these victories to their superior in-
trepidity and skill, the people of Vivenza were exceedingly
boisterous in their triumph ; raising such obstreperous
pæans that they gave themselves hoarse throats ; in-
somuch that, according to Mohi, some of the present
generation are fain to speak through their noses.

CHAPTER XLII

DOMINORA AND VIVENZA

THE three canoes still gliding on, some further particulars were narrated concerning Dominora ; and incidentally, of other isles.

It seems that his love of wide dominion sometimes led the otherwise sagacious Bello into the most extravagant actions. If the chance accumulation of soil and drift-wood about any detached shelf of coral in the lagoon held forth the remotest possibility of the eventful existence of an islet there, with all haste he dispatched canoes to the spot, to take prospective possession of the as yet nearly submarine territory ; and, if possible, eject the zoophytes.

During an unusually low tide, here and there baring the outer reef of the Archipelago, Bello caused his royal spear to be planted upon every place thus exposed, in token of his supreme claim thereto.

Another anecdote was this : that to Dominora there came a rumour, that in a distant island dwelt a man with an uncommonly large nose ; of most portentous dimensions, indeed ; by the soothsayers supposed to foreshadow some dreadful calamity. But disregarding these superstitious conceits, Bello forthwith dispatched an agent, to discover whether this huge promontory of a nose was geographically available ; if so, to secure the same, by bringing the proprietor back.

Now, by sapient old Mohi, it was esteemed a very happy thing for Mardi at large, that the subjects whom

173

Bello sent to populate his foreign acquisitions, were but too
apt to throw off their vassalage, so soon as they deemed
themselves able to cope with him.

Indeed, a fine country in the western part of Mardi, in
this very manner became a sovereign—nay, a republican
state. It was the nation to which Mohi had previously
alluded—Vivenza. But in the flush and pride of having
recently attained their national majority, the men of
Vivenza were perhaps too much inclined to carry a vauntful crest. And because entrenched in their fastnesses,
after much protracted fighting, they had eventually
succeeded in repelling the warriors dispatched by Bello
to crush their insurrection, they were unanimous in the
opinion that the hump-backed king had never before
been so signally chastised. Whereas, they had not so
much vanquished Bello, as defended their shores; even
as a young lion will protect its den against legions of
unicorns, though, away from home, he might be torn to
pieces. In truth, Braid-Beard declared, that at the time
of this war, Dominora couched ten long spears for every
short javelin Vivenza could dart; though the javelins
were as stoutly hurled as the spears.

But, superior in men and arms, why, at last, gave
over King Bello the hope of reducing those truculent
men of Vivenza? One reason was, as Mohi said, that
many of his fighting men were abundantly occupied
in other quarters of Mardi; nor was he long in
discovering that, fight he never so valiantly, Vivenza—
not yet its inhabitants—was wholly unconquerable.
Thought Bello, Mountains are sturdy foes; fate hard
to dam.

Yet, the men of Vivenza were no dastards; not to lie,
coming from lion-like loins, they were a lion-loined race.
Did not their bards pronounce them a fresh start in the
Mardian species; requiring a new world for their full

development ? For be it known, that the great land of Kolumbo, no inconsiderable part of which was embraced by Vivenza, was the last island discovered in the Archipelago.

In good round truth, and as if an impartialist from Arcturus spoke it, Vivenza was a noble land. Like a young tropic tree she stood, laden down with greenness, myriad blossoms, and the ripened fruit thick-hanging from one bough. She was promising as the morning.

Or Vivenza might be likened to St. John, feeding on locusts and wild honey, and with prophetic voice crying to the nations from the wilderness. Or, child-like, standing among the old robed kings and emperors of the Archipelago, Vivenza seemed a young Messiah, to whose discourse the bearded Rabbis bowed.

So seemed Vivenza in its better aspect. Nevertheless, Vivenza was a braggadocio in Mardi ; the only brave one ever known. As an army of spurred and crested roosters, her people chanticleered at the resplendent rising of their sun. For shame, Vivenza! Whence thy undoubted valour ? Did ye not bring it with ye from the bold old shores of Dominora, where there is a fulness of it left ? What isle but Dominora could have supplied thee with that stiff spine of thine ?—That heart of boldest beat ? Oh, Vivenza! know that true grandeur is too big for a boast ; and nations, as well as men, may be too clever to be great.

But what more of King Bello ? Notwithstanding his territorial acquisitiveness, and aversion to relinquishing stolen nations, he was yet a glorious old king ; rather choleric—a word and a blow—but of a right royal heart. Rail at him as they might, at bottom all the isles were proud of him. And almost in spite of his rapacity, upon the whole, perhaps, they were the better for his deeds. For if sometimes he did evil with no very virtuous intentions, he had fifty ways of accomplishing good with the best; and a thousand ways of doing good without meaning it. According to an ancient oracle, the hump-backed monarch was but one of the most conspicuous pieces on a board, where the gods played for their own entertainment.

But here it must not be omitted, that of late, King Bello had somewhat abated his efforts to extend his dominions. Various causes were assigned. Some thought it arose from the fact that already he found his territories too extensive for one sceptre to rule; that his more remote colonies largely contributed to his tribulations, without correspondingly contributing to his revenues. Others affirmed that his hump was getting too mighty for him to carry; others still, that the nations were waxing too strong for him. With prophetic solemnity, head-shaking sages averred that he was growing older and older; had passed his grand climacteric; and though it was a hale old age with him, yet it was not his lusty youth; that though he was daily getting rounder and rounder in girth, and more florid of face, that these, howbeit, were rather the symptoms of a morbid obesity than of a healthful robust-ness. These wise ones predicted that very soon poor Bello would go off in an apoplexy.

But in Vivenza there were certain blusterers, who often thus prated: ' The hump-back's hour is come; at last the old teamster will be gored by the nations he 's yoked; his game is done,—let him show his hand and throw up his sceptre; he cumbers Mardi,—let him be cut down and burned; he stands in the way of his betters,—let him sheer to one side; he has shut up many eyes, and now himself grows blind; he hath committed horrible atroci-ties during his long career, the old sinner!—now, let him quickly say his prayers and be beheaded.'

Howbeit, Bello lived on; enjoying his dinners, and

taking his jorums as of yore.   Ah, I have yet a jolly long lease of life, thought he over his wine ; and like unto some obstinate old uncle, he persisted in flourishing, in spite of the prognostications of the nephew nations, which at his demise perhaps hoped to fall heir to odd parts of his possessions : three streaks of fat valleys to one of lean mountains !

CHAPTER XLIII

THEY LAND AT DOMINORA

As erewhile recounted, not being on the best terms in
Mardi with the King of Dominora, Media saw fit to draw
nigh unto his dominions in haughty state ; he (Media)
being upon excellent terms with himself. Our sails were
set, our paddles paddling, streamers streaming, and Vee-
Vee in the shark's-mouth, clamorous with his conch. The
din was soon heard ; and sweeping into a fine broad bay
we beheld its margin seemingly pebbled in the distance
with heads ; so populous the land.

Winding through a noble valley, we presently came to
Bello's palace, couchant and bristling in a grove. The
upright canes composing its front projected above the
eaves in a long row of spear-heads fluttering with scarlet
pennons ; while below, from the intervals of the canes,
were slantingly thrust three tiers of decorated lances. A
warlike aspect ! The entire structure looking like the
broadside of the Macedonian phalanx, advancing to the
charge, helmeted with a roof.

'Ah, Bello,' said Media, 'thou dwellest among thy
quills like the porcupine.'

'I feel a prickly heat coming over me,' cried Mohi,
'my lord Media, let us enter.'

'Ay,' said Babbalanja, 'safer the centre of peril than
the circumference.'

Passing under an arch, formed by two pikes crossed, we
found ourselves targets in prospective, for certain flingers

of javelins, with poised weapons, occupying the angles of
the palace.

Fronting us, stood a portly old warrior, spear in hand,
hump on back, and fire in eye.

' Is it war ? ' he cried, pointing his pike, ' or peace ? '
reversing it.

' Peace,' said Media.

Whereupon advancing, King Bello courteously welcomed us.

He was an arsenal to behold : Upon his head the
hereditary crown of Dominora,—a helmet of the sea-
porcupine's hide, bristling all over with spikes, in front
displaying a river-horse's horn, levelled to the charge ;
thrust through his ears were barbed arrows ; and from
his dyed shark-skin girdle depended a kilt of strung
javelins.

The broad chest of Bello was the chart of Mardi.
Tattooed in sea-blue were all the groups and clusters of the
Archipelago ; and every time he breathed, rose and fell
the isles as by a tide : Dominora full upon his heart.

His sturdy thighs were his triumphal arch ; whereon in
numerous medallions, crests, and shields, were blazoned
all his victories by sea and land.

His strong right arm was Dominora's scroll of Fame,
where all her heroes saw their names recorded.—An
endless roll !

Our chronicler avouched, that on the sole of Bello's
dexter foot was stamped the crest of Franko's king, his
hereditary foe. ' Thus, thus,' cried Bello, stamping,
' thus I hourly crush him.'

In stature, Bello was a mountaineer ; but, as over some
tall tower impends the hillside cliff, so Bello's Athos hump
hung over him. Could it be, as many of his nobles held,
that the old monarch's hump was his sensorium and source
of strength : full of nerves, muscles, ganglions and

tendons ? Yet, year by year it grew, ringed like the bole of his palms. The toils of war increased it. But another skirmish with the isles, said the wiseacres of Porpheero, and Bello's mount will crush him.

Against which calamity to guard, his medicos and Sangrados sought the hump's reduction. But down it would not come. Then by divers mystic rites, his magi tried. Making a deep pit, many teeth they dropped therein. But they could not fill it. Hence, they called it the Sinking Pit, for bottom it had none. Nevertheless, the magi said, when this pit is filled, Bello's hump you 'll see no more. ' Then, hurrah for the hump ! ' cried the nobles, ' for he will never hurl it off. Long life to the hump ! By the hump we will rally and die ! Cheer up, King Bello ! Stand up, old king ! '

But these were they who, when their sovereign went abroad, with that Athos on his back, followed idly in its shade ; while Bello leaned heavily upon his people, staggering as they went.

Ay, sorely did Bello's goodly stature lean ; but though many swore he soon must fall ; nevertheless, like Pisa's Leaning Tower, he may long lean over, yet never nod.

Visiting Dominora in a friendly way, in good time, we found King Bello very affable ; in hospitality almost exceeding portly Borabolla : October-plenty reigned throughout his palace borders.

Our first reception over, a sumptuous repast was served, at which much lively talk was had.

Of Taji, Bello sought to know, whether his solar majesty had yet made a province of the moon ; whether the astral hosts were of much account as territories, or mere Motoos, as the little tufts of verdure are denominated here and there clinging to Mardi's circle reef ; whether the people in the sun vilified him (Bello) as they did in Mardi ; and what they thought of an event, so ominous to the liberties of the universe, as the addition to his navy of three large canoes.

Ere long, so fused in social love we grew, that Bello, filling high his can, and clasping Media's palm, drank everlasting amity with Odo.

So over their red cups, the two kings forgot their differences, and concerning the disputed islet nothing more was ever heard ; especially, as it so turned out, that while they were most hot about it, it had suddenly gone out of sight, being of volcanic origin.

CHAPTER XLIV

At last, withdrawing from the presence of King Bello, we went forth, still intent on our search.

Many brave sights we saw. Fair fields; the whole island a garden; green hedges all round; neat lodges, thick as white mice in the landscape; old oak woods, hale and hearty as ever; old temples buried in ivy; old shrines of old heroes, deep buried in broad groves of bay trees; old rivers laden down with heavy-freighted canoes; humped hills, like droves of camels, piled up with harvests; every sign and token of a glorious abundance, every sign and token of generations of renown. Rare sight! fine sight! none rarer, none finer in Mardi.

But roving on through this ravishing region, we passed through a cornfield in full beard, where a haggard old reaper laid down his hook, beseeching charity for the sake of the gods.—' Bread, bread! or I die mid these sheaves! '

' Thrash out your grain, and want not.'

' Alas, masters, this grain is not mine; I plough, I sow, I reap, I bind, I stack,—Lord Primo garners.'

Rambling on, we came to a hamlet, hidden in a hollow; and beneath weeping willows saw many mournful maidens seated on a bank; beside each, a wheel that was broken. ' Lo, we starve,' they cried, ' our distaffs are snapped; no more may we weave and spin! '

Then forth issued from vaults clamorous crowds of men, hands tied to their backs.—' Bread! Bread! ' they cried. ' The magician hath turned us out from our glen, where we

182

laboured of yore in the days of the merry Green Queen.
He has pinioned us hip and arm that we starve. Like
sheep we die off with the rot.—Curse on the magician.
A curse on his spell.'

Bending our steps toward the glen, roaring down the
rocks we descried a stream from the mountains. But ere
those waters gained the sea, vassal tribute they rendered.
Conducted through culverts and moats, they turned great
wheels, giving life to ten thousand fangs and fingers, whose
gripe no power could withstand, yet whose touch was soft
as the velvet paw of a kitten. With brute force they
heaved down great weights, then daintily wove and spun ;
like the trunk of the elephant, which lays lifeless a river-
horse, and counts the pulses of a moth. On all sides, the
place seemed alive with its spindles. Round and round,
round and round ; throwing off wondrous births at every
revolving ; ceaseless as the cycles that circle in heaven.
Loud hummed the loom, flew the shuttle like lightning,
red roared the grim forge, rung anvil and sledge ; yet no
mortal was seen.

'What ho, magician ! Come forth from thy cave ! '

But all deaf were the spindles, as the mutes that
mutely wait on the Sultan.

' Since we are born, we will live ! ' so we read on a
crimson banner, flouting the crimson clouds, in the van of
a riotous red-bonneted mob, racing by us as we came from
the glen. Many more followed : black, or blood-
stained :—

' Mardi is man's ! '
' Down with landholders ! '
' Our turn now ! '
' Up rights ! Down wrongs ! '
' Bread ! Bread ! '
' Take the tide, ere it turns ! '

Waving their banners, and flourishing aloft clubs,

hammers, and sickles, with fierce yells the crowd ran on toward the palace of Bello. Foremost, and inciting the rest by mad outcries and gestures, were six masks : ' This way ! This way ! ' they cried,—' by the wood ; by the dark wood ! ' Whereupon all darted into the groves ; when of a sudden, the masks leaped forward, clearing a long covered trench, into which fell many of those they led. But on raced the masks ; and gaining Bello's palace, and raising the alarm, there sallied from thence a woodland of spears, which charged upon the disordered ranks in the grove. A crash as of icicles against icebergs round Zembla, and down went the hammers and sickles. The host fled, hotly pursued. Meanwhile brave heralds from Bello advanced, and with chaplets crowned the six masks. —' Welcome, heroes ! worthy and valiant ! ' they cried. ' Thus our lord Bello rewards all those who, to do him a service, for hire betray their kith and their kin.'

Still pursuing our quest, wide we wandered through all the sun and shade of Dominora ; but nowhere was Yillah found.

CHAPTER XLV

THEY BEHOLD KING BELLO'S STATE CANOE

At last, bidding adieu to King Bello ; and in the midst of the lowing of oxen, breaking away from his many hospitalities, we departed for the beach. But ere embarking, we paused to gaze at an object, which long fixed our attention.

Now, as all bold cavaliers have ever delighted in special chargers, gaily caparisoned, whereon upon grand occasions to sally forth upon the plains : even so have maritime potentates ever prided themselves upon some holyday galley, splendidly equipped, wherein to sail over the sea.

When of old, glory-seeking Jason, attended by his promising young lieutenants, Castor and Pollux, embarked on that hardy adventure to Colchis, the brave planks of the good ship *Argos* he trod, its model a swan to behold.

And when Trojan Æneas wandered west, and discovered the pleasant land of Latium, it was in the fine craft *Bis Taurus* that he sailed : its stern gloriously emblazoned, its prow a levelled spear.

And to the sound of sackbut and psaltery, gliding down the Nile, in the pleasant shade of its pyramids to welcome mad Mark, Cleopatra was throned on the cedar quarter-deck of a glorious gondola, silk and satin hung ; its silver-plated oars musical as flutes. So, too, Queen Bess was wont to disport in old Thames.

And tough Torf-Egill, the Danish sea-king, reckoned in his stud, a slender yacht ; its masts young Zetland firs ; its prow a seal, dog-like holding a sword-fish blade. He called it the *Grayhound*, so swift was its keel ; the *Sea-hawk*, so blood-stained its beak.

And groping down his palace stairs, the blind old Doge Dandolo, oft embarked in his gilded barge, like the lord mayor setting forth in civic state from Guildhall in his chariot. But from another sort of prow leaped Dandolo, when at Constantinople, he foremost sprang ashore, and with a right arm ninety years old, planted the standard of St. Mark full among the long chin-pennons of the long-bearded Turks.

And Kumbo Sama, Emperor of Japan, had a dragon-beaked junk, a floating Juggernaut, wherein he burnt incense to the sea-gods.

And Kannakoko, King of New Zealand ; and the first Tahitian Pomaree ; and the Pelew potentate, each possessed long state canoes ; sea-snakes all ; carved over like Chinese card-cases, and manned with such scores of warriors, that dipping their paddles in the sea, they made a commotion like shoals of herring.

What wonder then that Bello of the Hump, the old sea-king of Mardi, should sport a brave ocean chariot ?

In a broad arbour by the waterside, it was housed like Alp Arslan's war-horse, or the charger Caligula deified ; upon its stern a wilderness of sculpture :—shell-work, medallions, masques, griffins, gulls, ogres, finned lions, winged walruses ; all manner of sea cavalry, crusading centaurs, crocodiles, and sharks ; and mermen, and mermaids, and Neptune only knows all.

And in this craft, Doge-like, yearly did King Bello stand up and wed with the Lagoon. But the custom originated not in the manner of the Doge's, which was as follows ; so, at least, saith Ghibelli, who tells all about it :—

When, in a stout sea-fight, Ziani defeated Barbarossa's son Otho, sending his feluccas all flying, like frightened water-fowl from a lake, then did his Holiness, the Pope, present unto him a ring, saying, ' Take this, oh Ziani, and with it the sea for thy bride ; and every year wed her again.'

So the Doge's tradition ; thus Bello's :—

Ages ago, Dominora was circled by a reef, which expanding in proportion to the extension of the isle's naval dominion, in due time embraced the entire lagoon ; and this marriage ring zoned all the world.

But if the sea was King Bello's bride, an Adriatic Tartar he wedded ; who, in her mad gales of passions, often boxed about his canoes, and led his navies a very boisterous life indeed.

And hostile prognosticators opined, that ere long she would desert her old lord, and marry again. Already, they held, she had made advances in the direction of Vivenza.

But truly, should she abandon old Bello, he would straightway after her with all his fleets ; and never rest till his queen was regained.

Now, old sea-king ! look well to thy barge of state : for, peradventure, the dry-rot may be eating into its keel ; and the wood-worms exploring into its spars.

Without heedful tending, any craft will decay ; yet, forever may its first, fine model be preserved, though its prow be renewed every spring, like the horns of the deer, if, in repairing, plank be put for plank, rib for rib, in exactest similitude. Even so, then, oh Bello ! do thou with thy barge.

CHAPTER XLVI

WHEREIN BABBALANJA BOWS THRICE

THE next morning's twilight found us once more afloat ; and yielding to that almost sullen feeling, but too apt to prevail with some mortals at that hour, all but Media long remained silent.

But now, a bright mustering is seen among the myriad white Tartar tents in the Orient ; like lines of spears defiling upon some upland plain, the sunbeams thwart the sky. And see ! amid the blaze of banners, and the pawings of ten thousand thousand golden hoofs, day's mounted Sultan, Xerxes-like, moves on : the Dawn his standard, East and West his cymbals.

' Oh, morning life ! ' cried Yoomy, with a Persian air ; ' would that all time were a sunrise, and all life a youth.'

' Ah ! but these striplings whimper of youth,' said Mohi, caressing his braids, ' as if they wore this beard.'

' But natural, old man,' said Babbalanja. ' We Mardians never seem young to ourselves ; childhood is to youth what manhood is to age :—something to be looked back upon, with sorrow that it is past. But childhood recks of no future, and knows no past ; hence, its present passes in a vapour.'

' Mohi, how's your appetite this morning ? ' said Media.

' Thus, thus, ye gods,' sighed Yoomy, ' is feeling ever scouted. Yet, what might seem feeling in me, I cannot express.'

188

' A good commentary on old Bardianna, Yoomy,' said
Babbalanja, ' who somewhere says, that no Mardian can
out with his heart, for his unyielding ribs are in the way.
And indeed, pride, or something akin thereto, often holds
check on sentiment. My lord, there are those who like
not to be detected in the possession of a heart.'

' Very true, Babbalanja ; and I suppose that pride was
at the bottom of your old ponderer's heartless, unsenti-
mental, bald-pated style.'

' Craving pardon, my lord is deceived. Bardianna was
not at all proud ; though he had a queer way of showing
the absence of pride. In his essay, entitled, " On the
Tendency to Curl in Upper Lips," he thus discourses :
" We hear much of pride and its sinfulness in this Mardi
wherein we dwell : whereas, I glory in being brimmed with
it ;—my sort of pride. In the presence of kings, lords,
palm-trees, and all those who deem themselves taller than
myself, I stand stiff as a pike, and will abate not one
vertebra of my stature. But accounting no Mardian my
superior, I account none my inferior ; hence, with the
social, I am ever ready to be sociable." '

' An agrarian ! ' said Media ; ' no doubt he would have
made the headsman the minister of equality.'

' At bottom we are already equal, my honoured lord,'
said Babbalanja, profoundly bowing. ' One way we all
come into Mardi, and one way we withdraw. Wanting
his yams a king will starve, quick as a clown ; and smote
on the hip, saith old Bardianna, he will roar as loud as
the next one.'

' Roughly worded, that, Babbalanja.—Vee-Vee ! my
crown !—So ; now, Babbalanja, try if you cannot polish
Bardianna's style in that last saying you father upon
him.'

' I will, my ever honourable lord,' said Babbalanja,
salaaming. ' Thus we 'll word it, then : In their merely

Mardian nature, the sublimest demi-gods are subject to infirmities ; for struck by some keen shaft, even a king ofttimes dons his crown, fearful of future darts.'

' Ha, ha !—well done, Babbalanja ; but I bade you polish, not sharpen the arrow.'

' All one, my thrice honoured lord ;—to polish is not to blunt.'

CHAPTER XLVII

BABBALANJA PHILOSOPHISES, AND MY LORD MEDIA PASSES ROUND THE CALABASHES

An interval of silence passed ; when Media cried, ' Out upon thee, Yoomy ! curtail that long face of thine.'

' How can he, my lord,' said Mohi, ' when he is thinking of furlongs ? '

' Fathoms you mean, Mohi ; see you not he is musing over the gunwale ?   And now, minstrel, a banana for thy thoughts.   Come, tell me how you poets spend so many hours in meditation.'

' My lord, it is because, that when we think, we think so little of ourselves.'

' I thought as much,' said Mohi, ' for no sooner do I undertake to be sociable with myself, than I am straightway forced to beat a retreat.'

' Ay, old man,' said Babbalanja, ' many of us Mardians are but sorry hosts to ourselves.   Some hearts are hermits.'

' If not of yourself, then, Yoomy, of whom else do you think ! ' asked Media.

' My lord, I seldom think,' said Yoomy, ' I but give ear to the voices in my calm.'

' Did Babbalanja speak ? ' asked Media.   ' But no more of your reveries ' ; and so saying Media gradually sunk into a revery himself.

The rest did likewise ; and soon, with eyes enchanted, all reclined : gazing at each other, witless of what we did.

It was Media who broke the spell ; calling for Vee-Vee our page, his calabashes and cups, and nectarines for all.

Eyeing his goblet, Media at length threw himself back, and said : ' Babbalanja, not ten minutes since, we were all absent-minded ; now, how would you like to step out of your body, in reality ; and, as a spirit, haunt some shadowy grove ? '

' But our lungs are not wholly superfluous, my lord,' said Babbalanja, speaking loud.

' No, nor our lips,' said Mohi, smacking his over his wine.

' But could you really be disembodied here in Mardi, Babbalanja ; how would you fancy it ? ' said Media.

' My lord,' said Babbalanja, speaking through half of a nectarine, ' defer putting that question, I beseech, till after my appetite is satisfied ; for, trust me, no hungry mortal would forfeit his palate, to be resolved into the impalpable.'

' Yet pure spirits we must all become at last, Babba-lanja,' said Yoomy, ' even the most ignoble.'

' Yes, so they say, Yoomy ; but if all boors be the immortal sires of endless dynasties of immortals, how little do our pious patricians bear in mind their magnificent destiny, when hourly they scorn their companionship. And if here in Mardi they cannot abide an equality with plebeians, even at the altar ; how shall they endure them, side by side, throughout eternity ?   But since the prophet Alma asserts that Paradise is almost entirely made up of the poor and despised, no wonder that many aristocrats of our isles pursue a career, which, according to some theologies, must forever preserve the social distinctions so sedulously maintained in Mardi.   And though some say, that at death everything earthy is removed from the spirit, so that clowns and lords both stand on a footing ; yet, according to the popular legends, it has ever been observed of the ghosts of boors when revisiting Mardi, that invari-

ably they rise in their smocks. And regarding our intellectual equality hereafter, how unjust, my lord, that
after whole years of days and nights consecrated to the
hard gaining of wisdom, the wisest Mardian of us all
should in the end find the whole sum of his attainments at
one leap outstripped by the veriest dunce, suddenly
inspired by light divine. And though some hold that all
Mardian lore is vain, and that at death all mysteries will
be revealed ; yet, none the less, do they toil and ponder
now. Thus, their tongues have one mind, and their
understanding another.'

'My lord,' said Mohi, ' we have come to the lees ; your
pardon, Babbalanja.'

'Then, Vee-Vee, another calabash ! Fill up, Mohi ;
wash down wine with wine. Your cup, Babbalanja ;
any lees ? '

'Plenty, my lord ; we philosophers come to the lees
very soon.'

'Flood them over, then ; but cease not discoursing ;
thanks be to the gods, your mortal palates and tongues can
both wag together ; fill up, I say, Babbalanja ; you are no
philosopher if you stop at the tenth cup ; endurance is
the test of philosophy all Mardi over ; drink, I say, and
make us wise by precept and example.—Proceed, Yoomy,
you look as if you had something to say.'

'Thanks, my lord. Just now, Babbalanja, you flew
from the subject ;—you spoke of boors ; but has not the
lowliest peasant an eye that can take in the vast horizon
at a sweep : mountains, vales, plains, and oceans ? Is
such a being nothing ? '

'But can that eye see itself, Yoomy ? ' said Babbalanja,
winking. ' Taken out of its socket, will it see at all ? Its
connection with the body imparts to it its virtue.'

'He questions everything,' cried Mohi. ' Philosopher,
have you a head ? '

' I have,' said Babbalanja, feeling for it ; ' I am finished off at the helm very much as other Mardians, Mohi.'

' My lord, the first yea that ever came from him.'

' Ah, Mohi,' said Media, ' the discourse waxes heavy. I fear me we have again come to the lees. Ho, Vee-Vee, a fresh calabash ; and with it we will change the subject. Now, Babbalanja, I have this cup to drink, and then a question to propound. Ah, Mohi, rare old wine this ; it smacks of the cork. But attention, philosopher. Supposing you had a wife—which, by the way, you have not— would you deem it sensible in her to imagine you no more, because you happened to stroll out of her sight ? '

' However that might be,' murmured Yoomy, ' young Nina bewailed herself a widow whenever Arhinoo, her lord, was absent from her side.'

' My lord Media,' said Babbalanja, ' during my absence, my wife would have more reason to conclude that I was not living, than that I was. To the former supposition, everything tangible around her would tend ; to the latter, nothing but her own fond fancies. It is this imagination of ours, my lord, that is at the bottom of these things. When I am in one place there exists no other. Yet am I but too apt to fancy the reverse. Nevertheless, when I am in Odo, talk not to me of Ohonoo. To me it is not, except when I am there. If it be, prove it. To prove it, you carry me thither ; but you only prove, that to its substantive existence, as cognisant to me, my presence is indispensable. I say that, to me, all Mardi exists by virtue of my sovereign pleasure ; and when I die, the universe will perish with me.'

' Come you of a long-lived race,' said Mohi, ' one free from apoplexies ? I have many little things to accomplish yet, and would not be left in the lurch.'

' Heed him not, Babbalanja,' said Media. ' Dip your beak again, my eagle, and soar.'

'Let us be eagles then, indeed, my lord : eagle-like, let us look at this red wine without blinking ; let us grow solemn, not boisterous, with good cheer.'

Then, lifting his cup, 'My lord, serenely do I pity all such who are stirred one jot from their centres by ever so much drinking of this fluid. Ply him hard as you will, through the live-long polar night, a wise man cannot be made drunk. Though, toward sunrise, his body may reel, it will reel round its centre ; and though he make many tacks in going home, he reaches it at last ; while scores of over-plied fools are foundering by the way. My lord, when wild with much thought 'tis to wine I fly, to sober me ; its magic fumes breathe over me like the Indian summer, which steeps all nature in repose. To me, wine is no vulgar fire, no fosterer of base passions ; my heart, ever open, is opened still wider ; and glorious visions are born in my brain ; it is then that I have all Mardi under my feet, and the constellations of the firmament in my soul.'

'Superb !' cried Yoomy.

'Pooh, pooh !' said Mohi, 'who does not see stars at such times ? I see the Great Bear now, and the little one, its cub ; and Andromeda, and Perseus' chain-armour, and Cassiopea in her golden chair, and the bright, scaly Dragon and the glittering Lyre, and all the jewels in Orion's sword-hilt.'

'Ay,' cried Media, 'the study of astronomy is wonderfully facilitated by wine. Fill up, old Ptolemy, and tell us should you discover a new planet. Methinks this fluid needs stirring. Ho, Vee-Vee, my sceptre ! be we sociable. But come, Babbalanja, my gold-headed aquila, return to your theme ;—the imagination, if you please.'

'Well, then, my lord, I was about to say, that the imagination is the Voli-Donzini ; or, to speak plainer, the unical, rudimental, and all-comprehending abstracted essence of the infinite remoteness of things. Without it, we were grasshoppers.'

'And with it, you mortals are little else; do you not chirp all over, Mohi? By my demi-god soul, were I not what I am, this wine would almost get the better of me.'

'Without it——' continued Babbalanja.

'Without what?' demanded Media, starting to his feet. 'This wine? Traitor, I'll stand by this to the last gasp; you are inebriated, Babbalanja.'

'Perhaps so, my lord; but I was treating of the imagination, may it please you.'

'My lord,' added Mohi, 'of the unical, and rudimental fundament of things, you remember.'

'Ah! there's none of them sober; proceed, proceed, Azzageddi!'

'My lord waves his hand like a banner,' murmured Yoomy.

'Without imagination, I say, an armless man, born blind, could not be made to believe that he had a head of hair, since he could neither see it, nor feel it, nor has hair any feeling of itself.'

'Methinks, though,' said Mohi, 'if the cripple had a Tartar for a wife, he would not remain sceptical long.'

'You all fly off at tangents,' cried Media, 'but no wonder: your mortal brains cannot endure much quaffing. Return to your subject, Babbalanja. Assume now, Babbalanja,—assume, my dear prince—assume it, assume it, I say!—Why don't you?'

'I am willing to assume anything you please, my lord: what is it?'

'Ah! yes!—Assume that—that upon returning home, you should find your wife had newly wedded, under the—the—the metaphysical presumption, that being no longer visible, you—*you*, Azzageddi, had departed this life; in

other words, out of sight, out of mind ; what then, my
dear prince ? '

' Why then, my lord, I would demolish my rival in a
trice.'

' Would you ?—then—then so much for your metaphysics, Bab—Babbalanja.'

Babbalanja rose to his feet, muttering to himself—' Is
this assumed, or real ?—Can a demi-god be mastered by
wine ?   Yet, the old mythologies make bacchanals of the
gods.   But he was wondrous keen !   He felled me, ere he
fell himself.'

' Yoomy, my lord Media is in a very merry mood to-day,'
whispered Mohi, ' but his counterfeit was not well done.
No, no, a bacchanal is not used to be so logical in his cups.'

CHAPTER XLVIII

THEY SAIL ROUND AN ISLAND WITHOUT LANDING ; AND TALK ROUND A SUBJECT WITHOUT GETTING AT IT

PURPOSING a visit to Kaleedoni, a country integrally united to Dominora, our course now lay northward along the western white cliffs of the isle. But finding the wind ahead, and the current too strong for our paddlers, we were fain to forgo our destination ; Babbalanja observing, that since in Dominora we had not found Yillah, then in Kaleedoni the maiden could not be lurking.

And now, some conversation ensued concerning the country we were prevented from visiting. Our chronicler narrated many fine things of its people ; extolling their bravery in war, their amiability in peace, their devotion in religion, their penetration in philosophy, their simplicity and sweetness in song, their loving-kindness and frugality in all things domestic :—running over a long catalogue of heroes, metaphysicians, bards, and good men.

But as all virtues are convertible into vices, so in some cases did the best traits of these people degenerate. Their frugality too often became parsimony ; their devotion grim bigotry ; and all this in a greater degree perhaps than could be predicated of the more immediate subjects of King Bello.

In Kaleedoni was much to awaken the fervour of its bards. Upland and lowland were full of the picturesque ; and many unsung lyrics yet lurked in her glens. Among her blue, heathy hills, lingered many tribes, who in their wild and tattooed attire still preserved the garb of the

198

mightiest nation of old times. They bared the knee, in
token that it was honourable as the face, since it had
never been bent.

While Braid-Beard was recounting these things, the
currents were sweeping us over a strait, toward a deep
green island, bewitching to behold.

Not greener that midmost terrace of the Andes, which
under a torrid meridian steeps fair Quito in the dews of a
perpetual spring ;—not greener the nine thousand feet of
Pirohitee's tall peak, which, rising from out the warm
bosom of Tahiti, carries all summer with it into the clouds ;
—nay, not greener the famed gardens of Cyrus,—than the
vernal lawn, the knoll, the dale of beautiful Verdanna.

' Alas, sweet isle ! Thy desolation is overrun with
vines,' sighed Yoomy, gazing.

' Land of caitiff curs ! ' cried Media.

' Isle, whose future is in its past. Hearthstone, from
which its children run,' said Babbalanja.

' I cannot read thy chronicles for blood, Verdanna,'
murmured Mohi.

Gliding near, we would have landed, but the rolling surf
forbade. Then thrice we circumnavigated the isle for a
smooth, clear beach ; but it was not found.

Meanwhile all still conversed.

' My lord,' said Yoomy, ' while we tarried with King
Bello, I heard much of the feud between Dominora and
this unhappy shore. Yet is not Verdanna as a child of
King Bello's ? '

' Yes, minstrel, a step-child,' said Mohi.

' By way of enlarging his family circle,' said Babbalanja,
' an old lion once introduced a deserted young stag to his
den ; but the stag never became domesticated, and would
still charge upon his foster-brothers.—Verdanna is not of
the flesh and blood of Dominora, whence, in good part,
these dissensions.'

' But, Babbalanja, is there no way of reconciling these foes ! '

' But one way, Yoomy :—By filling up this strait with dry land ; for, divided by water, we Mardians must ever remain more or less divided at heart. Though Kaleedoni was united to Dominora long previous to the union of Verdanna, yet Kaleedoni occasions Bello no disquiet ; for, geographically one, the two populations insensibly blend at the point of junction. No hostile strait flows between the arms, that to embrace must touch.'

' But, Babbalanja,' said Yoomy, ' what asks Verdanna of Dominora, that Verdanna so clamours at the denial ? '

' They are arrant cannibals, Yoomy,' said Media, ' and desire the privilege of eating each other up.'

' King Bello's idea,' said Babbalanja ; ' but, in these things, my lord, you demi-gods are ever unanimous. But, whatever be Verdanna's demands, Bello persists in rejecting them.'

' Why not grant everything she asks, even to renouncing all claim upon the isle,' said Mohi ; ' for thus, Bello would rid himself of many perplexities.'

' And think you, old man,' said Media, ' that, bane or blessing, Bello will yield his birthright ? Will a tri-crowned king resign his triple diadem ? And even did Bello what you propose, he would only breed still greater perplexities. For if granted, full soon would Verdanna be glad to surrender many things she demands. And all she now asks, she has had in times past ; but without turning it to advantage :—and is she wiser now ? '

' Does she not demand her harvests, my lord ? ' said Yoomy, ' and has not the reaper a right to his sheaf ? '

' Cant ! cant ! Yoomy. If you reap for me, the sheaf is mine.'

' But if the reaper reaps on his own harvest field, whose then the sheaf, my lord ? ' said Babbalanja.

' His for whom he reaps—his lord's ! '

' Then let the reaper go with sickle and with sword,' said Yoomy ; ' with one hand cut down the bearded grain, and with the other smite his bearded lords.'

' Thou growest fierce, in thy lyric moods, my warlike dove,' said Media, blandly. ' But for thee, philosopher, know thou that Verdanna's men are of blood and brain inferior to Bello's native race ; and the better Mardian must ever rule.'

' Verdanna inferior to Dominora, my lord !—Has she produced no bards, no orators, no wits, no patriots ? Mohi, unroll thy chronicles ! Tell me, if Verdanna may not claim full many a star along King Bello's tattooed arm of Fame ? '

' Even so,' said Mohi. ' Many chapters bear you out.'

' But, my lord,' said Babbalanja, ' as truth, omni-present, lurks in all things, even in lies : so does some germ of it lurk in the calumnies heaped on the people of this land. For though they justly boast of many lustrous names, these jewels gem no splendid robe. And though like a bower of grapes, Verdanna is full of gushing juices, spouting out in bright sallies of wit, yet not all her grapes make wine ; and here and there hang goodly clusters mildewed ; or half devoured by worms, bred in their own tendrils.'

' Drop, drop your grapes and metaphors ! ' cried Media. ' Bring forth your thoughts like men ; let them come naked into Mardi.—What do you mean, Babbalanja ? '

' This, my lord, Verdanna's worst evils are her own, not of another's giving. Her own hand is her own undoer. She stabs herself with bigotry, superstition, divided counsels, domestic feuds, ignorance, temerity ; she wills, but does not ; her East is one black storm-cloud, that never bursts ; her utmost fight is a defiance ; she showers reproaches where she should rain down blows. She stands a mastiff baying at the moon.'

'Tropes on tropes!' said Media. 'Let me tell the tale,—straightforward like a line. Verdanna is a lunatic——'

'A trope! my lord,' cried Babbalanja.

'My tropes are not tropes,' said Media, 'but yours are. —Verdanna is a lunatic, that after vainly striving to cut another's throat, grimaces before a standing pool and threatens to cut his own. And is such a madman to be entrusted with himself? No; let another govern him, who is ungovernable to himself. Ay, and tight hold the rein; and curb, and rasp the bit. Do I exaggerate?— Mohi, tell me, if, save one lucid interval, Verdanna, while independent of Dominora, ever discreetly conducted her affairs? Was she not always full of fights and factions? And what first brought her under the sway of Bello's sceptre? Did not her own chief Dermoddi fly to Bello's ancestor for protection against his own seditious subjects? And thereby did not her own king unking himself? What wonder, then, and where the wrong, if Henro, Bello's conquering sire, seized the diadem?'

'What my lord cites is true,' said Mohi, 'but cite no more, I pray; lest you harm your cause.'

'Yet for all this, Babbalanja,' said Media, 'Bello but holds lunatic Verdanna's lands in trust.'

'And may the guardian of an estate also hold custody of the ward, my lord?'

'Ay, if he can. What *can* be done, may be : that 's the creed of demi-gods.'

'Alas, alas!' cried Yoomy, 'why war with words over this poor, suffering land. See! for all her bloom, her people starve; perish her yams, ere taken from the soil; the blight of heaven seems upon them.'

'Not so,' said Media. 'Heaven sends no blights.

Verdanna will not learn. And if from one season's
rottenness, rottenness they sow again, rottenness must
they reap.   But Yoomy, you seem earnest in this matter ;
—come : on all hands it is granted that evils exist in
Verdanna ; now, sweet sympathiser, what must the royal
Bello do to mend them ? '

' I am no sage,' said Yoomy ; ' what would my lord
Media do ? '

' What would *you* do, Babbalanja ? ' said Media.

' Mohi, what you ? ' asked the philosopher.

' And what would the company do ? ' added Mohi.

' Now, though these evils pose us all,' said Babbalanja,
' there lately died in Verdanna, one, who set about curing
them in a humane and peaceable way, waving war and
bloodshed. That man was Konno. Under a huge
cauldron, he kept a roaring fire.'

' Well, Azzageddi, how could that answer his purpose ? '
asked Media.

' Nothing better, my lord.   His fire boiled his bread-
fruit ; and so convinced were his countrymen that he was
well employed, that they almost stripped their scanty
orchards to fill his cauldron.'

' Konno was a knave,' said Mohi.

' Your pardon, old man, but that is only known to his
ghost, not to us.   At any rate he was a great man ;   for
even assuming he cajoled his country, no common man
could have done it.'

' Babbalanja,' said Mohi, ' my lord has been pleased
to pronounce Verdanna crazy ; now, may not her crazi-
ness arise from the irritating, tantalising practices of
Dominora ? '

' Doubtless, Braid-Beard, many of the extravagances of
Verdanna are in good part to be ascribed to the cause you
mention ; but, to be impartial, none the less does Verdanna
essay to taunt and provoke Dominora ;   yet not with the

like result. Perceive you, Braid-Beard, that the Trade
wind blows dead across this strait from Dominora, and
not from Verdanna ? Hence, when King Bello's men
fling gibes and insults, every missile hits ; but those of
Verdanna are blown back in its teeth : her enemies
jeering her again and again.'

'King Bello's men are dastards for that,' cried Yoomy.

'It shows neither sense, nor spirit, nor humanity,' said
Babbalanja.

'All wide of the mark,' cried Media. 'What is to be
done for Verdanna ? '

'What will she do for herself ? ' said Babbalanja.

'Philosopher, you are an extraordinary sage ; and since
sages should be seers, reveal Verdanna's future.'

'My lord, you will ever find true prophets, prudent ;
nor will any prophet risk his reputation upon predicting
aught concerning this land. The isles are Oro's. Nevertheless, he who doctors Verdanna aright, will first medi-
cine King Bello ; who in some things is himself a patient,
though he would fain be a physician. However, my lord,
there is a demon of a doctor in Mardi, who at last deals
with these desperate cases. He employs only pills, picked
off the Conroupta Quiancensis tree.'

'And what sort of a vegetable is that ? ' asked Mohi.

'Consult the botanists,' said Babbalanja.

CHAPTER XLIX

THEY DRAW NIGH TO PORPHEERO ; WHERE THEY BEHOLD
A TERRIFIC ERUPTION

GLIDING away from Verdanna at the turn of the tide, we cleared the strait, and gaining the more open lagoon, pointed our prows for Porpheero, from whose magnificent monarchs my lord Media promised himself a glorious reception.

' They are one and all demi-gods,' he cried, ' and have the old demi-god feeling. We have seen no great valleys like theirs :—their sceptres are long as our spears ; to their sumptuous palaces, Donjalolo's are but inns :—their banquetting halls are as vistas ; no generations run parallel to theirs :—their pedigrees reach back into chaos.

' Babbalanja ! here you will find food for philosophy :— the whole land checkered with nations, side by side contrasting in costume, manners, and mind. Here you will find science and sages ; manuscripts in miles ; bards singing in choirs.

' Mohi ! here you will flag over your page ; in Porpheero the ages have hived all their treasures : like a pyramid, the past shadows over the land.

' Yoomy ! here you will find stuff for your songs :—blue rivers flowing through forest arches, and vineyards ; velvet meads, soft as ottomans : bright maidens braiding the golden locks of the harvest ; and a background of mountains that seem the end of the world. Or if nature will not content you, then turn to the landscapes of art. See ! mosaic walls, tattooed like our faces ; paintings, vast as horizons ; and into which you feel you could rush : See ! statues to which you could off turbans ; cities of columns standing thick as mankind ; and firmament domes forever shedding their sunsets of gilding : See ! spire behind spire, as if the land were the ocean, and all Bello's great navy were riding at anchor.

' Noble Taji ! you seek for your Yillah ;—give over despair ! Porpheero 's such a scene of enchantment, that there the lost maiden must lurk.'

' A glorious picture ! ' cried Babbalanja, ' but turn the medal, my lord ;—what says the reverse ? '

' Cynic ! have done.—But bravo ! we 'll ere long be in Franko, the goodliest vale of them all ; how long I to take her old king by the hand ! '

The sun was now setting behind us, lighting up the white cliffs of Dominora, and the green capes of Verdanna ; while in deep shade lay before us the long winding shores of Porpheero.

It was a sunset serene.

' How the winds lowly warble in the dying day's ear,' murmured Yoomy.

' A mild, bright night, we 'll have,' said Media.

' See you not those clouds over Franko, my lord,' said Mohi, shaking his head.

' Ah, aged and weather-wise as ever, sir chronicler ;—I predict a fair night, and many to follow.'

' Patience needs no prophet,' said Babbalanja. ' The night is at hand.'

Hitherto the lagoon had been smooth ; but anon, it grew black, and stirred ; and out of the thick darkness came clamorous sounds. Soon, there shot into the air a vivid meteor, which bursting at the zenith, radiated down the firmament in fiery showers, leaving treble darkness behind.

Then, as all held their breath, from Franko there

spouted an eruption, which seemed to plant all Mardi in the foreground.

As when Vesuvius lights her torch, and in the blaze, the storm-swept surges in Naples' bay rear and plunge toward it ; so now, showed Franko's multitudes, as they stormed the summit where their monarch's palace blazed, fast by the burning mountain.

'By my eternal throne !' cried Media, starting, 'the old volcano has burst forth again !'

'But a new vent, my lord,' said Babbalanja.

'More fierce this, than the eruption which happened in my youth,' said Mohi; 'methinks that Franko's end has come.'

'You look pale, my lord,' said Babbalanja, 'while all other faces glow ;—Yoomy, doff that halo in the presence of a king.'

Over the waters came a rumbling sound, mixed with the din of warfare, and thwarted by showers of embers that fell not, for the whirling blasts.

'Off shore! off shore !' cried Media ; and with all haste we gained a place of safety.

Down the valley now poured Rhines and Rhones of lava, a fire-freshet, flooding the forests from their fastnesses, and leaping with them into the seething sea.

The shore was lined with multitudes pushing off wildly in canoes.

Meantime, the fiery storm from Franko kindled new flames in the distant valleys of Porpheero ; while driven over from Verdanna came frantic shouts, and direful jubilees. Upon Dominora a baleful glare was resting.

'Thrice cursed flames !' cried Media. 'Is Mardi to be one conflagration ? How it crackles, forks, and roars ! —Is this our funeral pyre ?'

'Recline, recline, my lord,' said Babbalanja. 'Fierce flames are ever brief—a song, sweet Yoomy ! Your pipe,

old Mohi ! Greater fires than this have ere now blazed in
Mardi. Let us be calm ;—the isles were made to burn ;—
Braid-Beard ! hereafter, in some quiet cell, of this whole
scene you will but make one chapter ;—come, digest it
now.'

' My face is scorched,' cried Media.

' The last, last day ! ' cried Mohi.

' Not so, old man,' said Babbalanja, ' when that day
dawns 'twill dawn serene. Be calm, be calm, my potent
lord.'

' Talk not of calm brows in storm-time ! ' cried Media
fiercely. ' See ! how the flames blow over upon Dominora ! '

' Yet the fires they kindle there are soon extinguished,'
said Babbalanja. ' No, no ; Dominora ne'er can burn
with Franko's fires ; only those of her own kindling may
consume her.'

' Away ! Away ! ' cried Media. ' We may not touch
Porpheero now.—Up sails ! and westward be our course.'

So dead before the blast we scudded.

Morning broke, showing no sign of land.

' Hard must it go with Franko's king,' said Media,
' when his people rise against him with the red volcanoes.
Oh, for a foot to crush them ! Hard, too, with all who
rule in broad Porpheero. And may she we seek survive
this conflagration ! '

' My lord,' said Babbalanja, ' where'er she hide, ne'er
yet did Yillah lurk in this Porpheero ; nor have we missed
the maiden, noble Taji ! in not touching at its shores.'

' This fire must make a desert of the land,' said Mohi ;
' burn up and bury all her tilth.'

' Yet, Mohi, vineyards flourish over buried villages,'
murmured Yoomy.

' True, minstrel,' said Babbalanja, ' and prairies are
purified by fire. Ashes breed loam. Nor can any skill

make the same surface forever fruitful. In all times past, things have been overlaid ; and though the first fruits of the marl are wild and poisonous, the palms at last spring forth ; and once again the tribes repose in shade. My lord, if calms breed storms, so storms calms ; and all this dire commotion must eventuate in peace. It may be, that Porpheero's future has been cheaply won.'

CHAPTER L

' Ho, now ! ' cried Media, ' across the wide waters, for that New Mardi, Vivenza ! Let us indeed see, whether she who eludes us elsewhere be at last found in Vivenza's vales.'

' There or nowhere, noble Taji,' said Yoomy.

' Be not too sanguine, gentle Yoomy,' said Babbalanja.

' Does Yillah choose rather to bower in the wild wilderness of Vivenza, than in the old vineyards of Porpheero ? ' said Braid-Beard.

Sang Yoomy :—

> Her bower is not of the vine,
> But the wild, wild eglantine !
> Not climbing a mouldering arch,
> But upheld by the fir-green larch.
> Old ruins she flies :
> To new valleys she hies ;—
> Not the hoar, moss-wood,
> Ivied trees each a rood—
> Not in Maramma she dwells,
> Hollow with hermit cells.

> 'Tis a new, new isle !
> An infant's its smile,
> Soft-rocked by the sea.
> Its bloom all in bud ;
> No tide at its flood,
> In that fresh-born sea !

Spring ! Spring ! where she dwells,
In her sycamore dells,
Where Mardi is young and new :
Its verdure all eyes with dew.

There, there ! in the bright, balmy morns,
The young deer sprout their horns,
Deep-tangled in new-branching groves,
Where the red-rover robin roves,—

    Stooping his crest,
    To his moulting breast—
Rekindling the flambeau there !
Spring ! Spring ! where she dwells,
In her sycamore dells :—
Where, fulfilling their fates,
All creatures seek mates—
The thrush, the doe, and the hare !

'Thou art most musical, sweet Yoomy,' said Media,
'concerning this spring-land Vivenza. But are not the
old autumnal valleys of Porpheero more glorious than
those of vernal Vivenza ? Vivenza shows no trophies of
the summer time, but Dominora's full-blown rose hangs
blushing on her garden walls ; her autumn groves are
glory-dyed.'

'My lord, autumn soon merges in winter, but the spring
has all the seasons before. The full-blown rose is nearer
withering than the bud. The faint morn is a blossom ; the
crimson sunset the flower.'

CHAPTER LI

IN WHICH AZZAGEDDI SEEMS TO USE BABBALANJA
FOR A MOUTHPIECE

PORPHEERO far astern, the spirits of the company rose.
Once again, old Mohi serenely unbraided and rebraided
his beard; and sitting Turk-wise on his mat, my lord
Media, smoking his gonfalon, diverted himself with the
wild songs of Yoomy, the wild chronicles of Mohi, or the
still wilder speculations of Babbalanja; now and then,
as from pitcher to pitcher, pouring royal old wine down
his soul.

Among other things, Media, who at times turned over
Babbalanja for an encyclopaedia, however unreliable,
demanded information upon the subject of neap tides and
their alleged slavish vassalage to the moon.

When, true to his cyclopaediatic nature, Babbalanja
quoted from a still older and better authority than himself; in brief, from no other than eternal Bardianna. It
seems that that worthy essayist had discussed the whole
matter in a chapter thus headed: 'On Seeing into
Mysteries through Millstones'; and throughout his
disquisitions he evinced such a profundity of research,
though delivered in a style somewhat equivocal, that
the company were much struck by the erudition
displayed.

'Babbalanja, that Bardianna of yours must have been
a wonderful student,' said Media after a pause, 'no doubt
he consumed whole thickets of rush-lights.'

'Not so, my lord.—" Patience, patience, philosophers,"

said Bardianna ; " blow out your tapers, bolt not your
dinners, take time, wisdom will be plenty soon." '

' A notable hint ! Why not follow it, Babbalanja ? '

' Because, my lord, I have overtaken it, and passed on.'

' True to your nature, Babbalanja ; you stay nowhere.'

' Ay, keep moving is my motto ; but speaking of hard
students, did my lord ever hear of Midni the ontologist
and entomologist ? '

' No.'

' Then, my lord, you shall hear of him now. Midni
was of opinion that daylight was vulgar ; good enough
for taro planting and travelling ; but wholly unadapted to
the sublime ends of study. He toiled by night ; from
sunset to sunrise poring over the works of the old logicians.
Like most philosophers, Midni was an amiable man ; but
one thing invariably put him out. He read in the woods
by glowworm light ; insect in hand, tracing over his
pages, line by line. But glowworms burn not long ; and
in the midst of some calm intricate thought, at some imminent comma, the insect often expired, and Midni groped
for a meaning. Upon such an occasion, " Ho, ho," he
cried ; " but for one instant of sunlight to see my way to
a period ! " But sunlight there was none ; so Midni
sprang to his feet, and parchment under arm, raced about
among the sloughs and bogs for another glowworm.
Often, making a rapid descent with his turban, he thought
he had caged a prize ; but nay. Again he tried ; yet with
no better success. Nevertheless, at last he secured one,
but hardly had he read three lines by its light, when out
it went. Again and again this occurred. And thus he
forever went halting and stumbling through his studies,
and plunging through his quagmires after a glim.'

At this ridiculous tale, one of our silliest paddlers burst
into uncontrollable mirth. Offended at which breach of
decorum, Media sharply rebuked him.

But he protested he could not help laughing.

Again Media was about to reprimand him, when Babbalanja begged leave to interfere.

' My lord, he is not to blame. Mark how earnestly he struggles to suppress his mirth ; but he cannot. It has often been the same with myself. And many a time have I not only vainly sought to check my laughter, but at some recitals I have both laughed and cried. But can opposite emotions be simultaneous in one being ? No. I wanted to weep ; but my body wanted to smile ; and between us we almost choked. My lord Media, this man's body laughs ; not the man himself.'

' But his body is his own, Babbalanja ; and he should have it under better control.'

' The common error, my lord. Our souls belong to our bodies, not our bodies to our souls. For which has the care of the other ? which keeps house ? which looks after the replenishing of the aorta and auricles, and stores away the secretions ? Which toils and ticks while the other sleeps ? Which is ever giving timely hints, and elderly warnings ? Which is the most authoritative ?—Our bodies, surely. At a hint, you must move ; at a notice to quit, you depart. Simpletons show us, that a body can get along almost without a soul ; but of a soul getting along without a body we have no tangible and indisputable proof. My lord, the wisest of us breathe involuntarily. And how many millions there are who live from day to day by the incessant operation of subtle processes in them, of which they know nothing, and care less ? Little ween they, of vessels lacteal and lymphatic, of arteries femoral and temporal ; of pericranium or pericardium ; lymph, chyle, fibrin, albumen, iron in the blood, and pudding in the head ; they live by the charity of their bodies, to which they are but butlers. I say, my lord, our bodies are our betters. A soul so simple, that it prefers evil to good, is

lodged in a frame, whose minutest action is full of unsearchable wisdom. Knowing this superiority of theirs,
our bodies are inclined to be wilful : our beards grow in
spite of us ; and, as every one knows, they sometimes
grow on dead men.'

' You mortals are alive, then, when you are dead,
Babbalanja.'

' No, my lord ; but our beards survive us.'

' An ingenious distinction ; go on, philosopher.'

' Without bodies, my lord, we Mardians would be minus
our strongest motive passions, those which, in some way
or other, root under our every action. Hence, without
bodies, we must be something else than we essentially are.
Wherefore, that saying imputed to Alma, and which, by
his very followers, is deemed the most hard to believe of
all his instructions, and the most at variance with all
preconceived notions of immortality, I Babbalanja,
account the most reasonable of his doctrinal teachings.
It is this ;—that at the last day, every man shall rise in
the flesh.'

' Pray, Babbalanja, talk not of resurrections to a
demi-god.'

' Then let me rehearse a story, my lord. You will find
it in the " Very Merry Marvellings " of the Improvisitor
Quiddi ; and a quaint book it is. Fugle-fi is its finis :—
fugle-fi, fugle-fo, fugle-fogle-orum ! '

' That wild look in his eye again,' murmured Yoomy.

' Proceed, Azzageddi,' said Media.

' The philosopher Grando had a sovereign contempt for
his carcass. Often he picked a quarrel with it ; and
always was flying out in its disparagement. " Out upon
you, you beggarly body ! you clog, drug, drag ! You
keep me from flying ; I could get along better without
you. Out upon you, I say, you vile pantry, cellar, sink,
sewer ; abominable body ! what vile thing are you not ?

And think you, beggar! to have the upper hand of me? Make a leg to that man if you dare, without my permission. This smell is intolerable; but turn from it, if you can, unless I give the word. Bolt this yam!—it is done. Carry me across yon field!—off we go. Stop!—it's a dead halt. There, I've trained you enough for to-day; now, sirrah, crouch down in the shade, and be quiet.—I'm rested. So, here's for a stroll, and a revery homeward: —Up, carcass, and march." So the carcass demurely rose and paced, and the philosopher meditated. He was intent upon squaring the circle; but bump he came against a bough. "How now, clodhopping bumpkin! you would take advantage of my reveries, would you? But I'll be even with you"; and seizing a cudgel, he laid across his shoulders with right goodwill. But one of his backhanded thwacks injured his spinal cord; the philosopher dropped, but presently came to. "Adzooks! I'll bend or break you! Up, up, and I'll run you home for this." But wonderful to tell, his legs refused to budge; all sensation had left them. But a huge wasp happening to sting his foot, not him, for he felt it not, the leg incontinently sprang into the air, and of itself cut all manner of capers. "Be still! Down with you!" But the leg refused. "My arms are still loyal," thought Grando; and with them he at last managed to confine his refractory member. But all commands, volitions, and persuasions were as naught to induce his limbs to carry him home. It was a solitary place; and five days after, Grando the philosopher was found dead under a tree.'

'Ha, ha!' laughed Media, 'Azzageddi is full as merry as ever.'

'But, my lord,' continued Babbalanja, 'some creatures have still more perverse bodies than Grando's. In the fables of Ridendiabola, this is to be found: "A fresh water polyp, despising its marine existence, longed to live upon air. But all it could do, its tentacles or arms still continued to cram its stomach. By a sudden preternatural impulse, however, the polyp at last turned itself inside out ; supposing that after such a proceeding it would have no gastronomic interior. But its body proved ventricle outside as well as in. Again its arms went to work ; food was tossed in, and digestion continued." '

' Is the literal part of that a fact ? ' asked Mohi.

' True as truth,' said Babbalanja ; ' the polyp will live turned inside out.'

' Somewhat curious, certainly,' said Media.—' But methinks, Babbalanja, that somewhere I have heard something about organic functions, so called ; which may account for the phenomena you mention ; and I have heard too, methinks, of what are called reflex actions of the nerves, which, duly considered, might deprive of its strangeness that story of yours concerning Grando and his body.'

' Mere substitutions of sounds for inexplicable meanings, my lord. In some things science cajoles us. Now, what is undeniable of the polyp some physiologists analogically maintain with regard to us Mardians ; that forasmuch as the lining of our interiors is nothing more than a continuation of the epidermis, or scarf-skin, therefore, that in a remote age we too must have been turned wrong side out : an hypothesis which indirectly might account for our moral perversities : and also, for that otherwise nonsensical term—" the coat of the stomach " ; for originally it must have been a surtout, instead of an inner garment.'

' Pray, Azzageddi,' said Media, ' are you not a fool ? '

' One of a jolly company, my lord ; but some creatures besides wearing their surtouts within, sport their skeletons without : witness the lobster and turtle, who alive, study their own anatomies.'

' Azzageddi, you are a zany.'

'Pardon, my lord,' said Mohi, 'I think him more of a lobster; it's hard telling his jaws from his claws.'

'Yes, Braid-Beard, I am a lobster, a mackerel, anything you please; but my ancestors were kangaroos, not monkeys, as old Boddo erroneously opined. My idea is more susceptible of demonstration than his. Among the deepest discovered land fossils, the relics of kangaroos are discernible, but no relics of men. Hence, there were no giants in those days; but, on the contrary, kangaroos, and those kangaroos formed the first edition of mankind, since revised and corrected.'

'What has become of our finises, or tails, then?' asked Mohi, wriggling in his seat.

'The old question, Mohi. But where are the tails of the tadpoles, after their gradual metamorphosis into frogs? Have frogs any tails, old man? Our tails, Mohi, were worn off by the process of civilisation; especially at the period when our fathers began to adopt the sitting posture: the fundamental evidence of all civilisation, for neither apes, nor savages, can be said to sit; invariably, they squat on their hams. Among barbarous tribes benches and settles are unknown. But, my lord Media, as your liege and loving subject I cannot sufficiently deplore the deprivation of your royal tail. That stiff and vertebrated member, as we find it in those rustic kinsmen we have disowned, would have been useful as a supplement to your royal legs; and whereas my good lord is now fain to totter on two stanchions, were he only a kangaroo, like the monarchs of old, the majesty of Odo would be dignified, by standing firm on a tripod.'

'A very witty conceit! But have a care, Azzageddi; your theory applies not to me.'

'Babbalanja,' said Mohi, 'you must be the last of the kangaroos.'

'I am, Mohi.'

' But the old-fashioned pouch or purse of your gran-
dams ? ' hinted Media.

' My lord, I take it, that must have been transferred ;
nowadays our sex carries the purse.'

' Ha, ha ! '

' My lord, why this mirth ? Let us be serious. Although
man is no longer a kangaroo, he may be said to be an
inferior species of plant. Plants proper are perhaps in-
sensible of the circulation of their sap : we mortals are
physically unconscious of the circulation of the blood ; and
for many ages were not even aware of the fact. Plants
know nothing of their interiors :—threescore years and
ten we trundle about ours, and never get a peep at them ;
plants stand on their stalks :—we stalk on our legs ; no
plant flourishes over its dead root :—dead in the grave,
man lives no longer above ground ; plants die without
food :—so we. And now for the difference. Plants
elegantly inhale nourishment, without looking it up : like
lords, they stand still and are served ; and though green,
never suffer from the colic :—whereas, we mortals must
forage all round for our food : we cram our insides ; and
are loaded down with odious sacks and intestines. Plants
make love and multiply ; but excel us in all amorous
enticements, wooing and winning by soft pollens and
essences. Plants abide in one place, and live : we must
travel or die. Plants flourish without us : we must
perish without them.'

' Enough, Azzageddi ! ' cried Media. ' Open not thy
lips till to-morrow.'

CHAPTER LII

THE CHARMING YOOMY SINGS

THE morrow came; and three abreast, with snorting prows, we raced along; our mat-sails panting to the breeze. All present partook of the life of the air; and unanimously Yoomy was called upon for a song. The canoes were passing a long, white reef, sparkling with shells, like a jeweller's case : and thus Yoomy sang in the same old strain as of yore ; beginning aloud, where he had left off in his soul :—

Her sweet, sweet mouth !
  The peach-pearl shell :—
Red edged its lips,
  That softly swell,
Just oped to speak,
With blushing cheek,
  That fisherman
With lonely spear
  On the reef ken,
And lift to ear
Its voice to hear,—
  Soft sighing South !
Like this, like this,—
The rosy kiss !—
  That maiden's mouth.
A shell ! a shell !
A vocal shell !
  Song-dreaming,
In its inmost dell !

Her bosom !   Two buds half blown, they tell ;
 A little valley between perfuming ;
   That roves away,
   Deserting the day,—
 The day of her eyes illuming ;—
That roves away, o'er slope and fell,
Till a soft, soft meadow becomes the dell.

Thus far, old Mohi had been wriggling about in his seat, twitching his beard, and at every couplet looking up expectantly, as if he desired the company to think that he was counting upon that line as the last ; but now, starting to his feet, he exclaimed, ' Hold, minstrel ! thy muse's drapery is becoming disordered : no more ! '

' Then no more it shall be,' said Yoomy ; ' but you have lost a glorious sequel.'

CHAPTER LIII

THEY DRAW NIGH UNTO LAND

IN good time, after many days sailing, we snuffed the
land from afar, and came to a great country, full of inland
mountains, north and south stretching far out of sight.
' All hail, Kolumbo ! ' cried Yoomy.

Coasting by a portion of it, which Mohi called Kanneeda,
a province of King Bello's, we perceived the groves rocking
in the wind ; their flexible boughs bending like bows ;
and the leaves flying forth, and darkening the landscape,
like flocks of pigeons.

' Those groves must soon fall,' said Mohi.

' Not so,' said Babbalanja. ' My lord, as these violent
gusts are formed by the hostile meeting of two currents,
one from over the lagoon, the other from land ; they may
be taken as significant of the occasional variances between
Kanneeda and Dominora.'

' Ay,' said Media, ' and as Mohi hints, the breeze from
Dominora must soon overthrow the groves of Kanneeda.'

' Not if the land breeze holds, my lord ;—one breeze oft
blows another home.—Stand up, and gaze ! From cape
to cape, this whole main we see, is young and froward.
And far southward, past this Kanneeda and Vivenza, are
haughty, overbearing streams, which at their mouths dam
back the ocean, and long refuse to mix their freshness with
the foreign brine :—so bold, so strong, so bent on hurling
off aggression is this brave main, Kolumbo ;—last sought,
last found, Mardi's estate, so long kept back ;—pray Oro,
it be not squandered foolishly. Here lie plantations, held

in fee by stout hearts and arms ; and boundless fields, that
may be had for seeing.   Here, your foes are forests, struck
down with bloodless maces.—Ho ! Mardi's Poor, and
Mardi's Strong ! ye, who starve or beg ; seventh sons who
slave for earth's firstborn—here is your home ; pre-
destinated yours ; Come over, Empire-founders ! fathers
of the wedded tribes to come !—abject now, illustrious
evermore :—Ho : Sinew, Brawn, and Thigh ! '

   ' A very fine invocation,' said Media; 'now Babbalanja,
be seated ; and tell us whether Dominora and the kings of
Porpheero do not own some small portion of this great
continent, which just now you poetically pronounced as
the spoil of any vagabonds who may choose to settle
therein ?   Is not Kanneeda, Dominora's ? '

   ' And was not Vivenza once Dominora's also ?   And
what Vivenza now is, Kanneeda soon must be.   I speak
not, my lord, as wishful of what I say, but simply as fore-
knowing it.   The thing must come.   Vain for Dominora
to claim allegiance from all the progeny she spawns.   As
well might the old patriarch of the Flood reappear, and
claim the right of rule over all mankind, as descended
from the loins of his three roving sons.

   ' 'Tis the old law :—the East peoples the West, the
West the East ; flux and reflux.   And time may come,
after the rise and fall of nations yet unborn, that, risen
from its future ashes, Porpheero shall be the promised
land, and from her surplus hordes Kolumbo people it.'

   Still coasting on, next day we came to Vivenza ; and as
Media desired to land first at a point midway between its
extremities, in order to behold the convocation of chiefs
supposed to be assembled at this season, we held on our
way, till we gained a lofty ridge, jutting out into the
lagoon, a bastion to the neighbouring land.   It terminated
in a lofty natural arch of solid trap.   Billows beat against
its base.   But above, waved an inviting copse, wherein

was revealed an open temple of canes, containing one only image, that of a helmeted female, the tutelar deity of Vivenza.

The canoes drew near.

' Lo ! what inscription is that,' cried Media, ' there chiselled over the arch ? '

Studying those immense hieroglyphics awhile, antiquarian Mohi, still eyeing them, said slowly :—

' In-this-re-publi-can-land-all-men-are-born-free-and-equal.'

' False ! ' said Media.

' And how long stay they so ? ' said Babbalanja.

' But look lower, old man,' cried Media, ' methinks there's a small hieroglyphic or two hidden away in yonder angle.—Interpret them, old man.'

After much screwing of his eyes, for those characters were very minute, Champollion Mohi thus spoke—' Except-the-tribe-of-Hamo.'

' That nullifies the other,' cried Media. ' Ah, ye republicans ! '

' It seems to have been added for a postscript,' rejoined Braid-Beard, screwing his eyes again.

' Perhaps so,' said Babbalanja, ' but some wag must have done it.'

Shooting through the arch, we rapidly gained the beach.

CHAPTER LIV

THE throng that greeted us upon landing were exceedingly boisterous.

'Whence came ye?' they cried. 'Whither bound? Saw ye ever such a land as this? Is it not a great and extensive republic? Pray, observe how tall we are; just feel of our thighs; are we not a glorious people? Here, feel of our beards. Look round; look round; be not afraid; behold those palms; swear now, that this land surpasses all others. Old Bello's mountains are mole-hills to ours; his rivers, rills; his empires, villages; his palm-trees, shrubs.'

'True,' said Babbalanja. 'But great Oro must have had some hand in making your mountains and streams.— Would ye have been as great in a desert?'

'Where is your king?' asked Media, drawing himself up in his robe, and cocking his crown.

'Ha, ha, my fine fellow! We are all kings here; royalty breathes in the common air. But come on, come on. Let us show you our great Temple of Freedom.'

And so saying, irreverently grasping his sacred arm, they conducted us toward a lofty structure, planted upon a bold hill, and supported by thirty pillars of palm; four quite green; as if recently added; and beyond these, an almost interminable vacancy, as if all the palms in Mardi were, at some future time, to aid in upholding that fabric.

Upon the summit of the temple was a staff; and as we

drew nigh, a man with a collar round his neck, and the
red marks of stripes upon his back, was just in the act of
hoisting a tappa standard—correspondingly striped.
Other collared menials were going in and out of the
temple.

Near the porch stood an image like that on the top of
the arch we had seen. Upon its pedestal were pasted
certain hieroglyphical notices ; according to Mohi, offering
rewards for missing men, so many hands high.

Entering the temple, we beheld an amphitheatrical
space, in the middle of which a great fire was burning.
Around it were many chiefs, robed in long togas, and
presenting strange contrasts in their style of tattooing.

Some were sociably laughing, and chatting ; others
diligently making excavations between their teeth with
slivers of bamboo ; or turning their heads into mills, were
grinding up leaves and ejecting their juices. Some were
busily inserting the down of a thistle into their ears.
Several stood erect, intent upon maintaining striking
attitudes ; their javelins tragically crossed upon their
chests. They would have looked very imposing, were it
not, that in rear their vesture was sadly disordered.
Others, with swelling fronts, seemed chiefly indebted to
their dinners for their dignity. Many were nodding and
napping. And, here and there, were sundry indefatigable
worthies, making a great show of imperious and indispensable business ; sedulously folding banana leaves into
scrolls, and recklessly placing them into the hands of little
boys in gay turbans and trim little girdles, who thereupon
fled as if with salvation for the dying.

It was a crowded scene ; the dusky chiefs, here and
there, grouped together, and their fantastic tattooings
showing like the carved work on quaint old chimney-
stacks, seen from afar. But one of their number over-
topped all the rest. As when, drawing nigh unto old

Rome, amid the crowd of sculptured columns and gables, St. Peter's grand dome soars far aloft, serene in the upper air ; so, showed one calm grand forehead among those of this mob of chieftains. That head was Saturnina's. Gall and Spurzheim ! saw you ever such a brow ?—poised like an avalanche, under the shadow of a forest ! woe betide the devoted valleys below ! Lavatar ! behold those lips, —like mystic scrolls ! Those eyes,—like panthers' caves at the base of Popocatepetl !

' By my right hand, Saturnina,' cried Babbalanja, ' but thou wert made in the image of thy Maker ! Yet, have I beheld men, to the eye as commanding as thou ; and surmounted by heads globe-like as thine, who never had thy calibre. We must measure brains, not heads, my lord ; else, the sperm whale, with his tun of an occiput, would transcend us all.'

Near by, were arched ways, leading to subterranean places, whence issued a savoury steam, and an extra-ordinary clattering of calabashes, and smacking of lips, as if something were being eaten down there by the fattest of fat fellows, with the heartiest of appetites, and the most irresistible of relishes. It was a quaffing, guzzling, gobbling noise. Peeping down, we beheld a company, breasted up against a board groaning under numerous viands. In the middle of all was a mighty great gourd, yellow as gold, and jolly round like a pumpkin in October, and so big it must have grown in the sun. Thence flowed a tide of red wine. And before it stood plenty of paunches being filled therewith like portly stone jars at a fountain. Melancholy to tell, before that fine flood of old wine, and among those portly old topers, was a lean man ; who occasionally ducked in his bill. He looked like an ibis standing in the Nile at flood tide, among a tongue-lapping herd of hippopotami.

They were jolly as the jolliest ; and laughed so uproar-

iously, that their hemispheres all quivered and shook, like
vast provinces in an earthquake. Ha! ha! ha! how
they laughed, and they roared. A deaf man might have
heard them ; and no milk could have soured within a
forty-two-pounder ball shot of that place.

Now, the smell of good things is no very bad thing in
itself. It is the savour of good things beyond ; proof
positive of a glorious good meal. So snuffing up those
zephyrs from Araby the blest, those boisterous gales,
blowing from out the mouths of baked boars, stuffed with
bread-fruit, bananas, and sage, we would fain have gone
down and partaken.

But this could not be ; for we were told that those
worthies below were a club in secret conclave ; very busy
in settling certain weighty state affairs upon a solid basis.
They were all chiefs of immense capacity :—how many
gallons, there was no finding out.

Be sure, now, a most riotous noise came up from those
catacombs, which seemed full of the ghosts of fat Lamberts ;
and this uproar it was that heightened the din above-
ground.

But heedless of all, in the midst of the amphitheatre,
stood a tall, gaunt warrior, ferociously tattooed, with a
beak like a buzzard ; long dusky locks ; and his hands
full of headless arrows. He was labouring under violent
paroxysms ; three benevolent individuals essaying to hold
him. But repeatedly breaking loose, he burst anew into
his delirium ; while with an absence of sympathy, distress-
ing to behold, the rest of the assembly seemed wholly
engrossed with themselves ; nor did they appear to care
how soon the unfortunate lunatic might demolish himself
by his frantic proceedings.

Toward one side of this amphitheatrical space, perched
high upon an elevated dais, sat a white-headed old man
with a tomahawk in his hand : earnestly engaged in over-

seeing the tumult ; though not a word did he say. Occasionally, however, he was regarded by those present with a mysterious sort of deference ; and when they chanced to pass between him and the crazy man, they invariably did so in a stooping position ; probably to elude the atmospheric grape and canister, continually flying from the mouth of the lunatic.

' What mob is this ? ' cried Media.

' 'Tis the grand council of Vivenza,' cried a bystander. ' Hear ye not Alanno ? ' and he pointed to the lunatic.

Now, coming close to Alanno, we found, that with incredible volubility, he was addressing the assembly upon some all-absorbing subject connected with King Bello, and his presumed encroachments toward the north-west of Vivenza.

One hand smiting his hip, and the other his head, the lunatic thus proceeded ; roaring like a wild beast, and beating the air like a windmill :—

' I have said it ! the thunder is flashing, the lightning is crashing ! already there 's an earthquake in Dominora ! Full soon will old Bello discover that his diabolical machinations against this ineffable land must soon come to naught. Who dare not declare, that we are not invincible ? I repeat it, we are. Ha ! ha ! Audacious Bello must bite the dust ! Hair by hair, we will trail his gory gray beard at the end of our spears ! Ha, ha ! I grow hoarse ; but would mine were a voice like the wild bulls of Bullorom, that I might be heard from one end of this great and gorgeous land to its farthest zenith ; ay, to the uttermost diameter of its circumference. Awake ! oh Vivenza. The signs of the times are portentous; nay, extraordinary ; I hesitate not to add, peculiar ! Up ! up ! Let us not descend to the bathos, when we should soar to the climax ! Does not all Mardi wink and look on ? Is the great sun itself a frigid spectator ? Then let us double up our mandibles to the deadly encounter. Methinks I see it now. Old Bello is crafty, and his oath is recorded to obliterate us ! Across this wide lagoon he casts his serpent eyes ; whets his insatiate bill ; mumbles his barbarous tusks ; licks his forked tongues ; and who knows when we shall have the shark in our midst ? Yet be not deceived ; for though as yet Bello has forborne molesting us openly, his emissaries are at work ; his infernal sappers, and miners, and wet-nurses, and midwives, and gravediggers are busy ! His canoe yards are all in commotion ! In navies his forests are being launched upon the wave ; and ere long typhoons, zephyrs, white squalls, balmy breezes, hurricanes, and besoms will be raging round us ! '

His philippic concluded, Alanno was conducted from the place ; and being now quite exhausted, cold cobble-stones were applied to his temples, and he was treated to a bath in a stream.

This chieftain, it seems, was from a distant western valley, called Hio-Hio, one of the largest and most fertile in Vivenza, though but recently settled. Its inhabitants and those of the vales adjoining,—a right sturdy set of fellows,—were accounted the most dogmatically democratic and ultra of all the tribes in Vivenza ; ever seeking to push on their brethren to the uttermost ; and especially were they bitter against Bello. But they were a fine young tribe, nevertheless. Like strong new wine they worked violently in becoming clear. Time, perhaps, would make them all right.

An interval of greater uproar than ever now ensued ; during which, with his tomahawk, the white-headed old man repeatedly thumped and pounded the seat where he sat, apparently to augment the din, though he looked anxious to suppress it.

At last, tiring of his posture, he whispered in the ear

of a chief, his friend ; who, approaching a portly warrior present, prevailed upon him to rise and address the assembly. And no sooner did this one do so than the whole convocation dispersed, as if to their yams ; and with a grin, the little old man leaped from his seat, and stretched his legs on a mat.

The fire was now extinguished, and the temple deserted.

CHAPTER LV

As we lingered in the precincts of the temple after all
others had departed, sundry comments were made upon
what we had seen ; and having remarked the hostility of
the lunatic orator toward Dominora, Babbalanja thus
addressed Media :—

' My lord, I am constrained to believe that all Vivenza
cannot be of the same mind with the grandiloquent chief
from Hio-Hio. Nevertheless, I imagine, that between
Dominora and this land there exists at bottom a feeling
akin to animosity, which is not yet wholly extinguished ;
though but the smouldering embers of a once raging fire.
My lord, you may call it poetry if you will, but there are
nations in Mardi that to others stand in the relation of
sons to sires. Thus with Dominora and Vivenza. And
though, its majority attained, Vivenza is now its own
master, yet should it not fail in a reverential respect for its
parent. In man or nation, old age is honourable ; and a
boy, however tall, should never take his sire by the beard.
And though Dominora did indeed ill merit Vivenza's
esteem, yet by abstaining from criminations, Vivenza
should ever merit its own. And if in time to come, which
Oro forbid, Vivenza must needs go to battle with King
Bello, let Vivenza first cross the old veteran's spear with
all possible courtesy. On the other hand, my lord, King
Bello should never forget that whatever be glorious in
Vivenza redounds to himself. And as some gallant old

232

lord proudly measures the brawn and stature of his son ;
and joys to view in his noble young lineaments the likeness
of his own ; bethinking him, that when at last laid in his
tomb, he will yet survive in the long, strong life of his
child, the worthy inheritor of his valour and renown ; even
so, should King Bello regard the generous promise of this
young Vivenza of his own lusty begetting. My lord,
behold these two states ! Of all nations in the Archipelago, they alone are one in blood. Dominora is the last
and greatest Anak of Old Times ; Vivenza, the foremost
and goodliest stripling of the present. One is full of the
past ; the other brims with the future. Ah ! did this
sire's old heart but beat to free thoughts, and back his
bold son, all Mardi would go down before them. And
high Oro may have ordained for them a career little
divined by the mass. Methinks, that as Vivenza will
never cause old Bello to weep for his son ; so Vivenza will
not, this many a long year, be called to weep over the
grave of its sire. And though King Bello may yet lay
aside his old-fashioned cocked hat of a crown, and comply
with the plain costume of the times ; yet will his frame
remain sturdy as of yore, and equally grace any habiliments he may don. And those who say, Dominora is old
and worn out, may very possibly err. For if, as a nation,
Dominora be old—her present generation is full as young
as the youths in any land under the sun. Then, ho !
worthy twain ! Each worthy the other, join hands on
the instant, and weld them together. Lo ! the past is a
prophet. Be the future its prophecy fulfilled.'

CHAPTER LVI

A SCENE IN THE LAND OF WARWICKS, OR KING-MAKERS

WENDING our way from the temple, we were accompanied by a fluent, obstreperous wight, one Znobbi, a runaway native of Porpheero, but now an enthusiastic inhabitant of Vivenza.

'Here comes our great chief!' he cried. 'Behold him! It was *I* that had a hand in making him what he is!'

And so saying, he pointed out a personage, no way distinguished, except by the tattooing on his forehead—stars, thirty in number; and an uncommonly long spear in his hand. Freely he mingled with the crowd.

'Behold, how familiar I am with him!' cried Znobbi, approaching, and pitcher-wise taking him by the handle of his face.

'Friend,' said the dignitary, 'thy salute is peculiar, but welcome. I reverence the enlightened people of this land.'

'Mean-spirited hound!' muttered Media, 'were I him I had impaled that audacious plebeian.'

'There's a head chief for you, now, my fine fellow!' cried Znobbi. 'Hurrah! Three cheers! Ay, ay! All kings here—all equal. Everything's in common.'

Here, a bystander, feeling something grazing his side, looked down; and perceived Znobbi's hand in clandestine vicinity to the pouch at his girdle-end.

Whereupon the crowd shouted, 'A thief! a thief!' And with a loud voice the starred chief cried—'Seize him, people, and tie him to yonder tree.'

And they seized, and tied him on the spot.

234

' Ah,' said Media, ' this chief has something to say after all ; he pinions a king at a word, though a plebeian takes him by the nose. Beshrew me, I doubt not, that spear of his, though without a tassel, is longer and sharper than mine.'

' There 's not so much freedom here as these freemen think,' said Babbalanja, turning ; ' I laugh and admire.'

CHAPTER LVII

THEY HEARKEN UNTO A VOICE FROM THE GODS

NEXT day we retraced our voyage northward, to visit that section of Vivenza.

In due time we landed.

To look round was refreshing. Of all the lands we had seen, none looked more promising. The groves stood tall and green ; the fields spread flush and broad ; the dew of the first morning seemed hardly vanished from the grass. On all sides was heard the fall of waters, the swarming of bees, and the rejoicing hum of a thriving population.

' Ha, ha ! ' laughed Yoomy, ' Labour laughs in this land ; and claps his hands in the jubilee groves ! methinks that Yillah will yet be found.'

Generously entertained, we tarried in this land ; till at length, from over the lagoon, came full tidings of the eruption we had witnessed in Franko, with many details. The conflagration had spread through Porpheero ; and the kings were to and fro hunted, like malefactors by blood-hounds ; all that part of Mardi was heaving with throes.

With the utmost delight these tidings were welcomed by many ; yet others heard them with boding concern.

Those, too, there were, who rejoiced that the kings were cast down ; but mourned that the people themselves stood not firmer. A victory, turned to no wise and enduring account, said they, is no victory at all. Some victories revert to the vanquished.

But day by day great crowds ran down to the beach, in

236

wait for canoes periodically bringing further intelligence. Every hour new cries startled the air. ' Hurrah ! another kingdom is burnt down to the earth's edge ; another demi-god is unhelmed ; another republic is dawning. Shake hands, freemen, shake hands ! Soon will we hear of Dominora down in the dust ; of hapless Verdanna free as ourselves ; all Porpheero's volcanoes are bursting ! Who may withstand the people ? The times tell terrible tales to tyrants ! Ere we die, freemen, all Mardi will be free.'

Overhearing these shouts, Babbalanja thus addressed Media : ' My lord, I cannot but believe that these men are far more excited than those with whom they so ardently sympathise. But no wonder. The single discharges which are heard in Porpheero here come condensed in one tremendous report. Every arrival is a firing off of events by platoons.'

Now, during this tumultuous interval, King Media very prudently kept himself exceedingly quiet. He doffed his regalia ; and in all things carried himself with a dignified discretion. And many hours he absented himself ; none knowing whither he went, or what his employment.

So also with Babbalanja. But still pursuing our search, at last we all journeyed into a great valley, whose inhabitants were more than commonly inflated with the ardour of the times.

Rambling on, we espied a clamorous crowd gathered about a conspicuous palm, against which a scroll was fixed.

The people were violently agitated ; storming out maledictions against the insolent knave, who, overnight, must have fixed there that scandalous document. But whoever he may have been, certain it was he had con-trived to hood himself effectually.

After much vehement discussion, during which sundry

inflammatory harangues were made from the stumps of
trees near by, it was proposed that the scroll should be
read aloud, so that all might give ear.

Seizing it, a fiery youth mounted upon the bowed
shoulders of an old man, his sire ; and with a shrill voice,
ever and anon interrupted by outcries, read as follows :—

' Sovereign kings of Vivenza ! it is fit you should
hearken to wisdom. But well aware, that you give ear
to little wisdom except of your own ; and that as freemen,
you are free to hunt down him who dissents from your
majesties ; I deem it proper to address you anonymously.

' And if it please you, you may ascribe this voice to the
gods : for never will you trace it to man.

' It is not unknown, sovereign kings ! that in these
boisterous days, the lessons of history are almost discarded,
as superseded by present experiences. And that while
all Mardi's present has grown out of its past, it is becoming obsolete to refer to what has been. Yet, peradventure,
the past is an apostle.

' The grand error of this age, sovereign kings ! is the
general supposition that the very special Diabolus is
abroad ; whereas, the very special Diabolus has been
abroad ever since Mardi began.

' And the grand error of your nation, sovereign kings !
seems this :—the conceit that Mardi is now in the last
scene of the last act of her drama ; and that all preceding
events were ordained to bring about the catastrophe you
believe to be at hand,—a universal and permanent
republic.

' May it please you, those who hold to these things are
fools, and not wise.

' Time is made up of various ages ; and each thinks its
own a novelty. But imbedded in the walls of the pyramids, which outrun all chronologies, sculptured stones are
found, belonging to yet older fabrics. And as in the

mound-building period of yore, so every age thinks its
erections will forever endure.   But as your forests grow
apace, sovereign kings! overrunning the tumuli in your
western vales ; so, while deriving their substance from
the past, succeeding generations overgrow it ; but in time,
themselves decay.

'Oro decrees these vicissitudes.

'In chronicles of old, you read, sovereign kings! that
an eagle from the clouds presaged royalty to the fugitive
Taquinoo ; and a king, Taquinoo reigned ; No end to my
dynasty, thought he.

'But another omen descended, foreshadowing the fall of
Zooperbi, his son ; and Zooperbi returning from his camp,
found his country a fortress against him.   No more kings
would she have.   And for five hundred twelve-moons the
Regifugium or King's Flight, was annually celebrated like
your own jubilee day.   And rampant young orators
stormed out detestation of kings ; and augurs swore that
their birds presaged immortality to freedom.

'Then, Romara's free eagles flew over all Mardi, and
perched on the topmost diadems of the East.

'Ever thus must it be.

'For, mostly, monarchs are as gemmed bridles upon the
world, checking the plungings of a steed from the Pampas.
And republics are as vast reservoirs, draining down all
streams to one level; and so, breeding a fulness which cannot remain full, without overflowing.   And thus, Romara
flooded all Mardi, till scarce an Ararat was left of the
lofty kingdoms which had been.

'Thus, also, did Franko, fifty twelve-moons ago.   Thus
may she do again.   And though not yet, have you,
sovereign kings! in any large degree done likewise, it is
because you overflow your redundancies within your own
mighty borders ; having a wild western waste, which
many shepherds with their flocks could not overrun in a

day. Yet overrun at last it will be ; and then, the recoil must come.

'And, may it please you, that thus far your chronicles had narrated a very different story had your population been pressed and packed, like that of your old sire-land Dominora. Then, your great experiment might have proved an explosion ; like the chemist's who, stirring his mixture, was blown by it into the air.

'For though crossed, and recrossed by many brave quarterings, and boasting the great Bull in your pedigree ; yet, sovereign kings ! you are not meditative philosophers like the people of a small republic of old ; nor enduring Stoics, like their neighbours. Pent up, like them, may it please you, your thirteen original tribes had proved more turbulent than so many mutinous legions. Free horses need wide prairies ; and fortunate for you, sovereign kings ! that you have room enough, wherein to be free.

'And, may it please you, you are free, partly, because you are young. Your nation is like a fine, florid youth, full of fiery impulses, and hard to restrain ; his strong hand nobly championing his heart. On all sides, freely he gives, and still seeks to acquire. The breath of his nostrils is like smoke in spring air ; every tendon is electric with generous resolves. The oppressor he defies to his beard ; the high walls of old opinions he scales with a bound. In the future he sees all the domes of the East.

'But years elapse, and this bold boy is transformed. His eyes open not as of yore ; his heart is shut up as a vice. He yields not a groat ; and seeking no more acquisitions, is only bent on preserving his hoard. The maxims once trampled under foot are now printed on his front ; and he who hated oppressors is become an oppressor himself.

'Thus, often, with men ; thus, often, with nations. Then marvel not, sovereign kings ! that old states are different from yours ; and think not, your own must forever remain liberal as now.

'Each age thinks its own is eternal. But though for five hundred twelve-moons, all Romara, by courtesy of history, was republican ; yet, at last, her terrible king-tigers came, and spotted themselves with gore.

'And time was, when Dominora was republican, down to her sturdy backbone. The son of an absolute monarch became the man Karolus ; and his crown and head both rolled in the dust. And Dominora had her patriots by thousands ; and lusty Defences and glorious Areopagi-ticas were written, not since surpassed ; and no turban was doffed save in homage of Oro.

'Yet, may it please you, to the sound of pipe and tabor, the second King Karolus returned in good time ; and was hailed gracious majesty by high and low.

'Throughout all eternity, the parts of the past are but parts of the future reversed. In the old footprints, up and down, you mortals go, eternally travelling your sierras. And not more infallible the ponderings of the Calculating Machine than the deductions from the decimals of history.

'In nations, sovereign kings ! there is a transmigration of souls ; in you, is a marvellous destiny. The eagle of Romara revives in your own mountain bird, and once more is plumed for her flight. Her screams are answered by the vauntful cries of a hawk ; his red comb yet reeking with slaughter. And one East, one West, those bold birds may fly, till they lock pinions in the midmost beyond.

'But, soaring in the sky over the nations that shall gather their broods under their wings, that bloody hawk may hereafter be taken for the eagle.

'And though crimson republics may rise in constella-tions, like fiery Aldebarans, speeding to their culminations ;

yet, down must they sink at last, and leave the old sultan-sun in the sky ; in time, again to be deposed.

'For little longer, may it please you, can republics subsist now, than in days gone by. For assuming that Mardi is wiser than of old ; nevertheless, though all men approached sages in intelligence, some would yet be more wise than others ; and so, the old degrees be preserved. And no exemption would an equality of knowledge furnish, from the inbred servility of mortal to mortal ; from all the organic causes, which inevitably divide mankind into brigades and battalions, with captains at their head.

'Civilisation has not ever been the brother of equality. Freedom was born among the wild eyries in the moun-tains ; and barbarous tribes have sheltered under her wings, when the enlightened people of the plain have nestled under different pinions.

'Though, thus far, for you, sovereign kings ! your re-public has been fruitful of blessings ; yet, in themselves, monarchies are not utterly evil. For many nations they are better than republics ; for many they will ever so remain. And better, on all hands, that peace should rule with a sceptre, than that the tribunes of the people should brandish their broadswords. Better be the subject of a king, upright and just ; than a freeman in Franko, with the executioner's axe at every corner.

'It is not the prime end, and chief blessing, to be politically free. And freedom is only good as a means ; is no end in itself. Nor, did man fight it out against his masters to the haft, not then would he uncollar his neck from the yoke. A born thrall to the last, yelping out his liberty, he still remains a slave unto Oro ; and well is it for the universe that Oro's sceptre is absolute.

'World-old the saying, that it is easier to govern others than oneself. And that all men should govern themselves as nations, needs that all men be better, and wiser, than

the wisest of one-man rulers.   But in no stable democracy
do all men govern themselves.   Though an army be all
volunteers, martial law must . prevail.   Delegate your
power, you leagued mortals must.   The hazard you must
stand.   And though unlike King Bello of Dominora, your
great chieftain, sovereign kings ! may not declare war of
himself ; nevertheless, has he done a still more imperial
thing :—gone to war without declaring intentions.   You
yourselves were precipitated upon a neighbouring nation,
ere you knew your spears were in your hands.

' But, as in stars you have written it on the welkin,
sovereign kings ! you are a great and glorious people.
And verily, yours is the best and happiest land under the
sun.   But not wholly, because you, in your wisdom,
decreed it : your origin and geography necessitated it.
Nor, in their germ, are all your blessings to be ascribed
to the noble sires, who of yore fought in your behalf,
sovereign kings ! Your nation enjoyed no little independ-
ence before your declaration declared it.   Your ancient
pilgrims fathered your liberty ; and your wild woods
harboured the nursling.   For the state that to-day is
made up of slaves, cannot to-morrow transmute her bond
into free ; though lawlessness may transform them into
brutes.   Freedom is the name for a thing that is *not*
freedom ; this, a lesson never learned in an hour or an age.
By some tribes it will never be learned.

' Yet, if it please you, there may be such a thing as being
free under Caesar.   Ages ago, there were as many vital
freemen as breathe vital air to-day.

' Names make not distinctions ; some despots rule
without swaying sceptres.   Though King Bello's palace
was not put together by yoked men ; your federal temple
of freedom, sovereign kings ! was the handiwork of slaves.

' It is not gildings, and gold maces, and crown jewels
alone that make a people servile.   There is much bowing

and cringing among you yourselves, sovereign kings! Poverty is abased before riches, all Mardi over; anywhere, it is hard to be a debtor; anywhere, the wise will lord it over fools; everywhere, suffering is found.

'Thus, freedom is more social than political. And its real felicity is not to be shared. *That* is of a man's own individual getting and holding. It is not, who rules the state, but who rules me. Better be secure under one king, than exposed to violence from twenty millions of monarchs, though oneself be of the number.

'But superstitious notions you harbour, sovereign kings! Did you visit Dominora, you would not be marched straight into a dungeon. And though you would behold sundry sights displeasing, you would start to inhale such liberal breezes; and hear crowds boasting of their privileges; as you, of yours. Nor has the wine of Dominora a monarchical flavour.

'Now, though far and wide, to keep equal pace with the times, great reforms, of a verity, be needed; nowhere are bloody revolutions required. Though it be the most certain of remedies, no prudent invalid opens his veins to let out his disease with his life. And though all evils may be assuaged; all evils cannot be done away. For evil is the chronic malady of the universe; and checked in one place, breaks forth in another.

'Of late, on this head, some wild dreams have departed.

'There are many who erewhile believed that the age of pikes and javelins was passed; that after a heady and blustering youth, old Mardi was at last settling down into a serene old age; and that the Indian summer, first discovered in your land, sovereign kings! was the hazy vapour emitted from its tranquil pipe. But it has not so proved. Mardi's peaces are but truces. Long absent, at last the red comets have returned. And return they must, though their periods be ages. And should Mardi endure till mountain melt into mountain, and all the isles form one tableland ; yet, would it but expand the old battle-plain.

' Students of history are horror-struck at the massacres of old ; but in the shambles men are being murdered to-day. Could time be reversed, and the future change places with the past, the past would cry out against us, and our future, full as loudly as we against the ages fore-gone. All the Ages are his children, calling each other names.

' Hark ye, sovereign kings ! cheer not on the yelping pack too furiously. Hunters have been torn by their hounds. Be advised ; wash your hands. Hold aloof. Oro has poured out an ocean for an everlasting barrier between you and the worst folly which other republics have perpetrated. That barrier hold sacred. And swear never to cross over to Porpheero, by manifesto or army, unless you traverse dry land.

' And be not too grasping, nearer home. It is not free-dom to filch. Expand not your area too widely, now. Seek you proselytes ? Neighbouring nations may be free, without coming under your banner. And if you cannot lay your ambition, know this : that it is best served by waiting events.

' Time, but Time only, may enable you to cross the equator ; and give you the Arctic Circles for your boundaries.'

So read the anonymous scroll ; which straightway was torn into shreds.

' Old tory, and monarchist ! ' they shouted ; ' preaching over his benighted sermons in these enlightened times ! Fool ! does he not know that all the past and its graves are being dug over ? '

They were furious ; so wildly rolling their eyes after

victims, that well was it for King Media he wore not his crown; and in silence we moved unnoted from out the crowd.

' My lord, I am amazed at the indiscretion of a demi-god,' said Babbalanja, as we passed on our way; ' I recognised your sultanic style the very first sentence. This, then, is the result of your hours of seclusion.'

' Philosopher! I am astounded at your effrontery. I detected your philosophy the very first maxim. Who posted that parchment for you?'

So, each charged the other with its authorship: and there was no finding out, whether, indeed, either knew aught of its origin.

Now, could it have been Babbalanja? Hardly. For, philosophic as the document was, it seemed too dogmatic and conservative for him. King Media? But though imperially absolute in his political sentiments, Media delivered not himself so boldly, when actually beholding the eruption in Franko.

Indeed, the settlement of this question must be left to the commentators on Mardi, some four or five hundred centuries hence.

CHAPTER LVIII

WE penetrated farther and farther into the valleys around; but, though, as elsewhere, at times we heard whisperings that promised an end to our wanderings ;—we still wandered on ; and once again, even Yoomy abated his sanguine hopes.

And now, we prepared to embark for the extreme south of the land.

But we were warned by the people that, in that portion of Vivenza whither we were going, much would be seen repulsive to strangers. Such things, however, indulgent visitors overlooked. For themselves, they were well aware of those evils. Northern Vivenza had done all it could to assuage them ; but in vain ; the inhabitants of those southern valleys were a fiery and intractable race ; heeding neither expostulations nor entreaties. They were wedded to their ways. Nay, they swore, that if the northern tribes persisted in intermeddlings, they would dissolve the common alliance, and establish a distinct confederacy among themselves.

Our coasting voyage at an end, our keels grated the beach among many prostrate palms, decaying, and washed by the billows. Though part and parcel of the shore we had left, this region seemed another land. Fewer thriving things were seen ; fewer cheerful sounds were heard.

' Here labour has lost his laugh ! ' cried Yoomy.

It was a great plain where we landed ; and there, under a burning sun, hundreds of collared men were toiling in

trenches filled with the taro plant—a root most flourishing
in that soil.　Standing grimly over these, were men unlike
them ;　armed with long thongs, which descended upon the
toilers, and made wounds.　Blood and sweat mixed ;　and
in great drops fell.

'Who eat these plants thus nourished ? ' cried Yoomy.

'Are these men ? ' asked Babbalanja.

'Which mean you ? ' said Mohi.

Heeding him not, Babbalanja advanced toward the foremost of those with the thongs,—one Nulli : a cadaverous,
ghost-like man ;　with a low ridge of forehead ;　hair, steel-
gray ;　and wondrous eyes :—bright, nimble, as the twin
corposant balls, playing about the ends of ships' royal-
yards in gales.

The sun passed under a cloud ;　and Nulli, darting at
Babbalanja those wondrous eyes, there fell upon him a
baleful glare.

'Have they souls ? ' he asked, pointing to the serfs.

'No,' said Nulli, ' their ancestors may have had ;　but
their souls have been bred out of their descendants ;　as the
instinct of scent is killed in pointers.'

Approaching one of the serfs, Media took him by the
hand, and felt of it long ;　and looked into his eyes ;　and
placed his ear to his side ;　and exclaimed, ' Surely this
being has flesh that is warm ;　he has Oro in his eye ;　and
a heart in him that beats.　I swear he is a man.'

'Is this our lord the king ? ' cried Mohi, starting.

'What art thou ? ' said Babbalanja to the serf.　'Dost
ever feel in thee a sense of right and wrong ?　Art ever
glad or sad ?—They tell us thou art not a man :—speak,
then, for thyself ;　say, whether thou beliest thy Maker.'

'Speak not of my Maker to me.　Under the lash, I
believe my masters, and account myself a brute ;　but in
my dreams, bethink myself an angel.　But I am bond ;
and my little ones ;—their mother's milk is gall.'

' Just Oro ! ' cried Yoomy, ' do no thunders roll,—no
lightnings flash in this accursed land ! '

' Asylum for all Mardi's thralls ! ' cried Media.

' Incendiaries ! ' cried he with the wondrous eyes, ' come
ye, firebrands, to light the flame of revolt ?   Know ye not,
that here are many serfs, who, incited to obtain their
liberty, might wreak some dreadful vengeance ?   Avaunt,
thou king ! *thou* horrified at this ?   Go back to Odo, and
right her wrongs !   These serfs are happier than thine,
though thine no collars wear ; more happy as they are,
than if free.   Are they not fed, clothed, and cared for ?
Thy serfs pine for food : never yet did these ; who have
no thoughts, no cares.'

' Thoughts and cares are life, and liberty, and immortality ! ' cried Babbalanja ; ' and are their souls, then,
blown out as candles ? '

' Ranter ! they are content,' cried Nulli. ' They shed
no tears.'

' Frost never weeps,' said Babbalanja ; ' and tears are
frozen in those frigid eyes.'

' Oh fettered sons of fettered mothers, conceived and
born in manacles,' cried Yoomy ; ' dragging them through
life ; and falling with them, clanking in the grave :—
oh, beings as ourselves, how my stiff arm shivers to
avenge you !   'Twere absolution for the matricide, to
strike one rivet from your chains. My heart outswells
its home ! '

' Oro !   Art thou ? ' cried Babbalanja ; ' and doth this
thing exist ?   It shakes my little faith.'   Then, turning
upon Nulli, ' How can ye abide to sway this curs'd
dominion ? '

' Peace, fanatic !   Who else may till unwholesome fields,
but these ?   And as these beings are, so shall they remain ;
'tis right and righteous !   Maramma champions it !—*I*
swear it !   The first blow struck for them dissolves the

union of Vivenza's vales. The northern tribes well know it ; and know me.'

Said Media, ' Yet if——'

' No more ! another word, and, king as thou art, thou shalt be dungeoned :—here, there is such a law ; thou art not among the northern tribes.'

' And this is freedom ! ' murmured Media ; ' when heaven's own voice is throttled. And were these serfs to rise, and fight for it ; like dogs, they would be hunted down by her pretended sons ! '

' Pray, heaven ! ' cried Yoomy, ' they may yet find a way to loose their bonds without one drop of blood. But hear me, Oro ! were there no other way, and should their masters not relent, all honest hearts must cheer this tribe of Hamo on ; though they cut their chains with blades thrice edged, and gory to the haft ! 'Tis right to fight for freedom, whoever be the thrall.'

' These South savannahs may yet prove battlefields,' said Mohi, gloomily, as we retraced our steps.

' Be it,' said Yoomy. ' Oro will van the right.'

' Not always has it proved so,' said Babbalanja. ' Oft-times, the right fights single-handed against the world ; and Oro champions none. In all things, man's own battles man himself must fight. Yoomy : so far as feeling goes, your sympathies are not more hot than mine ; but for these serfs you would cross spears ; yet, I would not. Better present woes for some, than future woes for all.'

' No need to fight,' cried Yoomy, ' to liberate that tribe of Hamo instantly ; a way may be found, and no irretrievable evil ensue.'

' Point it out, and be blessed, Yoomy.'

' That is for Vivenza ; but the head is dull, where the heart is cold.'

' My lord,' said Babbalanja, ' you have startled us by

your kingly sympathy for suffering ; say thou, then, in
what wise manner it shall be relieved.'

' That is for Vivenza,' said Media.

' Mohi, you are old : speak thou.'

' Let Vivenza speak,' said Mohi.

' Thus, then, we all agree ; and weeping, all but echo
hard-hearted Nulli. Tears are not swords ; and wrongs
seem almost natural as rights. For the righteous to
suppress an evil is sometimes harder than for others to
uphold it. Humanity cries out against this vast enormity:
—not one man knows a prudent remedy. Blame not,
then, the North ; and wisely judge the South. Ere, as a
nation, they became responsible, this thing was planted
in their midst. Such roots strike deep. Place to-day
those serfs in Dominora ; and with them, all Vivenza's
past ;—and serfs, for many years, in Dominora, they would
be. Easy is it to stand afar and rail. All men are censors
who have lungs. We can say, the stars are wrongly
marshalled. Blind men say the sun is blind. A thousand
muscles wag our tongues ; though our tongues were
housed, that they might have a home. Whoso is free
from crime, let him cross himself—but hold his cross upon
his lips. That he is not bad, is not of him. Potter's clay
and wax are all moulded by hands invisible. The soil
decides the man. And, ere birth, man wills not to be
born here or there. These southern tribes have grown
up with this thing ; bondwomen were their nurses, and
bondmen serve them still. Nor are all their serfs such
wretches as those we saw. Some seem happy : yet not
as men. Unmanned, they know not what they are. And
though, of all the South, Nulli must stand almost alone in
his insensate creed ; yet, to all wrongdoers, custom backs
the sense of wrong. And if to every Mardian, conscience
be the awarder of its own doom ; then, of these tribes,
many shall be found exempted from the least penalty of

this sin. But sin it is, no less ;—a blot, foul as the crater-pool of hell ; it puts out the sun at noon ; it parches all fertility ; and, conscience or no conscience—ere he die—let every master who wrenches bond-babe from mother, that the nipple tear ; unwreathes the arms of sisters ; or cuts the holy unity in twain ; till apart fall man and wife, like one bleeding body cleft :—let that master thrice shrive his soul ; take every sacrament ; on his bended knees give up the ghost ;—yet shall he die despairing ; and live again, to die forever damned. The future is all hieroglyphics. Who may read ? But, methinks the great laggard Time must now march up apace, and somehow befriend these thralls. It cannot be, that misery is perpetually entailed ; though, in a land proscribing primogeniture, the first-born and last of Hamo's tribe must still succeed to all their sires' wrongs. Yes : Time—all-healing Time—Time, great philanthropist !—Time must befriend these thralls ! '

' Oro grant it ! ' cried Yoomy, ' and let Mardi say, amen ! '

' Amen ! amen ! amen ! ' cried echoes echoing echoes.

We traversed many of these southern vales ; but as in Dominora,—so, throughout Vivenza, North and South,—Yillah harboured not.

CHAPTER LIX

THEY CONVERSE OF THE MOLLUSCA, KINGS, TOADSTOOLS, AND OTHER MATTERS

ONCE more embarking, we gained Vivenza's south-western side ; and there beheld vast swarms of labourers discharging from canoes great loads of earth ; which they tossed upon the beach.

' It is true, then,' said Media, ' that these freemen are engaged in digging down other lands, and adding them to their own, piece-meal. And this, they call extending their dominions agriculturally, and peaceably.'

' My lord, they pay a price for every canoe load,' said Mohi.

' Ay, old man, holding the spear in one hand, and striking the bargain with the other.'

' Yet charge it not upon all Vivenza,' said Babbalanja. ' Some of her tribes are hostile to these things : and when their countrymen fight for land, are only warlike in opposing war.'

' And therein, Babbalanja, is involved one of those anomalies in the condition of Vivenza,' said Media, ' which I can hardly comprehend. How comes it, that with so many things to divide them, the valley-tribes still keep their mystic league intact ? '

' All plain, it is because the model, whence they derive their union, is one of nature's planning. My lord, have you ever observed the mysterious federation subsisting among the mollusca of the Tunicata order,—in other words, a species of cuttle-fish, abounding at the bottom of the lagoon ? '

'Yes : in clear weather about the reefs, I have beheld them time and again : but never with an eye to their political condition.'

'Ah ! my lord king, we should not cut off the nervous communication between our eyes and our cerebellums.'

'What were you about to say concerning the Tunicata order of mollusca, sir philosopher ? '

'My very honourable lord, I hurry to conclude. They live in a compound structure ; but though connected by membranous canals, freely communicating throughout the league—each member has a heart and stomach of its own ; provides and digests its own dinners ; and grins and bears its own gripes, without imparting the same to its neighbours. But if a prowling shark touches one member, it ruffles all. Precisely thus now with Vivenza. In that confederacy, there are as many consciences as tribes ; hence, if one member on its own behalf assumes aught afterward repudiated, the sin rests on itself alone; is not participated.'

'A very subtle explanation, Babbalanja. You must allude, then, to those recreant tribes ; which, while in their own eyes presenting a sublime moral spectacle to Mardi,—in King Bello's, do but present a hopeless example of bad debts. And these, the tribes that boast of boundless wealth.'

'Most true, my lord. But Bello errs when for this thing he stigmatises all Vivenza, as a unity.'

'Babbalanja, you yourself are made up of members :— then, if you be sick of a lumbago,—'tis not *you* that are unwell ; but your spine.'

'As you will, my lord. I have said. But to speak no more on that head—what sort of a sensation, think you, life is to such creatures as those mollusca ? '

'Answer your own question, Babbalanja.'

'I will ; but first tell me what sort of a sensation life is to you, yourself, my lord.'

'Pray answer that along with the other, Azzageddi.'

'Directly ; but tell me, if you will, my lord, what sort of a sensation life is to a toadstool.'

'Pray, Babbalanja, put all three questions together ; and then, do what you have often done before,—pronounce yourself a lunatic.'

'My lord, I beseech you, remind me not of that fact so often. It is true, but annoying. Nor will any wise man call another a fool.'

'Do you take me for a mere man, then, Babbalanja, that you talk to me thus ? '

'My demi-divine lord and master, I was deeply concerned at your indisposition last night :—may a loving subject inquire, whether his prince is completely recovered from the effect of those guavas ? '

'Have a care, Azzageddi ; you are far too courteous to be civil. But proceed.'

'I obey. In kings, mollusca, and toadstools, life is one thing and the same. The philosopher Dumdi pronounces it a certain febral vibration of organic parts, operating upon the *vis inertiae* of unorganised matter. But Bardianna says nay. Hear him : "Who put together this marvellous mechanism of mine ; and wound it up, to go for threescore years and ten ; when it runs out, and strikes Time's hours no more ? And what is it, that daily and hourly renews, and by a miracle creates in me my flesh and my blood ? What keeps up the perpetual telegraphic communication between my outpost toes and digits, and that domed grandee up aloft, my brain ?—It is not I ; nor you ; nor he ; nor it. No ; when I place my hand to that king muscle my heart, I am appalled. I feel the great God himself at work in me. Oro is life." '

'And what is death ? ' demanded Media.

'Death, my lord !—it is the deadest of all things.'

CHAPTER LX

WHEREIN THAT GALLANT GENTLEMAN AND DEMI-GOD,
KING MEDIA SCEPTRE IN HAND, THROWS HIMSELF
INTO THE BREACH

SAILING south from Vivenza, not far from its coast, we
passed a cluster of islets, green as new-fledged grass ; and
like the mouths of floating cornucopias, their margins
brimmed over upon the brine with flowers. On some,
grew stately roses ; on others stood twin-pillars ; across
others, tri-hued rainbows rested.

Cried Babbalanja, pointing to the last, ' Franko's pledge
of peace ! with that she loudly vaunts she 'll span the
reef !—Strike out all hues but red,—and the token 's nearer
truth.'

All these isles were prolific gardens ; where King Bello
and the Princes of Porpheero grew their most delicious
fruits,—nectarines and grapes.

But, though hard by, Vivenza owned no garden here ;
yet longed and lusted ; and her hottest tribes oft roundly
swore to root up all roses the half-reef over ; pull down
all pillars ; and dissolve all rainbows. ' Mardi's half is
ours,' said they. Stand back, invaders ! Full of
vanity ; and mirroring themselves in the future ; they
deemed all reflected there, their own.

'Twas now high noon.

' Methinks the sun grows hot,' said Media, retreating
deeper under the canopy. ' Ho ! Vee-Vee ; have you no
cooling beverage ? none of that golden wine distilled from
torrid grapes, and then sent northward to be cellared in an

iceberg ? That wine was placed among our stores.
Search, search the crypt, little Vee-Vee ! Ha, I see it !—
that yellow gourd !—Come : drag it forth, my boy.
Let 's have the amber cups : so : pass them round ;—fill
all ! Taji ! my demi-god, up heart ! Old Mohi, my babe,
may you live ten thousand centuries ! Ah ! this way you
mortals have of dying out at threescore years and ten is
but a craven habit. So, Babbalanja ! may you never die.
Yoomy ! my sweet poet, may you live to sing to me in
Paradise. Ha, ha ! would that we floated in this glorious
stuff, instead of this pestilent brine.—Hark ye ! were I
to make a Mardi now, I 'd have every continent a huge
haunch of venison ; every ocean a wine-vat ! I 'd stock
every cavern with choice old spirits, and make three
surplus suns to ripen the grapes all the year round.
Let 's drink to that !—Brimmers ! So : may the next
Mardi that 's made be one entire grape ; and mine the
squeezing ! '

'Look, look ! my lord,' cried Yoomy, ' what a glorious
shore we pass.'

Sallying out into the high golden noon, with golden-
beaming goblets suspended, we gazed.

'This must be Kolumbo of the South,' said Mohi.

It was a long, hazy reach of land ; piled up in terraces,
traced here and there with rushing streams, that worked
up gold dust alluvian, and seemed to flash over pebbled
diamonds. Heliotropes, sunflowers, marigolds gemmed,
or starred the violet meads, and vassal-like, still sunward
bowed their heads. The rocks were pierced with grottoes,
blazing with crystals, many-tinted.

It was a land of mints and mines ; its east a ruby ; west
a topaz. Inland, the woodlands stretched an ocean,
bottomless with foliage ; its green surges bursting through
cable-vines ; like Xerxes' brittle chains which vainly
sought to bind the Hellespont. Hence flowed a tide of

forest sounds ; of parrots, paroquets, macaws ; blent with
the howl of jaguars, hissing of anacondas, chattering of
apes, and herons screaming.

Out from those depths up rose a stream.

The land lay basking in the world's round torrid brisket,
hot with solar fire.

' No need here to land,' cried Yoomy, ' Yillah lurks
not here.'

' Heat breeds life, and sloth, and rage,' said Babbalanja.
' Here live bastard tribes and mongrel nations ; wrangling
and murdering to prove their freedom.—Refill, my
lord.'

' Methinks, Babbalanja, you savour of the mysterious
parchment, in Vivenza read :—Ha ? Yes, philosopher,
these are the men, who toppled castles to make way for
hovels ; these, they who fought for freedom, but find it
despotism to rule themselves. These, Babbalanja, are of
the race to whom a tyrant would prove a blessing.' So
saying he drained his cup.

' My lord, that last sentiment decides the authorship of
the scroll. But, with deference, tyrants seldom can prove
blessings ; inasmuch as evil seldom eventuates in good.
Yet will these people soon have a tyrant over them, if long
they cleave to war. Of many javelins, one must prove a
sceptre ; of many helmets, one a crown. It is but in the
wearing.—Refill, my lord.'

' Fools, fools ! ' cried Media, ' these tribes hate us kings ;
yet know not that Peace is War against all kings. We
seldom are undone by spears, which are our ministers.—
This wine is strong.'

' Ha, now 's the time ! In his cups learn kingcraft from
a king. Ay, ay, my lord, your royal order will endure, so
long as men will fight. Break the spears, and free the
nations. Kings reap the harvests that wave on battlefields. And oft you kings do snatch the aloe-flower,

whose slow blossoming mankind watches for a hundred years.—Say on, my lord.'

'All this I know ; and, therefore, rest content. My children's children will be kings ; though, haply, called by other titles. Mardi grows fastidious in names : we royalties will humour it. The steers would burst their yokes, but have not hands. The whole herd rears and plunges, but soon will bow again : the old, old way ! '

'Yet, in Porpheero, strong sceptres have been wrested from anointed hands. Mankind seems in arms.'

'Let them arm on. They hate us :—good ;—they always have ; yet still we 've reigned, son after sire. Sometimes they slay us, Babbalanja ; pour out our marrow, as I this wine ; but they spill no kinless blood. 'Twas justly held of old, that but to touch a monarch was to strike at Oro.—Truth. The palest vengeance is a royal ghost ; and regicides but father slaves. Thrones, not sceptres, have been broken. Mohi, what of the past ? Has it not ever proved so ? '

'Pardon, my lord ; the times seem changed. 'Tis held, that demi-gods no more rule by right divine. In Vivenza's land, they swear the last kings now reign in Mardi.'

'Is the last day at hand, old man ? Mohi, your beard is gray ; but, Yoomy, listen. When you die, look around ; mark then if any mighty change be seen. Old kingdoms may be on the wane ; but new dynasties advance. Though revolutions rise to high spring-tide, monarchs will still drown hard ;—monarchs survived the Flood ! '

'Are all our dreams, then, vain ? ' sighed Yoomy. 'Is this no dawn of day that streaks the crimson East ! Naught but the false and flickering lights which sometimes mock Aurora in the north ! Ah, man, my brother ! have all martyrs for thee bled in vain ; in vain we poets sang, and prophets spoken ? Nay, nay ; great Mardi, helmed and mailed, strikes at Oppression's shield, and challenges to battle ! Oro will defend the right, and royal crests must roll.'

' Thus, Yoomy, ages since, you mortal poets sang ; but the world may not be moved from out the orbit in which first it rolled. On the map that charts the spheres, Mardi is marked " the world of kings." Round centuries on centuries have wheeled by :—has all this been its nonage ? Now, when the rocks grow gray, does man first sprout his beard ? Or, is your golden time, your equinoctial year, at hand, that your race fast presses toward perfection ; and every hand grasps at a sceptre, that kings may be no more ? '

' But free Vivenza ! Is she not the star, that must, ere long, lead up the constellations, though now unrisen ? No kings are in Vivenza ; yet, spite her thralls, in that land seems more of good than elsewhere. Our hopes are not wild dreams : Vivenza cheers our hearts. She is a rainbow to the isles ! '

' Ay, truth it is, that in Vivenza they have prospered. But thence it comes not, that all men may be as they. Are all men of one heart and brain ; one bone and sinew ? Are all nations sprung of Dominora's loins ? Or, has Vivenza yet proved her creed ? Yoomy ! the years that prove a man, prove not a nation. But two kings' reigns have passed since Vivenza was a monarch's. Her climacteric is not come ; hers is not yet a nation's manhood even ; though now in childhood, she anticipates her youth, and lusts for empire like any czar. Yoomy ! judge not yet. Time hath tales to tell. Many books, and many long, long chapters, are wanting to Vivenza's history ; and what history but is full of blood ? '

' There stop, my lord,' said Babbalanja, ' nor aught predict. Fate laughs at prophets ; and of all birds, the raven is a liar ! '

CHAPTER LXI

THEY ROUND THE STORMY CAPE OF CAPES

LONG leagues, for weary days, we voyaged along that coast, till we came to regions where we multiplied our mantles.

The sky grew overcast. Each a night, black storm-clouds swept the wintry sea ; and like Sahara caravans, which leave their sandy wakes—so, thick and fleet, slanted the scud behind. Through all this rack and mist, ten thousand foam-flaked dromedary-humps uprose.

Deep among those panting, moaning fugitives, the three canoes raced on.

And now, the air grew nipping cold. The clouds shed off their fleeces ; a snow-hillock, each canoe ; our beards, white-frosted.

And so, as seated in our shrouds, we sailed in among great mountain passes of ice-isles ; from icy ledges scaring shivering seals, and white bears musical with icicles jingling from their shaggy ermine.

Far and near, in towering ridges, stretched the glassy Andes ; with their own frost shuddering through all their domes and pinnacles. Ice-splinters rattled down the cliffs, and seethed into the sea.

Broad away, in amphitheatres undermined by currents, whole cities of ice-towers, in crashes, toward one centre, fell.—In their earthquakes, Lisbon and Lima never saw the like. Churned and broken in the boiling tide, they swept off amain ;—over and over rolling ; like porpoises to vessels tranced in calms, bringing down the gale.

At last, rounding an antlered headland, that seemed a moose at bay—ere long, we launched upon blue lake-like waters, serene as Windermere, or Horicon. Thus, from the boisterous storms of youth, we glide upon senility.

But as we northward voyaged, another aspect wore the sea.

In far-off, endless vistas, colonnades of water-spouts were seen : all heaven's dome upholding on their shafts : and bright forms gliding up and down within. So at Luz, in his strange vision, Jacob saw the angels.

A boundless cave of stalactites, it seemed ; the cloud-born vapours downward spiralling, till they met the whirlpool-column from the sea ; then, uniting, over the waters stalked, like ghosts of gods. Or midway sundered —down, sullen, sunk the watery half ; and far up into heaven was drawn the vapoury. As, at death, we mortals part in twain ; our earthy half still here abiding ; but our spirits flying whence they came.

In good time we gained the thither side of great Kolumbo of the South ; and sailing on, long waited for the day ; and wondered at the darkness.

' What steadfast clouds ! ' cried Yoomy, ' yonder ! far aloft : that ridge, with many points ; it fades below, but shows a faint white crest.'

' Not clouds, but mountains,' said Babbalanja, ' the vast spine that traverses Kolumbo ; spurring off in ribs that nestle loamy valleys, veined with silver streams, and silver ores.'

It was a long, embattled line of pinnacles. And high posted in the East, those thousand bucklered peaks stood forth, and breasted back the dawn. Before their purple bastions bold, Aurora long arrayed her spears, and clashed her golden shells. The summons dies away. But now

her lancers charge the steep, and gain its crest aglow ;—
their glittering spears and blazoned shields triumphant
in the morn.

But ere that sight, we glided on for hours in twilight ;
when, on those mountains' farther side, the hunters must
have been abroad, morning glories all astir.

CHAPTER LXII

THEY ENCOUNTER GOLD HUNTERS

Now, northward coasting along Kolumbo's western shore, whence came the same wild forest-sounds, as from the eastern ; and where we landed not, to seek among those wrangling tribes ;—after many, many days, we spied prow after prow, before the wind all northward bound : sails widespread, and paddles plying : scaring the fish from before them.

Their inmates answered not our earnest hail.

But as they sped, with frantic glee, in one long chorus thus they sang :—

> We rovers bold,
> To the land of Gold,
> Over bowling billows are gliding :
> Eager to toil,
> For the golden spoil,
> And every hardship biding.
> See ! See !
> Before our prows' resistless dashes,
> The gold-fish fly in golden flashes !
> 'Neath a sun of gold,
> We rovers bold,
> On the golden land are gaining ;
> And every night,
> We steer aright,
> By golden stars unwaning !
> All fires burn a golden glare :
> No locks so bright as golden hair !

All orange groves have golden gushings :
All mornings dawn with golden flushings !
In a shower of gold, say fables old,
A maiden was won by the god of gold !
　In golden goblets wine is beaming :
　On golden couches kings are dreaming !
　The Golden Rule dries many tears !
　The Golden Number rules the spheres !
Gold, gold it is, that sways the nations :
Gold ! gold ! the centre of all rotations !
　On golden axles worlds are turning :
　With phosphorescence seas are burning !
　All fire-flies flame with golden gleamings :
　Gold-hunters' hearts with golden dreamings !
　With golden arrows kings are slain :
　With gold we 'll buy a freeman's name !
In toilsome trades, for scanty earnings,
At home we 've slaved, with stifled yearnings :
No light ! no hope ! Oh, heavy woe !
When nights fled fast, and days dragged slow.
　　　But joyful now, with eager eye,
　　　Fast to the Promised Land we fly :
　　　　Where in deep mines,
　　　　The treasure shines ;
　　　Or down in beds of golden streams,
　　　The gold-flakes glance in golden gleams !
　　　　How we long to sift,
　　　　That yellow drift !
　　　Rivers ! Rivers ! cease your going !
　　　　Sand-bars ! rise, and stay the tide !
　　　'Till we 've gained the golden flowing ;
　　　　And in the golden haven ride !

' Quick, quick, my lord,' cried Yoomy, ' let us follow
them ; and from the golden waters where she lies, our
Yillah may emerge.'

' No, no,' said Babbalanja,—' no Yillah there !—from
yonder promised land fewer seekers will return than go.

Under a gilded guise, happiness is still their instinctive
aim. But vain, Yoomy, to snatch at happiness. Of that
we may not pluck and eat. It is the fruit of our own toilsome planting ; slow it grows, nourished by many tears,
and all our earnest tendings. Yet ere it ripen, frosts may
nip ;—and then, we plant again ; and yet again. Deep,
Yoomy, deep, true treasure lies ; deeper than all Mardi's
gold, rooted to Mardi's axis. But unlike gold, it lurks in
every soil,—all Mardi over. With golden pills and
potions is sickness warded off ?—the shrunken veins of
age, dilated with new wine of youth ? Will gold the
heartache cure ? turn toward us hearts estranged ? will
gold on solid centres empires fix ? 'Tis toil world-wasted
to toil in mines. Were all the isles gold globes, set in a
quicksilver sea, all Mardi were then a desert. Gold is the
only poverty ; of all glittering ills the direst. And that
man might not impoverish himself thereby, Oro hath
hidden it, with all other banes,—saltpetre and explosives,
deep in mountain bowels, and river-beds. But man still
will mine for it ; and mining, dig his doom.—Yoomy,
Yoomy !—she we seek lurks not in the Golden Hills ! '
    ' Lo, a vision ! ' cried Yoomy, his hands wildly passed
across his eyes. ' A vast and silent bay, belted by silent
villages :—gaunt dogs howling over grassy thresholds at
stark corpses of old age and infancy ; gray hairs mingling
with sweet flaxen curls ; fields, with turned furrows,
choked with briers ; arbour-floors strewn over with hatchet-
helves, rotting in the iron ; a thousand paths, marked
with footprints, all inland leading, none villageward ; and
strewn with traces, as of a flying host. On : over forest
—hill and dale—and lo ! the golden region ! After the
glittering spoil, by strange river-margins, and beneath im-
pending cliffs, thousands delve in quicksands ; and,
sudden, sink in graves of their own making : with gold
dust mingling their own ashes. Still deeper, in more

solid ground, other thousands slave ; and pile their earth so high, they gasp for air, and die ; their comrades mounting on them, and delving still, and dying—grave pile on grave ! Here, one haggard hunter murders another in his pit ; and murdering, himself is murdered by a third. Shrieks and groans ! cries and curses ! It seems a golden hell ! With many camels, a sleek stranger comes—pauses before the shining heaps, and shows *his* treasures :' yams and bread-fruit. " Give, give," the famished hunters cry—" a thousand shekels for a yam !— a prince's ransom for a meal !—Oh, stranger ! on our knees we worship thee :—take, take our gold ; but let us live ! " Yams are thrown them ; and they fight. Then he who toiled not, dug not, slaved not, straight loads his caravans with gold ; regains the beach, and swift embarks for home. " Home ! home ! " the hunters cry, with bursting eyes. " With this bright gold, could we but join our waiting wives, who wring their hands on distant shores, all then were well. But we cannot fly ; our prows lie rotting on the beach. Ah ! home ! thou only happiness !—better thy silver earnings than all these golden findings. Oh, bitter end to all our hopes—we die in golden graves." '

CHAPTER LXIII

THEY SEEK THROUGH THE ISLES OF PALMS ; AND PASS THE ISLES OF MYRRH

Now, our prows we turned due west, across the blue lagoon.

Soon, no land appeared. Far as the eye could sweep, one azure plain ; all over flaked with foamy fleeces :—a boundless flock upon a boundless mead !

Again, all changed. Like stars in multitude, bright islets multiplied around. Emerald-green, they dotted shapes fantastic : circles, arcs, and crescents ;—atolls all, or coral carcanets, begemmed and flashing in the sun.

By these we glided, group after group ; and through the foliage, spied sweet forms of maidens, like Eves in Edens ere the Fall, or Proserpines in Ennas. Artless airs came from the shore ; and from the censer-swinging roses, a bloom, as if from Hebe's cheek.

'Here, at last, we find sweet Yillah !' murmured Yoomy. 'Here must she lurk in innocence ! Quick ! Let us land and search.'

'If here,' said Babbalanja, 'Yillah will not stay our coming, but fly before us through the groves. Wherever a canoe is beached, see you not the palm-trees pine ? Not so, where never keel yet smote the strand. In mercy, let us fly from hence. I know not why, but our breath here must prove a blight.'

These regions passed, we came to savage islands, where the glittering coral seemed bones imbedded, bleaching in the sun. Savage men stood naked on the strand, and brandished uncouth clubs, and gnashed their teeth like boars.

The full red moon was rising ; and in long review there passed before it phantom shapes of victims, led bound to altars through the groves. Death-rattles filled the air. But a cloud descended, and all was gloom.

Again blank water spread before us ; and after many days there came a gentle breeze, fraught with all spicy breathings ; cinnamon aromas ; and in the rose-flushed evening air, like glowworms, glowed the islets, where this incense burned.

' Sweet isles of myrrh ! oh crimson groves,' cried Yoomy. ' Woe, woe 's your fate ! your brightness and your bloom, like musky fire-flies, double-lure to death ! On ye the nations prey like bears that gorge themselves with honey.'

Swan-like, our prows sailed in among these isles ; and oft we landed ; but in vain ; and leaving them, we still pursued the setting sun.

CHAPTER LXIV

CONCENTRIC, INWARD, WITH MARDI'S REEF, THEY LEAVE THEIR WAKE AROUND THE WORLD

WEST, West ! West, West ! Whitherward point Hope and prophet-fingers ; whitherward, at sunset, kneel all worshippers of fire ; whitherward in mid-ocean, the great whales turn to die ; whitherward face all the Moslem dead in Persia ; whitherward lie Heaven and Hell !—West, West ! Whitherward mankind and empires—flocks, caravans, armies, navies ; worlds, suns, and stars all wend !—West, West !—Óh boundless boundary ! Eternal goal ! Whitherward rush, in thousand worlds, ten thousand thousand keels ! Beacon, by which the universe is steered !—Like the north star, attracting all needles ! Unattainable forever ; but forever leading to great things this side thyself !—Hive of all sunsets !—Gabriel's pinions may not overtake thee !

Over balmy waves, still westward sailing ! From dawn till eve the bright, bright days sped on, chased by the gloomy nights ; and, in glory dying, lent their lustre to the starry skies. So, long the radiant dolphins fly before the sable sharks ; but, seized, and torn in flames—die, burning :—their last splendour left, in sparkling scales that float along the sea.

Cymbals, drums and psalteries ! the air beats like a pulse with music !—High land ! high land ! and moving lights, and painted lanterns !—What grand shore is this ?

' Reverence we render thee, Old Orienda ! ' cried Media,

with bared brow. ' Original of all empires and emperors !
—a crowned king salutes thee ! '

' Mardi's fatherland ! ' cried Mohi, ' grandsire of the
nations,—hail ! '

' All hail ! ' cried Yoomy. ' Kings and sages hither
coming, should come like palmers,—scrip and staff ! Oh
Orienda ! thou wert our East, where first dawned song and
science, with Mardi's primal mornings ! But now, how
changed ! the dawn of light become a darkness, which we
kindle with the gleam of spears ! On the world's ancestral
hearth, we spill our brothers' blood ! '

' Herein,' said Babbalanja, ' have many distant tribes
proved parricidal. In times gone by, Luzianna hither sent
her proas ; Franko, her scores of captains ; and the
Dykemen, their peddler hosts, with yardstick spears !
But thou, oh Bello ! lord of the empire lineage ! Noah of
the moderns. Sire of the long line of nations yet in germ !
—thou, Bello, and thy locust armies, are the present
curse of Orienda. Down ancient streams, from holy
plains, in rafts thy murdered float ! The pestilence that
thins thy armies here is bred of corpses made by thee.
Maramma's priests, thy pious heralds, loud proclaim that
of all pagans, Orienda's most resist the truth !—ay ! vain
all pious voices, that speak from clouds of war ! The
march of conquest through wild provinces may be the
march of Mind ; but not the march of Love.'

' Thou, Bello ! ' cried Yoomy, ' wouldst wrest the
crook from Alma's hand, and place in it a spear. But vain
to make a conqueror of him, who put off the purple when
he came to Mardi ; and declining gilded mitres, entered
the nations meekly on an ass.'

' Oh, curse of commerce ! ' cried Babbalanja, ' that it
barters souls for gold. Bello ! with opium thou wouldst
drug this land, and murder it in sleep !—And what boot
thy conquests here ? Seed sown by spears but seldom

springs ; and harvests reaped thereby are poisoned by the
sickle's edge.'

Yet on, and on we coasted ; counting not the days.

' Oh, folds and flocks of nations ! dusky tribes innumerable ! ' cried Yoomy, ' camped on plains and steppes ; on
thousand mountains, worshipping the stars ; in thousand
valleys, offering up firstfruits, till all the forests seem in
flames ;—where, in fire, the widow's spirit mounts to meet
her lord !—Oh, Orienda, in thee 'tis vain to seek our
Yillah ! '

' How dark as death the night ! ' said Mohi, shaking the
dew from his braids, ' the heavens blaze not here with
stars, as over Dominora's land, and broad Vivenza.'

One only constellation was beheld ; but every star was
brilliant as the one that promises the morning.   That
constellation was the Crux-Australis,—the badge, and
type of Alma.

And now, south-west we steered, till another island vast
was reached—Hamora ! far trending toward the Antarctic Pole.

Coasting on by barbarous beaches, where painted men,
with spears, charged on all attempts to land, at length we
rounded a mighty bluff,—lit by a beacon ;   and heard a
bugle call :—Bello's ! hurrying to their quarters, the
World-End's garrison.

Here, the sea rolled high, in mountain surges : mid
which we toiled and strained, as if ascending cliffs of
Caucasus.

But not long thus. As when from howling Rhœtian
heights, the traveller spies green Lombardy below, and
downward rushes toward that pleasant plain ; so, sloping
from long rolling swells, at last we launched upon the
calm lagoon.

But as we northward sailed, once more the storm-trump
blew, and charger-like, the seas ran mustering to the call ;

and in battalions crouched before a towering rock, far
distant from the main. No moon, eclipsed in Egypt's
skies, looked half so lone. But from out that darkness,
on the loftiest peak, Bello's standard waved.

' Oh rifled tomb ! ' cried Babbalanja. ' Wherein lay
the Mars and Moloch of our times, whose constellated
crown was gemmed with diadems. Thou god of war !
who didst seem the devouring Beast of the Apocalypse ;
casting so vast a shadow over Mardi, that yet it lingers in
old Franko's vale ; where still they start at thy tremendous ghost ; and, late, have hailed a phantom, king !
Almighty hero-spell ! that after the lapse of half a century
can so bewitch all hearts ! But one drop of hero-blood
will deify a fool.

' Franko ! thou wouldst be free ; yet thy free homage is
to the buried ashes of a king ; thy first choice, the exalta-
tion of his race. In furious fires, thou burn'st Ludwig's
throne ; and over thy new-made chieftain's portal, in
golden letters print'st—" The Palace of our Lord ! " In
thy New Dispensation, thou cleavest to the exploded Law.
And on Freedom's altar—ah, I fear—still, may slay thy
hecatombs. But Freedom turns away ; she is sick with
burnt blood of offerings. Other rituals she loves ; and
like Oro, unseen herself, would be worshipped only by
invisibles. Of long-drawn cavalcades, pompous proces-
sions, frenzied banners, mystic music, marching nations,
she will none. Oh, may thy peaceful future, Franko,
sanctify thy bloody past. Let not history say : " To her
old gods she turned again." '

This rocky islet passed, the sea went down ; once more
we neared Hamora's western shore. In the deep darkness,
here and there, its margin was lit up by foam-white,
breaking billows rolled over from Vivenza's strand, and
down from northward Dominora ; marking places where
light was breaking in, upon the interior's jungle-gloom.

In heavy sighs, the night-winds from shore came over us.

'Ah, vain to seek sweet Yillah here,' cried Yoomy.—
'Poor land! curst of man, not Oro! how thou faintest for
thy children, torn from thy soil to till a stranger's.
Vivenza! did these winds not spend their plaints, ere
reaching thee, thy every vale would echo them. Oh,
tribe of Hamo! thy cup of woe so brims, that soon it must
overflow upon the land which holds ye thralls. No misery
born of crime, but spreads and poisons wide. Suffering
hunteth sin, as the gaunt hound the hare, and tears it in
the greenest brakes.'

Still on we sailed : and after many tranquil days and
nights, a storm came down, and burst its thousand bombs.
The lightnings forked and flashed ; the waters boiled ;
our three prows lifted themselves in supplication ; but the
billows smote them as they reared.

Said Babbalanja, bowing to the blast: 'Thus, oh
Vivenza! retribution works! Though long delayed, it
comes at last—Judgment, with all her bolts.'

Now, a current seized us, and like three darts our keels
sped eastward, through a narrow strait, far in, upon a
smooth expanse, an inland ocean, without a throb.

On our left, Porpheero's south-west point, a mighty rock,
long tiers of galleries within, deck on deck ; and flag-
staffs, like an admiral's masts : a line-of-battle ship, all
purple stone, and anchored in the sea. Here Bello's lion
crouched ; and, through a thousand port-holes, eyed the
world.

On our right, Hamora's northern shore gleamed thick
with crescents ; numerous as the crosses along the opposing strand.

'How vain to say that progress is the test of truth, my
lord,' said Babbalanja, ' when, after many centuries, those
crescents yet unwaning shine, and count a devotee for
every worshipper of yonder crosses. Truth and Merit

have other symbols than success ; and in this mortal race, all competitors may enter ; and the field is clear for all. Side by side, Lies run with Truths, and fools with wise ; but, like geometric lines, though they pierce infinity, never may they join.'

Over that tideless sea we sailed ; and landed right, and landed left ; but the maiden never found ; till, at last, we gained the water's limit ; and inland saw great pointed masses, crowned with halos.

' Granite continents,' cried Babbalanja, ' that seem created like the planets, not built with human hands. Lo, landmarks ! upon whose flanks Time leaves its traces, like old tide-rips of diluvian seas.'

As, after wandering round and round some purple dell, deep in a boundless prairie's heart, the baffled hunter plunges in ; then, despairing, turns once more to gain the open plain ; even so we seekers now curved round our keels ; and from that inland sea emerged. The universe again before us ; our quest, as wide.

CHAPTER LXV

SAILING ON

MORNING dawned upon the same mild, blue lagoon as erst ; and all the lands that we had passed, since leaving Piko's shore of spears, were faded from the sight.

Part and parcel of the Mardian isles, they formed a cluster by themselves ; like the Pleiades that shine in Taurus, and are eclipsed by the red splendour of his fiery eye, and the thick clusterings of the constellations round.

And as in Orion, to some old king-astronomer,—say, King of Rigel, or Betelguese,—this earth's four quarters show but four points afar ; so, seem they to terrestrial eyes, that broadly sweep the spheres.

And, as the sun, by influence divine, wheels through the Ecliptic ; threading Cancer, Leo, Pisces, and Aquarius ; so, by some mystic impulse am I moved, to this fleet progress, through the groups in white-reefed Mardi's zone.

Oh, reader, list ! I 've chartless voyaged. With compass and the lead, we had not found these Mardian Isles. Those who boldly launch, cast off all cables ; and turning from the common breeze, that 's fair for all, with their own breath fill their own sails. Hug the shore, naught new is seen ; and ' Land ho ! ' at last was sung, when a new world was sought.

That voyager steered his bark through seas untracked before ; ploughed his own path mid jeers ; though with a heart that oft was heavy with the thought that he might only be too bold, and grope where land was none.

So I.

And though essaying but a sportive sail, I was driven from my course by a blast resistless ; and ill-provided, young, and bowed to the brunt of things before my prime, still fly before the gale ;—hard have I striven to keep stout heart.

And if it harder be than e'er before to find new climes, when now our seas have oft been circled by ten thousand prows,—much more the glory !

But this new world here sought is stranger far than his, who stretched his vans from Palos.   It is the world of mind ; wherein the wanderer may gaze round, with more of wonder than Balboa's band roving through the golden Aztec glades.

But fiery yearnings their own phantom-future make, and deem it present.   So, if after all these fearful, fainting trances, the verdict be, the golden haven was not gained ; —yet, in bold quest thereof, better to sink in boundless deeps, than float on vulgar shoals ; and give me, ye gods, an utter wreck, if wreck I do.

CHAPTER LXVI

A FLIGHT OF NIGHTINGALES FROM YOOMY'S MOUTH

By noon, down came a calm.

'Oh Neeva! good Neeva! kind Neeva! thy sweet breath, dear Neeva!'

So from his shark's-mouth prayed little Vee-Vee to the god of Fair Breezes. And along they swept; till the three prows neighed to the blast; and pranced on their path like steeds of Crusaders.

Now, that this fine wind had sprung up; the sun riding joyously in the heavens; and the lagoon all tossed with white, flying manes; Media called upon Yoomy to ransack his whole assortment of songs :—warlike, amorous, and sentimental,—and regale us with something inspiring; for too long the company had been gloomy.

'Thy best,' he cried.

'Then will I e'en sing you a song, my lord, which is a song full of songs. I composed it long, long since, when Yillah yet bowered in Odo. Ere now, some fragments have been heard. Ah, Taji! in this my lay, live over again your happy hours. Some joys have thousand lives; can never die; for when they droop, sweet memories bind them up.—My lord, I deem these verses good; they came bubbling out of me, like live waters from a spring in a silver mine. And by your good leave, my lord, I have much faith in inspiration. Whoso sings is a seer.'

'Tingling is the test,' said Babbalanja. 'Yoomy, did you tingle, when that song was composing?'

'All over, Babbalanja.'

278

' From sole to crown ? '

' From finger to finger.'

' My life for it ! true poetry, then, my lord ! For this self-same tingling, I say, is the test.'

' And infused into a song,' cried Yoomy, ' it evermore causes it so to sparkle, vivify, and irradiate, that no son of man can repeat it without tingling himself. This very song of mine may prove what I say.'

' Modest youth ! ' sighed Media.

' Not more so, than sincere,' said Babbalanja. ' He who is frank will often appear vain, my lord. Having no guile, he speaks as freely of himself as of another ; and is just as ready to honour his own merits, even if imaginary, as to lament over undeniable deficiencies. Besides, such men are prone to moods, which to shallow-minded, un-sympathising mortals, make their occasional distrust of themselves appear but as a phase of self-conceit. Whereas, the man who, in the presence of his very friends, parades a barred and bolted front,—that man so highly prizes his sweet self, that he cares not to profane the shrine he worships, by throwing open its portals. He is locked up ; and Ego is the key. Reserve alone is vanity. But all mankind are egotists. The world revolves upon an I; and we upon ourselves ; for we are our own worlds :—all other men as strangers, from outlandish, distant climes, going clad in furs. Then, whate'er they be, let us show our worlds ; and not seek to hide from men what Oro knows.'

' Truth, my lord,' said Yoomy, ' but all this applies to men in mass ; not specially, to my poor craft. Of all mortals, we poets are most subject to contrary moods. Now, heaven over heaven in the skies ; now layer under layer in the dust. This, the penalty we pay for being what we are. But Mardi only sees, or thinks it sees, the tokens of our self-complacency : whereas, all our agonies operate unseen. Poets are only seen when they soar.'

'The song! the song!' cried Media. 'Never mind the metaphysics of genius.'

And Yoomy, thus clamorously invoked, hemmed thrice, tuning his voice for the air.

But here, be it said, that the minstrel was miraculously gifted with three voices; and, upon occasions, like a mocking-bird, was a concert of sweet sounds in himself. Had kind friends died, and bequeathed him their voices? But hark! in a low, mild tenor, he begins :—

Half-veiled above the hills, yet rosy bright,
   Stands fresh, and fair, the meek and blushing morn!
So Yillah looks! her pensive eyes the stars,
   That mildly beam from out her cheek's young dawn!

      But the still meek Dawn,
      Is not aye the form
      Of Yillah nor Morn!
        Soon rises the sun,
        Day's race to run:
      His rays abroad,
      Flash each a sword,—
        And merrily forth they flare!
        Sun-music in the air!
      So Yillah now rises and flashes!
      Rays shooting from out her long lashes,—
        Sun-music in the air!

      Her laugh! How it bounds!
      Bright cascade of sounds!
     Peal after peal, and ringing afar,—
     Ringing of waters, that silvery jar,
       From basin to basin fast falling!
       Fast falling, and shining, and streaming :—
     Yillah's bosom, the soft, heaving lake,
     Where her laughs at last dimple, and flake!

Oh, beautiful Yillah ! Thy step so free !—
  Fast fly the sea-ripples,
Revealing their dimples,
  When forth, thou hi'st to the frolicsome sea !

      All the stars laugh,
        When upward she looks :
      All the trees chat
        In their woody nooks :
      All the brooks sing ;
      All the caves ring ;
      All the buds blossom ;
        All the boughs bound ;
      All the birds carol ;
        And leaves turn round,
      Where Yillah looks !

  Light wells from her soul's deep sun,
  Causing many toward her to run !
  Vines to climb, and flowers to spring ;
  And youths their love by hundreds bring !

' Proceed, gentle Yoomy,' said Babbalanja.

' The meaning,' said Mohi.

' The sequel,' said Media.

' My lord, I have ceased in the middle ; the end is not yet.'

' Mysticism ! ' cried Babbalanja. ' What, minstrel ; must nothing ultimate come of all that melody ? no final and inexhaustible meaning ? nothing that strikes down into the soul's depths ; till, intent upon itself, it pierces in upon its own essence, and is resolved into its pervading original ; becoming a thing constituent of the all-embracing deific ; whereby we mortals become part and parcel of the gods ; our souls to them as thoughts ; and we privy to all things occult, ineffable, and sublime ? Then,

Yoomy, is thy song nothing worth ?   Alla-Malolla saith,
" That is no true, vital breath, which leaves no moisture
behind."   I mistrust thee, minstrel ! that thou hast not
yet been impregnated by the arcane mysteries ; that thou
dost not sufficiently ponder on the Adyta, the Monads, and
the Hyparxes ; the Dianoias, the Unical Hypostases, the
Gnostic powers of the Psychical Essence, and the Super-
mundane and Pleromatic Triads ; to say nothing of the
Abstract Noumenons.'

'Oro forbid !' cried Yoomy ; 'the very sound of thy
words affright me.'   Then, whispering to Mohi—' Is he
daft again ? '

' My brain is battered,' said Media.   ' Azzageddi ! you
must diet, and be bled.'

' Ah ! ' sighed Babbalanja, turning ; ' how little they
ween of the Rudimental Quincunxes, and the Hecatic
Spherula ! '

CHAPTER LXVII

THEY VISIT ONE DOXODOX

NEXT morning, we came to a deep green wood, slowly nodding over the waves ; its margin frothy-white with foam. A charming sight !

While delighted, all our paddlers gazed, Media, observing Babbalanja plunged in reveries, called upon him to awake ; asking what might so absorb him.

' Ah, my lord ! what seraphic sounds have ye driven from me ! '

' Sounds ! Sure, there 's naught heard but yonder murmuring surf ; what other sound heard you ? '

' The thrilling of my soul's monochord, my lord. But prick not your ears to hear it ; that divine harmony is overheard by the rapt spirit alone ; it comes not by the auditory nerves.'

' No more, Azzageddi ! No more of that. Look yonder ! '

' A most lovely wood, in truth. And methinks it is here the sage Doxodox, surnamed the Wise One, dwells.'

' Hark, I hear the hootings of his owls,' said Mohi.

' My lord, you must have read of him. He is said to have penetrated from the zoned, to the unzoned principles. Shall we seek him out, that we may hearken to his wisdom ? Doubtless he knows many things, after which we pant.'

The lagoon was calm, as we landed ; not a breath stirred the plumes of the trees ; and as we entered the voiceless shades, lifting his hand, Babbalanja whispered :

283

' This silence is a fit introduction to the portals of
Telestic lore. Somewhere, beneath this moss, lurks the
mystic stone Mnizuris ; whereby Doxodox hath attained
unto a knowledge of the ungenerated essences. Nightly,
he bathes his soul in archangelical circumlucencies. Oh,
Doxodox ! whip me the Strophalunian top ! Tell o'er
thy Jynges ! '

' Down, Azzageddi ! down ! ' cried Media. ' Behold :
there sits the Wise One ; now, for true wisdom ! '

From the voices of the party, the sage must have been
aware of our approach : but seated on a green bank, beneath the shade of a red mulberry, upon the boughs of
which many an owl was perched, he seemed intent
upon describing divers figures in the air, with a jet-black
wand.

Advancing with much deference and humility, Babbalanja saluted him.

' Oh wise Doxodox ! Drawn hither by thy illustrious
name, we seek admittance to thy innermost wisdom. Of
all Mardians, thou alone comprehendest those arcane
combinations, whereby to drag to day the most deftly
hidden things, present and to come. Thou knowest what
we are, and what we shall be. We beseech thee, evoke
thy Tselmns ! '

' Tetrads ; Pentads ; Hexads ; Heptads ; Ogdoads :—
meanest thou those ? '

' New terms all ! '

' Foiled at thy own weapons,' said Media.

' Then, if thou comprehendest not my nomenclature :—
how my science ? But let me test thee in the portico.—
Why is it, that as some things extend more remotely than
others ; so, Quadammodotatives are larger than Quali-
tatives ; forasmuch, as Quadammodotatives extend to
those things which include the Quadammodotatives
themselves.'

' Azzageddi has found his match,' said Media.

' Still posed, Babbalanja ? ' asked Mohi.

' At a loss, most truly ! But I beseech thee, wise Doxodox ! instruct me in thy dialectics, that I may embrace thy more recondite lore.'

' To begin then, my child :—all Dicibles reside in the mind.'

' But what are Dicibles ! ' said Media.

' Meanest thou, Perfect or Imperfect Dicibles ? '

' Any kind you please ;—but what are they ? '

' Perfect Dicibles are of various sorts : Interrogative ; Percontative ; Adjurative ; Optative ; Imprecative ; Execrative ; Substitutive ; Compellative ; Hypothetical ; and, lastly, Dubious.'

' Dubious enough ! Azzageddi ! forever, hereafter, hold thy peace.'

' Ah, my children ! I must go back to my Axioms.'

' And what are they ? ' said old Mohi.

' Of various sorts ; which, again, are diverse. Thus : my contrary axioms are Disjunctive, and Subdisjunctive ; and so, with the rest. So, too, in degree, with my Syllogisms.'

' And what of them ? '

' Did I not just hint what they were, my child ? I repeat, they are of various sorts : Connex, and Conjunct, for example.'

' And what of them ? ' persisted Mohi ; while Babbalanja, arms folded, stood serious and mute ; a sneer on his lip.

' As with other branches of my dialectics : so, too, in their way, with my Syllogisms. Thus : when I say,—If it be warm, it is not cold :—that's a simple Sumption. If I add, But it *is* warm :—that's an *As*sumption.'

' So called from the syllogist himself, doubtless,' said Mohi, stroking his beard.

' Poor ignorant babe ! no. Listen :—if, finally, I say,—
Therefore it is not cold :—that 's the final inference.'

' And a most triumphant one it is ! ' cried Babbalanja.
' Thrice profound, and sapient Doxodox ! Light of
Mardi ! and Beacon of the Universe ! didst ever hear of
the Shark-Syllogism ? '

' Though thy epithets be true, my child, I distrust thy
sincerity. I have not yet heard of the syllogism to which
thou referrest.'

' It was thus. A shark seized a swimmer by the leg ;
addressing him : " Friend, I will liberate you, if you
truly answer whether you think I purpose harm." Well
knowing that sharks seldom were magnanimous, he replied : " Kind sir, you mean me harm ; now go your
ways." " No, no ; my conscience forbids. Nor will I
falsify the words of so veracious a mortal. You were to
answer truly ; but you say I mean you harm :—so harm
it is :—here goes your leg." '

' Profane jester ! Wouldst thou insult me with thy
tomfoolery ? Begone—all of ye ! tramp ! pack ! I say :
away with ye ! ' and into the woods Doxodox himself
disappeared.

' Bravely done, Babbalanja ! ' cried Media. ' You
turned the corner to admiration.'

' I have hopes of our philosopher yet,' said Mohi.

' Outrageous impostor ! fool, dotard, oaf ! Did he
think to bejuggle me with his preposterous gibberish ?
And is this shallow phraseman the renowned Doxodox
whom I have been taught so highly to reverence ? Alas,
alas—Odonphi there is none ! '

' His fit again,' sighed Yoomy.

CHAPTER LXVIII

KING MEDIA DREAMS

THAT afternoon was melting down to eve ; all but Media broad awake ; yet all motionless, as the slumberer upon the purple mat. Sailing on, with open eyes, we slept the wakeful sleep of those who to the body only give repose, while the spirit still toils on, threading her mountain passes.

King Media's slumbers were like the helmed sentry's in the saddle. From them, he started like an antlered deer, bursting from out a copse. Some said he never slept ; that deep within himself he but intensified the hour ; or, leaving his crowned brow in marble quiet, unseen, departed to far-off councils of the gods. Howbeit, his lids never closed ; in the noonday sun, those crystal eyes, like diamonds, sparkled with a fixed light.

As motionless we thus reclined, Media turned and muttered : ' Brother gods, and demi-gods, it is not well. These mortals should have less or more. Among my subjects is a man, whose genius scorns the common theories of things ; but whose still mortal mind cannot fathom the ocean at his feet. His soul's a hollow, wherein he raves.'

' List, list,' whispered Yoomy—' our lord is dreaming ; and what a royal dream.'

' A very royal and imperial dream,' said Babbalanja ; ' he is arraigning me before high heaven ;—ay, ay ; in dreams, at least, he deems himself a demi-god.'

' Hist,' said Mohi—' he speaks again.'

'Gods and demi-gods! With one gesture all abysses we may disclose; and before this Mardi's eyes, evoke the shrouded time to come. Were this well? Like lost children groping in the woods, they falter through their tangled paths; and at a thousand angles, baffled, start upon each other. And even when they make an onward move, 'tis but an endless vestibule that leads to naught. In my own isle of Odo—Odo! Odo! How rules my viceroy there?—Down, down, ye madding mobs! Ho, spearmen, charge! By the firmament, but my halberdiers fly!'

'His dream has changed,' said Babbalanja. 'He is in Odo, whither his anxieties impel him.'

'Hist, hist,' said Yoomy.

'I leap upon the soil! Render thy account, Almanni! Where's my throne? Mohi, am I not a king? Do not thy chronicles record me? Yoomy, am I not the soul of some one glorious song? Babbalanja, speak.—Mohi! Yoomy!'

'What is it, my lord? thou dost but dream.'

Staring wildly; then calmly gazing round, Media smiled.

'Ha! how we royalties ramble in our dreams! I've told no secrets?'

'While he seemed to sleep, my lord spoke much,' said Mohi.

'I knew it not, old man; nor would now; but that ye tell me.'

'We dream not ourselves,' said Babbalanja, 'but the thing within us.'

'Ay?—good morrow, Azzageddi!—But come; no more dreams:—Vee-Vee! wine.'

And straight through that livelong night, immortal Media plied the can.

CHAPTER LXIX

Now suns rose, and set ; moons grew, and waned ; till, at last, the star that erewhile heralded the dawn, presaged the eve ; to us, sad token !—while deep within the deepest heart of Mardi's circle, we sailed from sea to sea ; and isle to isle ; and group to group ;—vast empires explored, and inland valleys, to their utmost heads ; and for every ray in heaven, beheld a king.

Needless to recount all that then befell ; what tribes and caravans we saw ; what vast horizons ; boundless plains ; and sierras, in their every intervale, a nation nestling.

Enough that still we roamed.

It was evening ; and as the red sun, magnified, launched into the wave, once more, from a wild strand, we launched our three canoes.

Soon, from her clouds, hooded Night, like a nun from a convent, drew nigh. Rustled her train, yet no spangles were there. But high on her brow, still shone her pale crescent ; haloed by bandelets—violet, red, and yellow. So looked the lone watcher through her rainbow-iris ; so sad, the night without stars.

The winds were laid ; the lagoon, still, as a prairie of an August noon.

' Let us dream out the calm,' said Media. ' One of ye paddlers, watch : Ho, companions ! who 's for Cathay ? '

Sleep reigned throughout the canoes, sleeping upon the waters. But nearer and nearer, low-creeping along, came mists and vapours, a thousand ; spotted with twinklings of will-o'-wisps from neighbouring shores. Dusky leopards, stealing on by crouches, those vapours seemed.

Hours silently passed. When startled by a cry, Taji sprang to his feet; against which something rattled; then, a quick splash! and a dark form bounded into the lagoon.

The dozing watcher had called aloud; and, about to stab, the assassin, dropping his stiletto, plunged.

Peering hard through those treacherous mists, two figures in a shallop, were espied; dragging another, dripping, from the brine.

'Foiled again, and foiled forever. No foe's corpse was I.'

As we gazed, in the gloom quickly vanished the shallop; ere ours could be reversed to pursue.

Then, from the opposite mists, glided a second canoe; and beneath the iris round the moon, shone now another: Hautia's flowery flag!

Vain to wave the syrens off; so still they came.

One waved a plant of sickly silver-green.

'The Midnight Tremmella!' cried Yoomy; 'the falling-star of flowers!—Still I come, when least foreseen; then, flee.'

The second waved a hemlock top, the spike just tapering to its final point. The third, a convolvulus, half-closed.

'The end draws nigh, and all thy hopes are waning.'

Then they proffered grapes.

But once more waved off, silently they vanished.

Again the buried barb tore at my soul; again Yillah was invoked, but Hautia made reply.

Slowly wore out the night. But when uprose the sun, fled clouds, and fled sadness.

CHAPTER LXX

THEY LAND AT HOOLOOMOOLOO

' KEEP all three prows for yonder rock,' cried Media ;
' no sadness on this merry morn ! And now for the Isle
of Cripples,—even Hooloomooloo.'

' The Isle of Cripples ? '

' Ay ; why not ? Mohi, tell how they came to club.'

In substance, this was the narration.

Averse to the barbarous custom of destroying at birth
all infants not symmetrically formed ; but equally desirous
of removing from their sight those unfortunate beings ;
the Islanders of a neighbouring group had long ago established an asylum for cripples ; where they lived, subject
to their own regulations ; ruled by a king of their own
election ; in short, forming a distinct class of beings by
themselves.

One only restriction was placed upon them : on no
account must they quit the isle assigned them. And to
the surrounding Islanders, so unpleasant the sight of a
distorted mortal, that a stranger landing at Hooloomooloo
was deemed a prodigy. Wherefore, respecting any knowledge of aught beyond them, the cripples were well-nigh as
isolated, as if Hooloomooloo was the only terra-firma
extant.

Dwelling in a community of their own, these unfortunates, who otherwise had remained few in number, increased
and multiplied greatly. Nor did successive generations
improve in symmetry upon those preceding them.

Soon, we drew nigh to the isle.

Heaped up, and jagged with rocks ; and, here and there, covered with dwarfed, twisted thickets, it seemed a fit place for its denizens.

Landing, we were surrounded by a heterogeneous mob ; and thus escorted, took our way inland, toward the abode of their lord, King Yoky.

What a scene !

Here, helping himself along with two crotched roots, hobbled a dwarf without legs ; another stalked before, one arm fixed in the air, like a lightning rod ; a third, more active than any, seal-like, flirted a pair of flippers, and went skipping along ; a fourth hopped on a solitary pin, at every bound, spinning round like a top, to gaze ; while still another, furnished with feelers or fins, rolled himself up in a ball, bowling over the ground in advance.

With curious instinct, the blind stuck close to our side ; with their chattering fingers, the deaf and the dumb described angles, obtuse and acute, in the air ; and like stones rolling down rocky ravines, scores of stammerers stuttered. Discord wedded deformity. All asses' brays were now harmonious memories ; all Calibans, as angels.

Yet for every stare we gave them, three stares they gave us.

At last, we halted before a tenement of rude stones ; crooked banian boughs its rafters, thatched with fantastic leaves. So rambling and irregular its plan, it seemed thrown up by the eruption, according to sage Mohi, the origin of the isle itself.

Entering, we saw King Yoky.

Ah ! sadly lacking was he, in all the requisites of an efficient ruler. Deaf and dumb he was ; and save arms, minus everything but an indispensable trunk and head. So huge his all-comprehensive mouth, it seemed to swallow up itself.

But shapeless, helpless as was Yoky,—as king of Hooloomooloo, he was competent ; the state being a limited monarchy, of which his highness was but the passive and ornamental head.

As his visitors advanced, he fell to gossiping with his fingers : a servitor interpreting. Very curious to note the rapidity with which motion was translated into sound ; and the simultaneousness with which meaning made its way through four successive channels to the mind—hand, sight, voice, and tympanum.

Much amazement his highness now expressed ; horrified his glances.

' Why club such frights as ye ? Herd ye, to keep in countenance ; or are afraid of your own hideousness, that ye dread to go alone ? Monsters ! speak.'

' Great Oro ! ' cried Mohi, ' are we then taken for cripples, by the very King of the Cripples ? My lord, are not our legs and arms all right ? '

' Comelier ones were never turned by turners, Mohi. But royal Yoky ! in sooth we feel abashed before thee.'

Some further stares were then exchanged ; when his highness sought to know whether there were any Comparative Anatomists among his visitors.

' Comparative Anatomists ! not one.'

' And why may King Yoky ask that question ? ' inquired Babbalanja.

Then was made the following statement.

During the latter part of his reign, when he seemed fallen into his dotage, the venerable predecessor of King Yoky had been much attached to an old gray-headed chimpanzee, one day found meditating in the woods. Rozoko was his name. He was very grave, and reverend of aspect ; much of a philosopher. To him, all gnarled and knotty subjects were familiar ; in his day he had cracked many a crabbed nut. And so in love with his

Timonean solitude was Rozoko, that it needed many bribes and bland persuasions to induce him to desert his mossy, hillside, misanthropic cave, for the distracting tumult of a court.

But ere long, promoted to high offices, and made the royal favourite, the woodland sage forgot his forests ; and, love for love, returned the aged king's caresses. Ardent friends they straight became ; dined and drank together ; with quivering lips, quaffed long-drawn, sober bumpers ; comparing all their past experiences ; and canvassing those hidden themes on which octogenarians dilate.

For when the fires and broils of youth are passed, and Mardi wears its truer aspect—then we love to think, not act ; the present seems more unsubstantial than the past ; then, we seek out graybeards like ourselves ; and hold discourse of palsies, hearses, shrouds, and tombs ; appoint our undertakers ; our mantles gather round us, like to winding-sheets ; and every night lie down to die. Then, the world's great bubble bursts ; then, Life's clouds seem sweeping by, revealing heaven to our straining eyes ; then, we tell our beads, and murmur paternosters ; and in trembling accents cry—' Oro ! be merciful.'

So, the monarch and Rozoko.

But not always were they thus. Of bright, cheerful mornings, they took slow, tottering rambles in the woods ; nodding over grotesque walking-sticks, of the chimpanzee's handiwork. For sedate Rozoko was a dilettante arbourist : an amateur in canes. Indeed, canes at last became his hobby. For half daft with age, sometimes he straddled his good staff and gently rode abroad, to take the salubrious evening air ; deeming it more befitting exercise, at times, than walking. Into this menage, he soon initiated his friend, the king ; and side by side they often pranced ; or, wearying of the saddle, dismounted ; and paused to ponder over prostrate palms decaying across the path.

Their mystic rings they counted ; and for every ring a year in their own calendars.

Now, so closely did the monarch cleave to the chimpanzee, that, in good time, summoning his subjects, earnestly he charged it on them, that at death, he and his faithful friend should be buried in one tomb.

It came to pass, the monarch died ; and poor Rozoko, now reduced to second childhood, wailed most dismally :— no one slept that night in Hooloomooloo. Never did he leave the body ; and at last, slowly going round it thrice, he laid him down ; close nestled ; and noiselessly expired.

The king's injunctions were remembered ; and one vault received them both.

Moon followed moon ; and wrought upon by jeers and taunts, the people of the isle became greatly scandalised, that a base-born baboon should share the shroud of their departed lord ; though they themselves had tucked in the aged Æneas fast by the side of his Achates.

They straight resolved, to build another vault ; and over it, a lofty cairn ; and thither carry the remains they reverenced.

But at the disinterring, a sad perplexity arose. For lo ! surpassing Saul and Jonathan, not even in decay were these fast friends divided. So mingled every relic,—ilium and ulna, carpus and metacarpus ;—and so similar the corresponding parts, that, like the literary remains of Beaumont and of Fletcher, which was which no spectacles could tell. Therefore, they desisted ; lest the towering monument they had reared might commemorate an ape, and not a king.

Such the narration ; hearing which, my lord Media kept stately silence. But in courtly phrase, as beseemed him, Babbalanja, turban in hand, thus spoke :—

' My concern is extreme, King Yoky, at the embarrassment into which your island is thrown. Nor less my grief, that I myself am not the man, to put an end to it. I could weep that Comparative Anatomists are not so numerous now, as hereafter they assuredly must become, when their services shall be in greater request ; when, at the last, last day of all, millions of noble and ignoble spirits will loudly clamour for lost skeletons ; when contending claimants shall start up for one poor, carious spine ; and, dog-like, we shall quarrel over our own bones.'

Then entered dwarf-stewards, and major-domos ; aloft bearing twisted antlers ; all hollowed out in goblets, grouped ; announcing dinner.

Loving not, however, to dine with misshapen Mardians, King Media was loth to move. But Babbalanja, quoting the old proverb—' Strike me in the face, but refuse not my yams,' induced him to sacrifice his fastidiousness.

So, under a flourish of ram-horn bugles, court and company proceeded to the banquet.

Central was a long, dislocated trunk of a wild banian ; like a huge centipede crawling on its hundred branches, sawn of even lengths for legs. This table was set out with wry-necked gourds; deformities of calabashes; and shape-less trenchers, dug out of knotty woods.

The first course was shrimp soup, served in great clamp - shells ; the second, lobsters, cuttle-fish, crabs, cockles, cray-fish ; the third, hunchbacked roots of the taro plant—plantains, perversely curling at the end, like the inveterate tails of pertinacious pigs ; and for dessert, ill-shaped melons, huge as idiots' heads, plainly suffering from water in the brain.

Now these viands were commended to the favourable notice of all guests ; not only for their delicacy of flavour, but for their symmetry.

And in the intervals of the courses, we were bored with hints to admire numerous objects of vertu : bow-legged stools of mangrove wood ; zigzag rapiers of bone ; armlets of grampus-vertebræ ; outlandish tureens of the calipees of terrapin ; and cannakins of the skulls of baboons.

The banquet over, with many congees, we withdrew.

Returning to the waterside, we passed a field, where dwarfs were labouring in beds of yams, heaping the soil around the roots by scratching it backward ; as a dog.

All things in readiness, Yoky's valet, a tri-armed dwarf, treated us to a glorious start, by giving each canoe a vigorous triple-push, crying, ' Away with ye, monsters ! '

Nor must it be omitted that just previous to embarking, Vee-Vee, spying a curious-looking stone, turned it over, and found a snake.

CHAPTER LXXI

' Now,' said Babbalanja, lighting his trombone as we sailed from the isle, ' who are the monsters, we or the cripples ? '

' You yourself are a monster, for asking the question,' said Mohi.

' And so, to the cripples I am ; though not, old man, for the reason you mention. But I am, as I am ; whether hideous, or handsome, depends upon who is made judge. There is no supreme standard yet revealed whereby to judge of ourselves ; " Our very instincts are prejudices," saith Alla-Malolla ; " our very axioms and postulates are far from infallible." " In respect of the universe, mankind is but a sect," saith Diloro ; " and first principles but dogmas." What ethics prevail in the Pleiades ? What things have the synods in Sagittarius decreed ? '

' Never mind your old authors,' said Media. ' Stick to the cripples ; enlarge upon them.'

' But I have done with them now, my lord ; the sermon is not the text. Give ear to old Bardianna. I know him by heart. Thus saith the sage in Book x. of the Ponderings, "Zermalmende," the title : " Je pense," the motto :—
" My supremacy over creation, boasteth man, is declared in my natural attitude : I stand erect ! But so do the palm-trees ; and the giraffes that graze off their tops. And the fowls of the air fly high over our heads ; and from the place where we fancy our heaven to be, defile the tops of our temples. Belike, the eagles, from their eyries look

298

down upon us Mardians, in our hives, even as upon the
beavers in their dams, marvelling at our incomprehensible
ways. And cunning though we be, some things hidden
from us may not be mysteries to them. Having five keys,
hold we all that open to knowledge ? Deaf, blind, and
deprived of the power of scent, the bat will steer its way
unerringly :—could we ? Yet man is lord of the bat and
the brute ; lord over the crows, with whom he must
needs share the grain he garners. We sweat for the fowls,
as well as ourselves. The curse of labour rests only on us.
Like slaves, we toil : at their good leisure they glean.

' " Mardi is not wholly ours. We are the least populous
part of creation. To say nothing of other tribes, a census
of the herring would find us far in the minority. And
what life is to us,—sour or sweet,—so it is to them. Like
us, they die, fighting death to the last ; like us, they spawn
and depart. We inhabit but a crust, rough surfaces, odds
and ends of the isles ; the abounding lagoon being its
two-thirds, its grand feature from afar ; and forever
unfathomable.

' " What shaft has yet been sunk to the antipodes ?
What underlieth the gold mines ?

' " But even here, above ground, we grope with the sun
at meridian. Vainly, we seek our North-West Passages
—old alleys, and thoroughfares of the whales.

' " Oh men ! fellow-men ! we are only what we are ;
not what we would be ; nor everything we hope for. We
are but a step in a scale, that reaches farther above us
than below. We breathe but oxygen. Who in Arcturus
hath heard of us ? They know us not in the Milky Way.
We prate of faculties divine : and know not how sprouteth
a spear of grass ; we go about shrugging our shoulders :
when the firmament-arch is over us ; we rant of ethereali-
ties : and long tarry over our banquets ; we demand
eternity for a lifetime : when our mortal half-hours too

often prove tedious. We know not of what we talk. The Bird of Paradise outflies our flutterings. What it is to be immortal has not yet entered into our thoughts. At will, we build our futurities ; tier above tier, all galleries full of laureates : resounding with everlasting oratorios ! Paternosters forever, or eternal Misereres ! forgetting that in Mardi, our breviaries oft fall from our hands. But divans there are, some say, whereon we shall recline, basking in effulgent suns, knowing neither Orient nor Occident. Is it so ? Fellow-men ! our mortal lives have an end ; but that end is no goal : no place of repose. Whatever it may be, it will prove but as the beginning of another race. We will hope, joy, weep, as before ; though our tears may be such as the spice-trees shed. Supine we can only be, annihilated.

' " The thick film is breaking ; the ages have long been circling. Fellow-men ! if we live hereafter, it will not be in lyrics ; nor shall we yawn, and our shadows lengthen, while the eternal cycles are revolving. To live at all, is a high vocation ; to live forever, and run parallel with Oro, may truly appal us. Toil we not here ? and shall we be forever slothful elsewhere ? Other worlds differ not much from this, but in degree. Doubtless, a pebble is a fair specimen of the universe.

' " We point at random. Peradventure at this instant, there are beings gazing up to this very world as their future heaven. But the universe is all over a heaven : nothing but stars on stars, throughout infinities of expansion. All we see are but a cluster. Could we get to Boötes, we would be no nearer Oro, than now ; he hath no place ; but is here. Already, in its unimaginable roamings, our system may have dragged us through and through the spaces, where we plant cities of beryl and jasper. Even now, we may be inhaling the ether which we fancy seraphic wings are fanning. But look round.

There is much to be seen here, and now.   Do the archangels
survey aught more glorious than the constellations we
nightly behold ?   Continually we slight the wonders we
deem in reserve.   We await the present.   With marvels
we are glutted, till we hold them no marvels at all.   But
had these eyes first opened upon all the prodigies in the
Revelation of the Dreamer, long familiarity would have
made them appear even as these things we see.   Now,
now, the page is outspread : to the simple, easy as a
primer ; to the wise, more puzzling than hieroglyphics.
The eternity to come is but a prolongation of time
present : and the beginning may be more wonderful than
the end.

' " Then let us be wise.   But much of the knowledge we
seek, already we have in our cores.   Yet so simple it is, we
despise it ; so bold, we fear it.

' " In solitude, let us exhume our ingots.   Let us hear
our own thoughts.   The soul needs no mentor, but Oro ;
and Oro, without proxy.   Wanting Him, it is both the
teacher and the taught.   Undeniably, reason was the first
revelation ; and so far as it tests all others, it has precedence over them.   It comes direct to us, without sup-
pression or interpolation ; and with Oro's indisputable
imprimatur.   But inspiration though it be, it is not so
arrogant as some think.   Nay, far too humble, at times
it submits to the grossest indignities.   Though in its best
estate, not infallible ; so far as it goes, for us, it is reliable.
When at fault, it stands still.   We speak not of vision-
aries.   But if this our first revelation stops short of the
uttermost, so with all others.   If, often, it only perplexes :
much more the rest.   They leave much unexpounded ;
and disclosing new mysteries, add to the enigma.   Fellow-
men ! the ocean we would sound is unfathomable ; and
however much we add to our line, when it is out, we
feel not the bottom.   Let us be truly lowly, then ; not

lifted up with a Pharisaic humility. We crawl not like worms ; nor wear we the liveries of angels.

' " The firmament-arch has no keystone ; least of all, is man its prop. He stands alone. We are everything to ourselves, but how little to others. What are others to us ? Assure life everlasting to this generation, and their immediate forefathers ;—and what tears would flow, were there no resurrection for the countless generations from the first man to five cycles since ? And soon we ourselves shall have fallen in with the rank and file of our sires. At a blow, annihilate some distant tribe, now alive and jocund—and what would we reck ? Curiosity apart, do we really care whether the people in Bellatrix are immortal or no ?

' " Though they smite us, let us not turn away from these things, if they really be thus.

' " There was a time, when near Cassiopeia, a star of the first magnitude, most lustrous in the North, grew lurid as a fire, then dim as ashes, and went out. Now, its place is a blank. A vast world, with all its continents, say the astronomers, blazing over the heads of our fathers ; while in Mardi were merry-makings, and maidens given in marriage. Who now thinks of that burning sphere ? How few are aware that ever it was ?

' " These things are so.

' " Fellow-men ! we must go and obtain a glimpse of what we are from the Belts of Jupiter and the Moons of Saturn, ere we see ourselves aright. The universe can wax old without us ; though by Oro's grace we may live to behold a wrinkle in the sky. Eternity is not ours by right ; and, alone, unrequited sufferings here form no title thereto, unless resurrections are reserved for mal-treated brutes. Suffering is suffering ; be the sufferer man, brute, or thing.

' " How small ;—how nothing, our deserts ! Let us

stifle all vain speculations ; we need not to be told what righteousness is ; we were born with the whole Law in our hearts. Let us do : let us act : let us down on our knees. And if, after all, we should be no more forever ;—far better to perish meriting immortality than to enjoy it unmeritorious. While we fight over creeds, ten thousand fingers point to where vital good may be done. All round us, Want crawls to her lairs ; and, shivering, dies un- relieved. Here, *here*, fellow-men, we can better minister as angels, than in heaven, where want and misery come not.

' " We Mardians talk as though the future was all in all ; but act as though the present was everything. Yet so far as, in our theories, we dwarf our Mardi ; we go not beyond an archangel's apprehension of it, who takes in all suns and systems at a glance. Like pebbles, were the isles to sink in space, Sirius, the dog-star, would still flame in the sky. But as the atom to the animalculae, so Mardi to us. And lived aright, these mortal lives are long ; looked into, these souls fathomless as the nethermost depths.

' " Fellow-men ! we split upon hairs ; but stripped, mere words and phrases cast aside, the great bulk of us are orthodox. None who think, dissent from the grand belief. The first man's thoughts were as ours. The paramount revelation prevails with us ; and all that clashes therewith we do not so much believe, as believe that we cannot disbelieve. Common sense is a sturdy despot ; that, for the most part, has its own way. It inspects and ratifies much independent of it. But those who think they do wholly reject it, are but held in a sly sort of bondage ; under a semblance of something else, wearing the old yoke." '

' Cease, cease, Babbalanja,' said Media, ' and permit me to insinuate a word in your ear. You have long been in the habit, philosopher, of regaling us with chapters from your old Bardianna; and, with infinite gusto, you have just recited the longest of all. But I do not observe, oh sage! that for all these things you yourself are practically the better or wiser. You live not up to Bardianna's main thought. Where he stands, he stands immovable; but you are a Dog-vane. How is this?'

'Gogle-goggle, fugle-fi, fugle-fogle-orum!'

'Mad, mad again,' cried Yoomy.

CHAPTER LXXII

BABBALANJA STARTS TO HIS FEET

FOR twenty-four hours, seated stiff and motionless, Babbalanja spoke not a word; then, almost without moving a muscle, muttered thus :—'At banquets surfeit not, but fill; partake, and retire; and eat not again till you crave. Thereby you give nature time to work her magic transformings; turning all solids to meat, and wine into blood. After a banquet you incline to repose :—do so : digestion commands. All this follow those who feast at the tables of Wisdom, and all such are they who partake of the fare of old Bardianna.'

'Art resuscitated, then, Babbalanja ? ' said Media.

'Ay, my lord, I am just risen from the dead.'

'And did Azzageddi conduct you to their realms ? '

'Fangs off ! fangs off ! depart, thou fiend !—unhand me ! or by Oro, I will die and spite thee ! '

'Quick, quick, Mohi ! let us change places,' cried Yoomy.

'How now, Babbalanja ? ' said Media.

'Oh my lord man—not *you*, my lord Media !—high and mighty Puissance ! great King of Creation !—thou art but the biggest of braggarts ! In every age, thou boastest of thy valorous advances :—flat fools, old dotards, and numskulls, our sires ! All the past, wasted time ! the present knows all ! right lucky, fellow-beings, we live now ! every man an author ! books plenty as men ! strike a light in a minute ! teeth sold by the pound ! all the elements fetching and carrying ! lightning running on

errands ! rivers made to order ! the ocean a puddle !—
But ages back they boasted like us ; and ages to come,
for ever and ever, they 'll boast. Ages back they black-
balled the past, thought the last day was come ; so wise
they were grown. Mardi could not stand long ; have to
annex one of the planets ; invade the great sun ; colonise
the moon ;—conquerors sighed for new Mardis ; and sages
for heaven—having by heart all the primers here below.
Like us, ages back they groaned under their books ; made
bonfires of libraries, leaving ashes behind, mid which we
reverentially grope for charred pages, forgetting we are so
much wiser than they.—But amazing times ! astounding
revelations ;   preternatural   divulgings !—How   now ?—
more wonderful than all our discoveries is this : that they
never were discovered before. So simple, no doubt our
ancestors overlooked them ; intent on deeper things—the
deep things of the soul. All we discover has been with us
since the sun began to roll ; and much we discover is not
worth the discovering. We are children, climbing trees
after birds' nests, and making a great shout, whether we
find eggs in them or no. But where are our wings, which
our forefathers surely had not ? Tell us, ye sages ! something worth an archangel's learning ; discover, ye dis-
coverers, something new. Fools, fools ! Mardi 's not
changed : the sun yet rises in its old place in the East ; all
things go on in the same old way ; we cut our eye-teeth
just as late as they did three thousand years ago.'

' Your pardon,' said Mohi, ' for beshrew me, they are
not yet all cut. At threescore and ten, here have I a
new tooth coming now.'

' Old man ! it but clears the way for another. The
teeth sown by the alphabet-founder were eye-teeth, not
yet all sprung from the soil. Like spring-wheat, blade by
blade, they break ground late ; like spring-wheat, many
seeds have perished in the hard winter glebe. Oh, my

lord ! though we galvanise corpses into St. Vitus' dances, we raise not the dead from their graves ! Though we have discovered the circulation of the blood, men die as of yore ; oxen graze, sheep bleat, babies bawl, asses bray— loud and lusty as the day before the Flood.   Men fight and make up ; repent and go at it ; feast and starve ; laugh and weep ; pray and curse ; cheat, chaffer, trick, truckle, cozen, defraud, fib, lie, beg, borrow, steal, hang, drown— as in the laughing and weeping, tricking and truckling, hanging and drowning times that have been.   Nothing changes, though much be new-fashioned : new fashions but revivals of things previous.   In the books of the past we learn naught but of the present ; in those of the present, the past.   All Mardi's history—beginning, middle, and finis—was written out in capitals in the first page penned.   The whole story is told in a title-page.   An exclamation point is entire Mardi's autobiography.'

' Who speaks now ? ' said Media ; ' Bardianna, Azza-geddi, or Babbalanja ? '

' All three : is it not a pleasant concert ? '

' Very fine : very fine.—Go on ; and tell us something of the future.'

' I have never departed this life yet, my lord.'

' But just now you said you were risen from the dead.'

' From the buried dead within me ; not from myself, my lord.'

' If you, then, know nothing of the future—did Bar-dianna ? '

' If he did, naught did he reveal.   I have ever observed, my lord, that even in their deepest lucubrations, the pro-foundest, frankest ponderers always reserve a vast deal of precious thought for their own private behoof.   They think, perhaps, that 'tis too good, or too bad ; too wise, or too foolish, for the multitude.   And this unpleasant vibration is ever consequent upon striking a new vein of ideas in the soul. As with buried treasures, the ground over them sounds strange and hollow. At any rate, the profoundest ponderer seldom tells us all he thinks; seldom reveals to us the ultimate, and the innermost; seldom makes us open our eyes under water; seldom throws open the totus-in-toto; and never carries us with him to the unconsubsistent, the idea-immanens, the super-essential, and the One.'

' Confusion ! Remember the Quadammodotatives ! '

' Ah ! ' said Braid-Beard, ' that's the crack in his calabash, which all the Dicibles of Doxodox will not mend.'

' And from that crazy calabash he gives us to drink, old Mohi.'

' But never heed his leaky gourd nor its contents, my lord. Let these philosophers muddle themselves as they will, we wise ones refuse to partake.'

' And fools like me drink till they reel,' said Babbalanja. ' But in these matters one's calabash must needs go round to keep afloat. Fogle-orum ! '

CHAPTER LXXIII

AT LAST, THE LAST MENTION IS MADE OF OLD BARDIANNA ;
AND HIS LAST WILL AND TESTAMENT IS RECITED AT
LENGTH

THE day was waning. And, as after many a tale of
ghosts, around their forest fire, Hungarian gypsies silent
sit, watching the ruddy glow kindling each other's faces ;
—so, now we solemn sat ; the crimson West our fire ; all
our faces flushed.

'Testators !' then cried Media, 'when your last wills
are all round settled, speak, and make it known !'

'Mine, my lord, has long been fixed,' said Babbalanja.

'And how runs it ?'

'Fugle-fogle——'

'Hark ye, intruding Azzageddi ! rejoin thy merry mates
below ;—go there, and wag thy saucy tail ; or I will nail
it to our bow, till ye roar for liberation. Begone, I say.'

'Down, devil ! deeper down !' rumbled Babbalanja.
'My lord, I think he's gone. And now, by your good
leave, I'll repeat old Bardianna's will. It's worth all
Mardi's hearing ; and I have so studied it, by rote I
know it.'

'Proceed, then ; but I mistrust that Azzageddi is not
yet many thousand fathoms down.'

'Attend, my lord :—"Anno Mardis 50,000,000 o.s.
I, Bardianna, of the island of Vamba, and village of the
same name, having just risen from my yams, in high health,
high spirits, and sound mind, do hereby cheerfully make
and ordain this my last will and testament.

309

' " Imprimis :

' " All my kith and kin being well to do in Mardi, I
wholly leave them out of this my will.

' " Item.   Since, in divers ways, verbally and otherwise,
my good friend Pondo has evinced a strong love for me,
Bardianna, as the owner and proprietor of all that capital
messuage with the appurtenances, in Vamba aforesaid,
called ' The Lair,' wherein I now dwell ; also for all my
bread-fruit orchards, palm groves, banana plantations,
taro patches, gardens, lawns, lanes, and hereditaments
whatsoever, adjoining the aforesaid messuage ;—I do
hereby give and bequeath the same to Bomblum of the
island of Adda ; the aforesaid Bomblum having never
expressed any regard for me, as a holder of real estate.

' " Item.   My esteemed neighbour Lakreemo having
since the last lunar eclipse called daily to inquire after the
state of my health : and having nightly made tearful
inquiries of my herb-doctor concerning the state of my
viscera ;—I do hereby give and bequeath to the aforesaid
Lakreemo all and sundry those vegetable pills, potions,
powders, aperients, purgatives, expellatives, evacuatives,
tonics, emetics, cathartics, clysters, injections, scarifiers,
cataplasms, lenitives, lotions, decoctions, washes, gargles,
and phlegmagogues; together with all the jars, calabashes,
gourds, and gallipots, thereunto pertaining ; situate, lying,
and being, in the west-by-north corner of my east-south-
east crypt, in my aforesaid tenement known as ' The Lair.'

' " Item.   The woman Pesti ; a native of Vamba,
having oftentimes hinted that I, Bardianna, sorely needed
a spouse, and having also intimated that she bore me a
conjugal affection ; I do hereby give and bequeath to the
aforesaid Pesti :—my blessing ; forasmuch, as by the
time of the opening of this my last will and testament, I
shall have been forever delivered from the aforesaid
Pesti's persecutions.

' " Item. Having a high opinion of the probity of my worthy and excellent friend Bidiri, I do hereby entirely, and wholly, give, will, grant, bestow, devise, and utterly hand over unto the said Bidiri, all that tenement where my servant Oram now dwelleth ; with all the lawns, meadows, uplands and lowlands, fields, groves, and gardens, thereunto belonging :—IN TRUST NEVERTHELESS to have and to hold the same for the sole use and benefit of Lanbranka Hohinna, spinster, now resident of the aforesaid island of Vamba.

' " Item. I give and bequeath my large carved drinking gourd to my good comrade Topo.

' " Item. My fast friend Doldrum having at sundry times, and in sundry places, uttered the prophecy, that upon my decease his sorrow would be great ; I do hereby give and bequeath to the aforesaid Doldrum, ten yards of my best soft tappa, to be divided into handkerchiefs for his sole benefit and behoof.

' " Item. My sensible friend Solo having informed me, that he intended to remain a bachelor for life ; I give and devise to the aforesaid Solo the mat for one person, whereon I nightly repose.

' " Item. Concerning my private arbour and palm groves, adjoining, lying, and being in the isle of Vamba, I give and devise the same, with all appurtenances whatsoever, to my friend Minta the Cynic, to have and to hold, in trust for the first through-and-through honest man, issue of my neighbour Mondi ; and in default of such issue, for the first through-and-through honest man, issue of my neighbour Pendidda ; and in default of such issue, for the first through-and-through honest man, issue of my neighbour Wynodo ; and in default of such issue, to any through-and-through honest man, issue of anybody, to be found through the length and breadth of Mardi.

' " Item. My friend Minta the Cynic to be sole judge of

all claims to the above-mentioned devise ; and to hold the
said premises for his own use, until the aforesaid person be
found.

' " Item.　Knowing my devoted scribe Marko to be
very sensitive touching the receipt of a favour ; I willingly
spare him that pain ; and hereby bequeath unto the
aforesaid scribe three milk-teeth, not as a pecuniary
legacy, but as a very slight token of my profound regard.

' " Item.　I give to the poor of Vamba the total contents of my red-labelled bags of bicuspids and canines
(which I account three-fourths of my whole estate) ; to
my body-servant Fidi, my staff, all my robes and togas,
and three hundred molars in cash ; to that discerning and
sagacious philosopher, my disciple Krako, one complete set
of denticles, to buy him a vertebral bone ring ; and to that
pious and promising youth Vangi, two fathoms of my best
kaiar rope, with the privilege of any bough in my groves.

' " All the rest of my goods, chattels, and household stuff
whatsoever ; and all my loose denticles, remaining after
my debts and legacies are paid, and my body is out of
sight, I hereby direct to be distributed among the poor of
Vamba.

' " Ultimo.　I give and bequeath to all Mardi this my
last advice and counsel :—videlicet : live as long as you
can ; close your own eyes when you die.

' " I have no previous wills to revoke ; and publish this
to be my first and last.

' " In witness whereof, I have hereunto set my right
hand ; and hereunto have caused a true copy of the tattooing of my right temple to be affixed, during the year first
above written.

' " By me, BARDIANNA." '

' Babbalanja, that 's an extraordinary document,' said
Media.

' Bardianna was an extraordinary man, my lord.'

' Were there no codicils ? '

' The will is all codicils ; all after-thoughts.   Ten thoughts for one act, was Bardianna's motto.'

' Left he nothing whatever to his kindred ? '

' Not a stump.'

' From his will, he seems to have lived single.'

' Yes : Bardianna never sought to improve upon nature ; a bachelor he was born, and a bachelor he died.'

' According to the best accounts, how did he depart, Babbalanja ? ' asked Mohi.

' With a firm lip, and his hand on his heart, old man.'

' His last words ? '

' Calmer, and better ! '

' Where think you, he is now ? '

' In his Ponderings.   And those, my lord, we all inherit ; for like the great chief of Romara, who made a whole empire his legatee ; so, great authors have all Mardi for an heir.'

CHAPTER LXXIV

A DEATH-CLOUD SWEEPS BY THEM, AS THEY SAIL

NEXT day, a fearful sight !

As in Sooloo's seas, one vast water-spout will, sudden, form : and whirling, chase the flying Malay keels ; so, before a swift-winged cloud, a thousand prows sped by, leaving braided, foaming wakes ; their crowded inmates' arms in frenzied supplications wreathed, like tangled forest boughs.

' See, see,' cried Yoomy, ' how the death-cloud flies ! Let us dive down in the sea.'

' Nay,' said Babbalanja. ' All things come of Oro ; if we must drown, let Oro drown us.'

' Down sails : drop paddles,' said Media : ' here we float.'

Like a rushing bison, sweeping by, the death-cloud grazed us with its foam ; and whirling in upon the thousand prows beyond, sudden burst in deluges ; and scooping out a maelstrom, dragged down every plank and soul.

Long we rocked upon the circling billows which, expanding from that centre, dashed every isle, till, moons afterward, faint, they laved all Mardi's reef.

' Thanks unto Oro,' murmured Mohi, ' this heart still beats.'

That sun-flushed eve we sailed by many tranquil harbours, whence fled those thousand prows. Serene, the waves ran up their strands ; and chimed around the unharmed stakes of palm, to which the thousand prows that morning had been fastened.

314

' Flying death, they ran to meet it,' said Babbalanja.
' But 'tis not that they fled, they died ; for maelstroms, of
these harbours, the death-cloud might have made.   But
they died because they might not longer live.   Could we
gain one glimpse of the great calendar of eternity, all our
names would there be found, glued against their dates of
death.   We die by land, and die by sea ; we die by earthquakes, famines, plagues, and wars ; by fevers, agues ;
woe, or mirth excessive.   This mortal air is one wide
pestilence, that kills us all at last.   Whom the death-
cloud spares, sleeping, dies in silent watches of the night.
He whom the spears of many battles could not slay, dies
of a grape-stone, beneath the vine-clad bower he built to
shade declining years.   We die, because we live.   But none
the less does Babbalanja quake.   And if he flies not, 'tis
because he stands the centre of a circle ; its every point a
levelled dart ; and every bow bent back :—a twang, and
Babbalanja dies.'

CHAPTER LXXV

THEY VISIT THE PALMY KING ABRAZZA

NIGHT and morn departed; and in the afternoon we drew nigh to an island, overcast with shadows; a shower was falling; and pining, plaintive notes forth issued from the groves : half-suppressed, and sobbing whisperings of leaves. The shore sloped to the water; thither our prows were pointed.

'Sheer off! no landing here,' cried Media, 'let us gain the sunny side; and like the care-free bachelor Abrazza, who here is king, turn our back on the isle's shadowy side, and revel in its morning meads.'

'And lord Abrazza :—who is he ?' asked Yoomy.

'The one hundred and twentieth in lineal descent from Phipora,' said Mohi ; 'and connected on the maternal side to the lord seigniors of Klivonia. His uttermost uncle was nephew to the niece of Queen Zmiglandi ; who flourished so long since, she wedded at the first Transit of Venus. His pedigree is endless.'

'But who is lord Abrazza ?'

'Has he not said ?' answered Babbalanja. 'Why so dull ?—Uttermost nephew to him who was nephew to the niece of the peerless Queen Zmiglandi ; and the one hundred and twentieth in descent from the illustrious Phipora.'

'Will none tell who Abrazza is ?'

'Cannot a man then be described by running off the catalogue of his ancestors ?' said Babbalanja. 'Or must we e'en descend to himself. Then, listen, dull Yoomy !

316

and know that lord Abrazza is six feet two : plump
thighs ; blue eyes ; and brown hair ; likes his bread-fruit
baked, not roasted ; sometimes carries filberts in his
crown : and has a way of winking when he speaks. His
teeth are good.'

' Are you publishing some decamped burglar,' said
Media, ' that you speak thus of my royal friend, the lord
Abrazza ? Go on, sir ! and say he reigns sole king of
Bonovona ! '

' My lord, I had not ended. Abrazza, Yoomy, is a fine
and florid king : high-fed, and affluent of heart ; of speech,
mellifluent. And for a royalty extremely amiable. He is
a sceptred gentleman, who does much good. Kind king !
in person he gives orders for relieving those who daily
dive for pearls to grace his royal robe ; and gasping hard,
with bloodshot eyes, come up from shark-infested depths,
and fainting, lay their treasure at his feet. Sweet lord
Abrazza ! how he pities those, who in his farthest woodlands day-long toil to do his bidding. Yet king-philoso-
pher, he never weeps ; but pities with a placid smile ;
and that but seldom.'

' There seems much iron in your blood,' said Media.
' But say your say.'

' Say I not truth, my lord ! Abrazza, I admire. Save
his royal pity all else is jocund round him. He loves to
live for life's own sake. He vows he 'll have no cares ;
and often says, in pleasant reveries,—" Sure, my lord
Abrazza, if anyone should be care-free, 'tis thou ; who
strike down none, but pity all the fallen ! " Yet none he
lifteth up.'

At length we gained the sunny side, and shoreward
tended. Vee-Vee's horn was sonorous ; and issuing
from his golden groves, my lord Abrazza, like a host
that greets you on the threshold, met us, as we keeled
the beach.

'Welcome! fellow demi-god, and king! Media, my pleasant guest!'

His servitors salaamed; his chieftains bowed; his yeoman-guard, in meadow-green, presented palm stalks, —royal tokens; and hand in hand, the nodding, jovial, regal friends, went up a lane of salutations; dragging behind, a train of envyings.

Much we marked Abrazza's jewelled crown; that shot no honest blaze of ruddy rubies; nor looked stern-white like Media's pearls; but cast a green and yellow glare; rays from emeralds, crossing rays from many a topaz. In those beams, so sinister, all present looked cadaverous: Abrazza's cheek alone beamed bright, but hectic.

Upon its fragrant mats a spacious hall received the kings; and gathering courtiers blandly bowed; and gushing with soft flatteries, breathed idol incense round them.

The hall was terraced thrice; its elevated end was curtained; and thence, at every chime of words, there burst a girl, gay scarfed, with naked bosom, and poured forth wild and hollow laughter, as she raced down all the terraces, and passed their merry kingships.

Wide round the hall, in avenues, waved almond-woods; their whiteness frosted into bloom. But every vine-clad trunk was hollow-hearted; hollow sounds came from the grottoes: hollow broke the billows on the shore: and hollow pauses filled the air, following the hollow laughter.

Guards, with spears, paced the groves, and in the inner shadows oft were seen to lift their weapons, and backward press some ugly phantom, saying, 'Subjects! haunt him not; Abrazza would be merry; Abrazza feasts his guests.'

So, banished from our sight seemed all things uncongenial; and pleasant times were ours in these dominions. Not a face passed by, but smiled; mocking-birds perched on the boughs; and singing, made us vow the woods were warbling forth thanksgiving, with a thousand throats! The stalwart yeomen grinned beneath their trenchers, heaped with citrons, pomegranates, grapes; the pages tittered, pouring out the wine; and all the lords loud laughed, smote their gilded spears, and swore the isle was glad.

Such the isle, in which we tarried; but in our rambles found no Yillah.

CHAPTER LXXVI

SOME PLEASANT, SHADY TALK IN THE GROVES, BETWEEN MY LORDS ABRAZZA AND MEDIA, BABBALANJA, MOHI, AND YOOMY

ABRAZZA had a cool retreat—a grove of dates; where we were used to lounge of noons, and mix our converse with the babble of the rills; and mix our punches in goblets chased with grapes. And as ever, King Abrazza was the prince of hosts.

'Your crown,' he said to Media; and with his own he hung it on a bough.

'Be not ceremonious!' and stretched his royal legs upon the turf.

'Wine!' and his pages poured it out.

So on the grass we lounged; and King Abrazza, who loved his antique ancestors; and loved old times; and would not talk of moderns;—bade Yoomy sing old songs; bade Mohi rehearse old histories; bade Babbalanja tell of old ontologies; and commanded all, meanwhile, to drink his old, old wine.

So, all round we quaffed and quoted.

At last, we talked of old Homeric bards :—those who, ages back, harped, and begged, and groped their blinded way through all this charitable Mardi; receiving coppers then, and immortal glory now.

ABRAZZA.—How came it, that they all were blind?

BABBALANJA.—It was endemical, your highness. Few grand poets have good eyes; for they needs blind must be, who ever gaze upon the sun. Vavona himself was blind;

320

when, in the silence of his secret bower, he said—' I will build another world. Therein, let there be kings and slaves, philosophers and wits ; whose chequered actions— strange, grotesque, and merry-sad, will entertain my idle moods.' So, my lord, Vavona played at kings and crowns, and men and manners; and loved that lonely game to play.

ABRAZZA.—Vavona seemed a solitary Mardian ; who seldom went abroad ; had few friends ; and shunning others, was shunned by them.

BABBALANJA.—But shunned not himself, my lord ; like gods, great poets dwell alone ; while round them roll the worlds they build.

MEDIA.—You seem to know all authors :—you must have heard of Lombardo, Babbalanja ; he who flourished many ages since.

BABBALANJA.—I have ; and his grand Koztanza know by heart.

MEDIA (*to Abrazza*).—A very curious work, that, my lord.

ABRAZZA.—Yes, my dearest king. But, Babbalanja, if Lombardo had aught to tell to Mardi—why choose a vehicle so crazy ?

BABBALANJA.—It was his nature, I suppose.

ABRAZZA.—But so it would not have been, to me.

BABBALANJA.—Nor would it have been natural, for my noble lord Abrazza, to have worn Lombardo's head :— every man has his own, thank Oro !

ABRAZZA.—A curious work : a very curious work. Babbalanja, are you acquainted with the history of Lombardo ?

BABBALANJA.—None better. All his biographies have I read.

ABRAZZA.—Then, tell us how he came to write that work. For one, I cannot imagine how those poor devils contrive to roll such thunders through all Mardi.

MEDIA.—Their thunder and lightning seem spontaneous combustibles, my lord.

ABRAZZA.—With which they but consume themselves, my prince beloved.

BABBALANJA.—In a measure, true, your highness. But pray you, listen ; and I will try to tell the way in which Lombardo produced his great Koztanza.

MEDIA.—But hark you, philosopher ! this time no incoherencies ; gag that devil, Azzageddi. And now, what was it that originally impelled Lombardo to the undertaking ?

BABBALANJA.—Primus and forever, a full heart :—brimful, bubbling, sparkling ; and running over like the flagon in your hand, my lord. Secundo, the necessity of bestirring himself to procure his yams.

ABRAZZA.—Wanting the second motive, would the first have sufficed, philosopher ?

BABBALANJA.—Doubtful. More conduits than one to drain off the soul's overflowings. Besides, the greatest fulnesses overflow not spontaneously ; and, even when decanted, like rich syrups, slowly ooze ; whereas, poor fluids glibly flow, wide-spreading. Hence, when great fulness weds great indolence ;—that man, to others, too often proves a cipher ; though, to himself, his thoughts form an infinite series, indefinite, from its vastness ; and incommunicable ;—not for lack of power, but for lack of an omnipotent volition, to move his strength. His own world is full before him ; the fulcrum set ; but lever there is none. To such a man, the giving of any boor's resoluteness, with tendons braided, would be as hanging a claymore to Valour's side, before unarmed. Our minds are cunning, compound mechanisms ; and one spring, or wheel, or axle wanting, the movement lags, or halts. Cerebrum must not overbalance cerebellum ; our brains should be round as globes ; and planted on capacious

chests, inhaling mighty morning inspirations. We have
had vast developments of parts of men ; but none of
manly wholes. Before a full-developed man, Mardi would
fall down and worship. We are idiot, younger sons of
gods, begotten in dotages divine ; and our mothers all
miscarry. Giants are in our germs ; but we are dwarfs,
staggering under heads overgrown. Heaped, our measures
burst. We die of too much life.

MEDIA (*to Abrazza*).—Be not impatient, my lord ; he 'll
recover presently. You were talking of Lombardo,
Babbalanja.

BABBALANJA.—I was, your highness. Of all Mardians,
by nature he was the most inert. Hast ever seen a yellow
lion, all day basking in the yellow sun :—in reveries, rending droves of elephants ; but his vast loins supine, and
eyelids winking ? Such, Lombardo ; but fierce Want,
the hunter, came and roused his roar. In hairy billows,
his great mane tossed like the sea ; his eyeballs flamed
two hells ; his paw had stopped a rolling world.

ABRAZZA.—In other words, yams were indispensable,
and, poor devil, he roared to get them.

BABBALANJA (*bowing*).—Partly so, my literal lord. And
as with your own golden sceptre, at times upon your royal
teeth, indolent tattoos you beat ; then, potent, sway it
o'er your isle ; so, Lombardo. And ere Necessity plunged
spur and rowel into him, he knew not his own paces. *That*
churned him into consciousness ; and brought ambition,
ere then dormant, seething to the top, till he trembled at
himself. No mailed hand lifted up against a traveller in
woods, can so appal, as we ourselves. We are full of
ghosts and spirits ; we are as graveyards full of buried
dead, that start to life before us. And all our dead sires,
verily, are in us ; *that* is their immortality. From sire to
son, we go on multiplying corpses in ourselves ; for all of
which are resurrections. Every thought 's a soul of some

past poet, hero, sage. We are fuller than a city. Woe it is, that reveals these things. He knows himself, and all that's in him, who knows adversity. To scale great heights we must come out of lowermost depths. The way to heaven is through hell. We need fiery baptisms in the fiercest flames of our own bosoms. We must feel our hearts hot—hissing in us. And ere their fire is revealed, it must burn its way out of us ; though it consume us and itself. Oh, sleek-cheeked Plenty ! smiling at thine own dimples ;—vain for thee to reach out after greatness. Turn ! turn ! from all your tiers of cushions of eiderdown —turn ! and be broken on the wheels of many woes. At white-heat, brand thyself ; and count the scars, like old war-worn veterans, over camp fires. Soft poet ! brushing tears from lilies—this way ! and howl in sackcloth and in ashes ! Know, thou, that the lines that live are turned out of a furrowed brow. Oh ! there is a fierce, a cannibal delight, in the grief that shrieks to multiply itself. That grief is miserly of its own ; it pities all the happy. Some damned spirits would not be otherwise, could they ?

ABRAZZA (*to Media*).—Pray, my lord, is this good gentleman a devil ?

MEDIA.—No, my lord ; but he's possessed by one. His name is Azzageddi. You may hear more of him. But come, Babbalanja, hast forgotten all about Lombardo ? How set he about that great undertaking, his Koztanza ?

ABRAZZA (*to Media*).—Oh, for all the ravings of your Babbalanja, Lombardo took no special pains ; hence, deserves small commendation. For, genius must be somewhat like us kings,—calm, content, in consciousness of power. And to Lombardo, the scheme of his Koztanza must have come full-fledged, like an eagle from the sun.

BABBALANJA.—No, your highness ; but like eagles, his thoughts were first callow ; yet, born plumeless, they came to soar.

ABRAZZA.—Very fine.   I presume, Babbalanja, the first thing he did was to fast, and invoke the muses.

BABBALANJA.—Pardon, my lord ; on the contrary, he first procured a ream of vellum, and some sturdy quills : indispensable preliminaries, my worshipful lords, to the writing of the sublimest epics.

ABRAZZA.—Ah ! then the muses were afterward invoked.

BABBALANJA.—Pardon again. Lombardo next sat down to a fine plantain pudding.

YOOMY.—When the song-spell steals over me, I live upon olives.

BABBALANJA.—Yoomy, Lombardo eschewed olives. Said he, ' What fasting soldier can fight ? and the fight of all fights is to write.'   In ten days Lombardo had written——

ABRAZZA.—Dashed off, you mean.

BABBALANJA.—He never dashed off aught.

ABRAZZA.—As you will.

BABBALANJA.—In ten days Lombardo had written full fifty folios ; he loved huge acres of vellum whereon to expatiate.

MEDIA.—What then ?

BABBALANJA.—He read them over attentively ; made a neat package of the whole : and put it into the fire.

ALL.—How ?

MEDIA.—What ! these great geniuses writing trash ?

ABRAZZA.—I thought as much.

BABBALANJA.—My lords, they abound in it ! more than any other men in Mardi.   Genius is full of trash.   But genius essays its best to keep it to itself ; and giving away its ore, retains the earth ; whence, the too frequent wisdom of its works, and folly of its life.

ABRAZZA.—Then genius is not inspired, after all.   How they must slave in their mines !   I weep to think of it.

BABBALANJA.—My lord, all men are inspired ; fools are inspired ; your highness is inspired ; for the essence of all ideas is infused. Of ourselves, and in ourselves, we originate nothing. When Lombardo set about his work, he knew not what it would become. He did not build himself in with plans ; he wrote right on ; and so doing, got deeper and deeper into himself ; and like a resolute traveller, plunging through baffling woods, at last was rewarded for his toils. ' In good time,' saith he, in his autobiography, ' I came out into a serene, sunny, ravishing region ; full of sweet scents, singing birds, wild plaints, roguish laughs, prophetic voices. Here we are at last, then,' he cried ; ' I have created the creative.' And now the whole boundless landscape stretched away. Lombardo panted ; the sweat was on his brow ; he off mantle ; braced himself ; sat within view of the ocean ; his face to a cool rushing breeze ; placed flowers before him ; and gave himself plenty of room. On one side was his ream of vellum——

ABRAZZA.—And on the other, a brimmed beaker.

BABBALANJA.—No, your highness ; though he loved it, no wine for Lombardo while actually at work.

MOHI.—Indeed ? Why, I ever thought that it was to the superior quality of Lombardo's punches that Mardi was indebted for that abounding humour of his.

BABBALANJA.—Not so ; he had another way of keeping himself well braced.

YOOMY.—Quick ! tell us the secret.

BABBALANJA.—He never wrote by rushlight. His lamp swung in heaven.—He rose from his East, with the sun ; he wrote when all nature was alive.

MOHI.—Doubtless, then, he always wrote with a grin ; and none laughed louder at his quips than Lombardo himself.

BABBALANJA.—Hear you laughter at the birth of a man

child, old man ?   The babe may have many dimples ; not so, the parent.   Lombardo was a hermit to behold.

MEDIA.—What ! did Lombardo laugh with a long face ?

BABBALANJA.—His merriment was not always merriment to him, your highness.   For the most part, his meaning kept him serious.   Then he was so intensely riveted to his work, he could not pause to laugh.

MOHI.—My word for it ; but he had a sly one, now and then.

BABBALANJA.—For the nonce, he was not his own master : a mere amanuensis writing by dictation.

YOOMY.—Inspiration, that !

BABBALANJA.—Call it as you will, Yoomy, it was a sort of sleep-walking of the mind.   Lombardo never threw down his pen : it dropped from him ; and then, he sat disenchanted : rubbing his eyes ; staring ; and feeling faint—sometimes, almost unto death.

MEDIA.—But pray, Babbalanja, tell us how he made acquaintance with some of those rare worthies he introduces us to in his Koztanza.

BABBALANJA.—He first met them in his reveries ; they were walking about in him, sour and moody : and for a long time were shy of his advances ; but still importuned, they at last grew ashamed of their reserve ; stepped forward ; and gave him their hands.   After that, they were frank and friendly.   Lombardo set places for them at his board ; when he died, he left them something in his will.

MEDIA.—What ! those imaginary beings ?

ABRAZZA.—Wondrous witty ! infernal fine !

MEDIA.—But, Babbalanja ; after all, the Koztanza found no favour in the eyes of some Mardians.

ABRAZZA.—Ay : the arch-critics Verbi and Batho denounced it.

BABBALANJA.—Yes : on good authority, Verbi is said to

have detected a superfluous comma ; and Batho declared
that, with the materials he could have constructed a far
better world that Lombardo's. But, didst ever hear of his
laying his axis ?

ABRAZZA.—But the unities ; Babbalanja, the unities !
they are wholly wanting in the Koztanza.

BABBALANJA. — Your highness ; upon that point,
Lombardo was frank. Saith he, in his autobiography :
' For some time, I endeavoured to keep in the good graces
of those nymphs ; but I found them so captious, and
exacting ; they threw me into such a violent passion with
their fault-findings ; that, at last, I renounced them.'

ABRAZZA.—Very rash !

BABBALANJA.—No, your highness ; for though Lombardo abandoned all monitors from without ; he retained
one autocrat within—his crowned and sceptred instinct.
And what, if he pulled down one gross world, and ran-
sacked the ethereal spheres, to build up something of his
own—a composite :—what then ? matter and mind,
though matching not, are mates ; and sundered oft, in
his Koztanza they unite :—the airy waist, embraced by
stalwart arms.

MEDIA.—Incoherent again ! I thought we were to have
no more of this !

BABBALANJA.—My lord Media, there are things infinite
in the finite ; and dualities in unities. Our eyes are
pleased with the redness of the rose, but another sense lives
upon its fragrance. Its redness you must approach, to
view : its invisible fragrance pervades the field. So, with
the Koztanza. Its mere beauty is restricted to its form :
its expanding soul past Mardi does embalm. Modak is
Modako ; but fogle-foggle is not fugle-fi.

MEDIA (to Abrazza).—My lord, you start again ; but
'tis only another phase of Azzageddi ; sometimes he 's
quite mad. But all this you must needs overlook.

ABRAZZA.—I will, my dear prince ; what one cannot see through, one must needs look over, as you say.

YOOMY.—But trust me, your highness, some of those strange things fall far too melodiously upon the ear to be wholly deficient in meaning.

ABRAZZA.—Your gentle minstrel, *this* must be, my lord. But Babbalanja, the Koztanza lacks cohesion ; it is wild, unconnected, all episode.

BABBALANJA.—And so is Mardi itself :—nothing but episodes ; valleys and hills ; rivers, digressing from plains ; vines, roving all over ; boulders and diamonds ; flowers and thistles ; forests and thickets ; and, here and there, fens and moors. And so, the world in the Koztanza.

ABRAZZA.—Ay, plenty of dead-desert chapters there ; horrible sands to wade through.

MEDIA.—Now, Babbalanja, away with your tropes ; and tell us of the work directly it was done. What did Lombardo then ? Did he show it to anyone for an opinion ?

BABBALANJA.—Yes, to Zenzori, who asked him where he picked up so much trash ; to Hanto, who bade him not be cast down, it was pretty good ; to Lucree, who desired to know how much he was going to get for it ; to Roddi, who offered a suggestion.

MEDIA.—And what was that ?

BABBALANJA.—That he had best make a faggot of the whole ; and try again.

ABRAZZA.—Very encouraging.

MEDIA.—Anyone else ?

BABBALANJA.—To Pollo, who, conscious his opinion was sought, was thereby puffed up ; and marking the faltering of Lombardo's voice, when the manuscript was handed him, straightway concluded that the man who stood thus trembling at the bar must needs be inferior to the judge. But his verdict was mild. After sitting up all

night over the work ; and diligently taking notes :—
' Lombardo, my friend ! here, take your sheets. I have
run through them loosely. You might have done better ;
but then you might have done worse. Take them, my
friend ; I have put in some good things for you.'

MEDIA.—And who was Pollo ?

BABBALANJA.—Probably someone who lived in Lombardo's time, and went by that name. He is incidentally
mentioned, and cursorily immortalised in one of the post-
humous notes to the Koztanza.

MEDIA.—What is said of him there ?

BABBALANJA.—Not much. In a very old transcript of
the work—that of Aldina—the note alludes to a brave line
in the text, and runs thus :—' Diverting to tell, it was this
passage that an old prosodist, one Pollo, claimed for his
own. He maintained he made a freewill offering of it to
Lombardo. Several things are yet extant of this Pollo,
who died some weeks ago. He seems to have been one of
those who would do great things if they could ; but are
content to compass the small. He imagined that the
precedence of authors he had established in his library
was their Mardi order of merit. He condemned the sublime poems of Vavona to his lowermost shelf. " Ah,"
thought he, " how we library princes, lord it over those
beggarly authors ! " Well read in the history of their
woes, Pollo pitied them all, particularly the famous ; and
wrote little essays of his own, which he read to himself.'

MEDIA.—Well : and what said Lombardo to those good
friends of his,—Zenzori, Hanto, and Roddi ?

BABBALANJA.—Nothing. Taking home his manuscript,
he glanced it over ; making three corrections.

ABRAZZA.—And what then ?

BABBALANJA.—Then, your highness, he thought to try
a conclave of professional critics ; saying to himself, ' Let
them privately point out to me, now, all my blemishes ;

so that, what time they come to review me in public, all will be well.' But curious to relate, those professional critics, for the most part, held their peace, concerning a work yet unpublished. And, with some generous exceptions, in their vague, learned way, betrayed such base, beggarly notions of authorship, that Lombardo could have wept, had tears been his. But in his very grief he ground his teeth. Muttered he, ' They are fools. In their eyes, bindings not brains make books. They criticise my tattered cloak, not my soul, caparisoned like a charger. He is the great author, think they, who drives the best bargain with his wares : and no bargainer am I. Because he is old, they worship some mediocrity of an ancient, and mock at the living prophet with the live coal on his lips. They are men who would not be men, had they no books. Their sires begat them not ; but the authors they have read. Feelings they have none : and their very opinions they borrow. They cannot say yea, nor nay, without first consulting all Mardi as an Encyclopædia. And all the learning in them is as a dead corpse in a coffin. Were they worthy the dignity of being damned, I would damn them ; but they are not. Critics ?—Asses ! rather mules ! so emasculated, from vanity, they cannot father a true thought. Like mules, too, from dunghills, they trample down gardens of roses : and deem that crushed fragrance their own.—Oh ! that all round the domains of genius should lie thus unhedged, for such cattle to uproot ! Oh ! that an eagle should be stabbed by a goose-quill ! But at best, the greatest reviewers but prey on my leavings. For I am critic and creator ; and as critic, in cruelty surpass all critics merely, as a tiger, jackals. For ere Mardi sees aught of mine, I scrutinise it myself, remorseless as a surgeon. I cut right and left ; I probe, tear, and wrench ; kill, burn, and destroy ; and what 's left after that the jackals are welcome to. It is *I* that stab false thoughts, ere hatched ; *I* that pull down wall and tower, rejecting materials which would make palaces for others. Oh ! could Mardi but see how we work, it would marvel more at our primal chaos, than at the round world thence emerging. It would marvel at our scaffoldings, scaling heaven ; marvel at the hills of earth, banked all round our fabrics ere completed.—How plain the pyramid ! In this grand silence, so intense, pierced by that pointed mass, —could ten thousand slaves have ever toiled ? ten thousand hammers rung ?—There it stands,—part of Mardi : claiming kin with mountains ;—was this thing piecemeal built ?—It was. Piecemeal ?—atom by atom it was laid. The world is made of mites.'

YOOMY (*musing*).—It is even so.

ABRAZZA.—Lombardo was severe upon the critics ; and they as much so upon him ;—of that, be sure.

BABBALANJA.—Your highness, Lombardo never presumed to criticise true critics ; who are more rare than true poets. A great critic is a sultan among satraps ; but pretenders are thick as ants, striving to scale a palm, after its aerial sweetness. And they fight among themselves. Essaying to pluck eagles, they themselves are geese, stuck full of quills, of which they rob each other.

ABRAZZA (*to Media*).—Oro help the victim that falls in Babbalanja's hands !

MEDIA.—Ay, my lord ; at times, his every finger is a dagger : every thought a falling tower that whelms ! But resume, philosopher—what of Lombardo now ?

BABBALANJA.—' For this thing,' said he, ' I have agonised over it enough.—I can wait no more. It has faults—all mine ;—its merits all its own ;—but I can toil no longer. The beings knit to me implore ; my heart is full ; my brain is sick. Let it go—let it go—and Oro with it. Somewhere Mardi has a mighty heart—*that* struck, all the isles shall resound ! '

ABRAZZA.—Poor devil ! he took the world too hard.

MEDIA.—As most of these mortals do, my lord. That 's the load, self-imposed, under which Babbalanja reels. But now, philosopher, ere Mardi saw it, what thought Lombardo of his work, looking at it objectively, as a thing out of him, I mean.

ABRAZZA.—No doubt, he hugged it.

BABBALANJA.—Hard to answer. Sometimes, when by himself, he thought hugely of it, as my lord Abrazza says ; but when abroad, among men, he almost despised it ; but when he bethought him of those parts, written with full eyes, half blinded ; temples throbbing ; and pain at the heart——

ABRAZZA.—Pooh ! pooh !

BABBALANJA.—He would say to himself, ' Sure, it cannot be in vain ! ' Yet again, when he bethought him of the hurry and bustle of Mardi, dejection stole over him. ' Who will heed it,' thought he ; ' what care these fops and brawlers for me ? But am I not myself an egregious coxcomb ? Who will read me ? Say one thousand pages —twenty-five lines each—every line ten words—every word ten letters. That 's two million five hundred thousand *a*'s and *i*'s and *o*'s to read ! How many are superfluous ? Am I not mad to saddle Mardi with such a task ? Of all men, am I the wisest, to stand upon a pedestal, and teach the mob ? Ah, my own Koztanza ! child of many prayers !—in whose earnest eyes, so fathomless, I see my own ; and recall all past delights and silent agonies :—thou mayst prove, as the child of some fond dotard—beauteous to me ; hideous to Mardi ! And methinks, that while so much slaving merits that thou shouldst not die ; it has not been intense, prolonged enough, for the high meed of immortality. Yet, things immortal have been written ; and by men as me ;—men, who slept and waked ; and ate ; and talked with tongues

like mine. Ah, Oro ! how may we know or not, we are
what we would be ? Hath genius any stamp and imprint,
obvious to possessors ? Has it eyes to see itself ; or is it
blind ? Or do we delude ourselves with being gods, and
end in grubs ? Genius, genius ?—a thousand years hence,
to be a household word ?—I ?—Lombardo ? but yesterday
cut in the market-place by a spangled fool !—Lombardo
immortal ?—Ha, ha, Lombardo ! but thou art an ass,
with vast ears brushing the tops of palms ! Ha, ha, ha !
Methinks I see thee immortal ! " Thus great Lombardo
saith ; and thus ; and thus ; and thus :—thus saith he—
illustrious Lombardo !—Lombardo, our great countryman !
Lombardo, prince of poets—Lombardo ! great Lombardo ! "—Ha, ha, ha !—go, go ! dig thy grave, and
bury thyself ! '

ABRAZZA.—He was very funny, then, at times.

BABBALANJA.—Very funny, your highness :—amazing
jolly ! And from my nethermost soul, would to Oro, thou
couldst but feel one touch of that jolly woe ! It would
appal thee, my right worshipful lord Abrazza !

ABRAZZA (to Media).—My dear lord, his teeth are
marvellously white and sharp : some she-shark must have
been his dam :—does he often grin thus ? It was infernal !

MEDIA.—Ah ! that 's Azzageddi. But, prithee, Babbalanja, proceed.

BABBALANJA.—Your highness, even in his calmer critic
moods, Lombardo was far from fancying his work. He
confesses, that it ever seemed to him but a poor scrawled
copy of something within, which, do what he would, he
could not completely transfer. ' My canvas was small,'
said he ; ' crowded out were hosts of things that came last.
But Fate is in it.' And Fate it was, too, your highness,
which forced Lombardo, ere his work was well done, to
take it off his easel, and send it to be multiplied. ' Oh, that
I was not thus spurred ! ' cried he ; ' but like many

another, in its very childhood, this poor child of mine must go out into Mardi, and get bread for its sire.'

ABRAZZA (*with a sigh*).—Alas, the poor devil! But methinks 'twas wondrous arrogant in him to talk to all Mardi at that lofty rate.—Did he think himself a god ?

BABBALANJA.—He himself best knew what he thought ; but, like all others, he was created by Oro to some special end ; doubtless, partly answered in his Koztanza.

MEDIA.—And now that Lombardo is long dead and gone—and his work, hooted during life, lives after him—what think the present company of it ?   Speak, my lord Abrazza ! Babbalanja ! Mohi ! Yoomy !

ABRAZZA (*tapping his sandal with his sceptre*).—I never read it.

BABBALANJA (*looking upward*).—It was written with a divine intent.

MOHI (*stroking his beard*).—I never hugged it in a corner, and ignored it before Mardi.

YOOMY (*musing*).—It has bettered my heart.

MEDIA (*rising*).—And I have read it through nine times.

BABBALANJA (*starting up*).—Ah, Lombardo ! this must make thy ghost glad !

CHAPTER LXXVII

THEY SUP

THERE seemed something sinister, hollow, heartless, about Abrazza, and that green-and-yellow evil-starred crown that he wore.

But why think of that ? Though we like not something in the curve of one's brow, or distrust the tone of his voice ; yet, let us away with suspicions if we may, and make a jolly comrade of him, in the name of the gods. Miserable ! thrice miserable he, who is forever turning over and over one's character in his mind, and weighing by nice avoirdupois the pros and the cons of his goodness and badness. For we are all good and bad. Give me the heart that's huge as all Asia ; and unless a man be a villain outright, account him one of the best tempered blades in the world.

That night, in his right regal hall, King Abrazza received us. And in merry good time a fine supper was spread.

Now, in thus nocturnally regaling us, our host was warranted by many ancient and illustrious examples.

For old Jove gave suppers ; the god Woden gave suppers ; the Hindoo deity Brahma gave suppers ; the Red Man's Great Spirit gave suppers :—chiefly venison and game.

And many distinguished mortals besides.

Ahasuerus gave suppers ; Xerxes gave suppers ; Montezuma gave suppers ; Powhattan gave suppers ; the Jews' Passovers were suppers ; the Pharaohs gave suppers ; Julius Caesar gave suppers :—and rare ones they were ; Great Pompey gave suppers ; Nabob Crassus gave suppers ; and Heliogabalus, surnamed the Gobbler, gave suppers.

It was a common saying of old, that King Pluto gave suppers ; some say he is giving them still. If so, he is keeping tip-top company, old Pluto :—Emperors and Czars ; Great Moguls and Great Khans ; Grand Lamas and Grand Dukes ; Prince Regents and Queen Dowagers : —Tamerlane hob-a-nobbing with Bonaparte ; Antiochus with Solyman the Magnificent; Pisistratus pledging Pilate ; Semiramis eating bon-bons with Bloody Mary, and her namesake of Medicis ; the Thirty Tyrants quaffing three to one with the Council of Ten ; and Sultans, Satraps, Viziers, Hetmans, Soldans, Landgraves, Bashaws, Doges, Dauphins, Infantas, Incas, and Caçiques looking on.

Again : at Arbela, the conqueror of conquerors, conquering son of Olympia by Jupiter himself, sent out cards to his captains—Hephestion, Antigonus, Antipater, and the rest—to join him at ten P.M. in the Temple of Belus ; there to sit down to a victorious supper off the gold plate of the Assyrian high priests. How majestically he poured out his old Madeira that night !—feeling grand and lofty as the Himalayas ; yea, all Babylon nodded her towers in his soul !

Spread, heaped up, stacked with good things ; and redolent of citrons and grapes, hilling round tall vases of wine ; and here and there, waving with fresh orange-boughs, among whose leaves, myriads of small tapers gleamed like fire-flies in groves,—Abrazza's glorious board showed like some banquet in Paradise : Ceres and Pomona presiding ; and jolly Bacchus, like a recruit with a mettlesome rifle, staggering back as he fires off the bottles of vivacious champagne.

In ranges, round about stood living candelabras :— lackeys, gaily bedecked, with tall torches in their hands ; and at one end stood trumpeters, bugles at their lips.

'This way, my dear Media!—this seat at my left.—
Noble Taji!—my right. Babbalanja!—Mohi—where you
are. But where's pretty Yoomy?—Gone to meditate
in the moonlight? ah!—Very good. Let the banquet
begin. A blast there!'

And charge all did.

The venison, wild boar's meat, and buffalo-humps were
extraordinary; the wine, of rare vintages, like bottled
lightning; and the first course, a brilliant affair, went off
like a rocket.

But as yet, Babbalanja joined not in the revels. His
mood was on him; and apart he sat; silently eyeing the
banquet; and ever and anon muttering,—' Fogle-foggle,
fugle-fi——'

The first fury of the feast over, said King Media, pouring
out from a heavy flagon into his goblet, ' Abrazza, these
suppers are wondrous fine things.'

' Ay, my dear lord, much better than dinners.'

' So they are, so they are. The dinner-hour is the
summer of the day : full of sunshine, I grant ; but not like
the mellow autumn of supper. A dinner, you know, may
go off rather stiffly ; but invariably suppers are jovial.
At dinners, 'tis not till you take in sail, furl the cloth, bow
the lady-passengers out, and make all snug; 'tis not
till then that one begins to ride out the gale with com-
placency. But at these suppers—Good Oro! your cup is
empty, my dear demi-god!—But at these suppers, I say,
all is snug and ship-shape before you begin; and when
you begin, you waive the beginning, and begin in the
middle. And as for the cloth,—but tell us, Braid-Beard,
what that old king of Franko, Ludwig the Fat, said of that
matter. The cloth for suppers, you know. It's down in
your chronicles.'

' My lord,'—wiping his beard,—' Old Ludwig was of
opinion that at suppers the cloth was superfluous, unless

on the back of some jolly good friar.   Said he, " For one,
I prefer sitting right down to the unrobed table." '

' High and royal authority, that of Ludwig the Fat,'
said Babbalanja, ' far higher than the authority of Ludwig
the Great :—the one, only great by courtesy ; the other,
fat beyond a peradventure.   But they are equally famous ;
and in their graves both on a par.   For after devouring
many a fair province, and grinding the poor of his realm,
Ludwig the Great has long since, himself, been devoured
by very small worms, and ground into very fine dust.
And after stripping many a venison rib, Ludwig the Fat
has had his own polished and bleached in the Valley of
Death ; yea, and his cranium chased with corrodings, like
the carved flagon once held to its jaws.'

' My lord ! my lord ! '—cried Abrazza to Media—
' this ghastly devil of yours grins worse than a skull.   I
feel the worms crawling over me !—By Oro, we must
eject him ! '

' No, no, my lord.   Let him sit there, as of old the
death's-head graced the feasts of the Pharaohs—let him
sit—let him sit—for death but imparts a flavour to life.—
Go on : wag your tongue without fear, Azzageddi !—But
come, Braid-Beard ! let 's hear more of the Ludwigs.'

' Well, then, your highness, of all the eighteen royal
Ludwigs of Franko——'

' Who like so many ten-pins, all in a row,' interposed
Babbalanja, ' have been bowled off the course by grim
death.'

' Heed him not,' said Media ; ' go on.'

' The Debonnaire, the Pious, the Stammerer, the Do-
Nothing, the Juvenile, the Quarreller :—of all these, I say,
Ludwig the Fat was the best table-man of them all.   Such
a full-orbed paunch was his, that no way could he devise of
getting to his suppers, but by getting right into them.
Like the Zodiac his table was circular, and full in the

middle he sat, like a sun ;—all his jolly stews and ragouts
revolving around him.'

'Yea,' said Babbalanja, 'a very round sun was Ludwig
the Fat.   No wonder he's down in the chronicles ; several
ells about the waist, and king of cups and Tokay.   Truly,
a famous king : three hundredweight of lard, with a
diadem on top : lean brains and a fat doublet—a demijohn of a demi-god ! '

'Is this to be longer borne ? ' cried Abrazza, starting
up.   'Quaff that sneer down, devil !   on the instant !
down with it, to the dregs !   This comes, my lord Media,
of having a slow drinker at one's board.   Like an iceberg,
such a fellow frosts the whole atmosphere of a banquet, and
is felt a league off.   We must thrust him out.   Guards ! '

'Back ! touch him not, hounds ! ' cried Media.   'Your
pardon, my lord, but we 'll keep him to it ; and melt him
down in this good wine.   Drink !   I command it, drink,
Babbalanja ! '

'And am I not drinking, my lord ?   Surely you would
not that I should imbibe more than I can hold.   The
measure being full, all poured in after that is but wasted.
I am for being temperate in these things, my good lord.
And my one cup outlasts three of yours.   Better to sip a
pint, than pour down a quart.   All things in moderation
are good ; whence, wine in moderation is good.   But all
things in excess are bad : whence wine in excess is bad.'

'Away with your logic and conic sections !   Drink !—
But no, no : I am too severe.   For of all meals a supper
should be the most social and free.   And going thereto we
kings, my lord, should lay aside our sceptres.—Do as you
please, Babbalanja.'

'You are right, you are right, after all, my dear demi-
god,' said Abrazza.   'And to say truth, I seldom worry
myself with the ways of these mortals ; for no thanks do
we demi-gods get.   We kings should be ever indifferent.

Nothing like a cold heart ; warm ones are ever chafing, and getting into trouble. I let my mortals here in this isle take heed to themselves ; only barring them out when they would thrust in their petitions. This very instant, my lord, my yeoman-guard is on duty without, to drive off intruders.—Hark !—what noise is that ?—Ho, who comes ? '

At that instant there burst into the hall a crowd of spearmen, driven before a pale, ragged rout, that loudly invoked King Abrazza.

' Pardon, my lord king, for thus forcing an entrance ! But long in vain have we knocked at thy gates ! Our grievances are more than we can bear ! Give ear to our spokesman, we beseech ! '

And from their tumultuous midst they pushed forward a tall, grim, pine-tree of a fellow, who loomed up out of the throng, like the Peak of Teneriffe among the Canaries in a storm.

' Drive the knaves out ! Ho, cowards, guards, turn about ! charge upon them ! Away with your grievances ! Drive them out, I say, drive them out !—High times, truly, my lord Media, when demi-gods are thus annoyed at their wine. Oh, who would reign over mortals ! '

So at last, with much difficulty, the ragged rout were ejected ; the Peak of Teneriffe going last, a pent storm on his brow ; and muttering about some black time that was coming.

While the hoarse murmurs without still echoed through the hall, King Abrazza refilling his cup thus spoke :—
' You were saying, my dear lord, that of all meals a supper is the most social and free. Very true. And of all suppers those given by us bachelor demi-gods are the best. Are they not ? '

' They are. For Benedict mortals must be home betimes : bachelor demi-gods are never away.'

' Ay, your highnesses, bachelors are all the year round
at home,' said Mohi : ' sitting out life in the chimney
corner, cosy and warm as the dog, whilome turning the
old-fashioned roasting-jack.'

' And to us bachelor demi-gods,' cried Media, ' our
to-morrows are as long rows of fine punches, ranged on a
board, and waiting the hand.'

' But, my good lords,' said Babbalanja, now brightening
with wine ; ' if, of all suppers those given by bachelors be
the best :—of all bachelors, are not your priests and monks
the jolliest ? I mean, behind the scenes ? Their prayers
all said, and their futurities securely invested,—who so
care-free and cosy as they ? Yea, a supper for two in a
friar's cell in Maramma is merrier far than a dinner for
five-and-twenty in the broad right wing of Donjalolo's
great Palace of the Morn.'

' Bravo, Babbalanja ! ' cried Media, ' your iceberg is
thawing. More of that, more of that. Did I not say, we
would melt him down at last, my lord ? '

' Ay,' continued Babbalanja, ' bachelors are a noble
fraternity : I 'm a bachelor myself. One of ye, in that
matter, my lord demi-gods. And if unlike the patriarchs
of the world, we father not our brigades and battalions ;
and send not out into the battles of our country whole
regiments of our own individual raising ;—yet do we oftentimes leave behind us goodly houses and lands ; rare old
brandies and mountain Malagas ; and more especially,
warm doublets and togas, and spatterdashes, wherewithal
to keep comfortable those who survive us ;—casing the
legs and arms, which others beget. Then compare not in-
vidiously Benedicts with bachelors, since thus we make an
equal division of the duties which both owe to posterity.'

' Suppers forever ! ' cried Media. ' See, my lord, what
yours has done for Babbalanja. He came to it a skeleton ;
but will go away, every bone padded ! '

'Ay, my lord demi-gods,' said Babbalanja, drop by drop refilling his goblet. 'These suppers are all very fine, very pleasant, and merry. But we pay for them roundly. Everything, my good lords, has its price, from a marble to a world. And easier of digestion, and better for both body and soul, are a half-haunch of venison and a gallon of mead, taken under the sun at meridian, than the soft bridal breast of a partridge, with some gentle negus, at the noon of night!'

'No lie that!' said Mohi. 'Beshrew me, in no well-appointed mansion doth the pantry lie adjoining the sleeping-chamber. A good thought: I'll fill up, and ponder on it.'

'Let not Azzageddi get uppermost again, Babbalanja,' cried Media. 'Your goblet is only half full.'

'Permit it to remain so, my lord. For whoso takes much wine to bed with him has a bedfellow more restless than a somnambulist. And though Wine be a jolly blade at the board, a sulky knave is he under a blanket. I know him of old. Yet, your highness, for all this, to many a Mardian, suppers are still better than dinners, at whatever cost purchased. Forasmuch, as many have more leisure to sup than dine. And though you demi-gods may dine at your ease; and dine it out into night: and sit and chirp over your burgundy till the morning larks join your crickets, and wed matins to vespers;—far otherwise, with us plebeian mortals. From our dinners we must hie to our anvils; and the last jolly jorum evaporates in a cark and a care.'

'Methinks he relapses,' said Abrazza.

'It waxes late' said Mohi; 'your highness, is it not time to break up?'

'No, no!' cried Abrazza: 'let the day break when it will: but no breakings for us. It's only midnight. This way with the wine; pass it along, my dear Media. We

are young yet, my sweet lord ; light hearts and heavy
purses ; short prayers and long rent-rolls.　Pass round the
Tokay !　We demi-gods have all our old age for a dormi-
tory.　Come !—Round and round with the flagons !　Let
them disappear like milestones on a racecourse ! '

' Ah ! ' murmured Babbalanja, holding his full goblet at
arm's length on the board, ' not thus with the hapless
wight, born with a hamper on his back, and blisters in his
palms.—Toil and sleep—sleep and toil, are his days and
his nights ;　he goes to bed with a lumbago, and wakes with
the rheumatics ;—I know what it is ;—he snatches lunches,
not dinners, and makes of all life a cold snack !　Yet praise
be to Oro, though to such men dinners are scarce worth the
eating ;　nevertheless, praise Oro again, a good supper is
something.　Off jack-boots ; nay, off shirt, if you will,
and go at it.　Hurrah !　the fagged day is done : the last
blow is an echo.　Twelve long hours to sunrise !　And
would it were an Antarctic night, and six months to to-
morrow !　But, hurrah !　the very bees have their hive,
and after a day's weary wandering hie home to their
honey.　So they stretch out their stiff legs, rub their lame
elbows, and putting their tired right arms in a sling, set
the others to fetching and carrying from dishes to dentals,
from foaming flagon to the demijohn which never pours
out at the end you pour in.　Ah ! after all, the poorest
devil in Mardi lives not in vain.　There 's a soft side to the
hardest oak-plank in the world ! '

' Methinks I have heard some such sentimental gabble
as this before from my slaves, my lord,' said Abrazza to
Media.　' It has the old gibberish flavour.'

' Gibberish, your highness ?　Gibberish ?　I 'm full of
it—I 'm a gibbering ghost, my right worshipful lord !
Here, pass your hand through me—here, *here*, and scorch
it where I most burn.　By Oro ! king ! but I will gibe
and gibber at thee, till thy crown feels like another skull

clapped on thy own.   Gibberish ? ay, in hell we 'll gibber
in concert, king! we 'll howl, and roast, and hiss together! '

'Devil that thou art, begone ! Ho, guards ! seize him ! '

'Back, curs ! ' cried Media.   'Harm not a hair of his
head.   I crave pardon, King Abrazza, but no violence
must be done Babbalanja.'

'Trumpets there ! ' said Abrazza ; 'so : the banquet is
done—lights for King Media !   Good night, my lord ! '

Now, thus, for the nonce, with good cheer, we close.
And after many fine dinners and banquets—through light
and through shade ; through mirth, sorrow, and all—
drawing nigh to the evening end of these wanderings wild
—meet is it that all should be regaled with a supper.

CHAPTER LXXVIII

THEY EMBARK

NEXT morning, King Abrazza sent frigid word to Media that the day was very fine for yachting ; but he much regretted that indisposition would prevent his making one of the party, who that morning doubtless would depart his isle.

'My compliments to your king,' said Media to the chamberlains, ' and say the royal notice to quit was duly received.'

' Take Azzageddi's also,' said Babbalanja ; ' and say, I hope his highness will not fail in his appointment with me :—the first midnight after he dies ; at the graveyard corner ;—there I 'll be, and grin again ! '

Sailing on, the next land we saw was thickly wooded : hedged round about by mangrove trees ; which growing in the water, yet lifted high their boughs.   Here and there were shady nooks, half verdure and half water.   Fishes rippled, and canaries sung.

' Let us break through, my lord,' said Yoomy, ' and seek the shore.   Its solitudes must prove reviving.'

' Solitudes they are,' cried Mohi.

' Peopled but not enlivened,' said Babbalanja.   ' Hard landing here, minstrel ! see you not the isle is hedged ? '

' Why break through, then,' said Media.   ' Yillah is not here.'

' I mistrusted it,' sighed Yoomy ; ' an imprisoned island ! full of uncomplaining woes : like many others we must have glided by, unheedingly.   Yet of them have I
346

heard.   This isle many pass, marking its outward brightness, but dreaming not of the sad secrets here embowered.
Haunt of the hopeless ! In those inland woods brood
Mardians who have tasted Mardi, and found it bitter—the
draught so sweet to others !—maidens whose unimparted
bloom has cankered in the bud ; and children, with eyes
averted from life's dawn—like those new-oped morning
blossoms which, foreseeing storms, turn and close.'

   ' Yoomy's rendering of the truth,' said Mohi.

   ' Why land, then ? ' said Media.   ' No merry man of
sense—no demi-god like me, will do it.   Let's away ; let's
see all that 's pleasant, or that seems so, in our circuit,
and, if possible, shun the sad.'

   ' Then we have circled not the round reef wholly,' said
Babbalanja, ' but made of it a segment.   For this is far
from being the first sad land, my lord, that we have
slighted at your instance.'

   ' No more.   I will have no gloom.   A chorus ! there,
ye paddlers ! spread all your sails ; ply paddles ; breeze
up, merry winds ! '

   And so, in the saffron sunset, we neared another shore.

   A gloomy-looking land ! black, beetling crags, rent by
volcanic clefts ;   ploughed up with watercourses, and
dusky with charred woods.   The beach was strewn with
scoria and cinders ; in dolorous soughs, a chill wind blew ;
wails issued from the caves ; and yellow, spooming surges,
lashed the moaning strand.

   ' Shall we land ? ' said Babbalanja.

   ' Not here,' cried Yoomy ; ' no Yillah here.'

   ' No,' said Media.   ' This is another of those lands far
better to avoid.'

   ' Know ye not,' said Mohi, ' that here are the mines of
King Klanko, whose scourged slaves, toiling in their pits,
so nigh approach the volcano's bowels, they hear its
rumblings ?   " Yet they must work on," cries Klanko,

" the mines still yield ! "   And daily his slaves' bones are brought above ground, mixed with the metal masses.'

' Set all sail there, men ! away ! '

' My lord,' said Babbalanja ; ' still must we shun the unmitigated evil ; and only view the good ; or evil so mixed therewith, the mixture 's both ? '

Half veiled in misty clouds, the harvest moon now rose ; and in that pale and haggard light all sat silent ; each man in his own secret mood : best knowing his own thoughts.

CHAPTER LXXIX

BABBALANJA AT THE FULL OF THE MOON

' Ho, mortals ! Go we to a funeral, that our paddles
seem thus muffled ? Up heart, Taji ! or does that witch
Hautia haunt thee ? Be a demi-god once more, and laugh.
Her flowers are not barbs ; and the avengers' arrows are
too blunt to slay. Babbalanja ! Mohi ! Yoomy ! up
heart ! up heart !—By Oro ! I will debark the whole
company on the next land we meet. No tears for me.
Ha, ha ! let us laugh. Ho, Vee-Vee ! awake ; quick,
boy,—some wine ! and let us make glad, beneath the glad
moon. Look ! it is stealing forth from its clouds. Perdition to Hautia ! Long lives, and merry ones to ourselves !
Taji, my charming fellow, here 's to you :—May your heart
be a stone ! Ha, ha !—will nobody join me ? My laugh
is lonely as his who laughed in his tomb. Come, laugh ;
will no one quaff wine, I say ? See ! the round moon is
abroad.'

' Say you so, my lord ? then for one, I am with you,'
cried Babbalanja. ' Fill me a brimmer. Ah ! but this
wine leaps through me like a panther. Ay, let us laugh :
let us roar : let us yell ! What if I was sad but just now ?
Life is an April day, that both laughs and weeps in a
breath. But whoso is wise, laughs when he can. Men fly
from a groan, but run to a laugh. Vee-Vee ! your gourd.
My lord, let me help you. Ah, how it sparkles ! Cups,
cups, Vee-Vee, more cups ! Here, Taji, take that :
Mohi, take that : Yoomy, take that. And now let us

drown away grief. Ha! ha! the house of mourning is deserted, though of old good cheer kept the funeral guests; and so keep I mine; here I sit by my dead, and replenish your wine-cups. Old Mohi, your cup: Yoomy, yours: ha! ha! let us laugh, let us scream! Weeds are put off at a fair; no heart bursts but in secret; it is good to laugh, though the laugh be hollow; and wise to make merry, now and for aye. Laugh, and make friends: weep and they go. Women sob, and are rid of their grief: men laugh, and retain it. There is laughter in heaven, and laughter in hell. And a deep thought whose language is laughter. Though wisdom be wedded to woe, though the way thereto is by tears, yet all ends in a shout. But wisdom wears no weeds; woe is more merry than mirth; 'tis a shallow grief that is sad. Ha! ha! how demoniacs shout; how all skeletons grin; we all die with a rattle. Laugh! laugh! Are the cherubim grave? Humour, thy laugh is divine; whence, mirth-making idiots have been revered; and therefore may I. Ho! let us be gay, if it be only for an hour, and Death hand us the goblet. Vee-Vee! bring on your gourds! Let us pledge each other in bumpers!—let us laugh, laugh, laugh it out to the last. All sages have laughed,—let us; Bardianna laughed,—let us; Demorkriti laughed,—let us; Amoree laughed,—let us; Rabeelee roared,—let us; the hyenas grin, the jackals yell,—let us.—But you don't laugh, my lord? laugh away!'

'No, thank you, Azzageddi, not after that infernal fashion; better weep.'

'He makes me crawl all over, as if I were an ant-hill,' said Mohi.

'He's mad, mad, mad!' cried Yoomy.

'Ay, mad, mad, mad!—mad as the mad fiend that rides me!—But come, sweet minstrel, wilt list to a song? —We madmen are all poets, you know:—Ha! ha!—

> Stars laugh in the sky :
> > Oh fugle-fi !
> The waves dimple below :
> > Oh fugle-fo !

The wind strikes her dulcimers ; the groves give a shout ;
the hurricane is only an hysterical laugh ; and the lightning that blasts, blasts only in play.   We must laugh or
we die ; to laugh is to live.   Not to laugh is to have the
tetanus.   Will you weep ? then laugh while you weep.
For mirth and sorrow are kin ; are published by identical
nerves.   Go, Yoomy : go study anatomy : there is much
to be learned from the dead, more than you may learn
from the living, and I am dead though I live ; and as soon
dissect myself as another ; I curiously look into my
secrets : and grope under my ribs.   I have found that the
heart is not whole, but divided ; that it seeks a soft
cushion whereon to repose ; that it vitalises the blood ;
which else were weaker than water : I have found that we
cannot live without hearts ; though the heartless live
longest.   Yet hug your hearts, ye handful that have
them ; 'tis a blessed inheritance !   Thus, thus, my lord,
I run on ; from one pole to the other ; from this thing to
that.   But so the great world goes round, and in one
somerset shows the sun twenty-five thousand miles of
a landscape ! '

   At that instant, down went the fiery full moon, and the
dog-star ; and far down into Media, a Tivoli of wine.

CHAPTER LXXX

MORNING

LIFE or death, weal or woe, the sun stays not his course. On : over battlefield and bower ; over tower and town he speeds ;—peers in at births and deathbeds ; lights up cathedral, mosque, and pagan shrine ;—laughing over all ; —a very Democritus in the sky ; and in one brief day sees more than any pilgrim in a century's round.

So, the sun ; nearer heaven than we :—with what mind, then, may blessed Oro downward look.

It was a purple, red, and yellow East ;—streaked, and crossed. And down from breezy mountains, robust and ruddy Morning came,—a plaided Highlander, waving his plumed bonnet to the isles.

Over the neighbouring groves the larks soared high ; and soaring, sang in jubilees ; while across our bows, between two isles, a mighty moose swam stately as a seventy-four ; and backward tossed his antlered wilderness in air.

Just bounding from fresh morning groves, with the brine he mixed the dew of leaves,—his antlers dripping on the swell, that rippled before his brown and bow-like chest.

' Five hundred thousand centuries since,' said Babbalanja, ' this same sight was seen. With Oro, the sun is co-eternal ; and the same life that moves that moose, animates alike the sun and Oro. All are parts of One. In me, in *me*, flit thoughts participated by the beings peopling all the stars. Saturn, and Mercury, and Mardi, are brothers, one and all ; and across their orbits to each

352

other talk, like souls. Of these things what chapters
might be writ! Oh! that flesh cannot keep pace with
spirit. Oh! that these myriad germ-dramas in me should
so perish hourly, for lack of power mechanic.—Worlds
pass worlds in space, as men, men,—in thoroughfares; and
after periods of thousand years, cry: "Well met, my
friend, again!"—To me, to *me*, they talk in mystic music;
I hear them think through all their zones.—Hail, farthest
worlds! and all the beauteous beings in ye! Fan me,
sweet Zenora! with thy twilight wings!—Ho! let's
voyage to Aldebaran.—Ha! indeed, a ruddy world!
What a buoyant air! Not like to Mardi, this. Ruby
columns: minarets of amethyst: diamond domes! Who
is this?—a god! What a lake-like brow! transparent as
the morning air. I see his thoughts like worlds revolving
—and in his eyes—like unto heavens—soft falling stars are
shooting.—How these thousand passing wings winnow
away my breath :—I faint :—back, back to some small
asteroid.—Sweet being! if by Mardian word I may
address thee—speak!—" I bear a soul in germ within
me; I feel the first, faint trembling, like to a harp-string,
vibrate in my inmost being. Kill me, and generations
die."—So, of old, the unbegotten lived within the virgin;
who then loved her God, as new-made mothers their babes
ere born. Oh, Alma, Alma, Alma!—Fangs off, fiend!—
will that name ever lash thee into foam?—Smite not my
face so, forked flames!'

'Babbalanja! Babbalanja! rouse, man! rouse! Art
in hell and damned, that thy sinews so snake-like coil and
twist all over thee? Thy brow is black as Ops! Turn,
turn! see yonder moose!'

'Hail! mighty brute!—thou feelest not these things:
never canst *thou* be damned. Moose! would thy soul
were mine; for if that scorched thing, mine, be immortal
—so thine; and thy life hath not the consciousness of

death.   I read profound placidity—deep—million—violet fathoms down, in that soft, pathetic, woman eye !   What is man's shrunk form to thine, thou woodland majesty ?— Moose, moose !—my soul is shot again—Oh, Oro ! Oro ! '

' He falls ! ' cried Media.

' Mark the agony in his waning eye,' said Yoomy ;— ' alas, poor Babbalanja ! Is this thing of madness conscious to thyself ?   If ever thou art sane again, wilt thou have reminiscences ?   Take my robe :—here, I strip me to cover thee and all thy woes.   Oro ! by this, thy being's side, I kneel :—grant death or happiness to Babbalanja ! '

CHAPTER LXXXI

L'ULTIMA SERA

THUS far, through myriad islands, had we searched : of
all, no one pen may write ; least, mine ;—and still no
trace of Yillah.

But though my hopes revived not from their ashes ; yet,
so much of Mardi had we searched, it seemed as if the long
pursuit must, ere many moons, be ended ; whether for
weal or woe, my frenzy sometimes recked not.

After its first fair morning flushings, all that day was
overcast. We sailed upon an angry sea, beneath an angry
sky. Deep scowled on deep ; and in dun vapours the
blinded sun went down, unseen ; though full toward the
West our three prows were pointed ; steadfast as three
printed points upon the compass card.

' When we set sail from Odo 'twas a glorious morn in
spring,' said Yoomy ; ' toward the rising sun we steered.
But now, beneath autumnal night-clouds, we hasten to its
setting.'

' How now ? ' cried Media ; ' why is the minstrel
mournful ?—He whose place it is to chase away despond-
ency : not be its minister.'

' Ah, my lord, so *thou* thinkest. But better can my
verses soothe the sad than make them light of heart.
Nor are we minstrels so gay of soul as Mardi deems us.
The brook that sings the sweetest, murmurs through the
loneliest woods :—

> The isles hold thee not, thou departed !
> From thy bower, now issues no lay :—
> In vain we recall perished warblings :
> Spring birds, to far climes, wing their way ! '

355

As Yoomy thus sang ; unmindful of the lay, with paddle
plying, in low, pleasant tones, thus hummed to himself our
bowsman, a gamesome wight :—

> Ho ! merrily ho ! we paddlers sail !
> Ho ! over sea-dingle, and dale !—
>   Our pulses fly,
>   Our hearts beat high,
> Ho ! merrily, merrily, ho !

But a sudden splash, and a shrill, gurgling sound, like
that of a fountain subsiding, now broke upon the air.
Then all was still, save the rush of the waves by our keels.

' Save him !   Put back ! '

From his elevated seat, the merry bowsman, too gleefully reaching forward, had fallen into the lagoon.

With all haste, our speeding canoes were reversed ; but
not till we had darted in upon another darkness than that
in which the bowsman fell.

As, blindly, we groped back, deep Night dived deeper
down in the sea.

' Drop paddles all, and list.'

Holding their breath, over the six gunwales all now
leaned ; but the only moans were the wind's.

Long time we lay thus ; then slowly crossed and recrossed our track, almost hopeless ; but yet loth to leave
him who, with a song in his mouth, died and was buried
in a breath.

' Let us away,' said Media ; ' why seek more ?   He is
gone.'

' Ay, gone,' said Babbalanja, ' and whither ?   But a
moment since, he was among us : now, the fixed stars are
not more remote than he.   So far off, can he live ?   Oh,
Oro ! this death thou ordainest unmans the manliest.
Say not nay, my lord.   Let us not speak behind Death's
back.   Hard and horrible is it to die : blindfold to leap

from life's verge ! But thus, in clouds of dust, and with a
trampling as of hoofs, the generations disappear ; death
driving them all into his treacherous fold, as wild Indians
the bison herds. Nay, nay, death is life's last despair.
Hard and horrible is it to die. Oro himself, in Alma, died
not without a groan. Yet why, why live ? Life is weari-
some to all : the same dull round. Day and night,
summer and winter, round about us revolving for aye.
One moment lived is a life. No new stars appear in the
sky ; no new lights in the soul. Yet, of changes there are
many. For though, with rapt sight, in childhood, we
behold many strange things beneath the moon, and all
Mardi looks a tented fair—how soon everything fades.
All of us, in our very bodies, outlive our own selves. I
think of green youth as of a merry playmate departed ;
and to shake hands, and be pleasant with my old age,
seems in prospect even harder than to draw a cold stranger
to my bosom. But old age is not for me. I am not of the
stuff that grows old. This Mardi is not our home. Up
and down we wander, like exiles transported to a planet
afar :—'tis not the world *we* were born in ; not the world
once so lightsome and gay ; not the world where we once
merrily danced, dined, and supped ; and wooed, and
wedded our long-buried wives. Then let us depart. But
whither ? We push ourselves forward—then, start back
in affright. Essay it again, and flee. Hard to live ; hard
to die ; intolerable suspense ! But the grim despot at
last interposes ; and with a viper in our winding-sheets
we are dropped in the sea.'

' To me,' said Mohi, his gray locks damp with night-
dews, ' death's dark defile at times seems at hand, with no
voice to cheer. That all have died, makes it not easier for
me to depart. And that many have been quenched in
infancy seems a mercy to the slow perishing of my old age,
limb by limb and sense by sense. I have long been the

tomb of my youth. And more has died out of me, already, than remains for the last death to finish. Babbalanja says truth. In childhood, death stirred me not ; in middle age, it pursued me like a prowling bandit on the road ; now, grown an old man, it boldly leads the way ; and ushers me on ; and turns round upon me its skeleton gaze : poisoning the last solaces of life. Maramma but adds to my gloom.'

' Death ! death ! ' cried Yoomy, ' must I be not, and millions be ? Must I go, and the flowers still bloom ? Oh, I have marked what it is to be dead ;—how shouting boys, of holydays, hide-and-seek among the tombs, which must hide all seekers at last.'

' Clouds on clouds ! ' cried Media, ' but away with them all ! Why not leap your graves, while ye may ? Time to die, when death comes, without dying by inches. 'Tis no death to die ; the only death is the fear of it. I, a demi-god, fear death not.'

' But when the jackals howl round you ? ' said Babbalanja.

' Drive them off ! Die the demi-god's death ! On his last couch of crossed spears, my brave old sire cried, " Wine, wine ; strike up, conch and cymbal ; let the king die to martial melodies ! " '

' More valiant dying, than dead,' said Babbalanja. ' Our end of the winding procession resounds with music, and flaunts with banners with brave devices :—" Cheer up ! " " Fear not ! " " Millions have died before ! "—but in the endless van, not a pennon streams ; all there is silent and solemn. The last wisdom is dumb.'

Silence ensued ; during which each dip of the paddles in the now calm water fell full and long upon the ear.

Anon, lifting his head, Babbalanja thus : ' Yillah still eludes us. And in all this tour of Mardi how little have we found to fill the heart with peace : how much to slaughter all our yearnings.'

'Croak no more, raven!' cried Media. 'Mardi is full of spring-time sights, and jubilee sounds. I never was sad in my life.'

'But for thy one laugh, my lord, how many groans! Were all happy, or all miserable,—more tolerable then, than as it is. But happiness and misery are so broadly marked, that this Mardi may be the retributive future of some forgotten past.—Yet vain our surmises. Still vainer to say, that all Mardi is but a means to an end; that this life is a state of probation; that evil is but permitted for a term; that for specified ages a rebel angel is viceroy.— Nay, nay. Oro delegates his sceptre to none; in his ever-lasting reign there are no interregnums; and Time is Eternity; and we live in Eternity now. Yet, some tell of a hereafter, where all the mysteries of life will be over; and the sufferings of the virtuous recompensed. Oro is just, they say.—Then always,—now, and evermore. But to make restitution implies a wrong; and Oro can do no wrong. Yet what seems evil to us may be good to him. If he fears not, nor hopes,—he has no other passion; no ends, no purposes. He lives content; all ends are com-passed in him; he has no past, no future; he is the everlasting now; which is an everlasting calm; and things that are,—have been,—will be. This gloom's enough. But hoot! hoot! the night-owl ranges through the woodlands of Maramma; its dismal notes pervade our lives; and when we would fain depart in peace, that bird flies on before:—cloud-like, eclipsing our setting suns, and filling the air with dolour.'

'Too true!' cried Yoomy. 'Our calms must come by storms. Like helmless vessels, tempest-tossed, our only anchorage is when we founder.'

'Our beginnings,' murmured Mohi, 'are lost in clouds; we live in darkness all our days, and perish without an end.'

' Croak on, cowards ! ' cried Media, ' and fly before the hideous phantoms that pursue ye.'

' No coward he, who hunted, turns and finds no foe to fight,' said Babbalanja. ' Like the stag, whose brow is beat with wings of hawks, perched in his heavenward antlers ; so I, blinded, goaded, headlong rush ! this way and that ; nor knowing whither ; one forest wide around ! '

CHAPTER LXXXII

THEY SAIL FROM NIGHT TO DAY

ERE long the three canoes lurched heavily in a violent
swell. Like palls, the clouds swept to and fro, hooding the
gibbering winds. At every head-beat wave, our arching
prows reared up, and shuddered ; the night ran out in
rain.

Whither to turn we knew not ; nor what haven to gain ;
so dense the darkness.

But at last the storm was over. Our shattered prows
seemed gilded. Day dawned ; and from his golden vases
poured red wine upon the waters.

That flushed tide rippled toward us ; floating from the
east, a lone canoe ; in which, there sat a mild old man ; a
palm-bough in his hand : a bird's beak, holding amaranth
and myrtles, his slender prow.

' Alma's blessing upon ye, voyagers ! ye look storm-
worn.'

' The storm we have survived, old man ; and many
more we yet must ride,' said Babbalanja.

' The sun is risen ; and all is well again. We but need
to repair our prows,' said Media.

' Then, turn aside to Serenia, a pleasant isle, where all
are welcome ; where many storm-worn rovers land at
last to dwell.'

' Serenia ? ' said Babbalanja ; ' methinks Serenia is
that land of enthusiasts, of which we hear, my lord ; where
Mardians pretend to the unnatural conjunction of reason
with things revealed ; where Alma, they say, is restored

to his divine original ; where, deriving their principles
from the same sources whence flow the persecutions of
Maramma,—men strive to live together in gentle bonds
of peace and charity ;—folly ! folly ! '

' Ay,' said Media, ' much is said of those people of
Serenia ; but their social fabric must soon fall to pieces ;
it is based upon the idlest of theories. Thanks for thy
courtesy, old man, but we care not to visit thy isle. Our
voyage has an object, which, something tells me, will not
be gained by touching at thy shores. Elsewhere we may
refit. Farewell ! 'Tis breezing ; set the sails ! Farewell,
old man.'

' Nay, nay ! think again ; the distance is but small ; the
wind fair,—but 'tis ever so, thither ;—come : we, people
of Serenia, are most anxious to be seen of Mardi ; so that
if our manner of life seem good, all Mardi may live as we.
In blessed Alma's name, I pray ye, come ! '

' Shall we then, my lord ? '

' Lead on, old man ! We will e'en see this wondrous
isle.'

So, guided by the venerable stranger, by noon we
descried an island blooming with bright savannas, and
pensive with peaceful groves.

Wafted from this shore, came balm of flowers, and
melody of birds : a thousand summer sounds and odours.
The dimpled tide sang round our splintered prows ; the
sun was high in heaven, and the waters were deep
below.

' The land of Love ! ' the old man murmured, as we
neared the beach, where innumerable shells were gently
rolling in the playful surf, and murmuring from their
tuneful valves. Behind, another, and a verdant surf
played against lofty banks of leaves ; where the breeze,
likewise, found its shore.

And now, emerging from beneath the trees, there came

a goodly multitude in flowing robes ; palm branches in
their hands ; and as they came, they sang :—

> Hail ! voyagers, hail !
> Whence e'er ye come, where'er ye rove,
>> No calmer strand,
>> No sweeter land,
> Will e'er ye view, than the land of Love !

> Hail ! voyagers, hail !
> To these, our shores, soft gales invite :
>> The palm plumes wave,
>> The billows lave,
> And hither point fix'd stars of light !

> Hail ! voyagers, hail !
> Think not our groves wide brood with gloom ;
>> In this, our isle,
>> Bright flowers smile :
> Full urns, rose-heaped, these valleys bloom.

> Hail ! voyagers, hail !
> Be not deceived ; renounce vain things ;
>> Ye may not find
>> A tranquil mind,
> Though hence ye sail with swiftest wings.

> Hail ! voyagers, hail !
> Time flies full fast ; life soon is o'er ;
>> And ye may mourn,
>> That hither borne,
> Ye left behind our pleasant shore.

CHAPTER LXXXIII

THEY LAND

THE song was ended; and as we gained the strand the crowd embraced us, and called us brothers; ourselves and our humblest attendants.

' Call ye us brothers, whom ere now ye never saw ? '

' Even so,' said the old man, ' is not Oro the father of all ? Then, are we not brothers ? Thus Alma, the master, hath commanded.'

' This was not our reception in Maramma,' said Media, ' the appointed place of Alma ; where his precepts are preserved.'

' No, no,' said Babbalanja ; ' old man ! your lesson of brotherhood was learned elsewhere than from Alma ; for in Maramma and in all its tributary isles true brotherhood there is none. Even in the Holy Island many are oppressed ; for heresies, many murdered ; and thousands perish beneath the altars, groaning with offerings that might relieve them.'

' Alas ! too true. But I beseech ye, judge not Alma by all those who profess his faith. Hast thou thyself his records searched ? '

' Fully, I have not. So long, even from my infancy, have I witnessed the wrongs committed in his name ; the sins and inconsistencies of his followers ; that thinking all evil must flow from a congenial fountain, I have scorned to study the whole record of your master's life. By parts I only know it.'

' Ah ! baneful error ! But thus is it, brothers ! that

364

the wisest are set against the Truth, because of those who
wrest it from itself.'

' Do ye then claim to live what your master hath
spoken ?   Are your precepts practices ? '

' Nothing do we claim : we but earnestly endeavour.'

' Tell me not of your endeavours, but of your life.
What hope for the fatherless among ye ? '

' Adopted as a son.'

' Of one poor, and naked ? '

' Clothed, and he wants for naught.'

' If ungrateful, he smite you ? '

' Still we feed and clothe him.'

' If yet an ingrate ? '

' Long, he cannot be ; for love is a fervent fire.'

' But what, if widely he dissent from your belief in
Alma ;—then, surely, ye must cast him forth ? '

' No, no ; we will remember, that if he dissent from us,
we then equally dissent from him ; and men's faculties are
Oro-given.   Nor will we say that he is wrong, and we are
right ; for this we know not, absolutely.   But we care
not for men's words ; we look for creeds in actions ; which
are the truthful symbols of the things within.   He who
hourly prays to Alma, but lives not up to world-wide love
and charity—that man is more an unbeliever that he who
verbally rejects the Master, but does his bidding.   Our
lives are our Amens.'

' But some say that what your Alma teaches is wholly
new—a revelation of things before unimagined, even by
the poets.   To do his bidding, then, some new faculty
must be vouchsafed, whereby to apprehend aright.'

' So have I always thought,' said Mohi.

' If Alma teaches love, I want no gift to learn,' said
Yoomy.

' All that is vital in the Master's faith, lived here in
Mardi and in humble dells, was practised long previous to

the Master's coming. But never before was virtue so
lifted up among us, that all might see ; never before did
rays from heaven descend to glorify it. But are Truth,
Justice, and Love, the revelations of Alma alone ? Were
they never heard of till he came ? Oh ! Alma but opens
unto us our own hearts. Were his precepts strange we
would recoil—not one feeling would respond ; whereas,
once hearkened to, our souls embrace them as with the
instinctive tendrils of a vine.'

'But,' said Babbalanja, 'since Alma, they say, was
solely intent upon the things of the Mardi to come—which
to all, must seem uncertain—of what benefit his precepts
for the daily lives led here ? '

'Would ! would that Alma might once more descend !
Brother ! were the turf our everlasting pillow, still would
the Master's faith answer a blessed end ;—making us more
truly happy *here*. *That* is the first and chief result ; for
holy here, we must be holy elsewhere. 'Tis Mardi, to
which loved Alma gives his laws ; not Paradise.'

'Full soon will I be testing all these things,' murmured
Mohi.

'Old man,' said Media, 'thy years and Mohi's lead ye
both to dwell upon the unknown future. But speak to me
of other themes. Tell me of this island and its people.
From all I have heard, and now behold, I gather that here,
there dwells no king ; that ye are left to yourselves ; and
that this mystic Love, ye speak of, is your ruler. Is it so ?
Then, are ye full as visionary as Mardi rumours. And
though for a time ye may have prospered,—long, ye cannot be, without some sharp lesson to convince ye that
your faith in Mardian virtue is entirely vain.'

'Truth. We have no king ; for Alma's precepts rebuke
the arrogance of place and power. He is the tribune of
mankind ; nor will his true faith be universal Mardi's, till
our whole race is kingless. But think not we believe in

man's perfection. Yet, against all good, he is not absolutely set. In his heart, there is a germ. *That* we seek to foster. To *that* we cling ; else, all were hopeless ! '

' Your social state ? '

' It is imperfect ; and long must so remain. But we make not the miserable many support the happy few. Nor by annulling reason's laws, seek to breed equality, by breeding anarchy. In all things, equality is not for all. Each has his own. Some have wider groves of palms than others ; fare better ; dwell in more tasteful arbours ; oftener renew their fragrant thatch. Such differences must be. But none starve outright, while others feast. By the abounding, the needy are supplied. Yet not by statute, but from dictates, born half dormant in us, and warmed into life by Alma. Those dictates we but follow in all we do ; we are not dragged to righteousness ; but go running. Nor do we live in common. For vice and virtue blindly mingled form a union where vice too often proves the alkali. The vicious we make dwell apart, until reclaimed. And reclaimed they soon must be, since everything invites. The sin of others rests not upon our heads : none we drive to crime. Our laws are not of vengeance bred, but Love and Alma.'

' Fine poetry all this,' said Babbalanja, ' but not so new. Oft do they warble thus in bland Maramma ! '

' It sounds famously, old man ! ' said Media, ' but men are men. Some must starve ; some be scourged. Your doctrines are impracticable.'

' And are not these things enjoined by Alma ? And would Alma inculcate the impossible ? of what merit his precepts unless they may be practised ? But, I beseech ye, speak no more of Maramma. Alas ! did Alma revisit Mardi, think you, it would be among those Morais he would lay his head ? '

' No, no,' said Babbalanja, ' as an intruder he came ;

and an intruder would he be this day. On all sides would he jar our social systems.'

' Not here, not here ! Rather would we welcome Alma hungry and athirst, than though he came floating hither on the wings of seraphs ; the blazing zodiac his diadem ! In all his aspects we adore him ; needing no pomp and power to kindle worship. Though he came from Oro ; though he did miracles ; though through him is life ;—not for these things alone, do we thus love him. We love him from an instinct in us ;—a fond, filial, reverential feeling. And this would yet stir in our souls were death our end, and Alma incapable of befriending us. We love him because we do.'

' Is this man divine ? ' murmured Babbalanja. ' But thou speakest most earnestly of adoring Alma :—I see no temples in your groves.'

' Because this isle is all one temple to his praise ; every leaf is consecrated his. We fix not Alma here and there ; and say, " Those groves for him, and these broad fields for us." It is all his own ; and we ourselves ; our every hour of life ; and all we are, and have.'

' Then, ye forever fast and pray ; and stand and sing ; as at long intervals the censer-bearers in Maramma supplicate their gods.'

' Alma forbid ! We never fast ; our aspirations are our prayers ; our lives are worship. And when we laugh, with human joy at human things,—*then* do we most sound great Oro's praise, and prove the merit of sweet Alma's love ! Our love in Alma makes us glad, not sad. Ye speak of temples ;—behold ! 'tis by not building *them*, that we widen charity among us. The treasures which, in the islands round about, are lavished on a thousand fanes ;—with these we every day relieve the Master's suffering disciples. In Mardi, Alma preached in open fields,—and must his worshippers have palaces ? '

'No temples, then no priests,' said Babbalanja, 'for few priests will enter where lordly arches form not the portal.'

'We have no priests, but one; and he is Alma's self. We have his precepts: we seek no comments but our hearts.'

'But without priests and temples, how long will flourish this your faith?' said Media.

'For many ages has not this faith lived, in spite of priests and temples? and shall it not survive them? What we believe we hold divine; and things divine endure forever.'

'But how enlarge your bounds? how convert the vicious, without persuasion of some special seers? Must your religion go hand in hand with all things secular?'

'We hold not, that one man's words should be a gospel to the rest; but that Alma's words should be a gospel to us all. And not by precepts would we have some few endeavour to persuade; but all, by practice, fix convictions that the life we lead is the life for all. We are apostles, every one. Where'er we go, our faith we carry in our hands and hearts. It is our chiefest joy. We do not put it wide away six days out of seven; and then, assume it. In it we all exult, and joy; as that which makes us happy here; as that, without which, we could be happy nowhere; as something meant for this time present, and henceforth for aye. It is our vital mode of being; not an incident. And when we die, this faith shall be our pillow; and when we rise, our staff; and at the end, our crown. For we are all immortal. Here, Alma joins with our own hearts, confirming nature's promptings.'

'How eloquent he is!' murmured Babbalanja. 'Some black cloud seems floating from me. I begin to see. I come out in light. The sharp fang tears me less. The forked flames wane. My soul sets back like ocean streams, that sudden change their flow. Have I been sane ? Quickened in me is a hope. But pray you, old man—say on ; methinks, that in your faith must be much that jars with reason.'

' No, brother ! Right reason, and Alma, are the same ; else Alma, not reason, would we reject. The Master's great command is Love ; and here do all things wise, and all things good, unite. Love is all in all. The more we love, the more we know ; and so reversed. Oro we love ; this isle ; and our wide arms embrace all Mardi like its reef. How can we err, thus feeling ? We hear loved Alma's pleading, prompting voice, in every breeze, in every leaf ; we see his earnest eye in every star and flower.'

' Poetry ! ' cried Yoomy, ' and poetry is truth ! He stirs me.'

' When Alma dwelt in Mardi, 'twas with the poor and friendless. He fed the famishing ; he healed the sick ; he bound up wounds. For every precept that he spoke he did ten thousand mercies. And Alma is our loved example.'

' Sure, all this is in the histories ! ' said Mohi, starting.

' But not alone to poor and friendless did Alma wend his charitable way. From lowly places he looked up ; and long invoked great chieftains in their state ; and told them all their pride was vanity ; and bade them ask their souls. " In *me*," he cried, " is that heart of mild content, which in vain ye seek in rank and title. I am Love : love ye then me." '

' Cease, cease, old man ! ' cried Media ; ' thou movest me beyond my seeming. What thoughts are these ? Have done ! Wouldst thou unking me ? '

' Alma is for all ; for high and low. Like heaven's own

breeze, he lifts the lily from its lowly stem, and sweeps, reviving, through the palmy groves. High thoughts he gives the sage, and humble trust the simple. Be the measure what it may, his grace doth fill it to the brim. He lays the lashings of the soul's wild aspirations after things unseen ; oil he poureth on the waters ; and stars come out of night's black concave at his great command. In him is hope for all ; for all, unbounded joys. Fast locked in his loved clasp no doubts dismay. He opes the eye of faith and shuts the eye of fear. He is all we pray for, and beyond ; all, that in the wildest hour of ecstasy, rapt fancy paints in bright Auroras upon the soul's wide, boundless Orient ! '

' Oh, Alma, Alma ! prince divine ! ' cried Babbalanja, sinking on his knees, ' in *thee*, at last, I find repose. Hope perches in my heart a dove ;—a thousand rays illume ;— all heaven 's a sun. Gone, gone ! are all distracting doubts. Love and Alma now prevail. I see with other eyes :—Are these my hands ? What wild, wild dreams were mine ;—I have been mad. Some things there are we must not think of. Beyond one obvious mark, all human lore is vain. Where have I lived till now ? Had dark Maramma's zealot tribe but murmured to me as this old man, long since had I been wise ! Reason no longer domineers ; but still doth speak. All I have said ere this, that wars with Alma's precepts, I here recant. Here I kneel, and own great Oro and his sovereign son.'

' And here another kneels and prays,' cried Yoomy. ' In Alma all my dreams are found, my inner longings for the love supreme that prompts my every verse. Summer is in my soul.'

' Nor now, too late for these gray hairs,' cried Mohi, with devotion. ' Alma, thy breath is on my soul. I see bright light.'

' No more a demi-god,' cried Media, ' but a subject to

our common chief. No more shall dismal cries be heard from Odo's groves. Alma, I am thine.'

With swimming eyes the old man kneeled ; and round him grouped king, sage, gray hairs, and youth.

There, as they kneeled, and as the old man blessed them, the setting sun burst forth from mists, gilded the island round about, shed rays upon their heads, and went down in a glory—all the East radiant with red burnings, like an altar-fire.

CHAPTER LXXXIV

BABBALANJA RELATES TO THEM A VISION

LEAVING Babbalanja in the old man's bower, deep in meditation ; thoughtfully we strolled along the beach, inspiring the musky, midnight air ; the tropical stars glistening in heaven, like drops of dew among violets.

The waves were phosphorescent, and laved the beach with a fire that cooled it.

Returning, we espied Babbalanja advancing in his snow-white mantle. The fiery tide was ebbing ; and in the soft, moist sand, at every step, he left a lustrous footprint.

' Sweet friends ! this isle is full of mysteries,' he said. ' I have dreamed of wondrous things. After I had laid me down, thought pressed hard upon me. By my eyes passed pageant visions. I started at a low, strange melody, deep in my inmost soul. At last, methought my eyes were fixed on heaven ; and there, I saw a shining spot, unlike a star. Thwarting the sky, it grew, and grew, descending ; till bright wings were visible : between them, a pensive face angelic, downward beaming ; and, for one golden moment, gauze-veiled in spangled Berenice's Locks.

' Then, as white flame from yellow, out from that starry cluster it emerged ; and brushed the astral crosses, crowns, and cups. And as in violet, tropic seas, ships leave a radiant-white and fire-fly wake ; so, in long extension tapering, behind the vision, gleamed another Milky Way.

' Strange throbbings seized me ; my soul tossed on its

own tides. But soon the inward harmony bounded in exulting choral strains. I heard a feathery rush; and straight beheld a form, traced all over with veins of vivid light. The vision undulated round me.

' " Oh! spirit! angel! god! whate'er thou art," I cried, " leave me; I am but man."

' Then, I heard a low, sad sound,—no voice. It said, or breathed upon me,—" Thou hast proved the grace of Alma: tell me what thou 'st learned."

' Silent replied my soul, for voice was gone,—" This have I learned, oh! spirit!—In things mysterious, to seek no more; but rest content, with knowing naught but Love."

' " Blessed art thou for that: thrice blessed," then I heard, " and since humility is thine, thou art one apt to learn. That which thy own wisdom could not find, thy ignorance confessed shall gain. Come, and see new things."

' Once more it undulated round me; its lightning wings grew dim; nearer, nearer; till I felt a shock electric,—and nested 'neath its wing.

' We clove the air; passed systems, suns, and moons: what seem from Mardi's isles, the glowworm stars.

' By distant fleets of worlds we sped, as voyagers pass far sails at sea, and hail them not. Foam played before them as they darted on; wild music was their wake; and many tracks of sound we crossed, where worlds had sailed before.

' Soon, we gained a point, where a new heaven was seen; whence all our firmament seemed one nebula. Its glories burned like thousand steadfast-flaming lights.

' Here hived the worlds in swarms: and gave forth sweets ineffable.

' We lighted on a ring, circling a space, where mornings seemed forever dawning over worlds unlike.

' " Here," I heard, " thou viewest thy Mardi's heaven.
Herein each world is portioned."

' As he who climbs to mountain tops pants hard for
breath ; so panted I for Mardi's grosser air. But that
which caused my flesh to faint was new vitality to my
soul. My eyes swept over all before me. The spheres
were plain as villages that dot a landscape. I saw most
beauteous forms, yet like our own. Strange sounds I heard
of gladness that seemed mixed with sadness :—a low,
sweet harmony of both. Else, I know not how to phrase
what never man but me e'er heard.

' " In these blest souls are blent," my guide discoursed,
" far higher thoughts and sweeter plaints than thine.
Rude joy were discord here. And as a sudden shout in
thy hushed mountain passes brings down the awful
avalanche ; so one note of laughter here might start some
white and silent world."

' Then low I murmured : " Is theirs, oh guide ! no
happiness supreme ? their state still mixed ? Sigh these
yet to know ? Can these sin ? "

' Then I heard : " No mind but Oro's can know all ;
no mind that knows not all can be content ; content alone
approximates to happiness. Holiness comes by wisdom ;
and it is because great Oro is supremely wise that he 's
supremely holy. But as perfect wisdom can be only
Oro's ; so, perfect holiness is his alone. And whoso is
otherwise than perfect in his holiness is liable to sin.

' " And though death gave these beings knowledge, it
also opened other mysteries, which they pant to know, and
yet may learn. And still they fear the thing of evil ;
though for them 'tis hard to fall. Thus hoping and thus
fearing, then, theirs is no state complete. And since Oro
is past finding out, and mysteries ever open into mysteries
beyond ; so, though these beings will for aye progress in
wisdom and in good ; yet, will they never gain a fixed

beatitude. Know, then, oh mortal Mardian! that when translated hither, thou wilt but put off lowly temporal pinings, for angel and eternal aspirations. Start not: thy human joy hath here no place : no name."

' Still, I mournful mused ; then said: "Many Mardians live who have no aptitude for Mardian lives of thought : how then endure more earnest, everlasting, meditations ? "

' " Such have their place," I heard.

' Then low I moaned, " And what, oh ! guide ! of those who, living thoughtless lives of sin, die unregenerate ; no service done to Oro or to Mardian ? "

' " They, too, have their place," I heard ; " but 'tis not here. And Mardian ! know, that as your Mardian lives are long preserved through strict obedience to the organic law, so are your spiritual lives prolonged by fast keeping of the law of mind. Sin is death."

' " Ah, then," yet lower moan made I ; " and why create the germs that sin and suffer, but to perish ? "

' " That," breathed my guide, " is the last mystery which underlieth all the rest. Archangel may not fathom it ; that makes of Oro the everlasting mystery he is ; that to divulge, were to make equal to himself in knowledge all the souls that are ; that mystery Oro guards ; and none but him may know."

' Alas ! were it recalled, no words have I to tell of all that now my guide discoursed, concerning things unsearchable to us. My sixth sense which he opened, sleeps again, with all the wisdom that it gained.

' Time passed ; it seemed a moment, might have been an age ; when from high in the golden haze that canopied this heaven, another angel came ; its vans like East and West ; a sunrise one, sunset the other. As silver-fish in vases, so in his azure eyes swam tears unshed.

' Quick my guide close nested me ; through its veins the waning light throbbed hard.

' " Oh, spirit ! archangel ! god ! whate'er thou art," it
breathed ; " leave me : I am but blessed, not glorified."
   ' So saying, as down from doves, from its wings dropped
sounds.   Still nesting me, it crouched its plumes.
   ' Then, in a snow of softest syllables, thus breathed the
greater and more beautiful : " From far away, in fields
beyond thy ken, I heard thy fond discourse with this lone
Mardian.   It pleased me well ; for thy humility was
manifest ; no arrogance of knowing.   Come *thou* and
learn new things."
   ' And straight it overarched us with its plumes ; which,
then, down-sweeping, bore us up to regions where my
first guide had sunk, but for the power that buoyed us,
trembling, both.
   ' My eyes did wane, like moons eclipsed in overwhelming
dawns : such radiance was around ; such vermeil light,
born of no sun, but pervading all the scene.   Transparent,
fleckless, calm, all glowed one flame.
   ' Then said the greater guide : " This is the night of all
ye here behold—its day ye could not bide.   Your utmost
heaven is far below."
   ' Abashed, smote down, I, quaking, upward gazed ;
where, to and fro, the spirits sailed, like broad-winged
crimson-dyed flamingos, spiralling in sunset-clouds.   But
a sadness glorified, deep-fringed their mystic temples,
crowned with weeping halos, bird-like, floating o'er them,
wheresoe'er they roamed.
   ' Sights and odours blended.   As when new-morning
winds, in summer's prime, blow down from hanging
gardens, wafting sweets that never pall ; so, from those
flowery pinions, at every motion, came a flood of fragrance.
   ' And now the spirits twain discoursed of things whose
very terms, to me, were dark.   But my first guide grew
wise.   For me, I could but blankly list ; yet comprehended naught ; and, like the fish that 's mocked with

wings, and vainly seeks to fly ;—again I sought my lower
element.

' As poised, we hung in this rapt ether, a sudden
trembling seized the four wings now folding me. And
afar off, in zones still upward reaching, suns' orbits off, I,
tranced, beheld an awful glory. Sphere in sphere, it
burned :—the one Shekinah ! The air was flaked with
fire ;—deep in which fell showers of silvery globes, tears
magnified—braiding the flame with rainbows. I heard a
sound ; but not for me, nor my first guide, was that unutterable utterance. Then, my second guide was swept
aloft, as rises a cloud of red-dyed leaves in autumn
whirlwinds.

' Fast clasping me, the other drooped, and, instant,
sank, as in a vacuum ; myriad suns' diameters in a breath ;
—my five senses merged in one, of falling ; till we gained
the nether sky, descending still.

' Then strange things—soft, sad, and faint, I saw or
heard ; as when, in sunny, summer seas, down, down, you
dive, starting at pensive phantoms that you cannot fix.

' " These," breathed my guide, " are spirits in their
essences ; sad, even in undevelopment. With these, all
space is peopled ;—all the air is vital with intelligence,
which seeks embodiment. This it is, that unbeknown to
Mardians, causes them to strangely start in solitudes of
night, and in the fixed flood of their enchanted noons.
From hence are formed your mortal souls ; and all those
sad and shadowy dreams, and boundless thoughts man
hath, are vague remembrances of the time when the soul's
sad germ wide wandered through these realms. And
hence it is, that when ye Mardians feel most sad, then ye
feel most immortal."

' Like a spark new-struck from flint, soon Mardi showed
afar. It glowed within a sphere, which seemed, in space,
a bubble, rising from vast depths to the sea's surface.

Piercing it, my Mardian strength returned; but the angel's veins once more grew dim.

' Nearing the isles, thus breathed my guide : " Loved one, love on ! But know, that heaven hath no roof. To know all is to be all. Beatitude there is none. And your only Mardian happiness is but exemption from great woes —no more. Great love is sad ; and heaven is love. Sadness makes the silence throughout the realms of space ; sadness is universal and eternal ; but sadness is tranquillity ; tranquillity the uttermost that souls may hope for."

' Then, with its wings it fanned adieu ; and disappeared where the sun flames highest.'

We heard the dream and, silent, sought repose, to dream away our wonder.

CHAPTER LXXXV

AT sunrise, we stood upon the beach.

Babbalanja thus :—' My voyage is ended. Not because what we sought is found ; but that I now possess all which may be had of what I sought in Mardi. Here, I tarry to grow wiser still :—then I am Alma's and the world's. Taji ! for Yillah thou wilt hunt in vain ; she is a phantom that but mocks thee ; and while for her thou madly huntest, the sin thou didst cries out, and its avengers still will follow. But here they may not come : nor those, who, tempting, track thy path. Wise counsel take. Within our hearts is all we seek : though in that search many need a prompter. Him I have found in blessed Alma. Then rove no more. Gain now, in flush of youth, that last wise thought, too often purchased, by a life of woe. Be wise : be wise.

' Media ! thy station calls thee home. Yet from this isle thou carriest that wherewith to bless thy own. These flowers that round us spring may be transplanted : and Odo made to bloom with amaranths and myrtles, like this Serenia. Before thy people act the things thou here hast heard. Let no man weep, that thou mayst laugh ; no man toil too hard, that thou mayst idle be. Abdicate thy throne : but still retain the sceptre. None need a king ; but many need a ruler.

' Mohi ! Yoomy ! do we part ? then bury in forgetfulness much that hitherto I 've spoken. But let not one syllable of this old man's words be lost.

' Mohi ! Age leads thee by the hand. Live out thy life ; and die, calm-browed.

' But Yoomy ! many days are thine. And in one life's span, great circles may be traversed, eternal good be done. Take all Mardi for thy home. Nations are but names ; and continents but shifting sands.

' Once more : Taji ! be sure thy Yillah never will be found ; or found, will not avail thee. Yet search, if so thou wilt ; more isles, thou sayst, are still unvisited ; and when all is seen, return, and find thy Yillah here.

' Companions all ! adieu.'

And from the beach he wended through the woods.

Our shallops now refitted, we silently embarked ; and as we sailed away the old man blessed us.

For a time, each prow's ripplings were distinctly heard : ripple after ripple.

With silent, steadfast eyes, Media still preserved his noble mien ; Mohi his reverend repose ; Yoomy his musing mood.

But as a summer hurricane leaves all nature still, and smiling to the eye ; yet, in deep woods, there lie concealed some anguished roots torn up :—so, with these.

Much they longed to point our prows for Odo's isle ; saying our search was over.

But I was fixed as fate.

On we sailed, as when we first embarked ; the air was bracing as before. More isles we visited :—thrice encountered the avengers : but unharmed ; thrice Hautia's heralds : but turned not aside ;—saw many chequered scenes—wandered through groves and open fields—traversed many vales—climbed hill-tops whence broad views were gained—tarried in towns—broke into solitudes —sought far, sought near :—Still Yillah there was none.

Then again they all would fain dissuade me.

' Closed is the deep blue eye,' said Yoomy.

' Fate's last leaves are turning, let me home and die,' said Mohi.

' So nigh the circuit 's done,' said Media, ' our morrow's sun must rise o'er Odo ; Taji ! renounce the hunt.'

' I am the hunter that never rests ! the hunter without a home ! She I seek still flies before ; and I will follow, though she lead me beyond the reef ; through sunless seas ; and into night and death. Her, will I seek through all the isles and stars ; and find her, whate'er betide ! '

Again they yielded ; and again we glided on ;—our storm-worn prows now pointed here, now there ;—beckoned, repulsed ;—their half-rent sails still courting every breeze.

But that same night, once more, they wrestled with me. Now, at last, the hopeless search must be renounced : Yillah there was none : back must I hie to blue Serenia.

Then sweet Yillah called me from the sea ;—still must I on ! but gazing whence that music seemed to come, I thought I saw the green corse drifting by : and striking 'gainst our prow, as if to hinder. Then, then ! my heart grew hard, like flint ; and black, like night ; and sounded hollow to the hand I clenched. Hyenas filled me with their laughs ; death-damps chilled my brow ; I prayed not, but blasphemed.

CHAPTER LXXXVI

THEY MEET THE PHANTOMS

THAT starless midnight there stole from out the darkness the iris flag of Hautia.

Again the syrens came. They bore a large and stately urn-like flower, white as alabaster, and glowing, as if lit up within. From its calyx, flame-like, trembled forked and crimson stamens, burning with intensest odours.

The phantoms nearer came ; their flower, as an urn of burning nitre. Then it changed, and glowed like Persian dawns ; or passive, was shot over by palest lightnings ;— so variable its tints.

' The night-blowing cereus ! ' said Yoomy, shuddering, ' that never blows in sunlight ; that blows but once ; and blows but for an hour.—For the last time I come ; now, in your midnight of despair, and promise you this glory. Take heed ! short time hast thou to pause ; through me, perhaps, thy Yillah may be found.'

' Away ! away ! tempt me not by that, enchantress ! Hautia ! I know thee not ; I fear thee not ; but instinct makes me hate thee. Away ! my eyes are frozen shut ; I will not be tempted more.'

' How glorious it burns ! ' cried Media. I reel with incense :—can such sweets be evil ? '

' Look ! look ! ' cried Yoomy, ' its petals wane, and creep ; one moment more, and the night-flower shuts up forever the last, last hope of Yillah ! '

' Yillah ! Yillah ! Yillah ! ' bayed three vengeful voices far behind.

' Yillah !   Yillah !—dash the urn !   I follow, Hautia !
though thy lure be death.'

The cereus closed ; and in a mist the syren prow went
on before ; we, following.

When day dawned, three radiant pilot-fish swam in
advance : three ravenous sharks astern.

And, full before us, rose the isle of Hautia.

CHAPTER LXXXVII

THEY DRAW NIGH TO FLOZELLA

As if Mardi were a poem, and every island a canto, the shore now in sight was called Flozella-a-Nina, or The-Last-Verse-of-the-Song.

According to Mohi, the origin of this term was traceable to the remotest antiquity.

In the beginning, there were other beings in Mardi besides Mardians ; winged beings, of purer minds, and cast in gentler moulds, who would fain have dwelt forever with mankind. But the hearts of the Mardians were bitter against them, because of their superior goodness. Yet those beings returned love for malice, and long entreated to virtue and charity. But in the end, all Mardi rose up against them, and hunted them from isle to isle ; till, at last, they rose from the woodlands like a flight of birds and disappeared in the skies. Thereafter, abandoned of such sweet influences, the Mardians fell into all manner of sins and sufferings, becoming the erring things their descendants were now. Yet they knew not that their calamities were of their own bringing down. For deemed a victory, the expulsion of the winged beings was celebrated in choruses throughout Mardi. And among other jubilations, so ran the legend, a pæan was composed, corresponding in the number of its stanzas to the number of islands. And a band of youths, gaily apparelled, voyaged in gala canoes all round the lagoon, singing upon each isle one verse of their song. And Flozella being the last isle in their circuit, its queen commemorated the circumstance by new naming her realm.

That queen had first incited Mardi to wage war against the beings with wings. She it was who had been foremost in every assault. And that queen was ancestor of Hautia, now ruling the isle.

Approaching the dominions of one who so long had haunted me, conflicting emotions tore up my soul in tornadoes. Yet Hautia had held out some prospect of crowning my yearnings. But how connected were Hautia and Yillah? Something I hoped; yet more I feared. Dire presentiments, like poisoned arrows, shot through me. Had they pierced me before, straight to Flozella would I have voyaged; not waiting for Hautia to woo me by that last and victorious temptation. But unchanged remained my feelings of hatred for Hautia; yet vague those feelings, as the language of her flowers. Nevertheless, in some mysterious way seemed Hautia and Yillah connected. But Yillah was all beauty, and innocence; my crown of felicity; my heaven below;—and Hautia, my whole heart abhorred. Yillah I sought; Hautia sought me. One openly beckoned me here; the other dimly allured me there. Yet now was I wildly dreaming to find them together. But so distracted my soul, I knew not what it was that I thought.

Slowly we neared the land. Flozella-a-Nina!—An omen? Was this isle, then, to prove the last place of my search, even as it was the Last-Verse-of-the-Song?

CHAPTER LXXXVIII

THEY LAND

A JEWELLED tiara, nodding in spray, looks flowery Flozella, approached from the sea. For, lo you ! the glittering
foam all round its white marge ; where, forcing themselves underneath the coral ledge, and up through its
crevices, in fountains, the blue billows gush. While,
within, zone above zone, thrice zoned in belts of bloom,
all the isle as a hanging-garden soars ; its tapering cone
blending aloft with heaven's own blue.

'What flies through the spray ! what incense is this ? '
cried Media.

'Ha ! you wild breeze ! you have been plundering the
gardens of Hautia,' cried Yoomy.

'No sweets can be sweeter,' said Braid-Beard, ' but no
Upas more deadly.'

Anon we came nearer ; sails idly flapping, and paddles
suspended ; sleek currents our coursers. And round
about the isle, like winged rainbows, shoals of dolphins
were leaping over floating fragments of wrecks :—dark-
green, long-haired ribs, and keels of canoes. For many
shallops, inveigled by the eddies, were oft dashed to pieces
against that flowery strand. But what cared the dolphins ? Mardian wrecks were their homes. Over and
over they sprang : from east to west : rising and
setting : many suns in a moment ; while all the sea, like
a harvest plain, was stacked with their glittering sheaves
of spray.

And far down, fathoms on fathoms, flitted rainbow

hues :—as seines-full of mermaids ; half-screening the bones of the drowned.

Swifter and swifter the currents now ran ; till with a shock, our prows were beached.

There, beneath an arch of spray, three dark-eyed maidens stood ; garlanded with columbines, their nectaries nodding like jesters' bells ; and robed in vestments blue.

' The pilot-fish transformed ! ' cried Yoomy.

' The night-heralds three ! ' said Mohi.

Following the maidens, we now took our way along a winding vale ; where, by sweet-scented hedges, flowed blue-braided brooks ; their tributaries, rivulets of violets, meandering through the meads.

On one hand forever glowed the rosy mountains with a tropic dawn ; and on the other lay an Arctic eve ;—the white daisies drifted in long banks of snow, and snowed the blossoms from the orange boughs. There, summer breathed her bridal bloom : her hill-top temples crowned with bridal wreaths.

We wandered on, through orchards arched in long arcades, that seemed baronial halls, hung o'er with trophies :—so spread the boughs in antlers. This orchard was the frontlet of the isle.

The fruit hung high in air, that only beaks, not hands, might pluck.

Here, the peach-tree showed her thousand cheeks of down, kissed often by the wooing winds ; here, in swarms, the yellow apples hived, like golden bees upon the boughs ; here, from the kneeling, fainting trees, thick fell the cherries, in great drops of blood ; and here, the pomegranate, with cold rind and sere, deep pierced by bills of birds, revealed the mellow of its ruddy core. So, oft the heart, that cold and withered seems, within yet hides its juices.

This orchard passed, the vale became a lengthening plain, that seemed the Straits of Ormus bared ; so thick it lay with flowery gems :—turquoise-hyacinths, ruby-roses, lily-pearls. Here roved the fragrant vines ; their flaxen ringlets curling over arbours, which laughed and shook their golden locks. From bower to bower flew the wee bird, that ever hovering, seldom lights ; and flights of gay canaries passed, like jonquils, winged.

But now, from out half-hidden bowers of clematis, there issued swarms of wasps, which, flying wide, settled on all the buds.

And, fifty nymphs preceding, who now follows from those bowers, with gliding, artful steps :—the very snares of love !—Hautia. A gorgeous amaryllis in her hand ; Circæa flowers in her ears ; her girdle tied with vervain.

She came by privet hedges, drooping ; downcast honey-suckles ; she trod on pinks and pansies, bluebells, heath, and lilies. She glided on : her crescent brow calm as the moon, when most it works its evil influences.

Her eye was fathomless.

But the same mysterious, evil-boding gaze was there, which long before had haunted me in Odo, ere Yillah fled. —Queen Hautia the incognito ! Then two wild currents met, and dashed me into foam.

' Yillah ! Yillah !—tell me, queen ! ' But she stood motionless ; radiant, and scentless : a dahlia on its stalk.

' Where ? Where ? '

' Is not thy voyage now ended ?—Take flowers ! Damsels, give him wine to drink. After his weary hunt, be the wanderer happy.'

I dashed aside their cups and flowers ; still rang the vale with Yillah !

' Taji ! did I know her fate, naught would I now disclose ! my heralds pledged their queen to naught. Thou but comest here to supplant thy mourner's night-shade with marriage roses. Damsels! give him wreaths; crowd round him; press him with your cups!'

Once more I spilled their wine, and tore their garlands.

'Is not that the evil eye that long ago did haunt me? and thou the Hautia who hast followed me, and wooed, and mocked, and tempted me, through all this long, long voyage? I swear! thou knowest all.'

'I am Hautia. Thou hast come at last. Crown him with your flowers! Drown him in your wine! To all questions, Taji! I am mute.—Away!—damsels, dance; reel round him; round and round!'

Then, their feet made music on the rippling grass, like thousand leaves of lilies on a lake. And, gliding nearer, Hautia welcomed Media; and said, 'Your comrade here is sad:—be ye gay. Ho, wine!—I pledge ye, guests!'

Then, marking all, I thought to seem what I was not, that I might learn at last the thing I sought.

So, three cups in hand I held; drank wine, and laughed; and half-way met Queen Hautia's blandishments.

CHAPTER LXXXIX

THEY ENTER THE BOWER OF HAUTIA

CONDUCTED to the arbour, from which the queen had emerged, we came to a sweet-brier bower within ; and reclined upon odorous mats.

Then, in citron cups, sherbet of tamarinds was offered to Media, Mohi, Yoomy ; to me, a nautilus shell, brimmed with a light-like fluid that welled and welled like a fount.

' Quaff, Taji, quaff ! every drop drowns a thought ! '

Like a blood-freshet, it ran through my veins.

A philtre ?—How Hautia burned before me ! Glorious queen ! with all the radiance, lighting up the equatorial night.

' Thou art most magical, oh queen ! about thee a thousand constellations cluster.'

' They blaze to burn,' whispered Mohi.

' I see ten million Hautias !—all space reflects her, as a mirror.'

Then, in reels, the damsels once more mazed, the blossoms shaking from their brows ; till Hautia glided near ; arms lustrous as rainbows : chanting some wild invocation.

My soul ebbed out ; Yillah there was none ! but as I turned round open-armed, Hautia vanished.

' She is deeper than the sea,' said Media.

' Her bow is bent,' said Yoomy.

' I could tell wonders of Hautia and her damsels,' said Mohi.

' What wonders ? '

'Listen; and in his own words will I recount the adventure of the youth Ozonna. It will show thee, Taji, that the maidens of Hautia are all Yillahs, held captive, unknown to themselves; and that Hautia, their enchantress, is the most treacherous of queens.

'"Camel-like, laden with woe," said Ozonna, "after many wild rovings in quest of a maiden long lost—beautiful Ady! and after being repelled in Maramma; and in vain hailed to land at Serenia, represented as naught but another Maramma;—with vague promises of discovering Ady, three syrens, who long had pursued, at last inveigled me to Flozella; where Hautia made me her thrall. But ere long, in Rea, one of her maidens, I thought I discovered my Ady transformed. My arms opened wide to embrace; but the damsel knew not Ozonna. And even, when after hard wooing, I won her again, she seemed not lost Ady, but Rea. Yet all the while, from deep in her strange, black orbs, Ady's blue eyes seemed pensively looking:—blue eye within black: sad, silent soul within merry. Long I strove, by fixed ardent gazing, to break the spell, and restore in Rea my lost one's past. But in vain. It was only Rea, not Ady, who at stolen intervals looked on me now. One morning Hautia started as she greeted me; her quick eye rested on my bosom; and glancing there, affrighted, I beheld a distinct, fresh mark, the impress of Rea's necklace-drop. Fleeing, 1 revealed what had passed to the maiden, who broke from my side: as I, from Hautia's. The queen summoned her damsels, but for many hours the call was unheeded; and when at last they came, upon each bosom lay a necklace-drop like Rea's. On the morrow, lo! my arbour was strewn over with bruised Linden-leaves, exuding a vernal juice. Full of forebodings, again I sought Rea: who, casting down her eyes, beheld her feet stained green. Again she fled; and again Hautia summoned her damsels: malicious triumph

in her eye ; but dismay succeeded : each maid had spotted
feet. That night Rea was torn from my side by three
masks ; who, stifling her cries, rapidly bore her away ;
and as I pursued, disappeared in a cave. Next morning,
Hautia was surrounded by her nymphs, but Rea was
absent. Then, gliding near, she snatched from my hair,
a jet-black tress, loose-hanging. ' Ozonna is the murderer ! See ! Rea's torn hair entangled with his ! '
Aghast, I swore that I knew not her fate. ' Then let the
witch Larfee be called ! ' The maidens darted from the
bower ; and soon after there rolled into it a green cocoa-
nut, followed by the witch, and all the damsels, flinging
anemones upon it. Bowling this way and that, the nut
at last rolled to my feet.—' It is he ! ' cried all.—Then
they bound me with osiers ; and at midnight, unseen and
irresistible hands placed me in a shallop ; which sped far
out into the lagoon, where they tossed me to the waves ;
but so violent the shock the osiers burst ; and as the
shallop fled one way, swimming another, ere long I gained
land.

' " Thus in Flozella, I found but the phantom of Ady,
and slew the last hope of Ady the true." '

This recital sank deep into my soul. In some wild way,
Hautia had made a captive of Yillah ; in some one of her
black-eyed maids, the blue-eyed One was transformed.
From side to side, in frenzy, I turned ; but in all those
cold, mystical eyes, saw not the warm ray that I sought.

' Hast taken root within this treacherous soil ? ' cried
Media.—' Away ! thy Yillah is behind thee, not before.
Deep she dwells in blue Serenia's groves ; which thou
wouldst not search. Hautia mocks thee ; away ! The
reef is rounded ; but a strait flows between this isle and
Odo, and thither its ruler must return. Every hour I
tarry here, some wretched serf is dying there, for whom,
from blest Serenia, I carry life and joy. Away ! '

'Art still bent on finding evil for thy good?' cried Mohi.—'How can Yillah harbour here?—Beware!—Let not Hautia so enthrall thee.'

'Come away, come away,' cried Yoomy. 'Far hence is Yillah! and he who tarries among these flowers must needs burn juniper.'

'Look on me, Media, Mohi, Yoomy. Here I stand, my own monument, till Hautia breaks the spell.'

In grief they left me.

Vee-Vee's conch I heard no more.

CHAPTER XC

TAJI WITH HAUTIA

As their last echoes died away down the valley, Hautia glided near ;—zone unbound, the amaryllis in her hand. Her bosom ebbed and flowed ; the motes danced in the beams that darted from her eyes.

' Come ! let us sin, and be merry. Ho ! wine, wine, wine ! and lapfuls of flowers ! let all the cane-brakes pipe their flutes. Damsels ! dance ; reel, swim, around me :— I, the vortex that draws all in. Taji ! Taji !—as a berry, that name is juicy in my mouth !—Taji, Taji ! ' and in choruses she warbled forth the sound, till it seemed issuing from her syren eyes.

My heart flew forth from out its bars, and soared in air ; but as my hand touched Hautia's, down dropped a dead bird from the clouds.

' Ha ! how he sinks !—but didst ever dive in deep waters, Taji ? Didst ever see where pearls grow ?—To the cave !—damsels, lead on ! '

Then wending through constellations of flowers, we entered deep groves. And thus, thrice from sunlight to shade, it seemed three brief nights and days, ere we paused before the mouth of the cavern.

A bow-shot from the sea, it pierced the hillside like a vaulted way ; and glancing in, we saw far gleams of water ; crossed, here and there, by long-flung distant shadows of domes and columns. All Venice seemed within.

From a stack of golden palm stalks, the damsels now made torches ; then stood grouped ; a sheaf of syrens in a sheaf of flame.

Illuminated, the cavern shone like a Queen of Kandy's casket ; full of dawns and sunsets.

From rocky roof to bubbling floor, it was columned with stalactites ; and galleried all round, in spiral tiers, with sparkling, coral ledges.

And now, their torches held aloft, into the water the maidens softly glided ; and each a lotus floated ; while, from far above, into the air Hautia flung her flambeau ; then bounding after,—in the lake, two meteors were quenched.

Where she dived, the flambeaux clustered ; and up among them, Hautia rose ; hands, full of pearls.

' Lo ! Taji ; all these may be had for the diving ; and beauty, health, wealth, long life, and the last lost hope of man. But through me alone may these be had. Dive thou, and bring up one pearl if thou canst.'

Down, down ! down, down, in the clear, sparkling water, till I seemed crystallised in the flashing heart of a diamond ; but from those bottomless depths I uprose empty-handed.

' Pearls, pearls ! thy pearls ! thou art fresh from the mines. Ah, Taji ! for thee, bootless deep diving. Yet to Hautia, one shallow plunge reveals many Golcondas. But come ; dive with me :—join hands—let me show thee strange things.'

' Show me that which I seek, and I will dive with thee, straight through the world, till we come up in oceans unknown.'

' Nay, nay ; but join hands, and I will take thee, where thy past shall be forgotten ; where thou wilt soon learn to love the living, not the dead.'

' Better to me, oh Hautia ! all the bitterness of my buried dead than all the sweets of the life thou canst bestow ; even, were it eternal.'

CHAPTER XCI

RETURNED from the cave, Hautia reclined in her clematis bower, invisible hands flinging fennel around her. And nearer, and nearer, stole dulcet sounds dissolving my woes, as warm beams, snow. Strange languors made me droop ; once more within my inmost vault, side by side, the Past and Yillah lay :—two bodies tranced ;—while like a rounding sun, before me Hautia magnified magnificence ; and through her fixed eyes slowly drank up my soul.

Thus we stood :—snake and victim : life ebbing out from me to her.

But from that spell I burst again, as all the Past smote all the Present in me.

' Oh Hautia ! thou knowest the mystery I die to fathom. I see it crouching in thine eye :—Reveal ! '

' Weal or woe ? '

' Life or death ! '

' See, see ! ' and Yillah's rose-pearl danced before me. I snatched it from her hand :—' Yillah ! Yillah ! '

' Rave on : she lies too deep to answer ; stranger voices than thine she hears :—bubbles are bursting round her.'

' Drowned ! drowned then, even as she dreamed :—I come, I come !—Ha, what form is this ?—hast mosses ? sea-thyme ? pearls ?—Help, help ! I sink !—Back, shining monster !—What, Hautia,—is it thou ?—Oh vipress, I could slay thee ! '

' Go, go,—and slay thyself : I may not make thee mine ; —go,—dead to dead !—There is another cavern in the hill.'

Swift I fled along the valley side; passed Hautia's cave'of pearls; and gained a twilight arch; within, a lake transparent shone. Conflicting currents met, and wrestled; and one dark arch led to channels, seaward tending.

Round and round, a gleaming form slow circled in the deepest eddies :—white, and vaguely Yillah.

Straight I plunged; but the currents were as fierce head-winds off capes, that beat back ships.

Then, as I frenzied gazed; gaining the one dark arch, the revolving shade darted out of sight, and the eddies whirled as before.

' Stay, stay ! let me go with thee, though thou glidest to gulfs of blackness ;—naught can exceed the hell of this despair !—Why beat longer in this corpse, oh, my heart ! '

As somnambulists fast-frozen in some horrid dream, ghost-like glide abroad, and fright the wakeful world ; so that night, with death-glazed eyes, to and fro I flitted on the damp and weedy beach.

' Is this spectre, Taji ? ' —and Mohi and the minstrel stood before me.

' Taji lives no more. So dead, he has no ghost. I am his spirit's phantom's phantom.'

' Nay, then, phantom ! the time has come to flee.'

They dragged me to the water's brink, where a prow was beached. Soon—Mohi at the helm—we shot beneath the far-flung shadow of a cliff; when, as in a dream, I hearkened to a voice.

Arrived at Odo, Media had been met with yells. Sedition was in arms, and to his beard defied him. Vain all concessions then. Foremost stood the three pale sons of him whom I had slain to gain the maiden lost. Avengers, from the first hour we had parted on the sea, they had drifted on my track ; survived starvation ; and lived to hunt me round all Mardi's reef ; and now at Odo, that last threshold, waited to destroy ; or there, missing the revenge they sought, still swore to hunt me round Eternity.

Behind the avengers raged a stormy mob, invoking Media to renounce his rule. But one hand waving like a pennant above the smoke of some sea-fight, straight through that tumult Media sailed serene : the rioters parting from before him, as wild waves before a prow inflexible.

A haven gained, he turned to Mohi and the minstrel :— ' Oh, friends ! after our long companionship, hard to part ! But henceforth, for many moons, Odo will prove no home for old age, or youth. In Serenia only, will ye find the peace ye seek ; and thither ye must carry Taji, who else must soon be slain, or lost. Go : release him from the thrall of Hautia. Outfly the avengers, and gain Serenia. Reck not of me. The state is tossed in storms ; and where I stand, the combing billows must break over. But among all noble souls, in tempest-time, the headmost man last flies the wreck. So, here in Odo will I abide, though every plank breaks up beneath me. And then,— great Oro ! let the king die clinging to the keel ! Farewell ! '

Such Mohi's tale.

In trumpet-blasts, the hoarse night-winds now blew ; the lagoon black with the still shadows of the mountains, and the driving shadows of the clouds. Of all the stars, only red Arcturus shone. But through the gloom, and on the circumvallating reef, the breakers dashed ghost-white.

An outlet in that other barrier was nigh.

' Ah ! Yillah ! Yillah !—the currents sweep thee oceanward ; nor will I tarry behind.—Mardi, farewell !—Give me the helm, old man ! '

' Nay, madman ! Serenia is our haven. Through yonder strait, for thee, perdition lies. And from the deep beyond, no voyager e'er puts back.'

' And why put back ? is a life of dying worth living o'er again ?—Let *me*, then, be the unreturning wanderer. The helm ! By Oro, I will steer my own fate, old man.— Mardi, farewell ! '

' Nay, Taji : commit not the last, last crime ! ' cried Yoomy.

' He 's seized the helm ! eternity is in his eye ! Yoomy : for our lives we must now swim.'

And plunging, they struck out for land : Yoomy buoying Mohi up, and the salt waves dashing the tears from his pallid face, as through the scud he turned it on me mournfully.

' Now, I am my own soul's emperor ; and my first act is abdication ! Hail ! realm of shades ! '—and turning my prow into the racing tide, which seized me like a hand omnipotent, I darted through.

Churned in foam, that outer ocean lashed the clouds ; and straight in my white wake, headlong dashed a shallop, three fixed spectres leaning o'er its prow : three arrows poising.

And thus, pursuers and pursued flew on, over an endless sea.

THE END

DATE DUE

GAYLORD PRINTED IN U.S.A.